THE
FORTUNATE
ONES

THE FORTUNATE ONES
Copyright © 2017 R.S. Grey

Published: R.S. Grey 2017
authorrsgrey@gmail.com
Editing: Editing by C. Marie
Proofreading: JaVa Editing
Cover Design: R.S. Grey
All rights reserved.
ISBN: **1977834108**
ISBN-13: **978-1977834102**

 CHAPTER ONE

This is the last outfit I would ever choose to wear, but it's not my choice to make. It's my work uniform: a skintight blue polo paired with a pleated khaki skirt that cuts off much closer to my crotch than my knees. Combine that with an embroidered baseball cap and gleaming white Keds, and I've become everything I hate in in this world: *a country club cabana girl.*

My name is embroidered on the shirt in a scrolling font. Above it sits the club's pretentious logo, a laurel wreath hugging the Twin Oak initials. It hasn't changed in 50 years, and that's just the way the members like it. Old money likes old things—except, of course, when it comes to the elite amenities in a place like this. Here, they want new, bigger, better. Acres of perfectly manicured lawns. 18 holes of world-class golf. An Olympic-sized swimming pool with all the kid-friendly accouterments any day-drinking lacrosse mom could ask for. From what I've seen, there's a members-only spa, formal dining room, and gentlemen's cigar lounge. Beyond that, there's no telling what else lies within the grounds of Twin Oaks. The scope of my job really only entails access to the pool and main clubhouse. Aside from that, I'm not particularly encouraged to roam.

When each member arrives, they drive through a bougainvillea-covered arched iron gate guarded by no less than three men at any given time. The level of security strikes me as overkill, as if the architects envisioned lower-middle-class hordes crashing through to get their first taste of crab legs. But, then again, I'm not dripping in diamonds like half the women here, so whatever. If Julio, Matt, and Nico make them feel safe, that's great.

The truth is, their only real talents are scanning ID cards and kissing the asses of wealthy members, like this guy.

"C'mon beautiful, give us a little smile."

I want to ignore him. I'm focused on the sleek black Porsche driving up the tree-lined drive. In a minute, it will pull into its designated parking spot between a white Mercedes SUV and some other car that costs more than most houses.

"Are you being shy darlin'?" the asshole asks, trying to get my attention.

His guests laugh and I know my time is up. I won't get to watch *him* get out of his Porsche today.

With a barely concealed sigh, I turn away from the drive and beam my pearly whites. The old fart claps his hands together and pulls out his wallet. Members pay for things at the club with their assigned ID number, but tips are usually doled out in cash. Every dime is supposed to pass through the cabana bar so it can be divvied up at the end of the day, but after schlepping back and forth around the pool all afternoon waiting on Mr. Oil Tycoon and his merry band of buttkissers, the crisp hundred-dollar bill he hands me feels more comfortable inside my pocket. Later, it will buy me takeout sushi and enough wine to drown this memory.

"Brookie, have I told you you're my favorite cabana girl?" he asks, making a show of plucking another

Benjamin from his wallet. "I like your...work ethic."

I can't argue with that. I am extraordinarily focused while I'm here, not because I care about this job, but because I've found that staying as busy as possible makes the shifts pass in a flash. No matter if Mr. Oil Tycoon asks me to slice two hundred limes so his board of directors can do rounds of tequila shots (my wrist is still recovering), rub sunscreen on his meatball head (my hands haven't felt clean since), or entertain his children while he and his wife get completely sloshed (c'mon kids, let's play *roll silverware*)—I'm going to do it all with a big, fake smile on my face.

I take the second bill out of his hand and dispense some version of the pleasant bullshit I've become remarkably adept at conjuring. My toolbox now includes a girlish laugh, a giddy thank-you, and a nauseating "Oh *you.*" I worry that someday I might slip and tell him to go screw himself, but from the looks of his saccharine stare, I've managed to hold off for at least one more day.

He dismisses me with a wave of his hand and I turn back for the cabana's bar. I'd like to take this moment to clarify that on my own time, I'm not a show dog, but here? At Twin Oaks? I have yet to encounter a situation that tests my dignity beyond the promise of a tip, and of course, the members take advantage of that knowledge. They want us at their beck and call, and our management encourages it. *Anything the guests request, make it happen.* If that means serving virgin daiquiris to spoiled brats until they puke, I'll do it. If that means pouring mommy's little cocktail into a Styrofoam cup so she can take a roadie with her, so be it. It's all part of the job.

When I make it back to the bar, I stuff the second hundred into the tip jar because I'm basically as generous as Jesus, except instead of turning water into wine, I turn misogyny into money. Also, coincidentally, I don't think I can stuff any more cash into my pocket without it becoming conspicuous.

I take off my Twin Oaks Country Club baseball cap and hang it on the back of the door then salute the poor schmuck who has arrived to relieve me. She's new, Cari or Cara, something like that. Behind her, Will and Kyle are manning the kitchen. Compared to the main dining room, the fare out here is simple at best: chicken salad sandwiches and fresh veggies, hotdogs and hamburgers for the kids. They do a pretty good job of it though, and I gratefully accept a club sandwich to-go. There would be no more freebie deli delights if they knew how many tips I keep for myself, but it's only fair. They get to listen to music and chat in the safety of the bar and kitchen while I'm stuck out there with the wildlife, trying to keep all my limbs intact.

"See you tomorrow?" Will calls from behind me.

"Nope. I have the day off."

I try not to sing the words.

He groans in annoyance, but I can't even feign sympathy.

It's going to be magnificent. I'm going to sleep in and go for a run, job search for a couple hours, and revel in the real world, where people carry Target purses instead of Birkin bags and children have to follow rules. At Twin Oaks, everyone is well connected. That little boy nearly drowning his sister in the pool right now? His mom is a senator. The teenager pouring vodka into her Sprite? Her dad owns half the commercial real estate in Austin. Nothing is scarier than a teen with powerful pedigree, and I steer clear of them as I weave around the pool and head inside.

The main clubhouse is referred to by most of the staff as The Manor because the sprawling two-story building looks as if it's been teleported from the English countryside. Symmetrical, ivy-covered, and old enough to harbor some pretty juicy secrets, it's a building I'd like to take out for a drink. Large, square windows line the first and second floor, and in the center of the limestone facade sits a massive porte cochère where guests can opt to leave their cars with a suited valet before swooping through the main entrance.

I've made the short walk from the pool to the clubhouse more times than I can count, but it's still exciting to pull open the heavy doors and step inside the foyer. Beneath a large coffered dome sits an antique marble table, there for the sole purpose of bearing a dramatic floral arrangement that gets changed out every morning. Today it's made up of a dozen cylindrical vases of varying heights. There are orchids and garden roses, hydrangeas and peonies. The guests in front of me breeze right past it without a second thought. I shake my head, walk around the table, and stroll down the large hallway that leads past a pair of bathrooms and a private lounge. Beyond lies the main dining room, the real gem of the clubhouse. In that room, the ceiling opens up, reaching heights that could rival any cathedral. Windows stretch across the back wall from floor to ceiling, showcasing the manicured gardens and the par-three eighth hole of the golf course.

The dining room itself looks as if an old French monarch rose from the dead and demanded that the entire room be decorated in an opulent shade of blue. There's plush wallpaper, starched table linens, and heavy drapes, all ranging from royal to robin's egg. My favorite detail is the pale blue and cream damask velvet that covers the antique

French dining chairs. It's completely impractical. I can't imagine the cost of upkeep over the years, but the chairs are beautiful and I'd take one home with me if I could get away with it.

This room is where I spend the other half of my time at Twin Oaks. If I'm not stationed for a shift out at the cabana, I'm perched behind the hostess podium for the lunch service. That spot is currently occupied by my older sister, Ellie, who's watching me with a smirk as I approach.

"Done with your shift, or are you about to quit in a blaze of glory?"

I grin and pat my pocket. "The first one, but if these tips keep coming, I should have enough saved for the latter soon."

She laughs. "You really have to swap with me one day for beer cart duty. You think you get good tips at the cabana, but you have no idea what you're missing."

"Thanks, but no thanks. The cabana is bad enough."

She rolls her eyes. "You act like I'm giving members blowies between holes."

I scrunch my nose. "Maybe you are, maybe you aren't. Whatever you do in, around, and between your holes is your business, sis."

She's about to respond when her attention shifts to someone behind me. From the familiar stench of heavily applied cologne, I know it's our manager, Mr. McDonald, though he insists we call him Brian.

"Is everything *tip top* here, Ellie? We start dinner service in 30 minutes."

She beams at him. "The tables have been set, I double-checked the crystal for fingerprints, and I've ensured the chef has been prepped on all the nutrition and allergy guidelines for the guests dining with us tonight."

He nods, scanning over the dining room as he continues, "I saw both the Daniels and Edwards family on the reservation list—"

"Already taken care of," Ellie says with practiced patience. "Their reservations are two hours apart, and if the Edwards family arrives early, I'll place them on the opposite side of the dining room. There shouldn't be any problems."

"Good." He gives her a final curt nod of approval before turning toward me. "Brooke, I haven't seen you in a few days. Is everything going well out in the cabana?"

"Nothing I can't handle."

I thought I would hate Brian when I first started working here. He's firmly lodged deep in his 40s with a thick, outdated mustache. He valiantly but unsuccessfully tries to hide his ever-burgeoning pudginess beneath shiny polyester suits, and while he definitely has the personality of a boiled potato, I appreciate that he's all business. The last thing I need is one more guy in this club trying to suck smiles out of me.

"The members have been speaking highly of you. Mr. Larson has requested that you pick up a few shifts out on the golf course."

Mr. Larson is Mr. Oil Tycoon, the man I can thank for the hundred-dollar bill stuffed in my pocket.

"I was actually just telling Brooke she would *love* working out there," Ellie prods.

I want to jab her with my elbow but the podium is in the way.

"Actually, Brian, I'm happy with where I'm at. I've only just now gotten the hang of the dining room and the cabana."

He seems disappointed, like he doesn't want to have to

tell Mr. Oil Tycoon I said no. "Right, well…Ellie, let me know if you need anything regarding the Edwards-Daniels situation."

When he's gone, it takes me all of two seconds to ask Ellie about "the situation".

She shrugs. "Didn't I tell you? Mr. Daniels was having an affair with Mrs. Edwards. After their spouses found out, each filed for divorce. Once everything was settled, the cheaters got married. As for the *cheatees*, well…either out of spite or a reluctance to give up their country club membership, they went ahead and married each other too! Now they just avoid each other like the plague."

"God this place is incestuous. You'd think if you were going to have an affair, you wouldn't just choose another dusty ol' cookie off the shelf."

She laughs. "They've *made* it that way. You know you can't even get a membership at this place if you aren't a legacy? All the families moving to Austin with new money would cut off their right arms to get in here, so it doesn't really shock me that Mrs. Daniels married Mr. Edwards. He might weigh 400 pounds and have a face like a shoe, but with an active club membership, he might as well be Daniel Craig."

I'm still stifling my laughter when Marissa joins us at the podium.

"What's funny?" she asks, scanning down the reservation list and scrunching her nose when she comes across a name she doesn't particularly like. She's one of my favorite waitresses in the dining room. Like every other front-of-the-house employee, she's young and beautiful—black with a short pixie haircut and legs that should probably be insured for a million bucks.

"I was filling Brooke in on the Edwards-Daniels

12

drama."

Marissa groans. "*Ugh*, who cares? That's old news. More importantly, did either of you see that *he's* here?"

"Who?" I ask, because even though I know exactly who she's talking about, I want to hear his name just for fun.

Marissa narrows her dark brown eyes at me. "You know who! Jared said he saw him go into the cigar lounge."

I wonder if he likes it in there because it's quiet or if he actually smokes.

Ellie leans in closer so the few members who just stepped into the foyer won't overhear us. "Are you sure? I didn't see his car in the parking lot when I got here. I heard he was traveling in Southeast Asia or something for the next few weeks."

"Well you"—Marissa playfully boops her on the nose—"were misinformed. I looked—his car is definitely out there."

"Whatever," I say on a sigh, and they jerk their heads to glare at me. "Sorry, it's just all a little ridiculous, the whispering and obsessing about him."

Ellie shoots a knowing glare to Marissa. "Oh, of course. How could I forget that Brooke is too cool to give a shit about James Ashwood. Every other female in this club has a GPS tracker on him, but not you. Why is that exactly?"

I pin on a bored expression. "Not my type."

They both crack up at that, which is fair. I'm not that good at lying.

"Riiiight. What else isn't your type? *Breathing*?"

In the three months I've worked at Twin Oaks, James Ashwood has been talked about way more than the bevy of professional athletes and famous locals who also frequent the club. *A royal asshole. A major dick. A shrewd businessman. A big tipper with an appetite for everything luxurious: beautiful women, top-shelf whiskey, and expensive cars.* I'm confident it's mostly fiction, made up by some kitchen staffer bored with plating $90 filets.

I'm about to tell both of them to go to hell when Ellie's face flushes light pink.

"It's him. *It's him,*" she hisses, stepping up to the podium and grabbing for a pen. She finds one, drops it, and then smooths down the front of her dress. Marissa straightens her back and pushes out her chest. It's mating season at the hostess stand.

I'm facing Ellie and Marissa as they watch him approach, and it takes all of my willpower to keep from joining in on their ogling. After all, Mr. Oil Tycoon forced me to miss James getting out of his Porsche when he first arrived; it's only fair that I should get to turn around and see him now, just for a second.

I swear if I concentrate hard enough, I can hear his deep voice over the soft ambient music playing overhead. He's getting closer. My hands fist at my sides and I know if I stay any longer, I'll cave and turn.

Instead, I wave goodbye to Ellie and Marissa and rush into the dining room—away from him. I pass through the bustling kitchen and head for the locker room so I can change back into clothes I feel comfortable in and get the hell out of here. Unfortunately, there are more women in here whispering about James. I swear, they make him seem larger than life. We have all sorts of rich and famous members in the club, but no one has a cult following quite like James Ashwood. I refuse to drink the Kool-Aid.

"Did you see him out there, Brooke?" someone asks as I bang my locker closed.

"Oh, I see a lot of things," I joke, deflecting any more talk about him.

Although, it is true—I do see a lot behind the scenes at Twin Oaks.

But I've never seen anything quite like him.

 **CHAPTER TWO**

Most members of the country club live tucked away inside gated mansions, within gated neighborhoods. They buy houses in which most rooms exist for the sole purpose of employing a squadron of maids to dust them. By contrast, I live in cooperative housing north of the University of Texas campus. The co-op itself is an old two-story bungalow that's been added on to and redesigned so many times over the years that it looks like a bad kindergarten art project, all popsicle sticks and macaroni.

There are 10 rooms total, full of creative types, mostly artists and musicians in their 20s. We each have our own bedroom, but the communal spaces are shared, one big hippie family. It has its drawbacks—like how my expensive toilet paper always seems to get shared when the others' scratchy one-ply hemp runs out—but the rent is cheap and I like the people that live here. They are the polar opposite of the people I wait on at the country club. My neighbor on the left, Jackie, is a performance artist who moonlights at a bakery, and my neighbor on the right, Ethan, is a documentarian. They hook up every so often, and in exchange for enduring the noise (the co-op has *very* thin walls), Jackie brings me day-old croissants from the bakery. It's an arrangement I'm pretty happy with.

I'm there now, in my room with Ellie. She's going on about something important, I'm sure, and I'm posed in front of my mirror, trying out different hairstyles.

"Just…no. No to the bangs. You'd look like an anime character."

I drop the hair I tucked under to mimic front bangs. I thought it looked good; Ellie clearly thinks differently.

"I want to change up my look."

She shrugs. "So cut your hair."

"No!"

I'm like Samson. If my hair goes, my power goes with it. It's jet-black, halfway down my back, and the singular feature of mine I truly treasure. Combined with my light blue eyes, it packs quite a punch—or so I've been told. Throughout high school, my gangly legs and saucer eyes were out of place among a sea of short, perky blondes. The only guys who were into my Hot Topic look were emo vampires themselves, more interested in making me the subject of their tortured teenage fantasies than actually getting to know me. I wasn't looking to be anyone's grunge-pop princess.

Through the tail end of puberty, my body's hormones acted like little general contractors that had fallen behind on a fixer-upper. I started noticing the effects freshman year of college, when my French TA asked me to meet him for coffee. I assumed he wanted to discuss my interpretation of *Amélie*, but when his hand hit my knee beneath the table, the truth set in quicker than my double espresso. It was new territory for me, being broadly desired, and I wasn't sure if I liked it. I always thought people that complained about their good looks were buffoons, but attractiveness does come with a unique set of challenges. For one, people have constantly underestimated me. Like in college, many of my classmates assumed I was seducing my professors (even the gay ones) in exchange for

As. Eventually, I stopped minding the whispers. I liked being underestimated. In fact, I still do.

After finishing my double major in French and Spanish, I spent a year traveling trying to "find myself". In reality, I was trying to find a job. Through a tutoring agency, I eventually found a position as an au pair with an American diplomat named Nicole and her young daughter Sophie. For a year and a half, we became a happy little family in the heart of Paris. During the day, Nicole worked at the embassy while I tutored Sophie in Spanish and French. We turned coffee houses, museums, and grassy parks into our classroom. I'd started to feel like a true *Parisien.* Life was grand.

That is, until Nicole joined Tinder.

Yeah, that's right. Even old, Ivy league-educated diplomats with bouffant hair are swiping right. It took Nicole two weeks to fall head over heels for some baguette-toting man named George, and another two weeks to promptly fire my ass. I was shocked, but I couldn't help but admire her honesty.

"You understand, don't you?" she prodded.

I didn't. "Do you need more room? I can get my own place."

Her smile fell, and I knew I'd missed the mark.

"I've just noticed that...well, when George is around, and you...I just don't think it would be wise to keep you around. Haven't you seen Pretty Woman*?"*

My mouth dropped. "What? Pretty Woman *is about a prostitute!"*

"Hmm...perhaps I'm thinking about a different movie," she muttered, confused. "Well nevertheless, I think it is time to part ways."

It made no sense.

"Do you seriously think I'm going to try to seduce George? His breath smells like sardines!"

She had the decency to blush. "No, not at all. It's just...George and I are ready to take our relationship to the next level, and no one keeps a pretty, young nanny around if they want their fledging relationship to succeed."

I lost all respect for Nicole that day, and though I would have loved to steal Sophie away in my suitcase, I wasn't ready to add kidnapping to my record just yet. A few days later, I moved back to Austin and Ellie put in a good word for me at Twin Oaks—a.k.a. where dreams go to die.

"When do you work again?" Ellie asks, drawing my attention away from the mirror.

"Tomorrow."

"What about Thursday?"

"I'm off."

She looks up from her magazine and grins. For a second, I'm taken aback by how similar we look nowadays. The two-year age gap between us used to be a big deal. Now, we could almost be twins—that is, if she stopped blowing $500 every few weeks to turn her light brown tresses platinum blonde. After all these years of hair dye, she should be walking around with frizzed-out straw for hair, but the trendy downtown salon she goes to must be filled with miracle workers, because even I sometimes forget Barbie blonde isn't her natural color.

"Perfect. I need you to cover my shift."

I scrunch my nose. "Yeah, no thanks. I'm not really looking to spend any more time at Twin Oaks than I have to."

She claps her hands together and juts her lower lip out pleadingly. In turn, I clap my hands together and flip her the double bird.

"Please Brooke! Tyler's band has a gig at Stubb's. They're opening for Vance Joy and I can't miss it."

I don't want to concede, not necessarily because I want Thursday off, but because Ellie works the dinner service at the club. I've only ever taken on lunchtime duties, and staff normally trains for at least a week before taking dinner service. *No*, I'm not worried about where the salad forks and dessert spoons go; I'm talking about the politics. You don't want to sit an Edwards next to a Daniels and provoke a food fight.

"Seriously, PLEASE. I'll owe you big time!" she says before pausing and tapping her chin, mulling it over. "Wait, actually, I *won't* owe you because I got you this job in the first place."

She's played the trump card.

"Fine. I'll do it. Text me any random things I need to know to cover my ass. I don't want to disappoint Brian."

She wags her eyebrows. "I thought you didn't care about the job."

"I don't, but that doesn't mean I want to be a shitty employee. Dad raised us better than that."

She nods, seemingly impressed with my wisdom. Little does she know, I'm just saying that to segue into the conversation I actually care about. "Speaking of Dad...does *he* know you're going to Tyler's gig on Thursday?"

She levels her blue eyes on me. They're ice cold. *Huh.* I need to remember that trick.

"No, he doesn't, and I'm not going to tell him."

"Smart. If we learned anything from binge-watching sitcoms as kids, it's that lying to your parents and sneaking out always goes off without a hitch."

She throws her magazine at me and I narrowly avoid a

paper cut to the cornea.

"He's not going to find out."

She's being naive. Ellie still lives at home with our dad and shiny new stepmother. If she comes home on Thursday (or early Friday morning) reeking of smoke and excuses, Dad will definitely do some sleuthing to figure out where she's been. He hates Tyler, and for good reason. Tyler has been arrested like 45 times for all sorts of fancy-sounding crimes, like possession of an illegal substance (weed) and driving while intoxicated (stupid), but Ellie is blind to his flaws. I blame the full-sleeve tattoos and hot, hot British accent.

Before Tyler tempted her with his bad-boy persona, Ellie had a clear type: hot, preppy rich kids, the type of guys she and I went to high school with. (*Yup. Shocking, isn't it? Ellie and I are from old money.*) We went to an expensive prep school in Austin and spent our childhood in the nice part of Westlake, where the houses are spaced acres apart and the views give you a glimpse of the entire cityscape. My experience growing up there is the exact reason I can't stand most members of the country club. I'll take my neighbors at the co-op any day.

"Didn't he threaten to kick you out if you kept seeing him? What are you going to do without Dad's infinity pool and fully stocked walk-in pantry?"

She smirks. "I'm spending the night at Tyler's place and heading straight to work on Friday afternoon. Dad will never know."

"You know, you wouldn't have to worry about sneaking around if you moved out."

"Why would I blow most of my paycheck on rent every month if I don't have to? Dad's house is massive, the fridge is always full, and I hardly have to see Martha."

"Really?"

I assumed our stepmom watched over the house like a gargoyle.

"Really. She has a very regimented life. Tennis at Twin Oaks every morning, then lunch with a few ladies from the Women's Philanthropic League of Austin. By midafternoon she's usually so exhausted from her hectic schedule that she has to have a 'lie down' that looks a lot like a white wine coma. I'm not allowed to play music or turn the TV on between the hours of 2 and 4 PM."

"*Jesus*. She's insane."

Ellie laughs. "She's not that bad. She makes Dad happy, and that's really all that matters, right?"

"I guess."

She points at me. "You two would actually get along if you made more of an effort to get to know her. She invited me to go with her to one of her charity meetings Thursday."

"And you said yes?"

She pushes to the end of the bed and swings her feet to the ground. "Yes. I agreed because Martha has been married to Dad for almost five years now."

"What about Mom?"

Her voice is devoid of emotion when she replies stubbornly, "What about her? She's halfway across the world at the moment."

"She said she'd be here for Christmas."

Ellie's laugh cuts deeper than it should. "Right. I'll leave out some milk and cookies for her."

She's putting her shoes on, getting ready to leave, when I offer up a sad suggestion.

"We could always visit her."

Her head snaps up and her eyes narrow. "Do you even know where she's stationed? Last I heard she and Jorge were still in Africa."

"They're in Argentina now."

"See? Do you see how ridiculous this is? You need to let it go, Brooke. I'm not saying you have to like Martha, but chasing after Mom is getting pathetic."

I flinch and she steps closer, wrapping me up in a hug before continuing.

"Sorry, I didn't mean that."

I don't hug her back, but I do inhale her shampoo. "Yes you did."

"Come with us to the charity meeting tomorrow. The event is benefitting a group that saves pigs from cosmetics testing labs."

"A bunch of old biddies in lipstick raising money for a bunch of little piggies in lipstick? No thanks, sis."

• • •

Thursday afternoon, despite my protests, I find myself smack dab in the middle of a Women's Philanthropic League of Austin luncheon. I recognize more than half of the injected lips in the room from Twin Oaks. This town is small, and these women's waistlines are (surgically) smaller.

"Brooke, I had no idea you were interested in joining the League!"

I glance up from my delicately arranged cucumber sandwich and force a smile for Jamie Mathers. "Oh, I don't think I am. My stepmom is a member, and I came to support her."

Jamie exchanges a knowing glance with the other women in our small circle. All five of them were in my graduating class in high school, and all five of them are currently carrying heavy rocks on their left ring fingers and supporting varying degrees of pregnant bellies. Jamie Mathers is the furthest along, and I'm slightly worried she'll go into labor on the spot. I wonder if it'd be rude to finish my cucumber sandwich before rendering aid.

"Well that's so nice of you," she says with a honey-dipped smile. "I'm glad you came. I haven't seen you since everyone left for college. What are you up to now?"

My eyebrows hit my hairline. "Oh…well, I'm kind of between positions at the moment."

"My mom mentioned you were working at the club with Ellie," Jessica Lindsey adds with a conniving grin.

It feels like a TMZ-style gotcha moment, and I'm reminded why I never liked Jessica.

"It's a temporary thing," I shoot back quickly.

They hum, and I decide that two can play this game. "What about you, Jamie? Jessica? What are you guys up to these days?"

They laugh and rub their swollen bellies like a pair of sequined Teletubbies. It's then that I decide I've officially stepped into the Twilight Zone. Compared to these women, I feel so young and ill-prepared for adulthood. There's so much life I want to live before I start wearing Lily Pulitzer rompers and joining mommy Facebook groups.

"Prepping for motherhood is a full-time job *in and of itself*," Jessica replies coolly.

As if it takes an advanced degree to pop out a placenta.

"Ah, I'm sure."

"Not to mention, Harry and I just moved into a new house in Tarrytown. It's going to take me *months* to decorate it. I just hope I can get everything done before Mary Grace arrives this fall."

The girls chat amongst themselves excitedly, talking about wallpaper swatches and Restoration Hardware cribs. I'm debating between the small cups of strawberry shortcake and crème brûlée circulating the room when they direct the conversation back toward me.

"What about you, Brooke?"

I snap my attention back to the group. "What?"

"Where are you living these days?"

They're expecting to hear the name of a ritzy Austin neighborhood, so when I explain my current living arrangement, they're all more than a little confused.

"What exactly is a *cowop*?" Jessica asks. "Isn't that where the weird art students live in West Campus?"

"Yeah…" Jamie adds, "I used to have to walk by one of those on my way to class. I swear everyone there was smoking—" She lowers her voice. "*Marijuana*. You could smell it a mile away."

They all glance back at me, waiting for my reply. I smile extra wide. "Yes. It's exactly like that, only north of campus."

"Oh." Jessica is stunned.

Jamie laughs nervously and tries to salvage the situation. "I don't know how you do it. I need my privacy. I can hardly manage sharing 3,000 square feet with Benjamin, let alone a dozen other people."

Benjamin (a.k.a. Ben Mackenzie) went to a neighboring high school, and regularly spent time at parties belching the letters of the alphabet. No one in their right mind ever referred to him as *Benjamin*. I want to call Jamie out for turning into a pretentious snob, but then I'd be just as bad as she is. So what if these women want to grow up and play house? Good for them. It's just not for me. Right now I want to eat another cucumber sandwich, avoid eye contact with Martha for the rest of this luncheon, and make it home in time to take a nap before I have to cover Ellie's shift at the club.

Ian is waiting for me by the curb outside when the luncheon wraps up. (Okay, that's a lie. I'm leaving an hour before everyone else because I ate my fill of artisanal cheeses and was bored out of my mind.) I'm surprised to see him because he's never been on time in his life—or at least not in the three months I've known him. Normally when he says, *Be right there!* he means, *Be right there when I finish smoking or jerking off,* or whatever the hell he does in that room of his.

"What's up, sexy?" he asks after leaning over to open his passenger-side door for me. He scoops all the empty coffee cups and organic granola wrappers onto the floor so I can sit down. *Romance.*

"Hey, thanks for picking me up."

I don't have a car. When I moved back to Austin, I bought a fixed-gear bike off Craigslist. It's old—on its dying leg—but it fits in well around the Austin bike lanes. It's great for getting around to most places, but for times like this, when I'm strapped into a cocktail dress and high heels, I have to rely on other people for transportation, hence why I called Ian—barista and model, fellow co-oper, short-term fling.

We're halfway back to the building when Ellie shoots me a text.

ELLIE: You left before I could give you the details about the shift!

BROOKE: Sorry. Had to get out of there. What should I know?

ELLIE: Make sure you check that the tables are

27

set up right when you get there. The servers are responsible for their own sections, but I'm pretty sure Jared works tonight and he always slacks off.

BROOKE: Got it. Anything else?

ELLIE: Check in with the chef and make sure he doesn't have any special requests for you. He likes to go over the specials with the hostess just in case a member asks about them.

I make a mental note to do both things before Ian speaks up.

"I took some new headshots today."

"Oh yeah?"

"Marco shot them for me before he left for a job. We posed in front of the graffiti wall downtown."

"That's great." I smile, feeling the buzz of another text in my lap.

ELLIE: Oh! I almost forgot! Guess who's coming in for dinner tonight.

"You don't sound very enthusiastic."

BROOKE: Who?

"Brooke."

"I *am* enthusiastic!" I insist, dropping my phone and turning my attention back to him. "New headshots will really help you book jobs."

My lap vibrates and I ignore it.

"Who are you texting anyway?"

"My sister," I answer honestly, though I don't like that

he's even asking me that question. Ian and I don't owe each other anything. We're friends, buds. We live in the co-op together, and sometimes he gives me a ride if he happens to be free. Twice in the last three months we've hooked up. It's the definition of a no-strings-attached fling, but when he glances over to me, I have a sneaking suspicion that he wants us to be something more.

"Do you want to hang out tonight? Like a date?"

Shit. Shit. Shit. For a while, I've been getting the feeling that Ian is looking for something a little more serious, and that question confirms it.

"Sorry. I have to work," I say, both relived to have an excuse and sad to have to turn him down. Ian is nice, even if his room at the co-op smells like a coffee roaster exploded inside of it and his greatest ambition in life is to become an "influencer" on Instagram. I just don't want a boyfriend at the moment. I'm actively trying to find a new position as an au pair or a tutor and chances are that when I do find one, I'll be forced to relocate for it. Ian knows this, and he's agreed to keep things light, but now I'm wondering if I need to take a step back.

When we arrive at the co-op, I make sure to thank him profusely for the ride and even offer him the extra cookie I stole from the charity luncheon. I was going to enjoy it after work—maybe with some cheap wine—but giving it to him helps assuage my guilt over potentially leading him on.

Damn. I wanted that cookie. Boys suck.

I don't remember that my sister texted me back until I'm upstairs in my room getting ready for my shift. I smooth down the silky material of my black cocktail dress and slide into some block-heeled black sandals before I reach for my phone and open our conversation.

His name jumps out at me in ALL CAPS, and my

stomach turns over in anticipation.

I read the last few texts again, just to confirm it says what I'm hoping it does.

ELLIE: Oh! I almost forgot! Guess who's coming in for dinner tonight.
BROOKE: Who?
ELLIE: JAMES ASHWOOD.

# CHAPTER THREE

James Ashwood is celebrating. That's what the note says by his reservation. He's requested a table near the fireplace for him and 10 guests. There will be champagne and multiple courses, and Brian has assigned three servers to the table so every need can be met right away. When I first arrived for my shift, the chef called an all-hands meeting just to go over *his* table specifically. The gist: don't fuck it up.

I'm standing behind the podium now, waiting for the first dinner guests to start arriving. It's 5:30 PM, and James' reservation is at 7:00 PM—an hour and a half that will feel like an eternity. Unlike when I work in the cabana, shifts in here tend to drag because I'm not constantly running around like a chicken with my head cut off. My job is to stand behind the podium in a semi-revealing yet sophisticated cocktail dress and greet guests as they walk in. I smile and offer up a polite hello then toss in a bit of tasteful small talk as I lead them on a short walk to their table. Easy peasy. In total, it takes about 30 seconds, maybe a minute if their table is across the dining room.

I use the time between guests to check my email. The tutoring agency should be getting back to me soon. They've informed me that positions are tight at the moment, but I have stellar references and a great education. The problem, I know, lies in the requisite headshot sitting at the bottom of my application. I wish I could add a little caption underneath that reads, *Hey, by the way, I'm not trying to sleep with your husband.*

"Hey! Brooke, right?"

I shove my phone beneath the podium with superhuman speed, slightly embarrassed to have been caught using it during my shift. Brian has threatened to chop fingers off if he catches us on them around the members. Fortunately, when I glance up, it's just one of the club's bartenders standing on the other side of the podium. I hardly recognize him outside of his usual post behind the dining room's mahogany bar, but his silver tie provides a helpful reminder. All the bartenders wear them. Beside it, his nametag proclaims him to be Garrett.

"Hey, yeah." I smile. "What's up?"

I glance to my right, where the dining room sprawls out before me. Surely I haven't already done something wrong. If I have, Ellie is going to kill me.

His smile turns crooked as he inches closer to the podium and lowers his voice.

"I know this is last minute, and you don't even know me, but I was wondering if you might be able to help me out."

My smile fades slightly. This dude is about to ask me to stay late. I can feel the request seeping out of his pores. He's going to beg, I know it, and then, of course, he does. Apparently Garrett has a "hot date" that he "really can't miss". It's with a woman he's been pursuing for months, and she's finally giving him the time of day. I feel for him, I do, but closing is for the birds, and I have plans with some cheap wine and a cookie—*oh, that's right*. I gave away my only excuse. What is it with men today?

"Garrett, I'd love to help you out, but—"

"Brooke, *please*. I'll pick up a shift for you! You name the day and I'll do it!"

It's sweet of him to offer, but somehow I don't think our members would enjoy seeing him traipse around the pool in a pleated skirt quite as much as he thinks. Unfortunately, I'd have to help him out with no promise of anything in return. Who does he think I am, Mother freaking Teresa?

But seeing a grown man beg is kind of awkward, and there are members walking in the door behind him. I don't want him to cause a scene, so before I fully realize what I'm doing, I agree and shoo him back to the bar.

"You're the best! Thank you!"

As it turns out, I am not the best. I am a sad sap, which Ellie confirms when I ask her what closing duties entail.

ELLIE: NO! Why did you agree?! You need to get out of that ASAP. Do you have any idea what that means?

I have no clue. Ellie does though, and she wastes no time informing me over a string of texts.

Basically, the club closes at 10 PM, but in reality, it closes when the last member decides to leave, and for top-paying members—the men and women whose perks extend well beyond the standard service—the doors are open 24/7.

ELLIE: You're going to be there all night! Tell Garrett to go screw himself! I bet he doesn't even have a date!

I glance up and lock eyes with Garrett behind the bar. He layers his hands over his heart and mouths another thank-you. I want to heed Ellie's directions, but the guy seems earnest, and what if he actually is going on a date? What if it's his potential soul mate? I'm selfish, but standing in the way of love just seems evil.

I wave back to him and toss my phone back beneath the podium with a grumble. The next time there's a break in guests, I head to the kitchen for a cup of coffee. Apparently, it's going to be a *long* night.

I'm not away from my post for more than a minute, and yet by the time I step back into the dining room, I spot *the* James Ashwood and his guests waiting at an *empty* hostess podium.

"Oh come on!" I hiss under my breath.

I pick up my pace right away, all but running across the room. Coffee spills across the front of my dress, but there's no time to worry about the smell of burning flesh because James Ashwood is watching me (*AHHH!*), and I'm watching Brian as he darts across the room in a mad dash to get to the podium. If he gets there before I do, I might as well clear out my locker right now…which wouldn't be so bad considering I hate this place, but I don't have another job. I can't get fired *yet*.

Thankfully, the spare tire around Brian's waist slows him down more than my high heels. I make it to the podium a few seconds before him.

"Good evening," I say, embarrassed by how exerted I am.

I work out, so I shouldn't be breathing like some sort of creepy man hovering over people's shoulders on the bus, but I attribute it to nerves. James Ashwood is standing a few feet away, and I'm smiling at him while the skin on my stomach sizzles.

Up close, he exudes a sort of aggressive authority, a

way of standing with his broad shoulders pushed back and his chin lifted high. He's used to moving through life unchecked, that much is clear.

"Are you all right?" he asks, pointing down at my cup. "Your coffee's half gone."

I glance down at my now-soaked dress and on cue, a few drops of coffee hit the floor. "Oh, yeah..." I laugh awkwardly. "I prefer to look at it as half full."

"Mr. Ashwood!" Brian says as he screeches to a halt behind me. "I'm so sorry for the wait!"

He shakes his head. "It's not a problem. Your hostess was just helping us."

It's here that I should probably clarify that I've only ever seen James Ashwood from afar. Maybe someday I'll stop referring to him by both his first and last name, but for now—and honestly, probably for always—he will remain James Ashwood. Without a doubt, he falls into the George Clooney category of men. From polling the women around the club, there isn't a single person walking around here with two X chromosomes who doesn't find him *extremely* attractive.

In the last month, I've heard numerous over-the-top phrases uttered about him.

From Janine, the sous chef in the kitchen: "He's so hot I want to bake him into a pie and sit on it."

From Hannah, one of the tennis pros: "His ass is like a perfect eclipse—you'll go blind if you stare directly at it."

I want to be impervious to his charms and looks because he seems like a royal pain in the ass, what with the cars, and the suits, and that soul-stealing smile he's aiming at one of his dinner dates right now. They're quite a group. Altogether, they could star in a 90210-esque drama about beautiful young people. There's a perky Asian girl with

35

cropped black hair, a svelte blonde with swoon-worthy red lipstick, a redhead with boobs they can probably make out from the space station, and a gaggle of men that compliment them well. I plan on getting a better look at them all as I lead their group to their table near the fireplace, but Brian steps forward and announces that he'll be taking them instead. Apparently, he doesn't trust my line-leading abilities, or maybe he's mad that I left my post for half a second.

I watch the backs of their shiny, privileged heads as they step past the podium. James is flanked by Nunga-Nunga Ginger and Svelte Blonde as he makes his way through the dining room, and I know for him, our short exchange is already forgotten.

Their servers are already in place, ready to start wine service. I can't hear what they're saying, but one of them presents him with a bottle of high-priced champagne. He nods and waves for his guests to claim their seats. I'm still staring, waiting for something. I'm not sure what it is until he glances back and his eyes meet mine across the dining room.

A ton of bricks fall on my chest.

I'm paralyzed.

And then he smiles, and it's small, *hidden*, like we're both in on a private joke, but there's no time to read into it. His attention sweeps back to his guests and there's a family walking up to the podium, ready to be seated. I shake my head. Clear my throat. Blink—again—and then force a wide smile for the members in front of me.

"Good morn—evening. Have you reservated…I mean, do you have a reservation?"

I use the next few hours during my shift to dissect James Ashwood, as if by breaking him down into chewable parts, he'll be easier to assess and subsequently dismiss. I suspect most of his power, like mine, comes from his hair. It seems odd, I know. There are few men known strictly for their locks. Fabio is, of course, one of them, but rest assured, the two have nothing in common. James' short hair is a rich, dark brown with a natural wave that's almost boyish, but with a touch of pomade the strands stay put in a business-friendly, panty-dropping look.

Separate from "the hair", there's his bone structure: firm jaw, straight nose. It makes me want to vomit in my mouth to say his face could be chiseled from marble, but it's the only way I can convey JUST HOW BEAUTIFULLY PROPORTIONED THIS MAN IS! *Roll over in your grave, Michelangelo. See if I care*.

I suspect his eyes are brown, but I feel like if I were ever close enough to notice the intricacies of his irises, I'd pass out before I could study them. As much as I'd love to go into detail about the rest of him, I can't because I don't *know* the details. His body definitely seems to be in good shape under his suits, but maybe that's the magic of expensive tailoring. He's definitely tall, but I couldn't rattle off an exact figure to save my life. Maybe one day I'll be with him when he robs a convenience store and I can use the ruler taped by the door to confirm whether he's 6'0'' or a little over.

I'm not satisfied. I want details, so I do what any responsible person would do: I try to Google him during my shift. I'm knee-deep in my investigation when Marissa joins me at the podium.

"What are you doing?" she asks, peering down at my phone. "Why are you looking at suits on Dolce & Gabbana's website?"

I hold up the medium-blue suit for her to inspect. "Do

you think James is wearing that right now?"

She snorts. "The dude buys custom. I hear he has a suit guy he flies in from Italy once a quarter."

I narrow my eyes in disbelief. "Who told you that?"

"Larry, from the kitchen."

"Oh, does 'Larry from the kitchen' know a lot about designer suits?"

"Maybe he moonlights at a dry cleaners? I dunno, but the suit guy thing seems plausible."

I shrug and slide my phone back to its hiding spot. "You're right. I guess it doesn't really matter anyway."

"Are you that bored?"

Yes. *Out of my mind*. It's 9:00 PM, so most of the diners have long since packed in the carbs and gone home. A few stragglers remain, and of course, James' entire group is still going strong. I've lost track of how many bottles of champagne they've managed to uncork. Let's just say the club's wine cellar might need to be restocked in the morning.

"Well at least we're both off soon. Let's go get a beer."

I level her with a death stare. "I wish, but Garrett somehow convinced me to cover for him."

She looks confused. "But Garrett is scheduled to close tonight…"

"Yep. Kill me now."

My misery does not find company with Marissa. She cracks up like I've said something hi-larious then claps her hand on the podium and tells me I'm a poor schmuck before she walks away.

"I'll remember that!" I call out after her.

She waves over her shoulder. "Have fun burning the midnight oil!"

I go back to Googling designer suits so I don't fall

asleep standing up. Another two groups of diners stroll out, a little obnoxious and a lot tipsy. Brian sees me twiddling my thumbs and instructs me to head back and help roll silverware for tomorrow's lunch service. *With pleasure.*

I spend an hour in the employee break room, divvying up knives and forks, and in that time, I add another quote to my collection.

"Do you think James Ashwood has his suits custom made?" I ask the coworker assembling cutlery with me.

From Yvonne, a member of the kitchen staff: "I don't care where he buys 'em as long as I know where the zipper is."

Alrighty then.

I finish up the rest of my closing duties and then head to check on Brian. Last time I saw him, he was on his way to confirm that James' group had everything they needed, but that was at least an hour ago. I've been chatting with the kitchen staff long enough that the dining room should be empty. *PLEASE GOD, LET IT BE EMPTY.* I want to go home and sleep before I have to wake up and do this all over again.

The club's chandeliers are set to dim continuously during dinnertime so that guests arriving at 5:30 PM are illuminated much more than those rolling in around 8:00. Now, as I leave the kitchen, the room is the darkest I've ever seen it. All the tea candles have been extinguished, and the hallway light that usually illuminates the hostess podium is off. Brian must have finished my closing duties for me, which means I'm that much closer to freedom.

I step into the dining room, prepared to make a beeline for the podium, grab my phone and purse, and get the hell out of this place before anyone can assign me last-minute duties. A quick glance toward the fireplace confirms that

James' group is gone, and the servers assigned to his table made quick work of the aftermath. It's almost like he was never there at all, except I have the open Google search on my phone to prove he was.

I make it another few steps before the sound of a glass being put down on the bar catches my attention. I whip my gaze across the space and there he sits.

Alone at the bar.

 CHAPTER FOUR

His rich brown hair glows beneath the dim, warm light, and his elbows are resting on the bar as his thumb brushes back and forth across the brim of a whiskey glass. I stand frozen as he pauses and takes a slow sip.

I don't think he knows I'm here. I glance back to the kitchen door and then across to the podium. I'm not supposed to leave until the last member is gone, I get that, but being here right now feels like an invasion of his privacy. Where is Brian when I need him? Surely the bartenders didn't leave James Ashwood to fend for himself? *Dear god, did he have to pour his own drink?* Brian will never let us hear the end of it. There will be 50 all-hands-on-deck meetings, maybe more.

I chew on my lip, willing Brian to magically appear. I need to know what I'm supposed to do here. James doesn't look like he wants company, but I don't want to get fired. I could ask him if he needs anything, but that's not my job. Where is the bartender? His waiter? How about a freaking bus boy?

I take a small step toward the podium, contemplating breaking out in a full sprint, but his voice catches me before I can.

"Come have a seat."

I freeze like a deer caught in headlights, and then I do the very ridiculous, very sitcom move of glancing over my shoulder to confirm that he is in fact talking to me.

There's no one else in the room.

I turn back to him. He's taking another sip of his drink. I clear my throat and try to speak without conveying how much he's caught me off guard.

"Oh, err, I'm on the clock. Actually, is there anything I can get you, Mr. Ashwood? The kitchen is still open."

That's a lie. When I passed by, the kitchen staff was wrapping up for the night, cleaning and prepping for tomorrow, but I don't care. I will force one of them to whip something up if James wants it, and if they don't agree, I'll do it myself. I've seen inside the refrigerators back there— there's more than enough fancy food to mask my ineptitude.

"You're still on the clock?" he asks, still facing away from me.

"Yes."

With that, he uses his foot to push aside the barstool beside him. Now it's angled to face him, and it's clearly an invitation for me to sit.

"So then there's no problem. I pay the club, the club pays you, and now I'm asking you to sit."

His words are demanding and clear. This man has entitlement seeping from his pores, but his tone catches me off guard. It's surprisingly gentle, almost…sad.

I step closer. "I really shouldn't. I have closing duties."

He chuckles, just once, like he knows I'm lying. "I'm sure they can manage without you."

And then finally, he turns and levels me with his searing gaze. As I suspected, his eyes are dark brown, almost black, and they pack quite a punch.

"Mr. Ashwood! I didn't realize you were still here."

It's Brian, finally. He's rushing into the room to aid

our last, lonely member, but James is still focused on me, studying me just like I'm studying him.

"I'd like Brooke to sit with me for a few minutes," he says to Brian. "Can you spare her?"

"Oh!" Brian's gaze volleys between us. "Of course, but it's up to Brooke. Her shift is ending soon."

I'm shocked by his answer. I assumed he would force me to sit and entertain James. Now, the decision is up to me, and that somehow makes it easier to step closer and accept the barstool he's moved aside for me. Brian says he'll be in his office if Mr. Ashwood needs anything, and before he leaves, he shoots me a warning with one look: *don't say anything stupid.*

Then we're alone again in the quiet dining room.

I situate myself on the barstool so my cocktail dress falls as far down my thighs as the silky material will allow. James acts like he doesn't notice as he takes a long pull of his drink. I wonder what number he's on. He doesn't seem drunk, but he's been in the club for hours, so there's no way he's exactly sober.

I turn and study his profile. At this proximity, I can see everything I've been imagining for the last few weeks. My gaze drags across his strong jawline and then higher, across his cheekbones. He's still clean-shaven, and I wonder if he usually has more stubble by this time of day.

Maybe I would have asked him, but he speaks up first.

"Tell me the real reason you didn't want to sit with me."

He asks the question with a small, teasing smirk, and it makes me want to tease back.

"I didn't want to get fired."

His smirk extends another inch and he turns to face me. I'm sad to lose his profile, but this is so much better. It's intoxicating to sit this close to him, with his full attention aimed at me. His eyes hold mine and I want to continue like that, meeting him spade for spade, but I cave. My gaze falls to my lap, and then over to the rows of expensive liquor lining the back of the bar.

"Having a drink with a member off the clock hardly seems like a fireable offense."

"Well if I'm *off the clock*, I might as well just head home," I say coyly.

"Something tells me you'll stay."

His voice is so smooth and enticing. It's confident, but not nearly as sharp as I'd imagined.

"I usually don't keep company with guys like you," I say, giving him the real reason. I catch his raised eyebrows out of the corner of my eyes. Maybe my honesty caught him off guard. "Sorry, you're probably used to staff members kissing your ass."

He nods. "Usually the right cheek, but your boss, Brian—he goes for both."

Is that genuine humor? It feels like a trap, as if he's trying to bait me into incriminating myself. I remain silent, half tempted to slide off the barstool and leave.

"Well if it matters, you're not my usual type either," he offers.

What's that supposed to mean?

"Well, yeah. I'd imagine you spend less time with *the help* and more time with *the helped*, like the group you came in with."

"Those women came with my friends, part of the celebration committee," he clarifies.

I remember that's why he came in tonight.

"What are we celebrating?"

"*We*? Technically I'm the only one with a drink."

He holds up his tumbler to prove his point.

Most of the veteran employees drink through their entire shift, so I don't feel bad hopping down and slinking around the bar to pour myself something. There's a ton of wine, but none of the bottles are open, so instead I settle for a Jack and Coke, heavy on the Coke. It's not my usual, but I enjoy the slight burn of acid in the back of my throat. It distracts me from the fact that James is watching me walk around the bar and reclaim my seat. *Jack and James.*

I take another sip and then brave a glance at him. He looks amused...by me. How nice. I've always wanted to amuse a man as hot as him. *Not.*

"Now what are we celebrating?" I ask again, trying to keep the topic of conversation away from anything too personal.

"My company just launched a new product."

"Oh yeah?" I'd heard he owned his own company. "What's the product?"

"A smart watch."

"Sounds fancy. What does this glorified pedometer do? Track how many steps housewives take between the wine aisle at Target and their kid's soccer practice?"

I'm caught off guard by my own boldness, but if I'm truly off the clock, I'm no longer being paid to put up a subservient veneer.

"Not quite. It's an early detection system for heart attacks."

My glass pauses on the way to my mouth. "What? *How?"*

"It'll bore you."

"Try me."

He sighs and sets his tumbler down. "Basically, a high-risk patient wears it around their wrist and the device's biosensors keep track of temperature, oxygen saturation, blood pressure, and respiratory rates."

"Sounds fancy," I say.

"All of that is basic. The real breakthrough is our proprietary software. It integrates these previously isolated data points within predictive algorithms."

He sees my raised eyebrow and decides to bring it down a notch.

"In 99% of the trial cases, it warned people about a myocardial infarction 10 minutes before it actually happened."

"Wow, okay. So I pay you for a watch that beeps and tells me I'm going to die?"

He looks down and laughs, shaking his head. "When it detects an oncoming attack, it dispenses a low dose of aspirin, dispatches an ambulance to your location, and calls your emergency contact."

I'm suddenly aware that I've started biting my lower lip. There's something about a man talking passionately about something. When I realize what I'm doing, I release it and reach for my drink. "I feel bad for calling it a glorified pedometer."

He laughs. "Well to be fair, it does track a user's steps too. I think most smart watches do these days."

I smile. "How long have you been working on it?"

"Five years."

"Five years?! And you're celebrating *here*?"

I sweep my hand across the dining room. It's nice, don't get me wrong, but if I'd spent five years working on something that SAVES PEOPLE'S LIVES, I'd celebrate anywhere but here. Disneyland, maybe.

"All day I've been pulled in different directions. Interviews, luncheons, a launch party…it feels good to sit here." Maybe he can tell I'm not convinced, because he continues, "I've been coming here since I was a kid. In a way, it's a second home for me."

That's surprising to hear. Most of the members who are legacies tend to have that old money stench to them— lazy, entitled, and more demanding than most. James Ashwood doesn't carry the stench. In fact, the man smells like an amalgam of all those sexy-sounding cologne things: spice and pine and sandalwood. *What the hell is sandalwood anyway?*

"How long ago was that? Were you here before they moved the golf course?" I ask.

"Are you just trying to figure out my age?"

Guilty.

I blush. "Maybe."

"I'm 36."

"Huh."

For some reason, I'm disappointed.

"How old did you think I was?"

"Just…younger."

I take another sip of my Jack and Coke. Soon I'm going to need a refill, or maybe by then James will be ready to leave.

"How old are you, Brooke?"

I still, somehow shocked that he knows my name. *Did Brian say it earlier?* I can't remember.

I slide my gaze to him. He's watching me with those eyes, a gaze that can cut straight through me. "I'm 25."

"25," he repeats with a nod before taking a sip of his drink.

"11 years."

"What?"

"That's the gap between us."

47

He smirks. "Am I allowed to have a drink with a woman 11 years younger than me?"

He sounds amused again. My cheeks are so red they might stay that way permanently, but I refuse to be anything other than cool and collected around James.

I shrug. "It's just a drink, right? I didn't mean to insinuate that we're—"

He cuts me off. "You didn't. Anyway, you told me I wasn't your type earlier, remember?"

I nearly choke. "Well, my type has been pretty hit-and-miss lately."

"You have a boyfriend?"

There's an authoritative edge to his tone when he asks that question—or maybe I'm reading too much into it.

"Soon to be ex, actually."

"Poor guy."

He doesn't sound the least bit empathetic.

"Maybe he deserves it," I point out.

"Maybe."

I look away and change the subject. "So, you make heart attack watches…is that what you used to tell people you wanted to do when you grew up?"

He sighs like my question just weighed him down. I glance back to find him staring down at his empty glass.

"It's just one part of my company…a means to an end."

"For what?"

He glances up at me from beneath his brows. "I started BioWear when I graduated from college, when I was…well, a bit more idealistic. I wanted to help people who *really* needed it, not just rich Americans. I wanted to combat neglected tropical diseases."

I laugh. "Okay, turn around—let me see if there's a

cape hanging off that suit."

He doesn't laugh with me. "I'm boring you. Let's talk about something else."

I've offended him.

I reach out and touch his shoulder. It's an intimate act between friends, but we aren't friends—we hardly know each other. We both freeze, and maybe I've gone too far, presumed too much. I yank my hand away and face the bar. It's an awkward couple of seconds, made worse by the fact that he doesn't rush to speak first.

"You can tell me about it if you want," I offer quietly. "I'd like to know more."

He doesn't continue right away. He's like a turtle coming out of his shell. Maybe he doesn't open up to many people like this, or maybe he thinks I really am bored, but in truth, this man could read off his junk mail folder and I'd be listening with bated breath.

"During my senior year of college, I took a global health seminar as a blow-off class. The professor didn't give tests, everyone knew it, so twice a week, I sat in the back row, bored and distracted while most of my friends didn't even bother showing up. I don't remember what most of the semester focused on, but one day, we had a guest lecturer, a project coordinator for Doctors Without Borders. She stood at the front of the class and flipped through a quick PowerPoint. Each slide presented some form of technology that could drastically impact the lives of people in third world countries—water filtration systems, solar panels, that sort of thing. At the end of it, she challenged us to be the next wave of inventors."

"And you listened."

He meets my gaze. "I guess so."

"So what's your focus?"

He answers quickly. "Mosquitos."

"*Mosquitos*?"

"They're the number one carrier of tropical diseases like malaria."

I've listened to enough NPR news hours to realize that's true, but short of eradicating the whole species, there's not much that can be done. *Unless...*

"So you want to buy a bunch of mosquito nets?"

He smiles. "The first piece of wearable tech I developed was a shirt—the BioShield."

"Sounds like something Iron Man would wear. What does it do?"

"It monitors the resting electric potential of human skin. The second a mosquito lands, the nanoprocessors in the device feel it. Before the mosquito can bite, an imperceptible electrical impulse is sent along the wearer's epidermis, just enough to deter the mosquito."

"Sounds awesome."

"It is. In testing, the prototype reduced the transmission of mosquito-born diseases by 98%."

"Have you guys started mass-producing it yet?"

He laughs. "To date, there have been three versions made. Each one cost about a million dollars."

I'd do a spit-take if my Jack and Coke weren't empty.

"I guess it's pretty hard to market in sub-Saharan Africa at that price."

"Exactly."

He stares down at his glass.

"So what are you going to do?" I ask, enjoying the fact that he's talking to me as if I'm an equal, not just some cabana girl.

"I've run the numbers, and with enough time and ingenuity, that number can be reduced to about $200 a shirt. So, while it won't ever be profitable…"

"It would be affordable," I finish, and he nods. "From a charity perspective. So your watch…it funds that project?"

He taps his glass on the bar twice in the affirmative. "Along with a few of our other mass-market consumer items."

"You know you could just kick back and buy a yacht or something, right?" I laugh.

"Yeah, but the upkeep on those things is ridiculous. It's better to rent, even if you have to give up that new yacht smell."

His slow-rolling smirk catches me off guard.

"Oh, the problems of the rich," I tease with an exaggerated eye roll.

It's clear James realizes how fortunate he is—fortunate, and getting more irresistible by the minute, which is a problem for a whole slew of reasons. He's 11 years older than me, and not once has he intimated that he invited me to sit for reasons beyond a platonic conversation. I should probably get up and leave before I accidentally fall into his bottomless brown eyes.

"Enough about me," he says, as if reading my mind. "What do you want to do with your life?"

Oh come on, like that's fair. It feels like I'm back in the third grade about to present my science fair project. Becky Olsen just went into detail about the efficacy and longevity of three popular sunscreen brands. Meanwhile, I'm picking my nose in front of a ragged poster that asks: *Are Cocoa Puffs Yummier than Fruity Pebbles?*

So, I deflect with humor. "You're looking at it."

"What? Working at a country club?"

Of course he sounds surprised, but for all he knows this is my dream job. Maybe I scraped by my entire life getting to this point and he just shit all over it.

"*Ohh yeah.* I love working at the cabana pool, serving margaritas to old geezers like you."

He smirks. "That's fine. I just don't see someone like you staying at a place like this for long."

"Someone like me? Because you know me so well?"

"I know *of* you."

Now I'm really confused.

"What does that mean?"

"You're pretty infamous around here."

I'm shocked. "For what exactly? I've only worked here for a few months."

Rumors travel fast through the club, regardless of whether they're based in fact or fiction. For all I know, some member has been going around with some story about how I gave him a blowjob down in the wine cellar. It wouldn't be that much of a stretch—Janice did it with Mr. Neal last week. I know because I caught them in the act.

"Nothing bad," he assures me. "Let's just say that every male member took notice the day you started working here."

Oh.

I don't know what he wants me to do with that information, giggle and fan my face? *You mean they like little ol' me?* The knowledge makes my skin itch. I want to deflect the attention away from me.

"Well, that's interesting considering every female employee is obsessed with you." I hold up my empty glass. "Cheers to being infamous."

By my tone, it's clear I don't really put much stock in what he's said. I've never wanted to be a woman who derives her self-worth from the opinions of lecherous old men.

He's quiet, probably confused by my reaction, and instead of pushing away from the bar and offering up some excuse to leave, I gift him with the same knowledge he just gave me: the truth.

"I double-majored at UT, Spanish and French. Ideally, I'd like to find an au pair position where I can tutor a child in those languages one on one."

"You speak French?"

"*Oui*," I say with a wink.

The information seems to interest him more than it should, but I don't get the chance to enquire as to why before I catch Brian approaching us out of the corner of my eye.

"Mr. Ashwood, how is everything going in here?" he asks with a light and pleasant tone. "The kitchen staff has left for the night"—*subtle hint at how late it is*—"but I'm happy to get you anything you need"—*not-so-subtle hint that James is a VIP member Brian doesn't want to piss off.*

James glances down at his watch. My guess is that it's probably past midnight.

"I should get going actually."

My heart deflates like a sad Mylar balloon. I don't want this encounter to end. I already know it's not going to happen again. I've worked here for three months and have never talked to James; tonight was a rare occurrence to say the least.

He scoots his barstool back and stands. *Yup, definitely over 6'0".* And the suit? *Absolutely custom.*

His eyes meet mine, and I think he knows I was just checking him out. I wonder what he thinks about it.

"Thanks for humoring an *old* man," he says, bending low so Brian can't hear.

I know he's firing back for my geezer comment from

earlier, but it almost feels like flirting. *Damn*. If I'm this excited by the prospect of him barely flirting with me, what would it feel like to be pursued and seduced by a man like him? My heart probably couldn't handle it. I'd have to get one of his fancy watches.

"I didn't mind," I quip. "Oh yeah—congrats."

He nods once and then he's strolling away with his hands in his pockets, taking the scent of rare spices and exotic wood with him.

• • •

When I make it outside, I'm still floating in a weird, drug-like haze—so much so that I'm surprised to see Ian's old blue Hyundai Accent sitting beneath the porte cochère. I forgot I asked him to give me a ride home earlier. *How long has he been waiting?*

I pick up my pace and cringe when I see how angry he is.

"Jesus, I've been here forever. Why didn't you answer your phone?"

"Sorry, sorry! I had to close and there was a member inside who wouldn't leave."

It's the truth, just not the *whole* truth.

"I was about to come in, but I'm not exactly dressed for it," he says, motioning down to his Bob Marley boxers and foam flip-flips.

I buckle up as he puts his car in drive and loops around, back toward the gatehouse. At this time of night, there shouldn't be any other cars exiting the club, but when we arrive at the fork where the parking lot and the valet entrance merge, we're met by a sleek black Porsche. Ian presses on the brake. So does the Porsche. I fidget in my seat.

Ian curses under his breath and then waves the car forward.

The Porsche pulls out in front of us and then we chug along behind it, down the winding tree-lined drive. At the entrance, the gate takes a few seconds to open, and I try as hard as I can to see through the tint of the Porsche's back windows. I can make out the silhouette of a man in the front seat, but no features. Most importantly, I can't tell if he's watching me in his rearview mirror. I hope he is.

I can hear the engine purring over the sound of Ian complaining about how he almost lost his high waiting so long, but I'm focused on the idea of James. I want to know what the interior of his car feels like. I want to know what kind of music he likes to play at this time of night. I want to know where he's heading when we hit the first main road and he turns right before we turn left.

I'm disappointed because I will never get those answers.

"Ian, I think we should talk."

 **CHAPTER FIVE**

I've called my mom five times in the past two weeks and she hasn't answered once. If we were dating, I would have probably picked up on her not-so-subtle attempt to get rid of me and moved on, but she's my mom, and therefore can't ignore me forever. To be fair, she did attempt to call me back last week, but it was at 1:27 AM. Silly me, I was asleep. Now, I try again, counting the rings as they tick by while simultaneously digesting the new decor in my dad's guest bathroom.

It's Wednesday, which means I should be hanging out at Flying Saucer with co-op friends, kicking ass in trivia. Music is my topic of choice. There isn't a late 90s, early 2000s song I cannot name, date, and sing (poorly) word for word. Tonight, however, my team is playing without me. I've already received three text messages asking me about various pop lyrics. Who doesn't know the full chorus to Britney's "Baby One More Time"? They should be ashamed.

The phone rings on and on.

I inspect the new pendant light hanging over the bathroom sink. Martha must be watching *Fixer Upper*. There's enough shiplap in this bathroom to build an actual ship.

"Hi, you've reached Laura Acosta. Sorry I missed your call. Leave a message after the beep."

I do *not* leave a message. Voicemails, like Britney, are a relic of decades gone by. I need immediate gratification.

I punch the little red circle repeatedly and end the call four times over.

Everyone is waiting for me at the dinner table, and I can hear Ellie chatting with my dad about the country club. He's been a member for as long as I can remember, but he's never there. Work keeps him busy, thank goodness. The only thing worse than working at the cabana would be working at the cabana while my dad hovers nearby, teasing in that adorable yet infuriating way only dads can manage. Martha's there a lot, but only to play tennis with her friends. She sometimes stays for brunch, but usually leaves before my shift starts.

It occurs to me that I've been in the restroom for a while now. They've probably concluded that Martha's carefully puffed soufflé is not sitting well with me. I know I'll have to leave the safety of this shiplap dungeon soon, but I was really hoping my mom would answer my call. I want to ask her about Christmas, just to prove Ellie wrong. *She is coming, see?!*

When I make it back to the dining room, I pause in the doorway for a moment and take in the charming tableau presented there. The three of them look like an all-American family enjoying their post-dinner coffee and dessert. Martha is wearing a brightly patterned blouse and white jeans. My dad admires her with a warm smile before he reaches across the table and takes her hand. There is a steaming cup of decaf waiting for me on my placemat and a half-devoured peach pie with a crumble top in the center of the table.

"Would you like some pie, Brooke?" Martha asks in her pleasant tone when she notices me standing there. It's not one of those nauseatingly pleasant tones of cordiality; it is, in fact, genuine, which I find worse. "Or I could get you something else if you aren't"—she drops her voice—"feeling well?"

She's trying to ask tactfully if I am having a case of the shits.

I point to the pie. "I'll just take a slice. Thank you."

"Are you feeling okay?" Ellie asks me from across the table. "You were in there for like 45 minutes."

Martha clears her throat, and my dad hides a laugh before adding, "Ellie, save the bathroom talk for after dinner. I'm still eating my pie."

We're grown adults, but it still makes me smile when Ellie gets reprimanded. Residual immaturity.

"I was actually checking out the new decor in there," I respond. "It looks great. Last time I was here, you'd just taken down the old wallpaper."

Martha beams as she hands me my slice of pie. "Oh! Well, thank you. I've been watching this show on HGTV and it's given me the renovation bug."

I smirk and give myself a mental pat on the back for being right about ol' Chip and Jo.

"Did you bring in a designer?" I ask, because I know she didn't.

She blushes. "No, actually I did it myself."

"Wow! It looks so professional!"

My dad is smiling at me because he likes when I play nice with Martha. It's like he and Ellie expect me to come to dinner and breathe fire, but I'm not that bad. Just because I don't want to actively pursue a relationship with Martha doesn't mean I hate the woman. She makes crumble-top pie, people—she's not the devil. I realize that, but I already have a mom. She might be a million miles away with a perpetually dead cell phone, but she's still alive.

"Martha and I were talking about doing a spa day soon," Ellie says after taking a sip of her coffee. "She went to some fundraiser last month and bid on a massive package from Milk + Honey."

Martha nods. "It includes massages, manicures, and pedicures—maybe facials too, I have to check. It's actually for four people, but we could divvy up the remaining treatments between the three of us and make a whole day of it."

They're both looking at me expectantly, but I'm hesitant to agree. While I love cucumber eye masks and tiny women digging their elbows into my back as much as the next person, I don't want to make this a habit—that is, this "girl time" thing with Martha and Ellie. I've spent the last few years keeping a healthy distance, which is why on Wednesdays, I usually opt for trivia night instead of family dinner. This week, Ellie convinced me to come, and now the stone is rolling down the hill trading moss for spa day invites.

"Can I get back to you?" I ask, and there is a collective sad sigh around the room like I've just turned on the Sarah McLachlan ASPCA commercial.

My dad is scowling at me, but Martha is quick to fill the silence. "Of course! Why don't you check your schedule and pick a day that works well for you? I'm pretty flexible."

I smile, and even though I have no intention of doing that, I agree anyway. "Sounds good."

Ellie pushes back from the table and comes around to collect my pie plate. "Done?"

"Wait! I was—"

I try to yank it back, but it's too late. She's carrying my plate to the kitchen before I even managed one bite. It's my punishment, and I know if I stick around, she's only going to make it worse. So, I request an Uber, thank my dad and Martha for a lovely dinner, and scurry out of the house before Ellie can hunt me down and scold me like Mr. Knightly in *Emma. Badly done, Brooke. Badly done.* Yeah? Well screw you, Mr. Knightly-Ellie.

• • •

Other than the family dinner and a few desperate phone calls to my mother, the last two weeks have been filled with the following:

- Two meetings with the au pair agency trying to place me with a family
- Nine shifts at the country club
- Three very awkward encounters with Ian in the co-op kitchen
- Six runs around Town Lake
- One afternoon spent reading Harry Potter en français (I laugh every time Neville Longbottom is mentioned in the French version as "Neville Londubat"—literally translated as "Neville Long-in-the-butt")
And, though I am ashamed to admit it...
- At least four hundred million thoughts about James

I haven't seen him since our late-night conversation at the bar. He hasn't been to the club, or if he has, it hasn't been during one of my shifts. I could ask Ellie if she's seen him in the dining room during dinner service, but that would only lead to questions about why I care. Up until this point, I've played it cool when it comes to James. My infatuation has remained low-key and hidden, but if Ellie gets ahold of it, there's no telling what she'll do. If history is any indication, she will march right up to him in the high school cafeteria and proclaim my love in front of the entire lacrosse team. *Joey Larson, just to be clear, I didn't want to "marry you and have your babies", I just thought you looked hot swinging that bat thing around the field—sue me.*

Since I can't rely on my sister for details, I'm on my own, and there's really nothing I can do. I don't have his phone number or email address, which means there's no way to contact him. Besides, what would I say if I could? I would love nothing more than to cyber-stalk him, scroll through his Instagram feed and get a feel for the type of person he is. Who knows, maybe I could find a photo of him stepping on puppy tails or something to moderate my rapidly developing schoolgirl crush, or maybe I'd find photos of him on a rented yacht with sleezy girls in bikinis. But, from what I know about him so far, I'd be much more likely to find a picture of him on a barge with nuns, delivering aid to Haiti after a hurricane.

One night, after a long shift, I type his name into Google just to confirm he has no Facebook. No Twitter. No Instagram. He's a rare breed of human, floating through life untethered to social media. Isn't he curious what every single person from his high school is up to at any given moment? He's missing out on such important events as Kathleen introducing little Josie to solid foods and Macy returning from her fourth trip to India, feeling #superenlightened.

The other possibility is that James is lying about who

he is. With such scant social media presence, it could be the case, but another quick Google search confirms that I'm just paranoid. There are enough articles about him published online to confirm everything he's told me. The Google rabbit hole leads me all the way back to his senior photo from some preppy boarding school. His dark hair was longer then, hanging over his forehead in the way only high school boys (and Justin Bieber circa 2009) can truly maintain. He is so handsome and confident in the photo, like he knows he's only a few years away from grabbing life by the balls. High School Me would have had a major crush on High School Him. Hopefully, Present Day Me will be smart enough to keep that information from Ellie.

The next day, I walk into the club for my lunch shift and casually peruse the reservations. James' name isn't on the list. *COME ON.* I breeze past the kitchen and employee locker room, running into one of the caddies for the golf course.

"Anyone good on the course today?" I ask like I couldn't care less.

The guy—Harrison—stops dead in his tracks and beams at me. We haven't talked before; I guess there's never been a reason.

"Hey! Yeah!" Then he shakes his head, as if coming out of whatever spell my attention put him under. "Oh, wait, no. The course is closed for maintenance today."

"Oh, bummer."

It is a bummer, because that means I have to go another day without seeing James.

My luck continues when a major rainstorm rolls in during my shift. There are flash flood warnings and clouds that look like they're coming directly from Mordor. I rode my bike to work today, and usually I would call Ian for a ride, but when we bumped into each other in the co-op hallway earlier, he pretended like he didn't see me. The days of him playing the part of my chauffeur are long gone, and I wasn't smart enough to cast an understudy.

My Uber arrives quickly and then promptly drives away without me once he sees my (now muddy) bike propped up beside me. I would have moved it off the bike rack earlier if I'd known it would get drenched.

My last hope is Ellie, but it's her day off and she's not answering her phone. Chances are she's sucking face with Tyler, but I send off a few desperate text messages just in case.

BROOKE: Hey! I need a ride! CALL ME.
BROOKE: Major rainstorm. Flash flooding. Could die. Please call me.
BROOKE: Currently floating down the Colorado River. Can't...hang on...much.........longeerrr...

Movement to my left catches my attention and I glance up before I can shoot off a text to Ellie outlining my death in great detail.

James is walking out of the entrance of the main clubhouse with a pretty woman in tow. I freeze, shocked that he's here after I didn't see his name on the reservation list, but I suppose it wouldn't be there. It's 3:30; whatever he's doing here, it's not for lunch or dinner. I assumed I'd have to endure another shift at the club without him, but here he is looking just as handsome as I remember.

I'm sure his date thinks so too. Date—I bristle at the idea. No, it's the middle of the afternoon, so they can't be on a date, right? It's too bad I can't hear what they're saying. I'm standing about 15 feet to their right, tucked beneath the porte cochère so I'm out of the way of the valet and protected from the rain pelting down from the sky.

It's completely awkward. If James looks up and sees me, I will look like a complete loser with my soggy bike and humidified hair. It's bound to happen any moment now. He's facing my direction, talking to the woman— who, by the way, is pulling off that shockingly red cocktail dress pretty well for midafternoon on a Thursday.

He leans forward and I think they're about to kiss (*DEAR GOD NO*) but instead, he reaches out and shakes her hand. She says something that makes him laugh as she accepts his handshake, and then I'm jealous of her palm for getting to touch his. *Did I touch him two weeks ago?* Yes. I remember—I put my hand on his shoulder to comfort him and then immediately yanked it away. It was nothing like this super erotic handshake taking place in front of me. I want to shout at them to get a room, but the valet whips around with James' car.

Where are they going now? To elope?

He steps back and waves to her.

Now.

Now is the moment in which he will look up, see me standing here like a damsel in distress, and offer me a ride. I will refuse at first because then he will think I'm kind— *Oh, I couldn't, I hate inconveniencing people*—but that's a lie. I will inconvenience the hell out of him if it means I'm allowed to get into that car and continue our conversation from the other night.

I'm still daydreaming about our exchange when he slides into the front seat of his Porsche and heads off down the winding drive.

Uh, dude?

You forgot me back here.

"Hey Brooke! Are you stuck?"

It's Harrison, the golf guy I spoke with earlier. I force myself to look away from James' receding car and offer him a reassuring smile.

"Just waiting out the rain for a few minutes."

"I can give you a ride home if you want?"

He's a nice-looking guy, probably a few years younger than me. I'd bet my entire life savings (which is maybe $37) that he goes to UT, belongs to a frat, and feels like a cultured man of the world for ordering chicken tikka masala. I would love a ride home, but what's that thing about history? If you don't learn from it then you're destined to repeat it? Whatever. The point is, I just cut Ian off my line, and I can't sink my hook into some other poor schmuck just because I don't have a car. It's not right, and this guy, with his earnest smile and big doe eyes, is begging for a broken heart.

So, in what I can only call a supremely pathetic act, I decline and bike home in the pouring rain. Water drips from my helmet into my eyes and I have to keep blinking to make out the road in front of me. My feet continuously slip off the pedals, and I suffer through it like a real champ. I commit all the bad parts to memory so I can wallow in my bedroom in peace while I continue to obsess over James…just for a minute, just to see if I can figure out who the woman was.

And I do.

I search #TwinOaksCountryClub on Instagram, and lo and behold, Little Miss Red Dress posted a photo of her afternoon meeting with James. It's not of him. No, she took a picture of their food and drinks to brag about how #goals her life is. The caption reads: *Having a great interview with THE #JamesAshwood at #TwinOaksCountryClub!*

#CrabCakes #GoatCheese #Yum #Yummy #Lucky #Blessed #Soblessed

I develop cataracts before I can finish reading all the hashtags she tacked on, but it doesn't matter. Her profile says she's a medical device rep, and she was interviewing with James at the club, so there it is, folks. She might soon be working for James' company, but she's not dating him. I might work at a country club, but clearly I missed my calling as a private investigator.

Ellie texts me when I'm about to go to sleep.

ELLIE: Oh whoops. Sorry, just seeing this. Are you still floating in the river? You should be nearing the Gulf of Mexico by morning. Should I pick you up in Galveston?

 **CHAPTER SIX**

On days like this, I'm tempted to take extreme measures to secure an au pair position. The next time the agency calls me with an interview opportunity, I'm going to give myself a reverse makeover. Fake braces, dopey glasses, maybe a lisp—anything to pick up a new job so I can drop this one.

"Um, yeahhhh, this is wrong...I asked for a virgin strawberry daiquiri and my friend asked for a virgin piña colada."

I take the drinks out of their barely-post-pubescent hands and swap them.

"There you go. Do you need anything else?"

The tween scowls. "But I already drank half of that one before I realized it wasn't the right drink. I want another one."

I take a calming breath and try to harness every drop of patience I have left inside of me.

"No problem. What's your member ID number?"

She pulls down her sunglasses so I can see her crystal-blue eyes. "I already gave it to you."

I want to drown her in that virgin strawberry daiquiri. Instead, I smile. "I'm sorry. I forgot it."

Her friend sneers. "Be nice to the help, Mercedes. She might be like...*special*."

Mercedes snickers and whispers loudly, "How sad. I mean, you'd kind of have to be to work here, right?"

Even though I want to, I don't engage. I keep my smile right where it is and ask again. "What's your member ID number?"

She rolls her eyes. "4387. The *Johnsons*."

She says it like she's proclaiming to be a Vanderbilt, but I know better. I didn't recognize her before, but now I do. From rumors passed around the club, I know her dad just got caught cheating on her mom with his tennis partner—his *male* tennis partner—and now it makes sense; this mean girl act is a defense mechanism. Soon enough, she'll find a good therapist and learn to get her anger out by taking up kickboxing. For now, I give her extra whipped cream on her strawberry daiquiri and vow to stay the hell away from her for the rest of the afternoon.

Another two hours pass, in which I schlepp food and drinks back and forth from the cabana bar to the kiddie pool. Fortunately, all the children over here are too young to be really mouthy. Plus, I'm the person bringing the candy and ice cream, so to them, I'm better than Elmo.

"Oooh, look who's over by the gate," one of the moms says as I'm clearing her table of empty margarita glasses.

"Oh god, he's so hot," her friend adds.

"Megan! You just got married six months ago!"

"Yeah, well, Mark isn't exactly a wizard in the bedroom. Staring at James is probably the most sexually fulfilling thing I'll do all week."

My neck nearly breaks at the mention of his name. I turn around, and sure enough, he's over by the gate, leaning on the ledge and scanning the pool area. I conclude that he's looking for someone a second before his brown eyes lock with mine. My stomach dips in a sensation I can only describe as euphoric and terrifying all at once, and that's before he smiles and nods for me to come over.

"Who is he looking at?" one of the moms asks.

"I think the hot cabana girl."

For their information, I am a cabana *woman*, thank you very much.

"Maybe he wants a margarita?" the first one asks.

"Um, if that's how he looks at you when he wants you to get him a margarita then sign me up for cabana duties."

My hand shakes as I reach for the last cup on their table.

"Do you know him?" Megan asks me.

I offer a hesitant smile and a quick shake of my head. It's better if they assume he just wants a drink; I'd rather not be the topic of the gossip continually spreading through Twin Oaks.

By the time I drop off my tray in the cabana kitchen and check my reflection in the back of a spoon (good, not great), James is standing just inside the pool gate, hands tucked in his pants pockets. It's early summer in Texas, which means the temperature is already creeping into the high 80s. I'd be sweating bullets if I were wearing a tailored suit out here, but James looks like he's hardly aware of the sun beating down overhead. Who knows? Maybe he doesn't have pores like the rest of us. Still, in an effort to save us both, I direct us over to the shaded porch near the bar then turn to face him.

"Going for a dip?" I tease.

I swear his smile turns devilish.

He nods toward the club entrance. "I just came from a lunch meeting. I need to get back to the office soon, but I wanted to talk to you."

I swallow down my eagerness. "Oh yeah?"

"You know," he says, brushing his hand along his smooth jaw, "I used to see you around the club all the time, but now that I have a reason to talk to you, you've been impossible to find."

The concept of him looking for me is hilarious given the biking-home-in-the-rain scenario I endured a few days ago.

"Well, I assure you, I've been here," I say, waving to the pool behind me. "Personally inebriating the rich, famous, and bratty."

That makes him smile just as the tweens screech in unison about a new Snapchat filter.

"Right. Of course," he says, glancing down to take in my Twin Oaks uniform in all its glory. I flush under his blatant perusal.

"So what did you need to talk to me about so desperately?" I ask, catching my hands in front of my waist and wringing them out.

He rocks back on his heels and glances away. His eyes narrow, and I almost think he's mulling over what he's about to say before he finally admits, "I could really use your help."

That's how he says it, just vague enough that I have no way of knowing what he's referring to.

"With what?"

He graciously ignores the high-pitched inflection of my words as he replies, "I'm attending a party soon, and I'd like you to accompany me." *A DATE? THIS IS AN INVITATION TO GO OUT ON A DATE.* "My company is in need of a new CFO and the man I'd like for the job will be in attendance, as will his French girlfriend."

I shake my head, confused. *Why is he giving me all these extraneous details?* It's a date—tell me what time you're picking me up and let's get this show on the road!

He smiles gently before he continues, "You mentioned

the other day that you're fluent in French…"

Of course. *Duh.* He doesn't want me for romance, he wants me for my Romance languages.

"So you want me to keep his date company for you?"

A normal, decent human would at least act embarrassed by the bluntness of my question. Not James.

He gazes directly at me as he replies, "Exactly."

I spend a moment trying to decide how his request makes me feel. It's not a date, that much is clear, but that doesn't mean I should turn him down. For the last two and a half weeks, I've been replaying our conversation in the bar so often that I could recite it word for word on a Broadway stage in sync with music. But, if I'm going to agree to this, I want to know exactly where I stand.

"So I'd be some sort of secret linguistic weapon?"

He smiles and then wipes it away, like he's entirely too amused by the question. God, he's good-looking up close, all hard lines and contours with a pair of lips he can maneuver into one hell of a tempting smile.

"I don't know how I feel about that," I continue on a shaky voice. "It feels a bit like being *used*."

"Would you rather I lied?" he asks with an arched brow.

Yes.

"No."

"Good, because I think honesty is important. Maybe I'm just old-fashioned."

I nod and do my best to slip into the persona he wants from me. "What's in it for me? Will there be good food?"

He chuckles. "Plenty, and of course, Jack and Coke."

He's alluding to my drink from the other night. I'm surprised he remembers; maybe he's replayed our encounter a time or two as well. The thought emboldens me.

I shrug. Cool. Effortless. "Fine, I'll go."

Still, I need to know my role. Online, I wasn't able to find anything about a girlfriend or wife, but it's not like his entire life is plastered on Google. He's not a celebrity, at least not outside of Austin.

"So you'll introduce me as your friend then?" I ask before quickly adding, "I just want to play my part right."

Beneath dark brows, his coffee-brown eyes regard me with bold interest. "I'll introduce you however you'd like."

The way he says it ensures I catch his meaning. It's an invitation.

But then he's tugging out his phone and tapping away, dowsing the tension between us with a big bucket of ice water.

"I'll have my assistant drop off something for you to wear. What's your email address? She'll need to know your dress size."

I'm offended. "I can pick something up myself."

Thanks to my dad and Martha, I've attended plenty of fundraisers and galas. I know how to dress for an occasion.

He shakes his head, no room for negotiations as he hands over his iPhone, open to a new contact page. I fill in my name, and though he only asked for my email, I give him my number too. Maybe it's forward, or maybe it's expected. I'll never know, because just then Little Miss Virgin Piña Colada shouts about how slow the service is here. I have to get back to work.

The moms stationed by the kiddie pool spend the rest of my shift trying to pry details of our conversation out of me. I keep my lips zipped, but it doesn't help. By the end of the day, the entire club has heard about my poolside rendezvous with James.

 **CHAPTER SEVEN**

It's Saturday, and James' party is tonight. I know this thanks to Beth, his assistant. She and I have been in constant communication since I agreed to be James' secret weapon. Thank goodness for her, because the man himself has yet to use those nine digits I programmed into his phone. Would it have killed him to call or text to confirm that I still wanted to go? Maybe that way we could have gotten to know each other a little better and I wouldn't be so freaking nervous about tonight. The details I've gleaned from Beth aren't nearly sufficient.

What is the fundraiser called? Have I heard of it?

The party doesn't have a name, and no, you haven't heard of it.

Who's throwing it?

The host committee wishes to remain private.

Where is the party located?

That information hasn't been released to the public at this time.

I'm half-convinced Beth is a robot, like Siri. Her responses are so austere and impersonal. I've even attempted to crack a few jokes, and I got crickets in response. I guess my humor doesn't translate into robot binary. (Good to know in case they one day take over the planet.)

Beth *did* tell me what time the party starts.

9:00 PM.

Now, it's 5:10 PM, and I'm sitting in Milk + Honey in downtown Austin. You see, I'm a genius. I knew I needed to take extreme measures the moment I found out I would be attending a party on James' arm—well, in the vicinity of his arm, at least. The point is, after I'm done at Milk + Honey, I hope I'll be able to show James I'm so much more than an interpreter for hire.

The genius part comes in because while I wanted to look my best, I also figured it might be a good time to give in to Martha a little bit. She wanted me to join her and Ellie for a spa day, so here we are. I think this is called killing two birds with one hot stone massage.

We started the morning with manicures and pedicures. From there, we had hydrating facials and massages. During a short break, we snacked on quinoa salad with spinach and red wine vinaigrette and caprese skewers with balsamic drizzle. I've been dipped, lathered, waxed, and rinsed. I'm pretty sure the entire top layer of my epidermis has been stripped off at this point, and though I'm hesitant to admit it, I am actually having a good time with Martha and Ellie.

The details aren't that noteworthy. Our conversation has included such titillating topics as home renovations and Martha's nagging tennis elbow. I did confide in them about how hard it's been to find another position as a tutor, and Martha listened intently while encouraging me to keep looking. It's the longest amount of time I've spent with her in years, and I'm finding it harder to dislike her as the day continues, which is annoying. I've grown comfortable with the distance between us, and I'm not sure what to do with these new feelings. I am the Grinch with an enlarged heart.

Fortunately, we split up after a late lunch since they want to continue spa treatments (because somehow there are still more to be had) and I need start getting ready for the party. I have the hair stylist give me a Brazilian blowout so my dark hair hangs in glossy waves down my back, and then a nice woman named Linda starts applying my makeup.

"So tell me, what's the occasion?"

Of course she has to ask—no one gets this gussied up without a place to go. Trouble is, I don't know exactly where I'm off to tonight. I checked my email at lunch, but there was nothing new from Beth. The last I heard, I needed to be at home and ready to go by 8:30 PM.

I give Linda a generic lie.

"Just a fancy party thing." I shrug. "I forget the name."

She waggles her eyebrows as if my ambiguity intrigues her even more. "What does your dress look like?"

I still technically don't have a dress. I gave Beth my measurements a few days ago, and I was tempted to tack on a few requirements—no ruffles, nothing too sparkly—but I resisted. For all I know, Beth the robot has more fashion sense than I do.

All that is probably too much to unload on a complete stranger, so I tell her what I imagine the dress will look like. It's a party, no doubt at some ritzy downtown hotel, so it will need to be floor-length and fitted, sleeveless and tight in all the right places.

She hums in appreciation of my fictitious description. "I remember when I used to be able to wear slinky numbers like that. What color?"

I smile. "Light blue."

To match my eyes.

• • •

When I return home, I'm a sore thumb inside the co-op. Fortunately, no one is in the living room, so I scurry to the stairs and run smack into Ian, the absolute last person I want to see.

His eyes widen at my appearance. "Whoa…"

I blanch. "Oh, hey Ian."

He doesn't oblige when I try to skirt around him. "You look…" His gaze drags down my body, and I'm thankful I'm still wearing the tank top and yoga pants I threw on before the spa. "Amazing."

This is too awkward for words, so I smile and nod. "Thanks."

He steps aside and I head for my room.

"Where are you headed?" he asks, his tone more curious than anything. "I've never seen you done up like this."

I swallow and choose my next words carefully. Most of my roommates at the co-op—Ian included—make fun of my job at the country club. It's kind of funny when you think about it: they make fun of the rich people who choose to spend their time and money at Twin Oaks, and my old classmates and members at Twin Oaks balk at the idea of these artist types living together in a co-op. I guess being judgey crosses all class lines.

"Oh, yeah…just going to some party."

"For your dad?"

Ian knows I come from a wealthy family.

"Uhh, something like that."

He quirks his brow, and I can tell he wants to keep pushing the subject, but I don't have time. It's already 8:00 PM, and according to Beth, James will be here at 8:30. I wave bye to Ian and then bolt down the hallway. When I get closer to my door, I spot a black satin box with a matching ribbon sitting on the floor. Beside it, there's another box, much smaller, but no less fancy. I turn back to confirm Ian's gone, grab the boxes, and push into my room with a massive smile on my face.

It's my dress. I know it, and I have a hard time keeping myself from squealing with excitement. I've had romantic experiences in the past. College boyfriends packed me the occasional soggy picnic or threw together a mix CD full of songs about other peoples' love, but this—this feels special, even if James didn't pick out the dress himself. He definitely cared enough to ensure I'd have something beautiful to wear for the party.

For him.

No. Wrong.

I'm attending so I can keep his business associate's date occupied, and I need to remember that…but what was that he said at the end of our conversation by the pool? That I could be introduced however I chose? Surely he meant that to mean what I think he did.

Whatever. Who cares. I have more important things to worry about, like these two boxes (!!!).

I kick my door closed and drop them carefully on my bed. First, I open the big one. The ribbon is silky between the pads of my fingers as I release the bow and slide the top of the box to the side. Inside, there's black tissue paper for miles. I pull apart the layers gently, like an archeologist handling a delicate artifact. Finally, I reach the bottom and lay eyes on the dress. My breath catches.

It's silky and black, just like the box. The name on the label catches my attention: Vivian Palermo. She's a local Austin designer whose dresses usually retail for the price of a prize pony—I know because Ellie and I saw one hanging inside Nordstrom last week and started drooling until we saw the price tag. My dad might have money, but that doesn't mean I do. I work for every dollar I have, so while designers like Palermo hang abundantly in my imagination, they are nowhere to be found in my closet.

Until now.

I carefully extract the dress from the box and hold it up.

A laugh erupts out of me before I can stop it. Something is wrong. The dress is nothing more than a slip, really. The thin straps give way to a plunging neckline, and though the skirt seems like it will fall to a decent length on my thighs, it's deceiving—the short fringe on bottom won't conceal a thing once I have it on. It's a modern take on a 1920s flapper dress, and I'll be lucky if I make it through the night without at least one boob and most of my vulva being on full display. *Thanks for nothing, Beth.*

In the smaller box, I find a pair of Manolo Blahnik stilettos. The heel is sky high and thin, completely impossible to walk in save for the slender ankle strap. The shoes are delicate and sexy, and I want to find them as ridiculous as the dress, but I don't. Even if James asks for the outfit back, I won't forfeit these. They're mine now.

The outfit I described to Linda back at Milk + Honey was nothing like this. I was anticipating some kind of dress worthy of a gala or fundraiser. This dress, despite its beauty, is more fit for a Halloween superstore. I cringe at that thought; I'm not giving it enough credit. The designer knew what she was doing, and as I slip it on—just to see how it fits—I'm not sure how I feel about it. I spin and take in the dress from every angle using my thin floor-length mirror. It fits like a glove, tight across my chest and stomach before it flares out slightly below my waist. I add the shoes, because well, I have to, and when the whole ensemble is complete, I feel like someone else, someone who wears dresses like this and accepts party invitations from total strangers. I've had my fair share of wild nights and spontaneous adventures, but never with someone like James. I know I'm out of my league, and that only intrigues me more.

In the end, the dress stays on, but it gets concealed beneath a giant wool coat. It's early summer, so I'll burn up the moment I step outside, but the alternative is walking through the halls of the co-op in nothing but a wisp of silk.

There's no phone call or text waiting for me at 8:30 PM. No new emails either. So, once I've checked and rechecked my makeup and hair and adjusted my dress so it's concealing as much as possible beneath the coat, I head downstairs.

His Porsche is waiting at the curb in front of the co-op—I know because half of my roommates are pushed up against the living room window, trying to get a good look. When I make it to the bottom of the stairs, I pause and listen for a second.

"Who is that?"

"Batman?"

"I don't know. He just pulled up."

"Do you KNOW what kind of car that is?"

"Jerry, since when do you care about cars?"

"Is someone selling drugs for the cartel?"

"Oh shit, what if he's here to collect on debts or something? Should we, like, hit the deck?"

Ian is among the small group of twittering numskulls, and he's the first the see me. I pull my coat closed. He glances from me, to the waiting car, and then back.

"I think your carriage is here, Cinderella."

Half a dozen heads swing in my direction. I put on an

awkward smile and wave as I scurry toward the door.

"Brooke!" one of them yells after me. "ARE YOU SELLING DRUGS?"

That question is followed by an audible oomph. "No, you idiot. *Look at her*. She's going on a date."

"Huh. Must be some place fancy…"

"Can you ask him if I can get a ride in his car when he drops you off?!"

Sure. Yeah. Whatever. I say what I need to before I rip open the front door and spill out onto the paved walkway. The driver's side door of the Porsche opens and James steps out wearing a fitted tuxedo. James in a tux is the human equivalent of ice-cold milk with warm chocolate chip cookies. On their own, they're each pretty great. Together, they're otherworldly.

His hair is styled more formally than I've seen it, the short waves tamed and smoothed back. He's sharp edges and dark brows, almost more intimidating than handsome—almost. I don't want to overplay just how devastatingly handsome he looks. I mean, the heavens *do* crack open and tiny angels *do* start singing from above. That part is real, but I'm not sure if the earth really does tilt on its axis or if I'm just feeling unsteady perched on these Manolos. I'll have to confer with a seismologist at a later date.

James steps forward to catch my hand before I step off the curb, and though it's meant as a polite gesture, it becomes abundantly necessary as I step down and lose my balance, teetering on my heels for a moment. I blush. I'm a five-year-old girl who raided her mother's closet. No, *worse*—I'm a woman 11 years his junior. I half-expect him to come to his senses, drop my hand, and drive away in his very fast, very sexy car, but instead, he smiles down at me.

"That's some coat."

His tone is teasing, and his hand is still wrapped around mine. I'm sweating. I want to rip the coat off and swallow big gulps of air. I want to look away from his clean-shaven jaw and come-hither eyes, but I can't. Moth, flame.

"Well..." I counter. "This is some dress."

I'm breathy, like the way I sound right after really good sex.

He nods and drops my hand, but his smirk doesn't budge. "I asked Beth to send me a link so I could see it, but she said it should be a surprise."

I love Beth.

"I'd like to see it now," he continues, "but I'm assuming you want to wait until we aren't in full view of your...housemates."

I cringe as I turn around to find even more of my roommates crowded around the window, peering out. They wave excitedly and Jerry mouths, *Ask about the ride!*

"*Yeah*...they're kind of an eclectic bunch," I say fondly.

"I'd love to meet them, but we're running a little late."

Of course. I nod and turn back to the car. He leads me to the passenger side and opens the door for me. I'm very aware of the fact that I'm about to get into James' car. Not three weeks ago I wondered what it would be like inside, and I'm not disappointed. There are buttery leather seats and a fancy-looking computer system on the dashboard. "I Can't Go On Without You" by Kaleo—a sexy, crooning rock song—is playing from the speakers.

James: 1.

Actually, James: 6. The tuxedo counts for at least 5 points.

He slides behind the wheel and glances over, his gaze locking with mine as he asks if I'm ready to go. There's a hidden meaning to his question, I'm sure of it, but instead of running for my life (while I still have one), I smile and nod. "Let's go."

As he pulls away from the house, I fire off a quick text to Ellie.

BROOKE: I'm in James Ashwood's car at the moment. If you don't hear from me by morning, don't bother sending a search party. Wherever I am, I want to be there.

CHAPTER EIGHT

It takes 10 minutes to get from the co-op to the party, and James takes two phone calls in that time. The first is from Beth, who calls with important news about a distribution center in East Asia. I only follow every other word, and that isn't enough to clue me in on what's going on. The second phone call is even more coded, though it doesn't seem intentional. I consider myself a lover of language, but I don't speak techie.

We pull up to a red light and I turn to meet his eyes.

Sorry, he mouths.

I offer him a small smile and a shrug. It's not a big deal. I almost prefer this. With him on the phone, I don't have to worry about making small talk. I can just sit here and think deeply about what to do with my hands. He turns back and focuses on the road. I do the same for a moment, but it's not long before my gaze wanders back to him.

Out of the corner of my eye, I take in the details I'll be too busy to notice later: the perfectly crisp edge of his tuxedo shirt, his tan hands as they grip the steering wheel, the fit of his pants against his hard thigh. I can't go higher than his shoulder; he'll know I'm watching him if I do. It's too bad, because I'm desperate for a look at his profile—I know it will punch me in the gut—but instead, I turn my focus out through the front window and revel in the sound of his voice. It's deep and low, and during his second call, it turns gruff. I've never been so intrigued by the way someone speaks, but then again, I've never been in a car with James.

He hangs up and apologizes again, but I assure him it's fine.

"I've been trying to figure out where you're taking me."

He smiles. "It's just around the corner."

He's not kidding. A moment later, he pulls over to the curb on 5th street, gets out, and rounds the front of the car. The valet opens my door and I step out just as James is handing off his keys, but before the eager-faced teenager can get behind the wheel, James holds up his finger for him to wait.

I glance to the valet and then back to James.

"Want to leave that in the car?" he says, pointing to my coat. "I doubt they'll have a coat check inside."

Of course not—why would they? It's a million degrees out here.

I blush and reach for the top button. I'd forgotten I was even wearing it. It was slightly chilly in James' car, but now the humidity and heat have set in and I'm almost thankful to get rid of the thick wool—that is, until I catch the valet's eyes nearly bugging out when he gets a glimpse at my dress underneath.

I hate Beth.

I can't even look at James. I know he'll see how uncomfortable I am wearing this out in public. Maybe I should have rooted through my closet for another option, but now it's too late. I'm here and I'm wearing the dress, so I might as well embrace it. I stand tall and push my shoulders back. My silky hair falls over my shoulder and down my back.

James steps forward and takes my hand, blocking my view of the valet. His grip is warm and strong as he leads me away from the curb.

"You look beautiful," he says, low enough so I know the compliment is meant only for me to hear.

I love Beth.

The building we walk up to is simple: a one-story made of black brick with no name and no windows on the facade. Ahead of us there's a single black door serving as the main entrance. It's oversized and shiny, flanked by black pillars and two bouncers on either side.

A gray-haired man nods to the bouncer on the left and the hulking man steps back and opens the door. No one speaks or makes eye contact as we pass. It's the weirdest experience of my life, and I'm half-convinced I'm about to step into some creepy illuminati meeting with Robert Langdon.

We step inside and James lets go of my hand so he can lead me down a long hallway with his palm pressed to the small of my back. I can feel the warmth of his touch through the thin material of my dress, and I'm glad I left my coat in the car.

Whoever designed the facade of the building clearly had a hand in the interior as well, and they subscribed to the notion that black is back to being the new black. The hallway is monochromatic: black marble floors, black walls, and black metal orb chandeliers. At first, my heels clacking against the marble is the only sound, but as we continue toward another door at the end of the hall, low, bluesy jazz music starts to spill out.

There's another bouncer. Another man with a subtle nod and no words exchanged.

The second door is whisked open, and finally, we've

arrived—or rather, we've gone back in time.

My dress makes much more sense as we step into a room decorated as a 1920s speakeasy. Heavy chandeliers burning large Edison bulbs illuminate the black and white checkered marble floors. A long bar on the left is lined with thousands of backlit liquor bottles. Tufted dark leather sofas surround low coffee tables, and a few refurbished whiskey barrels serve as cocktail tables. A 12-person jazz band performs on a small stage across from the bar. I can't tell how far the room extends. It's more of a ballroom than a bar, and when I press up on my toes, I think I spot gambling tables at the other end.

"What *is* this place?"

The question is meant to be rhetorical, but James answers anyway.

"The best kept secret in town."

• • •

I can't remember if James ever told me he was taking me to a hoity-toity fundraiser or if I assumed that on my own. Looking back, I don't think he ever misled me. Still, he didn't willingly offer details about tonight. As we make our way through the room, James is continuously stopped by men with hearty laughs and strong handshakes. Without much context, they remind me of my dad's friends. They're movers and shakers in Austin, and maybe if I were in that world, I'd recognize them. It's clear from the suits and the watches and the beautiful women that they have all done well for themselves; I don't think they'd be in this room otherwise.

It's the beautiful women that catch my attention the

most though. They smile knowingly at me when we're in a small group together, as if I'm in on the secret. At first, I'm not, but I catch on fast.

The first couple we stop and chat with is comprised of an overweight man nearing 60 and a sexy, young blonde. He's wearing a wedding ring; she isn't. The next couple, though much closer in age, follow the same pattern—he's wearing a ring, but she isn't. Scantily clad cocktail waitresses pass through the crowd delivering moonshine cocktails and old fashioneds—or for men like James, bourbon on the rocks. They're beautiful and blinding, eye candy for the men here out on the town with their mistresses. That's what they are, mistresses, and perhaps I'm one of them.

"Ah, Michael, there you are," James says as a new man approaches our group.

He's younger than most of the men here, close to James' age. By his side is a striking black woman wearing a fitted tuxedo jacket and pants, clearly designed with her lithe body in mind. While at first the outfit seems conservative compared to most of the dresses in the room, she chose to forego a shirt beneath the jacket so it looks more like a low-cut top. It's daring and bold. She looks like she just stepped off the runways of Paris, and with that face and those legs, chances are she probably did.

The men exchange handshakes and then James introduces me to Michael's date, Celeste.

"It's a pleasure to meeting you," she says with a soft French accent.

Ah, so *she's* my target for the night, the whole reason I'm here in the first place.

She holds her hand out for me to take, and her palm is silky smooth. I'm not a tiny girl, but Celeste still has a few inches on me. My model theory grows more roots.

"*Enchanté. I love your outfit*," I say in French, grateful that I don't have to lie.

Her eyes light up.

"*Vous parlez Francais?*" she asks, intrigued.

I nod.

"*Ah, I was worried I would have to keep quiet tonight,*" she continues in French. "*My English isn't very good.*"

I open my mouth to continue our conversation, but Michael beats me to it.

"James, it seems you found a beautiful French girl as well," he says, his eyes pinned on me. "Who is this delicate creature?"

The hairs on the back of my neck stand on end. It's not that Michael is bad-looking; it's worse. He has all the attributes women usually look for accompanied by an air of unchecked arrogance. I'm not a girl, and I'm not a "delicate creature", and most importantly, I haven't been *found*.

James glances down at me, his expression unreadable. "This is my friend Brooke."

I know most women don't want to be referred to as a friend while they're supposedly on a date with a man, but for some reason, the word strikes me. In this setting, where we're surrounded by every form of debauchery known to man, I'd rather be James' friend than his date. It holds more weight, and I think Michael realizes it for a split second before his smile twists into something more sinister.

"If you're only James' friend, I'd love to get to know you better. Care for a drink?"

I hold up my cocktail. "I'll let you know when I'm dry."

"*Smart girl,*" Celeste says in French. My gaze whips to her and she shrugs and looks away. "*He's a controlling prick.*"

"*Then why are you here with him? As his date?*"

Her eyes slice back to me. "*There's a little more to it than that.*" She inclines her head to James. "*You of all people should realize that. Friends, eh? Does that word mean something different in English? Because this man can't take his eyes off you.*"

Michael nudges James jocularly. "Why do I get the feeling they're talking about us?"

Celeste offers him a sugary smile and then leans over to press a chaste kiss to his cheek. "Because we were, *mon amour*, but don't worry, it's all sweet things."

That's enough to placate Michael, but I can feel James studying me. It's like the heat of a thousand suns burning into the side of my face, but I refuse to glance over. He brought me here, stuck me in this room with these people for one purpose, and she's standing right in front of me.

"Come freshen up with me?" I ask Celeste.

She steps away from Michael.

He reaches out for her hand, holding her back for a moment. "Don't be gone too long. It drives me crazy when you disappear at these parties."

There's an edge to his tone, and I suspect that's the controlling side Celeste was talking about.

• • •

The bathroom is as exquisitely decorated as the rest of the club and includes a powder room as big as my bedroom back at the co-op. That's where I find Celeste after I wash my hands. She's in front of the mirror, applying another layer of dark red lipstick. It's intoxicating, the color of spilled blood.

"There's a drink for you there," she says, pointing to a small side table beside a love seat in the center of the room.

I stroll over to pick up the pink cocktail. "How'd you get these?"

She inclines her head toward the antechamber, where an attendant is standing with her arms by her sides and her gaze laser-focused on the wall in front of her. Clearly, she's been trained to blend into the landscape.

"Thank you," I say in English, just in case she *is* listening.

Like the first drink I had, this one tastes like it has enough alcohol in it to strip the varnish off a boat.

"*Jeez. How is everyone still standing out there?*" I ask, setting it back down. "*If I drink all of this, I'll hit the floor in five minutes.*"

She meets my eyes in the mirror and laughs. "*You get used to them. Trust me.*"

I don't think I believe her.

"*Here. Come put some of this on.*"

She's holding out the dark red lipstick for me to take.

Yeah right.

"*It would look too dark on me. Garish.*"

She smirks. "*It'll look completely different on you. Besides, it's Chanel. It wouldn't look 'garish' on a clown.*"

Earlier at the spa, my makeup artist applied a pale pink lipstick, but it's long gone now. Besides, this isn't a night for pale pink. She hands over the tube and I step closer to the mirror, taking my time as I meticulously swipe it across my lips. With a color like this, it has to be perfect. She hands me a tissue for blotting and when I step back and take in the look, I realize she was right. On me, the color looks more like deep pomegranate.

"*See?*" she asks, retrieving the tube out of my hand, capping it and dropping it back in her small black clutch. "*I've been wearing this color for years, since back when I was still modeling.*"

"*You don't anymore?*"

"*No. I used to travel all over the world, but then I met Michael.*"

Interesting.

"*Do you love him?*"

She thinks over the question for a moment before replying. "*I love him more than I hate him,*" she says, meeting my eyes in the mirror. "*Does that make sense?*"

It sounds very French. Still...

"*It would give me a headache.*"

She laughs. "*Oh, it does. But the sex?*" She waggles her brows. "*I've never had anything like it, you know?*"

I don't know, not really, but I nod anyway.

She steps back and takes a seat on the tufted velvet love seat in the center of the powder room.

"*You don't want any more of your drink?*" she asks as she picks hers up. "*I don't want it to go to waste.*"

I should say no. I already feel a little lightheaded, but I don't want to offend her. She went to the trouble to order it, so I pick it back up and vow to take tiny baby sips in hopes that it'll last me the rest of the night.

That seems to appease her, because she leans back and assesses me coolly.

"*How long have you been with James?*"

I take a sip.

"*Not long.*" Her eyes narrow, and I feel like a sitting duck. "*Shouldn't we be getting back? Michael said he doesn't like it when you disappear.*"

She laughs and then leans back even more, making

93

herself at home. "*He doesn't like it, he* loves *it. It drives him wild to think I'm out there talking to another man. Later, when we get home, he'll show me just how much it bothered him.*"

Her admission stuns me into silence long enough for her to lean forward and smirk. "*Now, how long have you known James?*"

I look away. "*A few weeks, though I hardly know him. We've only spoken a few times.*"

"*Then why did he invite you here tonight?*"

For a moment I'm not sure I should admit the truth, but something tells me Celeste can smell bullshit from a mile away. "*Let's just say it isn't a coincidence that I'm fluent in French.*"

"*Ha!*" She flings her head back in laughter. "*Brilliant. I always knew I liked James.*"

That surprises me. "*You know him well?*"

"*Oh, not really. He doesn't come here often, hardly at all in fact, which is how I know I like him.*"

Interesting. "*But he has been here before?*"

She nods and sets her drink down on the side table. I watch as she pulls out a little bottle of perfume so she can dab a few drops behind each ear. The scent is flowery and delicate, a complete contrast to the confident vixen before me.

"*A few times,*" she says, narrowing her eyes and thinking back. "*I think I saw him last at the Halloween party.*"

"*Did he bring a date?*"

She grins, seeing my question for what it is. "*A man like that does not arrive alone. But, I recall her as a generic-looking brunette. Nothing like you.*"

Nothing like me.

"We're friends," I reiterate.

"Friends, lovers…we do not make such harsh distinctions where I come from."

I glance away and pretend to take in the room around me. *"I hardly know him. He's a lot older than me, and I'm not looking for a relationship right now. I might be relocating for a job soon."*

"Wow," she says with raised brows. *"What is that, four reasons? You've put a lot of thought into why you shouldn't be with him."* I shoot her a warning glare, but she continues, *"When I don't want a man, I don't think of him at all."*

She stands, drops her perfume back into her clutch, and grabs her drink.

"We should get back. They'll be wondering where we are."

I'm exhausted as I follow Celeste out of the bathroom. It's been months since I've really stretched my French muscles, but I don't think that's the reason my head is pounding. I take another small sip of my drink and then instantly regret it. I'm supposed to be nursing it, but I've already downed half thanks to Celeste's interrogation. I hand it off to a passing waiter when she isn't looking and decide water will be the only thing passing my lips the rest of the night.

The crowd pushes in on us as we walk through the club. I can't remember if there were this many people when we first arrived, but now I feel like I can hardly breathe. The jazz band is gone, replaced by loud music. That coupled with raucous laughter and conversation overpowers my ability to think. I blink and try to clear my head. I blink again and realize Celeste isn't in front of me anymore. She was leading the way back to the guys, but now she's nowhere to be found.

"Celeste?"

I turn in a circle, trying to spot her long black hair or the color of dried blood staining her lips. My vision cuts to a black tuxedo jacket similar to the one she was wearing. *No.* A woman with the same length of hair. *No.* I think I catch a whiff of her perfume, but when I turn toward the scent, I nearly fall onto a couple wrapped around one another. The man has his hand up the woman's dress, she's moaning into his mouth, and they don't notice me. To them, I'm just another warm body.

A hand brushes across my back, then lower.

"Are you lost, sweetheart?" a deep voice asks close to my ear.

I jerk away.

Even in this state, my fight-or-flight instincts kick in. I push through the crowd quicker than before, jostling people out of my way.

Glass shatters on the floor behind me, but I don't stop.

"Hey! EASY!" someone shouts at me.

I shake my head and blink harder, trying to clear my fuzzy vision, but it doesn't work. It feels like I'm trying to wake myself up out of a deep sleep.

I need to find James. He's the only person I know here, but he's not where I left him.

At least, I *think* this is where I left him. *Were we by the bar? Or did we wander toward the gambling tables in the back?* My heart rate kicks up another notch and I try not to panic. It seems futile. The more I try to catch my breath, the harder it becomes.

Then I spot them up ahead: Celeste and Michael. I push down the urge to cry as I rush toward them, too scared to blink for fear that they'll disappear and I'll be left on my own again.

They're among the crowd of people playing craps, and she's pressed up against his side as he grips a pair of dice in his hands. He holds out his fist and she kisses it. Another few shakes and then he tosses the dice out onto the table. The crowd erupts with a mixture of cheers and groans. He turns to Celeste and kisses her hard enough that they nearly topple over. I'm almost to them when Michael starts to string a line of kisses down her neck. She turns to give him better access and her eyes light up when she spots me.

"Brooke! There you are!" She breaks away from him to reach for me. *"Come, come. We're playing craps. I'm Michael's lucky charm!"*

She grips my arm and tugs me closer. I lose my footing and stumble into the leggy blonde on the other side of Celeste. She curses and turns to scold me, but Celeste levels her with a stare. "Fuck off, will you?"

The blonde mutters something under her breath but still moves to the side, making space for me.

"Where have you been?" Celeste asks as she wraps an arm around my shoulders and draws me against her.

She sounds giggly and carefree—in complete contrast to how I feel.

I try to collect enough words to form a reply but my head is too cluttered. I can't grip hold of English, let alone French.

My struggle makes her laugh.

"Enjoying that drink I gave you?" She winks.

I swallow and find my voice. "Wh-What?"

She leans closer and whispers, *"That drink—did you finish it?"* I shake my head and she continues, *"Good. I probably put too much in."*

Wait.

What?

My body breaks out in a cold sweat.

"*Too much?*" I repeat.

Her laughter sounds like the evil cackle of a hyena.

"*Jesus, calm down.*" She's rubbing my back, trying to soothe me. "*Don't cry.*"

I didn't realize I was.

"James?"

The name falls out of my mouth with no context.

She shrugs. "*I haven't seen him since we left for the bathroom, but who cares! He can be so boring.*"

Can he? I can't remember.

"*Ugh! Cheer up. C'mon, I want to have fun! Look, here—*" She forces a pair of dice into my clammy hands. "*You want a turn being Michael's lucky charm?*"

Somewhere in the back of my mind, I know I don't want to be here, playing along with Celeste. I know something is wrong, but the alarm bells aren't loud enough to overpower the crowd around the craps table.

A handsome man with a sinister smile is telling me to kiss the dice.

Michael.

Celeste helps me by wrapping her delicate hand around my neck and forcing my face down to his fist.

"*Kiss!*"

I do as I'm told and then Michael tosses the dice out onto the green felt. The crowd erupts again and I get jostled between bodies. My rib smarts and I hiss, trying to place the pain. It's the blonde on the other side of me, jabbing her elbow into my side, seeking retribution for earlier.

I shove her back just before a strong hand wraps around my upper arm.

"Where've you been?"

My stomach dips.

I look over my shoulder and there he is—the man I've been trying to find.

"James! My man!" Michael says, clapping him on the shoulder. "C'mon, we're just getting started."

James doesn't shift his attention off me. His brown eyes trace along my features, and he looks concerned; maybe he should be. I was trying to find him earlier, but now I can't remember why.

"Are you okay?" he asks, his grip tightening on my arm a little more.

It's nearly painful.

I nod because I am. *Right?* I look around me. The room sways, and I can't focus my vision no matter how hard I try.

"Hey, Brooke. Are you okay?" he asks again, his tone a little more gruff than it was a moment before.

Celeste laughs and presses herself against me. I focus on the feel of her tuxedo jacket. It's cool and silky, and maybe I'm overheated because I like the way the fabric feels against my skin.

"Relax, will you?" she says in English. "We wanted to have a little fun."

I think her accent is so beautiful, and maybe I say so because she laughs and presses a kiss to my cheek.

"I don't have the accent. All of you do!"

I smile because she makes "the" sound like "zee" and it's so charming. Michael must have fallen in love with her so easily.

"What did you take?" James asks. I turn my attention back to him, but he's not looking at me anymore. Of course he's not—how could he focus on me for long with so many beautiful people around?

How terrible.

I want him—this confident, sexy, older man—to focus on me, to *want me.*

It feels like a challenge, one I can't pass up. I sidle closer to him and press my body against his. My hands drag across his muscled biceps and I shiver. I have to tip my head back to stare up at his eyes, and maybe I expect to see lust brewing there, but there's nothing but annoyance. His lips—the lips I want to taste—are pulled in a tight line. His dark brows are furrowed. He's looking down at me with a level of disdain usually reserved for snot-nosed kids, not a woman you find irresistible.

"What'd you take?" he asks again.

"I don't—"

Michael laughs and slaps his shoulder. "It's a party drug, James. It's not going to kill her."

No. This isn't right.

I shake my head. "I didn't know. I didn't t-take...anything."

I think my words will clarify things, but he shakes his head and steps back, taking me with him. "Right. C'mon, let's go."

Celeste protests, yanking on my other arm. "She doesn't have to go with you!" She turns to Michael. "*Mon amour*, tell him!"

The searing stare James aims at Michael is enough to override whatever spell Celeste has over him. He puts his hands in the air in innocence and tells Celeste to let go of me. She pouts, but finally releases me. I don't even get the chance to say goodbye before James is pulling me through the crowd so fast I'm tripping over my feet.

I tell him to slow down, that his hold on my arm is hurting me, but I don't think he can hear over the music—

or maybe he doesn't care.

His car is waiting out by the curb and he doesn't let go of me until I'm inside and safely buckled. He rounds to the driver's side and I stare down at where his hand was touching my arm. My skin still tingles.

When he gets in, I can feel the anger emanating off him. Every movement he makes is done with a little too much force. The engine roars, his foot hits the gas, and we're speeding away from the party without a second glance.

"We didn't have to leave," I say, wondering if that's why he's upset. The party was still in full swing. His warm eyes glare over at me and I get the message loud and clear: *shut up.*

When we pull up to the curb in front of the co-op, I'm dipping in and out of sleep, content to stay right where I am, but James opens my door and hauls me out of the car. His hands are too rough, not at all how I imagined they would be. He lets go of me and I sway. By now it's impossible to walk on my heels, so I stop and yank them off one at a time. When I stand back up, James dwarfs me even more.

I smile.

He frowns and nods to the house.

"At least your roommates are asleep."

"My roommates?" I ask, confused. "Do you know them?"

He sighs and shakes his head, continuing past me up the front path. I think he's just going to walk me to the front door, but he continues inside and up the stairs behind me. I'm not sure what we're doing.

James Ashwood is in my house, which probably only means one thing.

"Are we going to have sex?"

Is that why we left the club?

"Just concentrate on walking," he chides.

I think I used to amuse him, but now he's treating me like his annoying kid sister.

"This is my room," I say, presenting my door with a proud smile.

"Hey!" someone shouts from behind a closed door. "SHUT UP OUT THERE!"

I barely manage to stifle a laugh as James opens my door with another sigh—God, I must really be exasperating—and then we're both standing in my small room. It's a little messy, but I'm not embarrassed. I'm proud of how I decorated it. One entire wall is covered in framed prints I bought off one of my roommates. She would have given them to me for free, but I love her art and wanted to support her.

"It's called a gallelly—garelly—gallery wall." I laugh, pointing to it.

"Can you get ready for bed on your own?" he asks, ignoring me.

I move to a bookshelf I found on the side of the road. Some college kid was moving home for summer and didn't need it anymore. I took it, sanded it down, and painted it a sunflower yellow. "And this is where I put my books. Well, just the paperbacks. I have a Kindle too."

"Brooke."

Right.

I turn away from my bookshelf to find him standing with his hands on his hips. He doesn't belong in my room with the art prints and yellow bookshelves. He's much too serious. Right now, he's scowling. Scowling, scowling, scowling—it's all he ever does. His tuxedo is so black it burns. The light in his eyes is so intoxicating I want to step closer, press onto my toes, and get a really good look at them, just so I'll know exactly what shade of brown I should make my coffee in the morning.

His thick hair—*THE HAIR*—is mussed up now.

"You shouldn't run your hands through your hair so much. You messed it all up."

He steps toward my chest of drawers and starts pulling them open.

"Where do you keep your pajamas?"

I laugh and clap my hands over my mouth when he opens my top drawer. "Not *there*!"

That's where I keep the fancy underwear—a.k.a. the stuff that never gets worn. There are lacy underthings and delicate brassieres, most of which I purchased in France during a short and spicy affair with a young French guy. He ended up being more interested in my friend, but I guess it wasn't a total waste because now James is likely imagining me in those instead of the 5 for $25 panties from Target I actually wear.

I expect him to be flustered. Guys my age would be, but James pushes the drawer closed as disaffectedly as he opened it and opens the one beneath it. I'm too lost in a fit of laughter to care when he tosses a t-shirt and sleeping shorts at me.

"I think you can manage from here. I'll see you."

What?

He's leaving already?

I reach for his hand and am relieved when he doesn't immediately yank it away.

"I never got to thank you for my dress."

He stays stock-still, staring down at me.

"And tonight…"

103

I think his face softens just a bit, but it's hard to tell.

Fortunately, his words are clear enough on their own. "I'm going."

"Fine." I drop his hand. "But the next time you want me to be your date or your little secret weapon, don't bother. Michael's secret weapon was stronger. Tonight was awful."

He pauses for a moment with his hand on the door and I'm hopeful that my words finally penetrated his perfect facade, but then he yanks it open and walks out. I decide if I never saw him again, it'd be too soon.

 **CHAPTER NINE**

FROM: BrookeSDavenport@Gmail.com
TO: BethAssist@BioWear.com

Beth, since I have no way of contacting your boss, could you please forward this email to him for me?

Thanks,
Brooke

PS the heels were killer.

————

Dear James,

I've thought a lot about what happened last week. Although I don't think I owe you any kind of explanation, I would like to set the record straight.

You brought me to that party.

You introduced me to *your* friends and one of *your* friends slipped something into my drink while I was in the bathroom.

I still have no clue what she gave me. I was pretty out of it the next day. My sister almost took me to the hospital.

Thank you for giving me the benefit of the doubt.

Thank you for ensuring that I wasn't having an adverse reaction.

Thank you for staying with me and making sure I made it through the night.

Oh wait, you didn't.

Fuck off,
Brooke

• • •

It's been a week since the party and two days since I sent James that carefully crafted email. While I would love a response or—CALL ME CRAZY—maybe even an apology, I'm not holding my breath. The entire night was a disaster. I remember bits and pieces of it and I cringe thinking back on some of my behavior, but then I quash that line of thinking. I didn't willingly take those drugs. Celeste dosed my drink while we were in the bathroom. Jesus Christ, who *does* that? I still can't believe it actually happened. I should contact the authorities. I could draw so much unwanted attention to that little "hidden gem" of theirs. I've wavered back and forth about it a few times. While I don't think Celeste should go around drugging people without their consent, I don't really know how I would go about seeking retribution. I don't know Michael or Celeste—I'm not even sure those are their real names. The only person I could really pin the incident on is James and I might hate him at the moment, but I don't necessarily want to drag him into a police report and potential investigation.

Out of curiosity, I hunt down the club a few days later. The black brick building is easy enough to find downtown, but there's a new, massive banner hanging across the side of it, proudly announcing the block as a future site for Austin's newest and most luxurious condominiums. The front door swings open and construction workers march in and out, carrying tools and supplies with them. I think back on all the decadence from that night—the chandeliers, the furniture, the pristine marble floors—and wonder where it's all gone.

I can't find anything about the club online; putting in search terms like "secret Austin club" and "downtown speakeasy" only brings up weird Craigslist sex ads. After perusing a few (okay, like 20), I decide none of them have anything to do with the party and I'd be wise to avoid the bushes at Pease Park at night.

I'd rather just forget about the entire ordeal.

I'm hanging out with Ellie in her room at our dad's house. We're both off from work, and while our morning was spent productively (SoulCycle, brunch, laundry), our afternoon has been anything but (Real Housewives, homemade face masks, enough Instagram scrolling to make my thumb cramp. Hello millennial arthritis).

"Hey, isn't this the guy you said James wanted to hire?"

Ellie holds her laptop out for me so I can see the article on the screen. It's from the Austin American-Statesman and includes a large, majestic photo of James on the homepage. I tell myself they photoshopped it to make him look that good.

The headline reads: *BioWear Names New CFO.*

I cringe and wave it away. There's no point in reading it.

Ellie insists, all but flinging her laptop at me. It almost topples off the bed before I catch it. "Okay! Jeez, I'll read it."

I skim.

"Blah blah blah thought they would pick Michael Felch, blah blah blah they picked someone else." I hand her laptop back to her and turn back to the TV, where Countess Luann (*once a countess, always a countess*) is currently going on about her wedding. "Why do I care?"

Ellie groans in annoyance, but it doesn't faze me.

I flip the channel and land on Ellen, America's sweetheart.

"Don't be so obtuse!"

"Wow, someone's using the word of the day."

"James wanted to hire Michael Felch up until last week, made you come to the party to schmooze him and his girlfriend, yet now *suddenly* his company hires someone else?"

"Yup."

I flip another channel and land on Judge Judy, America's strict but fair nanny.

"I bet he didn't hire Michael because of what went down at the club."

"Or *maybe*—and this might sound insane, so stay with me—there was *more than one* highly qualified candidate."

"No. I swear this is his way of letting you know he believes you, that he's sorry for what happened."

You see, this is why I don't like bringing Ellie into my personal life. Sure, we share the same parents, and I spend most of my waking non-work hours (and some of my waking work hours) with her, but she loves nothing more than going off on fanatical tangents supported by flimsy notions. If I believe James took my email into consideration when hiring his new CFO, I'm putting way too much faith in him. I've learned my lesson. I got burned last week, and I'm not going to fall into the same trap again.

I point to the TV. "Can't a woman watch her daytime TV in peace?"

She plunks me in the head with her pointer finger and thumb.

"Consider the situation from his side for a second. The last woman he dated had a major drug problem—"

"What? How do you know that?"

"Social media. Anyway, she was a real partier, and now, a year later, he's into you, someone he hopes will be different. He's super excited about taking you to the party, maybe even hopes something will come from it, and then BOOM, you come back from the bathroom blitzed out of your mind."

"Because Celeste drugged me."

"Right! But from his perspective, it looks like you're a crazy party girl. I don't really blame him for being annoyed that night."

I sit up and reach for my shoes. "That's some good psychoanalysis, Freud."

My sarcasm flies right over her head.

"Yeah, I know."

It's time to go. Martha is downstairs in the kitchen baking and will probably insist that I stop and chat with her for a good 45 minutes, but that's fine—I'd stick my head into the oven if it meant getting out of this room.

"Wait, don't leave!" She scrambles off her bed. "You were just about to agree to cover another one of my shifts."

"Yeah, that's a hard no."

"C'mon! It's this Friday." She's at her dresser, slamming drawers, looking for something. "Tyler has a gig playing at this local festival in the afternoon and he's nervous the crowd won't be very big. I have to be there to support him."

"Sounds miserable, but not as miserable as I'll be if I agree. Ask Marissa to cover it."

"I already did. She's going to the festival too."

She finally pulls something white out of the drawers and turns to me with big puppy dog eyes. Fortunately, I'm more of a cat person.

"I promise I won't ask you for another favor for a month."

"That's what you said last week."

"A year then!"

I laugh because it's ridiculous, but her desperation tells me she won't be giving up any time soon.

"Sweeten the deal for me."

"Fine. If you cover my shift, I won't bring up any more of my theories about James."

I arch my brows. *Now we're talking.*

"And…?"

"I'll bring back a funnel cake from the festival."

"Deal."

"Yay!" she says as she shoves the white thing in my arms.

"What's this?" I ask, holding it up so the fabric unfolds and hangs limp in the air.

It's a dress.

Actually, it's a uniform…

She smiles sheepishly. "My shift is out on the golf course."

"No." I drop the dress like it's on fire and head for her door. "Not going to happen. I'm ripping up our verbal contract."

"It's too late!" she calls out after me. "You already agreed!"

Absolutely not. No amount of day-old funnel cake will convince me to prance around as the beverage cart girl on the golf course.

Over.

My.

Dead.

Body.

• • •

Welp, I'm a dead body. I'm sitting in the employee locker room at the country club, and my shift starts in 15 minutes—correction, *Ellie's* shift starts in 15 minutes. I hate that I'm here, sitting in her white polo dress. The material is some kind of thick cotton blend that is sure to suffocate me the moment I step out into the Texas heat.

I could be preparing for my shift—after all, I've never worked out there before—but Ellie filled me in on most of the details when she dropped the dress off last night. I was staying strong in my refusal until the tutoring agency contacted me about an interview next week. Sadly, I need Ellie to cover my shift so I can go.

I think her exact words were, *Oh, how the tables have turned.*

So now I'm here and Ellie is wearing a flower crown and smoking a bowl while her boyfriend bangs on a tattered tambourine.

Conversation on the other end of the locker room trickles over to me.

"—saw him just now."

"I think he's eating lunch."

Two new waitresses are gossiping about one of the guests, and I'd bet a million dollars I know who it is. I still haven't heard from him. My email gets checked every hour on the hour, but I tell myself that's in case the agency has another interview invitation for me.

"I think the hostess put him in Sammy's section. Lucky bitch."

My stomach knots into a tight ball.

I look down at my watch.

14 minutes left.

I don't want to listen to their conversation, but I don't want to start my shift any earlier than necessary, so I reach for my phone and dial the first number I ever memorized.

I don't expect her to answer, but then the FaceTime call starts to connect and my heart drops.

"Brooke?!"

The excitement in her voice makes my heart sore.

"Hey Mom."

"Hold on. I didn't realize this was FaceTime. Let me just step inside. The connection is a little better in there."

There's a mixture of indiscernible sounds and I'm pretty sure she drops the phone at one point, but about a minute later, her face appears on my phone screen and a wave of homesickness hits me.

"There you are! My little Bwookie. Where are you?" She squints her eyes. "Is that a locker behind your head?"

I swallow down the sudden—and strange—urge to cry as best as possible and plaster on a big smile. "Yeah, I'm at work. I only have a few minutes to talk."

She holds the phone out a little so more than just her eyes and nose fit into the frame, and I get a better look at her. She looks to be ready for bed with her long light brown hair wrapped up in a bun and a loose-fitting kimono wrapped around her shoulders. She's in her late 40s, but she doesn't look it. Good genes, I guess. Light blue glasses sit on the brim of her nose, the only sign that she's aging at all. She pushes them up onto her head and smiles.

"I guess that's why you're wearing that polo shirt?"

I cringe. "Yeah, it's a dress actually."

"Why does it have Ellie's name embroidered on it?"

"Oh." I glance down and brush my finger across her name. "I'm covering a shift for her."

"That's nice of you. I didn't know you two were working together."

Yes she did; I told her about it the last time we FaceTimed.

"We're both at the country club, remember?"

"Oh yes! Of course."

From the tone of her voice, I can tell she's lying. She doesn't remember.

"How are you, Mom? I've been trying to reach you for the last few weeks."

She frowns. "I'm sorry, honey. Jorge and I were stationed in a remote village in Argentina for the last month and a half and there weren't any cell towers within a few miles of the village. I thought I told you I'd be out of contact for a bit?"

She didn't, but I nod. "Yeah, I must have forgotten."

I walk a tight rope when it comes to my mom because I'm too scared to rock the boat. We talk so rarely and though I'd love nothing more than to berate her for falling off the face of the earth without any warning, I don't want to spend these precious few minutes arguing. Instead, I fill her in on what I've been up to lately. I tell her about the book I just finished and brag about the interview I have next week with the tutoring agency.

She grins. "That sounds awesome, Brooke. I know you'd rather be working with a family than dealing with that job at the country club, but hang in there. It'll work out when it's supposed to."

I try to take her words to heart.

"Thanks Mom."

"If I text you my address, would you mind sending me that book? *The Nightingale*? It's hard to get paperbacks down here."

"Of course." The request fills me with hope. "Do you need anything else? I can put together a little care package."

She shakes her head. "No. We won't be here much longer. We're headed back to Syria next month."

"How long will you be there?"

"I'm not sure. I'll have to ask Jorge."

"Do you think you'll have any time off around the holidays?"

Her smile falls. "I'm sorry, honey. The Peace Corps really needs us right now. War and famine have devastated the entire region. If you could see the images of these children…"

Of course. How can I compete with starving children? I feel evil for even considering it.

A locker slams a few rows down, reminding me of where I am. I check the time and cringe. "Mom, I gotta go. My shift is starting soon."

"Oh, right. Hey, how about I try to call you tomorrow?"

"I'm working late, but I could talk in the morning?"

"We've got an all-staff meeting pretty early, but I'll try you after that."

"Sounds good."

When we hang up, I regret calling her in the first place. It's time to start working and I feel like I've just been sucker-punched in the stomach. My emotions are brewing right at the surface, which is a bad starting point for the beginning of the shift. If I run into Mr. Oil Tycoon or any of the other more demanding members, I might not be able to offer up an oh-so-sunny smile. Knowing that, I try to avoid everyone as I weave through the kitchen and main dining room, heading for the loading dock out back where the beverage carts have been left to charge.

The club has three of them, basically souped-up golf carts with coolers on the sides and a small table built into the back for prepping drinks. The person assigned to the beverage cart shift before me was responsible for restocking it and when I open the first cooler, I confirm it's full of sodas and mixers. Ellie said that on a good shift, I'd have to head back to the club midway through to restock, but I doubt I'll be able to get through all of this alcohol in the next few hours—unless I run across a rowdy bachelor party or something, which for my sanity's sake, I really hope I don't.

I'm finishing up inventory when Brian comes out to check on me.

"Did Ellie explain everything to you?" he asks with his hands on his hips.

He's the one who wanted me to try out the new job, but now he doesn't seem so sure it's a good idea, probably because I'm currently scowling. Before I respond, I painstakingly turn my frown upside down.

"Just about. I haven't driven the cart yet, but I'm assuming it handles like a normal golf cart?"

He nods and points out the gas, brake, and emergency brake. "It's top-heavy, so avoid any sharp turns. Other than that, you'll be okay."

"Sounds good."

"And not to put any pressure on you, but we've got some important members scheduled to play golf this afternoon, so attempt to look like you know what you're doing."

I laugh. "I think I'll manage just fine. I just have to drive this thing around and make drinks, right?"

Wrong.

The golf course is packed. The club scheduled tee times back to back, so I'm left scrambling from hole to hole like a chicken with my head cut off. Worse, compared to working in the cabana, being out on the golf course is like trying to survive in the wild west. There are rules and social norms inside the clubhouse; guests have to carry themselves with a certain level of decorum. Out here, anything goes.

I'm no prude, but if I have to listen to one more of these golfers drone on about their girlfriend's tits or ass, I'm going to drive my golf cart into a sand trap. Currently, I'm mixing up three margaritas for a group of retirees who are requesting everything under the sun.

"Do you have top-shelf tequila?"

"Don't skimp on the limes."

"Make sure my drink is ice cold."

"Could I get a little more bourbon in this?"

"You know what? I'll just take a beer instead."

I squeeze fresh lime juice until my hands are numb and narrowly miss slicing my finger open on a soda can tab.

"You almost done there, sweetie?" one of them asks.

"Sure thing, asshole."

"What was that?"

"Oh!" I tilt my head around the side of the beverage cart and smile sweetly. "I said, 'Sure, when you finish this hole!'"

He grins, drags his gaze down to my breasts, and then turns back to his red-faced friends.

I make sure to give him a little less tequila than everyone else. It feels like a silent victory when he tips me fifty bucks.

"Meet up with us again at hole 9, will you?"

He holds out another fifty.

I smile, take it, and agree to see them there.

So this is what it feels like to sell your soul to the devil. Funny, I knew it would happen eventually, but I guess I always thought it would hurt.

• • •

I get my first break toward the end of my shift, when I pull up to hole 7. There's a group of four men getting ready to tee off and as I drive closer, I prep myself for more of the same bullshit I've dealt with all day.

"Goddamn, I didn't know angels drove golf carts!"

"$15 for a beer? Do you come with it?"

"I've been slicing my tee shots, do you mind givin' me a little back rub, honey?"

I pull the cart to a stop a safe distance from their group, a trick I learned early on. If I park far enough away, I don't have to listen to their conversations while I'm mixing their drinks.

117

I straighten my Twin Oaks baseball cap so the late afternoon sun isn't in my eyes and then stroll closer to the men to get drink orders. From my vantage point, I can tell they're younger and definitely more in shape than most of the other guys I've seen on the course today, so much so that they actually make their boring golf outfits pretty hot. It's all about the pants, specifically the derrière, and yes, I realize men have objectified me all day and now I'm doing the same to these unsuspecting golfers, but that's life, and sometimes it's pretty fun to be a hypocrite. So, I stare at their butts as much as I want until one of them sees me approaching and nudges his friend. Like dominoes, they turn toward me, anxious for a drink, and I assess them from right to left. Cute…Cuter…Cutest…James.

Shit.

I can't believe he's there, standing at the end of the group, watching me approach like I don't hate his stinking guts. Worse, I just totally checked out his butt without realizing it. What an unsettling thought considering I've spent the last few days telling myself I don't find him attractive anymore—and I don't. Like one shapely butt cheek is going to change that. *Pfft.*

"Hey guys," I say with a broad smile. "Can I get you anything from the beverage cart?"

"Is this a mirage?" Cute asks Cuter. "Is she an angel or something, because I've been wanting a beer for the last 30 minutes."

He's laying on the charm pretty thick, but it's still kind of funny. "Well, it's your lucky day. We carry every beer that's on the menu back at the clubhouse, foreign and domestic."

"I'll take a Dos Equis," Cutest says.

Cuter nods. "Same for me."

"Lime?"

They both nod.

"Can you do any mixed drinks out here?" Cute asks with a hopeful smile.

"Simple ones. Margarita on the rocks, vodka soda, Jack and Coke—that sort of thing."

He nods. "Great. I'll take a vodka soda."

That leaves just one person: Mr. James Suddenly-Silent Ashwood.

"James? Want anything?" Cutest asks, nudging him.

I work up enough courage to stare at the grass at James' feet. It's a start.

"I didn't realize you worked out here, Brooke."

His voice is a warm hand around my neck.

"Uhh, her dress says her name's Ellie dude."

"That's not her dress," he points out with a confident tone.

I ignore their conversation. "Would you like something or not?"

My tone is biting, but when I get called into Brian's office later to address this complaint—as I undoubtedly will—I'll describe it as gentle and kind.

He still doesn't reply, so I nod and turn on my heel. "Well I'll get those drinks started while Mr. Ashwood thinks over what he would like."

There's shuffling of feet and the awkward sounds of clearing throats. It's obvious we know each other, and the second before I step out of earshot, they ask him what's going on. I wish now that I'd pulled my beverage cart close enough to hear his reply. I'm sure it'd be amusing.

I pop tops off beers, slice limes, and whip up a vodka soda faster than I've done anything all day. The drinks are in their hands and a cool tip is in mine before I've had time

119

to process my body's reaction to James.

"Manna from heaven," Cuter says, clinking his bottle with his friend's.

I smile and attempt once more to get a drink for James. I don't want to get accused of denying him service or anything.

"I'm fine, thanks."

Three words said in a tone that oozes disdain and annoyance. I want to roll my eyes and flip him off a thousand times, but I don't even think that would cool my jets at this point. I clench my teeth to keep expletives from spilling out and then taking a calming breath.

"Right, well…enjoy your golf game."

Cutest steps forward with an easy smile. "Can't you stay? We're not even halfway through and we're all sick of each other. I promise I'll order a new drink every hole."

Cute nods enthusiastically.

I smile and am about to reply when James beats me to the punch. "She can't."

I whip my gaze up, finally, *finally* giving in to the urge to look at him.

He's wearing a Nike hat and matching shirt, both black—the color of his soul. I realize, as I focus on just how tan and muscular they are, that I've never seen his arms. He's always dressed in a suit when he's inside the club. Out here, he almost looks like a regular guy—a very hot, very in shape, regular guy.

"Well this is awkward as shit," Cute says with a laugh.

The guys chuckle, but James' face is an impenetrable mask of hatred, and it's directed right at me.

If I stay another second, there's going to be a scene, and I refuse to let that happen. I only have an hour left of my shift. I'll wrap it up, earn as many tips as I can, and then do what any self-respecting woman would do in this situation: wait for James in the parking lot when I'm no longer on the clock and give him a piece of my mind.

CHAPTER TEN

By the time I've exchanged my dress for jeans and a tank top, I've almost talked myself out of confronting James. Key word: almost. At this point, I'm a missile that's already been launched. My momentum is too strong to be overridden by silly things like common sense and consequences.

There's a Tesla SUV parked in James' spot. It's his second fancy car, one I don't see all that often, and I'm trying to decide how satisfying it would be to pull a Carrie Underwood when I hear him call my name.

That didn't take long. So much for taking a Louisville Slugger to both headlights.

I turn to find him walking out of the club and heading straight for me. I'd assumed he would take longer with his golfing buddies; maybe they didn't play the full course, or maybe he cut things off early. Either way, I'm happy I didn't have to wait all night. As it is, the sun is barely setting behind him. I'd probably think it was lovely if I wasn't a burning ball of fury.

I cross my arms and lean against the side of his car.

He scowls.

I grimace with the intensity of a thousand toddlers being made to eat broccoli.

It takes him an obnoxiously long time to reach me. It's like he's walking the wrong way on a moving airport walkway, and I think he likes to watch me squirm. He doesn't stop walking until he's right in front of me. I can smell his cologne, the stuff he puts on in the morning to make women swoon. *How pathetic.* I inhale deeply.

"Where's your dress?" he asks, tipping his head to the side.

"Stuffed in Ellie's locker."

He nods and I think…*dear god, is he actually smiling right now?!*

"I can see you're furious." He says it like he's happy at the prospect.

I nod. "I am. Did your stupid watch detect that?"

"What exactly are you upset about?"

"Let's recount." I hold up my fingers and start ticking things off. "Your friend drugged me, you blamed me, you didn't stay to see if I was okay, and you still haven't apologized."

"She's not my friend."

I throw my hands up in anger. "Who cares?! You assumed I did that to myself, and you were wrong."

He arches a brow. "Can you blame me? It didn't look good. You disappeared and then returned out of your mind."

"So? You were wrong and you should have apologized."

He nods.

I wait.

Silence.

"So…apologize!"

He smiles and steps around me. He's going to leave, but I'm not done.

"Why were you acting like that back there?" I ask. "On the course?"

He unlocks his car, sets down his golf clubs, and then starts to fold down the back row of seats. "I was curious."

"Curious?"

He stashes his clubs, closes the door, and turns back to me. "Yeah. Where's your bike?"

"Locked to the rack behind the clubhouse."

He starts to walk away, and I'm forced to follow if I want to continue the conversation.

"Curious about what?"

"What your plan was—besides refusing to look at me. It was actually pretty funny."

I seethe.

"I wouldn't look at you because I didn't want to make a scene in front of your friends."

"They're business associates," he clarifies as we round the side of the clubhouse.

"What does that matter?!"

"Because it's an important distinction. Is Brian your friend?"

"Stop changing the subject!"

He points to my bike lock.

"What's the combo?"

I cross my arms, looking every bit of four years old. "Like I'm telling you."

The stare he levels at me could slice through granite. It seems to say, *If I wanted to steal your bike, I could just buy this entire country club.*

"10-17-38."

He puts in the combo, pops the lock, and proceeds to wheel my bike back in the direction of the parking lot. I'm left to speed walk after him again.

"What are you doing?"

There are a handful of members out in the parking lot,

and every one of them is watching me trail after James as he steals my bike. They do nothing.

I finally catch up with him enough to try to yank it out of his hold.

"Give me my bike, James."

But it's too late. We're back at his parking spot. He pops the trunk of his Tesla and pauses for a moment, assessing something. Then he leans down and detaches the front wheel with a few flicks of his wrist. Without it in place, the bike slides easily into the trunk space. He tosses the wheel in after it and slams the door closed.

I cross my arms. "Great. You've stolen a bike from a woman. What's next? Gonna go steal those little tennis balls off some granny's walker? Or what about a rattle from a baby?"

He chuckles, shakes his head, and heads for the passenger side door. "Get in the car, Brooke."

I can feel people watching us, completely enthralled no doubt. Soon Brian is going to wander out and join the crowd. I don't want to get in trouble for causing a scene in the parking lot, although truthfully, that's exactly what I had originally planned to do. I just didn't expect James to do it for me.

He opens my door, rounds the front of the car, and gets in behind the wheel. He doesn't have to ask me to get in again; the empty seat taunts me enough as it is. I glance back to the clubhouse and seriously contemplate booking an Uber to get home. He changes radio stations, puts the car in reverse, and before I can truly acknowledge my actions, I get in.

Neither of us speaks for the first few minutes. I sit like a statue, my arms crossed in front of my chest, my gaze laser-focused out the front window. James, by contrast, has apparently reached the highest level of nirvana. He couldn't be more relaxed. He turns up the music and drums his thumb on the steering wheel. I bet if I glanced over, I'd even find a hint of a smile.

He drives us down the winding drive and away from the country club. I could ask him where we're going, but alas, I'd be breaking the silence first, and I will not lose this battle. Besides, I get my answer soon enough when he pulls up in front of 24 Diner at 6th and Lamar. I've driven by the restaurant a million times, but I've never stopped for a meal.

He didn't even ask if I was hungry. He just assumed if he parked here and hopped out of the car, I would follow along after him—and what's more frustrating is that I do. It's getting annoying. I feel like a puppy or a victim with Stockholm syndrome.

"Table for two please," he says to the hostess.

She leads us to a small booth in the back of the restaurant. James stakes a claim on one side, and I take the other. The waiter swoops down on us, and James speaks up for me. "We'll take an order of the chicken and waffles."

I peer at him over the top of my menu.

"I'm not hungry."

I am, but if he's going to be difficult, then so am I.

"That's too bad."

He takes my menu and hands it to the waiter along with his.

We're left to ourselves. Silence descends again, and I can't handle it. I've never been around someone so infuriating. Sure, first dates are awkward, but that awkwardness is usually felt by both parties. James seems totally oblivious. He's staring off down the hallway past my head, content within his own thoughts.

So, I try to be too.

I think over what I need to buy at the grocery store tomorrow. Chicken. Maybe some of that fancy gelato I stroll past every week and try very hard to avoid. I remind myself to text Ellie about our SoulCycle class Monday— she has a tendency to forget about them unless I hound her. All in all, I think I do a good job of ignoring him completely.

Our food arrives and my mouth waters. I've had chicken and waffles a few times in my life, but it's never looked like this. In the center of a large plate sits a perfect, golden waffle. On top of that, they've arranged four pieces of crispy fried chicken. The smell hits me before my other senses can even catch up. I want to fall forward and face-plant into it. That's how delicious this food smells.

James puts a quarter of the waffle and some chicken onto a spare plate and pushes it toward me.

"I know you aren't hungry," he says, "but if you're going to try a bite, I'd add a little bit of the brown sugar butter."

He points to a small bowl off to the side I hadn't noticed due to my waffle blinders. At this point, I'm drooling out of the corner of my mouth. I'm sure in some alternate universe, Brooke 1,342 stands up, flips the table over, and skips all the way home...but in this life, I swallow my pride right before dipping my knife into the brown sugar butter and drizzling syrup all over my plate.

I'm ashamed, and I do not meet his eyes as I fork my first bite into my mouth. It is, of course, a perfect combination of chicken and waffle and butter and syrup— all the main food groups.

It's heaven on earth.

"Oh my god," I moan before realizing what I'm doing.

I whip my gaze to James, and thankfully he pretends like he doesn't hear me—that is, until I notice the little smirk he's trying to hide behind his napkin as he wipes his mouth.

I ignore him, and just to be sure the first bite wasn't a fluke, I take another.

My plate is cleared before James has finished half of his. I dab my mouth like a proper lady and then recline against the booth.

I watch him eat, studying the meticulous way he loads his fork. One bite of waffle, one bite of chicken, one small dab of brown sugar butter—if all the parts aren't there, he doesn't eat it.

I smile to myself and tuck away that bit of information.

"This is my way of apologizing," he says, pulling us out of what could now be described as pleasant silence. Funny how that happens.

I glance up to find him studying me. Our eyes lock for one heated moment, and then he looks back down at his food.

"It doesn't come naturally to me," he continues.

"I would have never guessed," I tease.

"It's something I want to work on."

I smirk. "No time like the present."

He laughs, sets his fork down, and then leans back, hooking his elbow on the back of the booth. Reclined like that, he looks every bit the confident businessman, aloof and unattainable. "You're right."

I wait, and he continues, "I owe you an apology."

I squint as if I'm thinking really hard. "Yeah, I still don't think those are quite the words I'm looking for."

"I'm sorry."

"What was that?"

He clears his throat then leans forward like he's about to divulge state secrets. "I'm sorry."

The table seems too small now with him leaning toward me. While I probably smell like I just dipped myself in brown sugar butter, James smells like his woodsy cologne. I'm hyperaware of that scent and the way our legs are all but twined underneath the table.

"I accept your apology, under one condition."

My smile is wicked and from the gleam in his eye, I can tell he likes it.

"What's that?"

I pick up my fork and smirk. "I want another one of these. No sharing."

• • •

After dinner, we don't talk about where we're headed next, but I think he's taking me home. We head north on Lamar, away from downtown. In 10 minutes, he'll drop me off outside the co-op and this weird exchange will be over. I wanted an apology from him, and now I have it. Beyond that, I don't think there's any reason for James to see me again. I don't think we're friends. He wanted me to be a pawn in his game, and I fulfilled my duty. Sure, I've wondered what would have happened that night if Celeste hadn't slipped something into my drink. James and I might have enjoyed the party, and maybe at some point he would have admitted to inviting me to attend for reasons that didn't include buttering up a potential hire.

Beyond a few smoldering glances and the compliment paid to me before the party, James hasn't made it clear that he even sees me as an attractive woman. By now, most other guys would have made their feelings toward me a bit more obvious, but it seems James does more of his thinking above the belt.

I wonder if the age difference is too much for him. I tried to find information about his last girlfriend, the one Ellie said had a drug problem, but it didn't look like they were anything serious. She was only pictured alongside him at one or two events before she reportedly checked herself into Passages Malibu, the luxury rehab center where all the celebrities pretend to get their life in order. I don't get the feeling he's lovesick over her.

He presses the brake and I glance over. His eyes meets mine, and there's something there—questions in his gaze that mimic my own. I think he's going to ask me something, but instead, he turns his attention back to the road.

So, I take matters into my own hands.

"Are you dating anyone right now?"

He accelerates.

"Of course not. I wouldn't have taken you to that party if I was."

"But what about your last relationship? Was it a tough breakup?"

"Not at all. I haven't dated anyone serious in a few years."

Even better.

"Why?" he asks.

"Asking for a friend."

"Oh, okay." He's willing to play along. "Is your friend cute?"

I glance out the window so he can't see my smile. By now, the sun has set and the bright lights of the businesses along Lamar whip past us.

"Blindingly."

"Does she work at the club?"

I chuckle. "Yes, unfortunately."

"Is she interested in me?"

His question catches me off guard.

"Who knows? You'd have to ask her," I reply tentatively.

That surprises him. He does one of those curious *huh* noises like I've just told him something incredibly interesting.

I turn back toward him. "She doesn't know you very well. If she were interested in you at this point, it would be for superficial reasons, like your wealth. Hell, she might just want a membership to Twin Oaks," I tease. "You have to be careful these days."

His gaze slices over me. "Maybe she finds me attractive and it has nothing to do with my country club membership."

I chew on my bottom lip. "Maybe." But because I feel like I revealed too much, I add, "But she really wants that membership."

He laughs as he pulls up to a red light. We're about to turn right and head into the heart of north campus; there's only another minute or two until he drops me off. Suddenly, I want to stall, but beyond asking him to take me back to his place, I can't think of a good reason. I could suggest that we continue our night somewhere else, a bar maybe? But he's still dressed in his golf clothes and my jeans are pretty casual. I just threw them on to get me back home from the club.

I tap my finger on my knee, trying to come up with something. We could take a walk somewhere or do something outside. Peter Pan Mini-Golf would be perfect for our ensembles, but it's all the way in the opposite direction. I should have suggested it when we left the diner.

"James? Do you want to—"

Words are spilling out of my mouth before I even have a solid plan. I'm kind of hoping the second half of the sentence will come to me through divine intervention, but it never has the chance.

Bright headlights expand behind us so quickly that we both twist to look back at the precise moment a car slams into James' Tesla. I whip forward from the intensity of the impact, arms flailing to catch myself against the dashboard as we're pushed into the intersection, right in the way of oncoming traffic.

"JAMES!"

I scream just before another car comes into the intersection and slams into the side of us. We spin out, fishtailing in the center of the chaos. The airbags deploy with a loud POP, so quickly that I feel nothing, see nothing. One second I'm aware of my screams, and the next my ears are ringing so loudly I can't hear myself breathe. White powder fills the air like snow and the sharp smell of chemicals stings my nostrils. I collect parts of the scene, quickly wondering if more will come or if the crash is over.

One of my hands grips the door. The other is on James' arm, clinging for dear life.

My chest rises and falls so quickly I don't feel as if I get any air at all.

I squeeze my eyes closed again, scared it's not over.

James is saying something, but I can't listen. I blink and blink until I can focus beyond the white powder in the air. There's wreckage sprinkled across the road in front of us, another car, badly damaged, a man stumbling out of it. His head is bleeding.

James covers my hand with his and squeezes. It's the first feeling that comes back to me.

"Are you okay? BROOKE, ARE YOU OKAY?"

He's shouting at me now, so worried I'm hurt.

Am I?

I look down and assess that I still have two legs and two arms. I stare at the deflated airbag hanging limp in front of me, now useless.

"What happened?"

The sound of my voice surprises me. I'm crying—no, *sobbing*—and though I try to plug the waterworks, it's no use.

"Brooke. *Brooke*. Brooke."

He says my name so many times that it doesn't sound like a word anymore. I turn and he cups my face between his hands. His dark, worried gaze darts back and forth between my eyes, desperately trying to focus.

"I think I'm okay," I repeat, holding my hand up to grip his. My other hand is still on his arm, stuck there. I've probably branded his skin, but I don't think I could move it if I tried.

Police sirens wail somewhere in the distance. The lights from an ambulance flicker through the front windshield, and now that the powder is starting to settle, it's easier to see just how bad the wreck was.

A fist raps on James' window. It's a paramedic asking if we're okay, telling us not to move until they assess our injuries.

"Check her," James insists. "Check her. I'm fine."

The next hour is spent being checked out by EMS (Yes, I can feel and move all my limbs. No, I don't have a headache.) and relaying our version of events to the police officers. There were four cars involved in the crash, and multiple witnesses who can attest to what happened. The man who slammed into us was taken to the emergency room before I got to see him. I suspect he was driving drunk, but overheard whispers from a few of the medics clarify that wasn't the case, something about prescription drugs that shouldn't have been mixed.

After we speak with the police and James shares his insurance and contact information with the other drivers, we're free to leave—except James' car is totaled, along with my bike. I don't bring it up at the moment because it's the least of anyone's concerns, but when the driver slammed into the back of us, he basically squashed my bike like a pancake. For the time being, if I need to get somewhere, it's going to have to be on foot or by bus.

While James deals with the tow truck driver, I stand off to the side, out of the way of the police officers and firefighters cleaning up the wreckage on the road. After his damaged Tesla is loaded onto the back of a truck, he comes over to get me.

"C'mon, the driver is going to drop us off."

James takes my hand in his and together, we walk toward the tow truck. The cab has one long bench seat, so I scoot to the middle and look for a seatbelt, panicking that there might not be one.

"Here."

James holds it out for me and I loop it across my body, hissing as it rubs the raw skin across my chest. My only injuries were abrasions from the seatbelt in James' car as I lurched forward during the crash. The medics checked the bruising and redness along the path of the seatbelt, but there wasn't much else they could do for it besides offering me some over-the-counter pain reliever, which I refused. Now that the adrenaline and shock are wearing off, I regret

135

my decision.

"Does it hurt?" James asks as he buckles up beside me.

The driver hops in on the other side and I shake my head. "It's not too bad."

"Where to, folks?"

"Head toward Mount Bonnell Road and I'll direct you from there," James replies.

I stay silent, content to let James take control of the next few minutes. When I blink, the wreck replays in my mind. The point of impact flashes again and again until I'm desperate to focus on something else, like the fact that James is still holding my hand.

Fortunately, James and the driver carry on their own conversation for the short drive, and once we get closer, James directs him into a gated community I've heard whispers about at the country club: Island at Mount Bonnell Shores.

"Huh," the driver says, leaning forward to inspect the sprawling estates surrounding us. "I always wondered who lived here."

"It's just up ahead," James says, ignoring the man's awestruck tone as he points to the left. "There."

We pull up in front of a gated estate sitting on a few oak-covered acres. The house isn't visible from the road, but the dark-stained wooden fence running around the property and the mid-century address numbers give the property a clean, modern look.

The driver pulls up to the curb and James hops out, reaching back for my hand so he can help me jump down. I step out onto the street and realize right away that the air smells different here—fresher—and I swear there's a slight breeze where none existed before. I smile, because of course James would have waterfront property on Lake

Austin. Every house in this exclusive community probably has its own boat dock.

James hammers out the details about his Tesla with the tow truck driver. Cash is exchanged, the driver tips his hat, and then he leaves James and me standing on the curb in front of his house.

"I like your fence," I say with a small smile. I come from wealth, but James' is a kind that exists in another stratosphere, the kind that intimidates most people—me included.

He shakes his head and starts to head up the paved walkway.

"C'mon. I think we could both use a drink."

CHAPTER ELEVEN

James' house is a modern take on a traditional Texas farmhouse: a mix of dark woods, copper, glass, and cut limestone. Ahead of the entry gallery, a tall light shaft illuminates the space from above and gives it a museum aesthetic. Stone walls contrast with bright burnished plaster and concrete floors. I wouldn't be surprised to find it's been featured in *Architectural Digest*, or at least on a couple fancy home blogs.

"It must have taken you forever to build this," I say as he leads me past the foyer and into the streamlined kitchen.

He glances back at me with a smooth smile. "I can't take the credit. The previous owner was an architect."

"Well they had great taste."

He nods and tells me to make myself comfortable while he goes to change out of his golf clothes.

I take a seat on one of his kitchen barstools just long enough to hear him close a door somewhere in another part of the house. Then I hop up and snoop around as much as I can. I'm not stupid enough to wander far; the place is a maze and I didn't bring any breadcrumbs to lead me back to the kitchen. I play it safe by peeking my head into nearby rooms. There's a formal dining room, office, some sort of sitting area, and an expansive living room—at least, I think that's what it is. It's hard to tell any of the rooms apart because most of them are empty.

At first, I think it's a fluke, or even some kind of minimalist design strategy I'm too uncultured to appreciate, but the more rooms I see, the more I realize that isn't the case. One or two bare rooms can be written off, but they're *all* bare. In one room, I stumble on a few pieces of mismatched furniture, but they aren't arranged in any sort of thoughtful way. In fact, it looks like James just moved in and only brought a few items with him from his old place. Framed photos and paintings sit against the wall of a sitting room, waiting to be hung. A mismatched chair and end table sit in one corner underneath a floor lamp. An open paperback rests on the table, flipped on its face.

The vignette is so depressing that I turn on my heel and book it back to the kitchen before I see anything worse, like a room full of discarded frozen dinners for one. Unfortunately, James is back before I am, pouring a finger's worth of amber-colored liquor into a glass tumbler.

I blush at having been caught nosing around his house and grapple for the first excuse that comes to mind. "Just looking for a bathroom."

His brow arches, but he doesn't look up. "Find one?"

"Mhmm."

"Good," he says, pushing the tumbler across the gleaming white kitchen island then pouring one for himself. "I hope you like Maker's Mark. It's all I have."

I hate it, in fact, but I'm not going to admit that. I reach for the drink and down a long swallow, hissing as it burns my throat.

He laughs. "Yeah, sorry. It was a gift, and I don't have anything better—I don't really drink unless I'm at the club or a social event."

"Or after a near-death experience," I choke out, trying not to wheeze at the aftertaste.

I'm sure people who enjoy drinking alcohol straight are very cool and badass, but I like my alcohol diluted and masked to oblivion. In fact, just give me the soda.

"You okay? Do you want something else?"

"It's fine. I just usually mix it with something," I admit sheepishly.

He turns to his industrial refrigerator and pulls open the door to check inside. I, of course, pop up on my toes to peer over his shoulder. There are a few takeout cartons, a half-full bottle of white wine, and the requisite condiments like ketchup and mustard. The fare is as depressing as the art sitting on the floor in his sitting room, but at least there's a glimmer of hope.

"I'll take that wine," I say, hopeful that I won't have to finish my drink.

He chuckles. "Yeah, I wouldn't drink that if I were you. I don't even remember opening it. Looks like you're stuck with the bourbon."

Why hath God forsaken me?

He pulls the bottle out of the refrigerator and pours the contents down the sink—as sacrilegious a behavior as I've ever seen.

"Did you just move in?" I ask, returning my attention back to the liquor I plan on nursing.

"Maybe a year ago."

"What?!"

My shock is out there, spilling across his kitchen along with the sip of bourbon I spit out. I wipe it away with the sleeve of my shirt before he turns back to me.

"I guess it's been a year and a few months, actually."

No. That doesn't make sense.

I turn back to the empty rooms behind me. "But what about your stuff?"

141

"The furniture? Yeah, I've been meaning to get around to that."

"And the artwork…"

"I haven't decided where I should hang it."

He says it like it all makes sense, and maybe it does. Maybe I'm the weird one.

I turn back to his kitchen and see the pieces of his life I missed before. On top of a thick slab of Carrera marble there are paper plates and solo cups. The glasses and china you might expect to find in a house like this *are* in the custom cabinets, but they're still bubble wrapped.

"Honestly, it doesn't even look like you live here."

"I don't really." I turn in time to see him shrug. "I hardly spend any time here. I work long days, and when I'm not at the office, I'm at the club."

I frown. "That's so…"

"Depressing?" he fills in for me before he downs the rest of his drink and sets the tumbler down in the sink. "Yeah, well, I don't bring many people here for a reason."

He's being defensive, and I don't blame him. I feel bad for poking at his life. I could have easily gone home after the wreck—we were only a few minutes away from the co-op—but instead he brought me here. I don't want him to regret that decision.

"Well, if it matters, I'd rather live in your empty house than my ridiculous co-op."

He turns back and smiles. "I think you have more furniture crammed in that tiny room than I have in this whole house."

That thought makes me laugh. "And most of it I found on the side of the street."

That surprises him. "Really? That bookshelf?"

I beam. "Yup. I sanded it down and repainted it."

He nods, impressed. "Maybe I'll commission you to furnish this place."

I snort. "Yeah right. This is the sort of house you fill with Eames armchairs and Rothko originals."

"I'm more of a paint-by-numbers kind of guy."

I laugh at the absurdity of that statement. "Yeah, right. I'll make sure to bring you one the next time I see you."

He smiles and crosses his arms, leaning back against the counter on the other side of the island. I take in the black lounge pants and Caltech t-shirt he changed into. The dark gray material looks like it's been washed a million times, soft and worn. His feet are bare, which is adorable in its own right.

Then it hits me, like a stiff punch to the gut—I AM IN JAMES ASHWOOD'S HOUSE. I'm in his kitchen, *hanging out*, and he feels so comfortable he's not even wearing socks!

Maybe he's noticed that I've gone silent, but he doesn't try to coax me out of it. It's infuriating, how comfortable he is in his own skin. I'm squirming on his barstool with a bourbon-soaked sleeve, sifting through lame topics of conversation until I land on one that is probably inappropriate, but interesting nonetheless.

I decide to lead into it slowly, so I don't spook him and his bare feet—and no, I don't have a weird foot fetish. *Except, maybe I do...he does have nice feet...*

"What's on your mind?" he asks.

Your stupid feet.

"Oh, um, I was actually wondering about your last girlfriend? Someone told me she had a drug problem or something?"

Well, so much for leading into it slowly.

He sighs, like the subject still weighs heavily on him.

"I'm guessing you mean Rebecca?"

Shouldn't he know who his last girlfriend was?

"Um, I guess so? Pretty blonde?"

"Yeah, that's Rebecca. We weren't anything serious."

Silence follows, which means if I want answers, I'm going to have to ask the questions outright.

"And she was into drugs?"

He clears his throat and stalls, clearly irritated by the topic. "Among other things." He's focused on a point just over my shoulder, and maybe I should take his closed-off demeanor as a sign to change the subject, but I'm interested. I want to know if he's truly single or if he has a druggie ex-girlfriend who keeps him up at night. "It was a hard time. Rebecca and I weren't together long, but those few weeks happened to coincide with her downward spiral. When we first started dating, I didn't even realize she was using."

"Wow."

"She's doing well now. Last I heard, she was in California at a rehab facility." He frowns and drags his hands through his hair. "I don't know. I'm coming off callous about the whole thing, but I hardly knew her. She was my date for a few public functions. I never even brought her here."

My heart is a drum during a Dave Grohl solo—THUMP KICK POUND THUMP KICK POUND.

"So you only bring certain women here?" I ask, probing just a liiiiittttle further.

His eyes meet mine, and I'm surprised to find a hint of amusement there. "As you can see, it's not some big prize. In fact, I think you might be the only woman I've ever brought here."

SWOON.

"Because you're embarrassed by your red plastic cups?" I quip, because I'm incapable of enduring an intimate moment without making a joke.

His focus shifts to his stack of disposable cups and then back to me. "Well, most of the time they invite me back to their place."

REVERSE SWOON. Of course. I hadn't even considered that.

"Oh. So none of the women you've been involved with have asked to come here?"

"In my line of work, you get pretty good at saying no. I'm not into the idea of someone moving in and spending a bunch of money decorating a place I hardly spend time in."

I grin. "So you just leave it empty. You're either a much simpler creature than I thought you were, or you're deeply troubled."

"Probably a little of both. What about you?"

I lean back on the barstool, as if I'm trying to put distance between myself and whatever question he's about to ask.

"What about me?"

"You mentioned a boyfriend a few weeks ago. Are you still seeing him?"

"*Seeing* him? Yes. He lives at the co-op with me. Dating him? No."

My focus is pinned on the countertop, so I can't tell if he smiles when he says, "Thanks for the clarification."

Then I remember something that will amuse him even more.

"You know, he was actually at the window the night you picked me up for that party."

His brows rise in surprise. "So he saw you in that dress?"

My cheeks flush. "No. I had the coat on, remember?"

He nods, and I swear I see him replaying that night in his head. I wonder if he remembers the dress like I do. The feel of it against my skin is hard to forget, even when I want nothing more than to put that entire night behind me.

I shift on my barstool and wince when my tank top brushes across the seatbelt burn on my chest.

"Oh shit," he says, pushing off the counter. "I can't believe I just remembered. Do you want something for the pain?"

I glance down at my chest and am surprised at how angry and raw the scratches look around my tank top. Under my gaze, the skin seems to throb even more. "Yeah, I guess so. It wasn't hurting too much until I looked down at it."

He tells me to stay put, and I do. I learned my lesson last time, and I don't think he'd buy it if I said I was searching for a bathroom a second time. He comes back quickly with a small, rattling bottle of Tylenol. I expect him to hand it over, but instead, he fills a small glass of water and doles out two pills into the palm of my hand. His hand grips mine to keep it steady so the pills don't fall onto the ground. It's something you'd do for a child, but I don't mind him touching me, and I don't mind how close he is now compared to earlier. He was standing half a kitchen away from me, but now we'd be toe to toe if I weren't sitting on the stool.

When I'm finished taking the medicine, he takes the glass and sets it on the countertop. Even though he's done playing nurse, he doesn't move away. His attention is on my chest, and I will my breathing to slow down when he reaches out gently, brushing his fingertip across my skin, just barely touching the edge of the wound.

146

"How badly does it hurt?" he asks. "One to ten."

My breath catches in my throat when his fingertips brush across my collarbone.

Does what hurt? Him touching me?

It *burns*.

I shake my head, aware that it doesn't really answer his question, but it's the best I can do right now. I don't trust my voice with words.

His fingers brush higher, up near my shoulder, and they light a fire beneath them. My stomach squeezes tight, and my chest is rising and falling so fast it feels like I'm spiraling through the car accident all over again.

It would be different if his touch was hard and deep, but this thing he's doing feels more like torture. The light drag of fingertips across my skin means I can't control the goose bumps or the shiver that rolls down my spine.

Every nerve ending in my body is focused on his movements, on where they might go.

"I don't know," I whisper.

He shakes his head. "It'll leave a bruise, I'm sure."

He seems pissed by the notion and drops his hand, turning away to drop my glass in the sink. In the blink of an eye, the atmosphere in his kitchen has shifted. There's enough pressure brewing in the space to kick-start a hurricane. I can't stand the awkwardness, and I consider trying to bring the conversation back to the pleasant topics from earlier, but it seems futile. Besides, who am I kidding? I am currently equal parts hot and bothered, all because James platonically stroked my clavicle. It's embarrassing, and my opaque cloud of emotions suddenly crystallizes into an intense urge to flee. I'm afraid to find out just how much sway James has over my libido.

Best to not overstay my welcome, I think in a desperate

attempt to rationalize my feelings. We all have that one friend who's the last to leave the party, ignoring the fact that you're cleaning up in your pajamas. It's not like James invited me back to his place at the end of a sexy date. He is definitely not trying to seduce me. He probably just wanted to make sure I wasn't going to drop dead of a brain hemorrhage.

I slide off the stool and clear my throat, lest any residual hormones try to make me sound like a lust-filled schoolgirl.

"I should probably get going."

He glances back at me, his eyes matching the stormy atmosphere. "What?"

"I don't want to keep you."

"Keep me?"

I nod. "Yeah, you know…" I glance around. "Like you said, if I stay too long, I might start decorating!"

That makes him smile again, and his smile is worse than the storm clouds.

"Let me take you home at least," he says, moving around the island, presumably to get his shoes.

"It's okay, I can just ride my—"

Shit.

I completely forgot about my bike. I didn't remember to grab it from James' car before the tow truck driver drove off, but it's just as well. Last I saw, it looked like it'd been folded into an origami swan. The repair job would likely cost more than a new bike.

He frowns, presumably thinking the same thing I am.

"Did that bike have any sentimental value?"

Sentimental value? Well no, other than being my only means of transportation.

"No." I shrug, trying to play it off. "Like most of the

inanimate objects in my life, it was a fixer-upper I found on Craigslist. It probably would have crapped out in the next few months anyway."

His handsome face is a mask of disapproval.

"Good thing there's Uber, right?" I add with a weak smile.

He nods and pulls his phone out of his pocket. "That's probably for the best."

I want to know what he means, and usually I would bite my tongue, but he's requested an Uber for me and I'm about to leave. No doubt another few weeks will go by before I get to see him again, so I bite the bullet.

"Why is it for the best?"

He looks up at me from beneath his brows. "You know why."

His response is an arrow to my heart.

"I don't, actually."

"We're fooling ourselves here, Brooke."

"Oh yeah? Why's that?"

He leans forward and props his hands on the counter. His head falls and his gaze is focused down at his bare feet. It takes him a second to collect his thoughts, but when he does, he glances back up and asks me with a stiff tone, "What do you want out of the next five or ten years?"

Easy. "I want to find another job teaching French or Spanish. I want to travel and see as much of the world as I can. I lived in Europe after college for a few years, and I might want to try that again."

I think my answer will make him happy, but his smile, half twisted in sadness, proves me wrong.

"That's great. I want those things for you too, but I want to be honest about what I want. I'm sick of serial dating, sick of living out of an empty house I don't want to come home to at the end of the day."

"Okay, and what does this have to do with—"

"I want a wife and a family, and I want it soon."

His words coil around my neck like a noose.

"A wife?" I clarify with a squeaky lilt to my tone.

"And kids."

"Doesn't that sound a little too, I dunno—*forward*?"

He laughs and pushes off the counter. "I'm not proposing marriage, but I've gotten to where I am today by looking into the future. In five years, you want to be traveling the world. I want to be married and settled down."

My voice is barely a whisper when I reply, "So what are you asking?"

"It's obvious that we're attracted to one another, but we have to be realistic, don't you agree? The math just doesn't work."

He looks down at his phone, and I can tell from his furrowed brow that my Uber must have arrived.

Oookay, it's time to go. I gather my purse from the counter and laugh, realizing something.

"You know, you played this all wrong," I quip.

He looks back up, curious about the shift in my tone.

"You're right, there is an attraction. We were supposed to fool around for a few months, ignore reality for as long as possible, and then have this discussion after a nasty blowout. Things should have gotten messy and complicated."

He chuckles and shakes his head. "I don't want to rob you of your 20s."

"Well this way you're robbing me of a few months of what would undoubtedly be *really* good sex."

"Is that right?" His scorching gaze nearly makes me regret my joke. "Is it too late to choose door number three?"

My mouth goes dry and before I can embarrass myself any further, I turn toward the front door. We walk alongside one another like two well-adjusted adults who don't tumble into bed just because it would feel really good. We look toward the future and plan our lives accordingly. I've never regretted acting responsibly so much in my life.

"You know you have it easy, really," I say, peering up at him as we walk. "There must be thousands of women in Austin ready to ovulate at the mention of a five-year family plan."

He arches his brow. "Do you know of any?"

My stomach drops. We're joking around, but still, the thought of setting him up with someone else isn't funny yet. I refuse to drop the cool-girl act though, so I force a laugh.

"Maybe you should just post a job opening through your business—or better yet, make a Tinder account. Slap on a photo with you wearing a suit, maybe link to this address, and make sure to mention that annoying little dimple that appears when you really think something is funny."

His gaze is hot on the side of my face when he replies. "Thanks for the advice."

A car honks out front.

It's time to leave.

"Thanks for the ride. Sorry about your car."

He smiles. "Thanks for the talk. Sorry about your bike."

"Is that what it was? A talk? It felt more like a therapy session."

"If that's how you feel, you should come back for

another appointment, lie down on my couch…"

I roll my eyes.

"I'll see you at the club," I counter, taking one last look at him as he holds the front door open for me.

Though, for sanity's sake, I hope I don't.

CHAPTER TWELVE

"Where do you see yourself in five years?"

The question snaps me out of my brief reverie and I straighten in my chair, smoothing nonexistent wrinkles out of my skirt. It's the second time someone has asked me that recently, and my answer is the same.

"Ideally, I'd like a long-term position with a family either here in the States or somewhere abroad."

The woman sitting across from me —Mrs. Lancing— smiles and glances back down at her clipboard. She's been interviewing me for the last 30 minutes, making her way down what I presume is a list of a million and one questions. We've gone through the gritty details about my resume and experience. I recounted the work with my last family, careful to leave out the irksome details of my departure. Still, Mrs. Lancing is curious.

"Was there any reason that position didn't work for you?"

I smile sweetly, trying hard to keep my focus on her and not the large mounted moose behind her head. Their entire house is filled with animal carcasses, mainly deer heads and elk antlers. On the way to the sitting room where we're conducting the interview, I had to walk past a taxidermied black bear twice my size. Apparently Mr. Lancing is a big game hunter, a masculine hobby I can only assume helps him compensate for a particular anatomical shortcoming.

I swear the moose's eyes follow me when I shift in my seat and reply, "Not at all. I loved Sophie—my student— and I had a very professional relationship with her mother, Ms. Bannon."

She sets her clipboard down on her lap. "Then why aren't you still working there?"

I swallow hard. "Ms. Bannon asked me to leave. She felt there was no longer a need for—"

Her smile falls. "You were terminated."

"Well…yes. I was fired, but not for reasons on my end."

Her eyes narrow.

"If you call Beatrice at the agency, she can fill you in on all the details—"

"Of course. I'll give her a call." She smiles, just to save face, and then she stands, signaling the end of the interview. "Thank you for taking the time to meet with me, Ms. Davenport."

I stand and shake her hand, fully aware that I will not be getting the job all thanks to that five letter word: F-I-R-E-D.

She offers to show me the way out, but I tell her I'm fine on my own. I can't stand another minute of small talk, especially if she's not even going to offer me the job at the end of it. I'm frustrated that another potential position fell through my fingers because of this bizarre black mark on my record—although, would I really want to work for a family crazy enough to fill their house with dead animals? *Stop killing bears, you psychos.*

Outside, the bike I borrowed from one of my roommates sits on the sidewalk waiting for me. The neighborhood where the Lancings live is so nice that I didn't even bother locking it up. Unfortunately, it's also about a 30-minute bike ride from where I live, and worse, it's hilly. I had to wear nice clothes for my interview, and while I strip off my blazer and stuff it in my purse, I'm still left in my skirt and blouse. At least I thought ahead and packed tennis shoes.

I know I could call an Uber and save myself from biking home in a Texas sauna, but money is tight at the moment. I'm trying to save up as much as I can, just in case I never find another tutoring position, not to mention the fact that I need a new bike since my old one was turned into an aluminum pretzel. I'm assuming it's beyond repair, as I haven't spoken to James since the night of the accident. *One week and two days, but who's counting?* I figure he would have reached out if there were any part of my bike worth salvaging.

By the time I make it back to the co-op, my blouse is stuck to me like a second skin. My roommate, Jackie, gives me a wide berth as I pass her in the hallway.

"Rough day?"

I shoot her a *don't ask* glare.

"I'm headed to the bakery. I'll bring home the leftovers after my shift."

That means she and Ethan have plans to get it on later and she wants to butter me up with flaky croissants and iced pastries. I don't necessarily want to spend my evening listening to them bang it out next door, but that's my loneliness talking. I refuse to be a sad, loveless loser. I'd rather be a hyperglycemic loveless loser, so I nod in consent and demand one of the bakery's cinnamon rolls as reparation.

On the floor inside my room there's a yellow sticky note that was clearly shoved under my door. I straighten out the crease and interpret Ian's scratchy handwriting.

Hit me up when you're back. Chase stopped by this afternoon.

Let me decode that:

Hit me up = come to my room.

Chase stopped by this afternoon = my dealer came by and sold me weed and I want to smoke with you.

WHO SAYS ROMANCE IS DEAD?

I crumple up the note and toss it in the trashcan underneath my desk. Though tempting, I have more important things to do than waste the day half-blazed out of my mind. I rip off my interview clothes and throw them in the hamper before I shower and change into a mismatched pair of pajamas. Yes, technically it's still the middle of the afternoon, but these are my *getting shit done* jammies.

After that, I spend five minutes cleaning my room, which makes me feel marginally more in control of my life. Next, I check my bank account, which makes me feel marginally *less* in control of my life. The gratuities at the country club are great, but somehow paychecks sift through my fingers like sand. Every month I pay my rent, cell phone bill, health insurance premium, and the partial balance of a credit card bill (thanks to the few weeks I endured before starting at the country club). My goal is to put half of each paycheck into savings so I can ditch the country club and travel. To date, I've managed to sock away a couple thousand dollars, but now that I need a new bike, that figure isn't going to increase any time soon.

I close my laptop, postpone my problems for tomorrow, and flop back on my bed.

Ellie is working at the club covering my shift so I could go to that interview, which means I can't hang out with her, and I'm too broke to go out and buy happiness, which leaves me with very few options. I could head over to my dad's house and raid his refrigerator. I might feel bad taking his money, but I don't feel bad taking his food that's just going to go bad. Unfortunately, that scenario involves running into Martha, and I don't have the energy for her today. I could search online for a new bike, but there's no point in looking into it until I have funds to purchase one.

Sometime between falling into a never-ending pit of misery and half-wondering if I *should* spend my evening getting blazed with Ian, I fall asleep. The next thing I know, my phone is buzzing on my chest, jerking me out of an unsatisfying, restless nap.

"Yup, *hey there!*" I say after I answer, which is officially the weirdest greeting ever.

"Brooke?"

The voice doesn't register right away. I blink sleep out of my eyes and turn to check my bedside clock. It's 7:42 PM. I got back from my interview around 2:00 PM. *So much for getting shit done.*

I remember I'm on the phone one second before the person asks, "Are you there?"

Hearing his voice floods me with warmth.

"James?"

"Hey."

My brain is still groggy from sleeping away the afternoon. I can't figure out why exactly I'm on the phone with James. He's never called or texted me before, not even last week when I broke down and texted him when I was weak.

It was pathetic and read like this:

BROOKE: Hey, how certain are you that we should stay away from each other? 50%? 100%?

When he didn't respond in 30 minutes, I did.

BROOKE: HAHA. Just kidding. Good night!

Yeah, I know, not my proudest moment. When Ellie saw it, she didn't stop laughing for 15 whole minutes. She was rolling back and forth on my bed, howling with joy. I walked downstairs, toasted a bagel, smeared cream cheese all over it, and walked slowly back upstairs. She was still laughing when I got there, so I didn't share my bagel with her.

"Sorry if this is a bad time," he continues, sounding adorably earnest.

"No! *No*!" I sit up and smooth out my hair, like that will somehow help the situation. "What's up?"

"I just wanted to call and let you know I'm having a courier drop off a replacement bike at the co-op."

"A bike? For me?"

"Yes. Consider it a gift."

My emotions are everywhere. Half of me wants to jump at the opportunity to solve one of the dozen problems crushing me at the moment. The other half of me is smart enough not to accept a gift from James without knowing his intentions first.

"I don't know, I don't want to be in your debt," I reason. "Besides, my mother taught me not to take gifts from strangers."

Calling him a stranger is a petty jab, but the rest is true. I don't know what kind of strings come attached to gifts from James Ashwood.

"Brooke." He sighs as if he doesn't have the energy for an argument. "I forced you to get in my car. I put your bike in the trunk. Forget that I called it a gift. It's the least I can do for putting you through that wreck."

"But it wasn't your fault."

"Please just let me do this. It's nothing."

I stare down at my finger twisting my duvet cover into a tight spiral. "So you bought it for me out of guilt?"

"Does it matter why I bought it?"

Yes. I want to know the real reason, because if it is just out of guilt, that's one thing, and maybe I'd keep it if that were the case. But, if it's something else, a motive that runs a little deeper, I'd like to know. Still, he sounds exasperated, and I need a new bike. James feels like he owes me one, so I'll accept the gift, and when I've saved up enough to buy my own, I'll give it back.

"Okay," I concede. "Well, thank you."

"He should be there in a few minutes."

"I'll head outside in a second."

I'm standing up, pulling a sweatshirt on over my pajamas, when he admits, "I wasn't sure what color to get."

"You didn't outsource the job to Beth?"

"No. It only took a few minutes," he says, quick to downplay the significance.

Even so, I smile thinking of him picking out my bike himself. Then I frown, thinking of him picking out my bike himself.

Outside, the sun is setting behind the houses across the street, and cicadas nearly drown out the sound of children playing a few blocks over. I plop down on the curb and glance left and right, checking for the courier.

"Okay, well, I'm outside now."

A long pause follows and I wait for the inevitable goodbye. Instead, he says, "I saw your text the other day."

My cheeks flush, and I'm grateful he can't see my

159

face. "You saw it, but didn't reply."

"I saw it, but didn't reply," he echoes.

I chuckle. "I know you're a little older, but text messages aren't like paper letters—you're allowed to respond immediately."

His tone doesn't carry the same amusement as mine when he replies, "I thought it was probably best to give you a little space."

"Yeah?"

"I don't think this is a good idea."

"This phone call?"

I know what he's really hinting at, but I refuse to acknowledge his concerns because they're my concerns too, and if we both agree that this is a bad idea, it'll end. No reason for any more phone calls.

"How was your day today?" I ask. He doesn't answer right away, so I sigh, "C'mon, it's a platonic question. Pretend I'm your friend."

"My day was fine. Busy. I'm still at the office, actually."

"But the sun's about to set."

"I missed it rising too."

I frown thinking of him locked away in his office all day and all night.

"Well, spoiler: it looks the same as it did yesterday and the day before that and the day before that."

He laughs, and then I hear the hinges of his chair squeal. I picture him sitting behind his desk, loosening his tie and tilting his head toward the ceiling. Maybe it's the first time he's taken a deep breath all day.

"I took our new CFO to the club for lunch today. I didn't see you there."

Was he hoping to?

"I had a job interview."

"How'd it go?"

"Oh, you know." I drag my Birkenstocks back and forth along the concrete. "Not that great."

"Why do you think that?"

I laugh, thinking over the worst parts of the interview. "I could just tell, but it's fine, because I was actually hoping to work at Twin Oaks until I die. I bet the mortician will let me wear my uniform to my grave."

He chuckles. "You won't stay forever."

"No, probably just until forever isn't very long anymore."

"I could hire you."

I burst out laughing.

"Yeah, c'mon," he goads. "You could teach me French."

"Uh huh, right."

"*Bonsoir.*"

Oh Jesus, even his terrible French accent is sexy.

"Say something," he urges.

"*Si suelement les choses avaient été différentes.*"

"What does that mean?" he asks with a dark, husky tone.

I tell him to look it up if he wants to know.

A car turns down my street and I perk up, hoping it's the courier, but he passes right by.

"What were you doing before I called you?" he asks.

"Power napping," I admit sheepishly. "I had plans to be more productive, but I fell asleep before I got around to actually doing anything."

"I can't remember the last time I slept a full eight hours, let alone took a nap during the day."

"You should try it. You're getting bags under your

161

eyes," I tease.

"I'll stick to caffeine. I feel like I've never needed much sleep. At Caltech, my buddy and I would go stretches where we slept on pallets in the computer lab. We'd wake up, code, eat, code, sleep, and shower in the gym on campus when we couldn't stand the stench any longer."

That sounds horrible.

"*Why?*"

"We were building BioWear. There wasn't time for anything else."

"But now your company is successful," I point out. "Shouldn't you be enjoying the fruits of your labor?"

He chuckles like the idea is completely preposterous. "Now I have even less time than I did then. I believe a wise 20th-century poet said it best: mo' money, mo' problems."

I laugh and the hinges on his chair squeal again. There are footsteps and then the sound of ice clinking against glass. He's sitting in his office, pouring himself a drink. He should go home, but why would he? It's not like there's anything better waiting for him there. The thought is almost too much to bear, so I come up with a simple solution.

"I think you should get a pet."

He laughs. "A pet?"

"Yeah, like a dog or a hamster. Something to keep you company."

"A hamster." Another laugh. I can practically see him rubbing his brow and giving in to the conversation. "I don't have time for a pet."

"What about a fish?" I ask. "You could put it in a gigantic tank in that empty house of yours and just swim around with it in SCUBA gear."

A white delivery truck turns onto my street. His headlights flash across me and I jump to my feet, waving him over. "Wait, I think my bike is here!"

"I'll let you go then."

He sounds disappointed, and I am too. I'd like to stay on the phone with him the rest of the night. I'd like to be the one to coax him out of his loneliness, but that's not in the cards for us.

"James?"

"Yeah?"

The sadness in his tone eats away at me.

"Thanks for calling," I say, hoping he deciphers everything left unsaid.

He pauses before replying, "Thanks for answering."

By the time I hang up, the delivery truck has pulled up in front of the curb, and I watch as a tall skinny guy hops out with a clipboard in hand.

"Brooke Davenport?"

"That's me."

He nods and then I watch as he pops open the back doors and wheels my new bike down the ramp and onto the sidewalk. I was expecting something similar to what I had, but this is one of those fancy bikes I've always dreamed about owning one day. Even better, it's the same color as my bookshelf: sunflower yellow. I beam.

"I've never seen a bike this color before," I say, stepping forward to brush my hand across the polished body.

He shrugs. "Had to pick it up from a paint shop this afternoon."

My stomach knots into a tight ball. There's the answer I was seeking earlier. No one takes the time to get a bike custom painted out of guilt. No, this is something special.

The next day, I force Ellie to drive me to a pet shop and then to James' office downtown. He's in a meeting, so

I leave the goldfish with Beth, along with fish food and a note.

This is Harry. He needed a friend. Take good care of him!
XO, Brooke.

PS I love the yellow.

CHAPTER THIRTEEN

Two weeks later, Ellie and I are changing out of our work clothes in the employee locker room at Twin Oaks. I'm sweaty and hot from working in the cabana during the peak of summer. Ellie is annoyingly fresh-faced and beautiful from her shift working the lunch service.

"Here…can I just—"

Sweet-smelling mist hits the back of my head, and I turn to find Ellie holding her body spray at arm's length with one hand while pinching her nose closed with the other. She spritzes me again.

"Stop Febreezing me like I'm a sofa!"

"You stink!"

I reach forward to try to slap the bottle out of her hand, but she drops it back into her locker with a gloating smile.

"Well it's like a million degrees out at the cabana and some old geezer spilled his Bloody Mary on me. I get it, I smell like a frat party."

"Well now you smell like Strawberry Breeze," she announces proudly.

I glare at her before turning back to finish changing into my workout clothes.

"Need a ride home?"

"Nah, I have my bike."

"The one from *Mr. Ashwood*?"

She's taken to addressing James as Mr. Ashwood and

tacking on a snooty British accent to go along with it. I find it excruciatingly annoying, but I can't tell her that or she'll do it even more.

"That's the one."

"Isn't it kind of weird that he gifted you that expensive bike and then ignored you for the two weeks?"

I straighten my shoulders. "He hasn't ignored me."

"Oh? I thought you said the two of you hadn't talked since he called you?"

Well that's true, we haven't talked, but a few days ago, I was working at the cabana when I saw his Porsche zipping down the drive. I paused in the middle of making a drink and stepped around the corner so I could watch him park. He was with a work associate or something, another guy in an expensive suit. I stood frozen as they headed toward the entrance of the clubhouse. He seemed to be listening intently to his friend then suddenly he turned and caught me staring. A rush of adrenaline tingled through my body as his gaze captured mine. A small, enigmatic smile tugged at the corners of his mouth, just enough to bring out that dimple, and I fought the urge to wave or do something equally lame. Fortunately, his friend tapped his shoulder and reclaimed his attention before I could make a fool of myself.

I picked apart every detail of his smile for the next 24 hours before I finally found enough sense to force myself to move on. Other than that, there have been no texts, no phone calls. I don't even know if Harry has adjusted to his new goldfish life or if he's swimming in a porcelain graveyard.

"Brooke?" Ellie says, flicking my arm and tugging me out of my reverie. "You haven't talked to him, have you?"

"No."

"Because Marissa showed me something earlier, and I wasn't sure if I wanted to tell you."

I pause, pulling my shirt on over my head. "What are you talking about? Does it have to do with James?"

"Yeah. I guess he went to some sort of fundraiser last night? There are pictures of him on Instagram."

I finish tugging my shirt down and then get to work on my tennis shoes. "He doesn't have an Instagram."

"His date posted the photo."

I ignore the burning sensation in my chest and the sudden urge to vomit all over the employee locker room. I'd have to clean that shit up, and that is not happening.

"Do you wanna see it?"

It's feels like she's asking me to check out a dead body she found in the woods.

"No thank you."

"Are you sure?" she asks, her phone already open to the photo.

Ugh.

I yank it out of her hand and take in the sight for myself. Jealousy is such a rare sensation for me that it's hard to identify as I stare down at what can only be described as the most photogenic couple on earth. James' date is a petite blonde with curls that cascade down her back. The volume alone is something I've never been able to achieve—bitch must have gone to Drybar. Her dress is tight and clingy, just like her. I swear there's not a single iota of space between her and James. She has her arm wrapped around his waist and she's leaning into him like they're posing for an engagement announcement.

James is hard to look at, depressingly handsome in his fitted tuxedo, perhaps the very same one he wore when he took me to the 1920s party. He isn't smiling, but he doesn't exactly look angry to have the blonde wrapped around him either. His impenetrable dark eyes stare straight into the camera…straight at me.

"I swear he has the most beautiful face I've ever seen," Ellie says. "But it's not *too* beautiful, y'know? There's some ruggedness to it."

I hadn't realized she was looking at the photo over my shoulder, registering my reaction. I quickly pass the phone back to her and offer a weak excuse for why I need to leave immediately. I pedal back to the co-op faster than usual with the summer sun burning overhead, and then, because I can't stand the idea of holing up in my room and moping, I keep pedaling past my street and continue my workout through the afternoon. By the time I make it home, my legs are jelly and Ellie's stupid strawberry spray has mixed with my sweat to create an odor so foul I can barely breathe. I lock up my bike and head straight for a shower.

Later that night, when the co-op is quiet and my roommates are asleep, I look up the photo again. Yes, I memorized his date's Instagram handle because I want to rub salt in this wound. The burn is better than nothing. At the country club, I didn't read the caption, but now I do.

Having such a blast with my handsome date at the @AustinPetsAlive Summer Gala. This organization is one of a kind and one very close to my heart. It's so important to give back and take care of Austin's furry friends, y'all!

Her love of philanthropy sparks my memory. I knew I recognized her when I first looked at the photo at Twin Oaks, and when I scroll through her Instagram feed, I connect the dots. Her name is Lacy Nichols, and she's as close to a society belle as Austin has. I mean, this isn't the 1880s, but it *is* the south. She's the (#youngest) vice president of the Women's Philanthropic League of Austin in history, and there's even a photo on her Instagram where she's posed with my stepmom for a council meeting. This town is too damn small.

I remember now that she was at the tea Martha and Ellie dragged me to at the beginning of summer. She was tasked with giving a speech before we were allowed to stuff our faces with finger sandwiches. I can't remember what she said, as I wasn't listening, but now I wish I had been.

Further Instagram stalking (of which I am not proud) reveals that she's everything James is looking for. At 31, she's 6 years older than me, and in her prime. She's been in a dozen weddings in the last year and always captions those posts with some adorable self-deprecating joke about always being a bridesmaid, never a bride. Her friends follow suit with ridiculously positive comments like, *GIRL, you'll be the next one walking down the aisle!!!!!* Not to mention, she clearly adores kids. She posts photos with her nieces and nephews like four times a week. This girl's ovaries are practically screaming at me through my iPhone screen.

She is, to quote her friend's comment, *total wifey material*, and by contrast, I'm a loose cannon. Being in that many weddings and wearing *that* much chiffon would make me break out in hives. I don't want to babysit tiny children. I want to hike to Macchu Picchu and swim in the Mediterranean. I want to spend a summer in the south of France, drinking my way from one vineyard to another. I want to miss my train in Germany and hop on the next one no matter where it's headed.

I am not so delusional that I can't see how precisely

169

Lacy Nichols fits into James' five-year plan, but I still don't want them together because I am a selfish person with envy in my heart and melted chocolate on my fingers. The chocolate is from me attempting to eat my feelings, but it didn't work; I'm just as annoyed by the fact that he took Lacy as his date as I was before I ate the Reese's Peanut Butter Cup. Lesson learned.

CHAPTER FOURTEEN

My mom and dad married really young, and it didn't work out. I don't quite know all the details, but I do remember my mom sitting Ellie and me down and explaining that she was shagging our neighbor, Jorge. He was a few years younger, and sexual in a way that awoke a yearning desire in her. I don't know, it was all pretty gross, so I repressed most of the conversation. I do recall the moment a few years later when she told us she was moving, though. I think it went something like this: *I'm in love like I've never been before, and sometimes love takes you to strange places. I'm moving to Africa.* I think she even said it in a breezy, heart-struck tone, definitely not the way a mom should sound when telling her two daughters that, for all intents and purposes, she'd rather spend her time around civil war and famine than with them.

"What? Why?" I cried.

"Jorge is a member of the Peace Corps. He's been stationed in Sudan, and I need to go with him. Those people need us."

I'm paraphrasing, but you get the gist. None of it made sense at the time. Obviously she had to divorce our dad if she was going to continue having sex with our neighbor—even my adolescent brain could compute that—but why did she have to move? Didn't she know we needed her too?

I'm almost embarrassed to admit that this whole

episode in my life still bothers me. Being a teenager without a mom present changed me; I really haven't felt normal since the day she waved goodbye to us from beyond the airport gate. I try not to dwell on those thoughts though. They aren't healthy, and thankfully I've realized since then that I don't have to fear love. Not every person I get close to in my life is going to abandon me just because my mom did. However, I have learned from her mistakes. Lesson 1: Don't get married young. Lesson 2: Don't have kids if you don't really want them around.

Got it, loud and clear.

Thanks Mom.

It's actually kind of a relief that James and I have five-year plans that don't match up, because now I'm off the hook. I don't have to process how I feel about him (MORE THAN I SHOULD). I don't have to consider that it's been weeks since we last spoke (AND I CAN'T STOP THINKING ABOUT HIM).

He called me a few days ago, totally out of the blue. My heart raced when I saw his name flash across my screen, but I couldn't bring myself to answer it. It eventually went to voicemail, and he didn't leave a message. For all I know, it was a butt dial. I need it to have been a butt dial, in fact, because if we're going to stay away from each other, no communication is probably the way to go. A platonic friendship won't work for us. James has only been in my life for a few months, and already he's consuming too much of me.

What would an older, wiser version of myself say? *Walk away—no, run as fast as you can. James is going to eat you alive if you let him. Stay focused on what's important. Double your efforts to find a new tutoring position so you can quit your dead-end job. Accept that date from the nice guy who works at the cafe down the block and revel in the lack of chemistry. Thoughts about cafe guy won't keep you up at night.*

It sounds like a solid plan, right up until I leave for work the next morning and nearly trip over three massive bouquets of peonies sitting outside my door. I search for a card and find one tucked into the middle bunch.

From Harry.

• • •

I'm sitting in Ellie's car as we head back to the co-op. We've just stuffed our faces at Madam Mam's, a Thai restaurant near UT campus that I've been craving for the last few days. The chicken pad thai temporarily distracted me from all the thoughts about James swirling around my mind, but as we turn another corner closer to home, I dread the moment when she drops me off.

I'm growing weaker by the day when it comes to staying away from him. He called again last night, and I didn't answer. One call can be written off as a mistake, but not two. His toned behind isn't that clumsy.

I'm not sure why he's calling. It could be about something innocuous (*Where did you buy Harry's fish food?*), but I know better.

Ellie turns and the seatbelt rubs against my chest. I pre-wince, expecting pain, but nothing comes. The burn from the crash has healed and now there's one less thing tethering me to James.

"Should we stop at Amy's?" Ellie asks, and my heart sinks.

She's not a big ice cream fan. If she's going to pig out, it's going to be on cake or pie, so the fact that she's suggesting Amy's tells me she can tell I'm upset.

"I don't need ice cream. I'm fine," I say with forced cheer.

"You've been quiet all night. What's going on?"

I turn to look out the window so she can't read my emotions. I've been told I have a terrible poker face.

"I've just been thinking about job prospects," I offer, because it's a half-truth, and it's easier than delving into the whole truth.

"Are you sure that's all?"

"Positive."

When Ellie drops me off at home, I'm surprised to find a black Porsche sitting by the curb. The doors are open, but the driver is missing. A few of my roommates are there though, kicking the tires and checking out the interior. They don't even notice me until I'm beside the car, asking what they're doing.

They nod their head toward the house. "James Bond's inside waiting for you."

My heart soars.

I want to twirl and skip up the front path, but I take my time and gather my wits as much as possible. With the flowers and the phone calls, I knew something like this was bound to happen. James might have been the one to initiate this forced separation, but he's also the one who's been pushing the boundaries. I wonder if he regrets his decision, and I suppose I'm about to find out because he's here now, in the co-op living room, chatting with my roommate Maggie.

I have no clue how this tableau came about exactly, but Maggie and James are side by side on the ground, making posters, open paint cans and used brushes scattered all around them. The man is wearing designer clothes. Sure, it's just jeans and a t-shirt, but the thread count on that cotton is probably higher than my bed sheets, and now it's speckled with paint.

There are already a dozen signs completed and drying in one corner of the room.

CAPTIVITY IS NOT CONSERVATION!

EMPTY THE TANKS!

ORCAS ARE DYING TO ENTERTAIN YOU!

Maggie is in the middle of a passionate speech: "They can't claim they're capturing these animals and breeding them in glorified swimming pools for educational purposes, not anymore. That notion is absolutely ridiculous. Did you know that in the wild, orcas usually swim over a hundred miles in one day?!"

James shakes his head with a thoughtful frown, unaware that I'm standing in the doorway, watching. "Wow. I didn't know that."

Maggie sits back on her heels and surveys her handiwork. "That's why my friends and I are staging a protest. I can't sit idly by any longer."

"The signs look really good, Maggie," I say, announcing my presence.

James' attention sweeps to me and I meet his dark gaze. A timid smile spreads across his lips.

"Oh, well there's your girl," Maggie says, taking the paintbrush out of his hand. "I can take it from here. Thanks for your help. Glad to know you're not just some suit."

I tip back on my heels, nodding my head toward the stairs. He follows without a word and once we're both in my room, I close the door and slowly turn back to face him. He's near my bed, eclipsing everything around him as he tugs a hand through his hair. He's nervous, an odd emotion to see on a man as self-assured as James.

"You didn't answer your phone," he says with a frown.

I focus my attention just over his shoulder, appreciating the reprieve. I haven't seen him this close in weeks, and maybe I forgot just how much he affects me. Now I certainly remember, and my heart is racing. My hands feel clammy, and if I were smart, I would have taken Ellie up on her offer for ice cream.

"Brooke?"

I chew on my bottom lip and look away. "Yeah, it was sort of a self-preservation thing."

"So you weren't ignoring me because you aren't interested anymore?"

A chuckle tumbles out of me.

"Can you look at me?"

I swallow and glance down. "No, actually, I can't."

"Why?"

Because I'm crumbling. Because your face hurts— HURTS—to look at. Because I think you're going to break my heart. Because there are a dozen solid reasons for why we should steer clear of one another, some of which you've already admitted yourself.

I settle on giving him the reason that bothers me the most.

"Because you're seeing someone else, and you shouldn't be here."

"Seeing someone else?" he says, his tone hard and unyielding. "What are you talking about?"

My focus is on my shoes, but he steps forward and captures my chin, raising it gently until I'm forced to meet his eyes. Desire ripples through me.

"Lacy Nichols."

176

"Was a friend who invited me to a fundraiser."

"Nothing else?"

He takes another step toward me. I step back and my heels hit my bedroom door. There's nowhere to go, no way to escape the fact that James is crushing me against the door with his body, not enough to hurt me, but enough to make my breathing erratic. My chest brushes against his and my heart leaps as if trying to reach him. His hand still holds my chin, and slowly he tips it up, up, so when his head bends and he captures my mouth, our lips are perfectly in sync.

The kiss is so unexpected that at first, I freeze from the initial shock of contact. For seconds, I don't do much more than stand there. He increases the pressure and slips his hand from my chin to the nape of my neck. His fingers stroke and soothe, making it too easy to give in to him. I tilt my head and my hands find his waist. I grip the bottom of his shirt and tug him closer until our hips meet. His hard thigh presses against mine. He shifts us closer to the door, and a heavy need starts to build between us. My lungs don't have room to inflate as he continues to kiss me endlessly, teasing and coaxing out soft moans.

By the time his hand starts to slide up from my waist, my body is a mess of sensations. He skims along my ribs and then brushes his fingers just below my breast, testing the limits. When I don't protest, his hand moves higher until he's cupping it in his palm, rolling his hand back and forth. His kiss is nearly punishing, but his touch is so gentle I want to melt.

He's playing a game with me, seeing how long I can endure the sweet torture before I break down and openly beg him for more. A fire is building within me, burning hotter by the second. Soon he'll get exactly what he wants.

I'll have turned to putty in his hands.

I grip his shirt tighter and our hips grind together as if the friction will help dispel some of the pressure mounting between us.

Out of nowhere, a knock pounds against my bedroom door behind me and we leap apart.

"Hey dude! Is it cool if we take your car around the block?"

I press the back of my hand to my lips to hide my laugh.

My roommates have impeccable timing.

James' hand rests against the door beside my head and he pinches his eyes closed, obviously annoyed at being interrupted.

"I know it's an expensive car," Jerry says. "But you probably have some pretty good insurance, huh?"

"Go! I don't care," James replies, his voice booming so loud that I jump.

"Thanks man!"

The sound of receding footsteps echoes down the hall and neither one of us speaks. It feels just like the aftermath of our car crash. The pieces of the scene filter back to me slowly and then, with embarrassment, I realize I'm still gripping his shirt. I let go and step aside to put space between us.

"Don't," he says, turning to me.

"What?"

"Don't do the thing where you regret what just happened."

I laugh. "Believe me, I don't regret that."

He nods and pushes off the door, straightening back to his full height. "Good, because that wasn't a mistake. I came here with clear intentions."

A lazy grin spreads across my lips. "Of ravishing me?"

He shakes his head and steps back to assess me. "Of asking you to accompany me on a trip I need to take for work."

"What?"

"There's a conference in Vegas. I go every year, *alone*, but this year I'd like you to come with me."

He's making it sound extremely simple, but it's not.

I shake my head. "It's not a good idea. It would only make this more confusing."

"I don't care."

I narrow my eyes at him, angry at having to be the responsible one all of a sudden. "Come on, James. This has been the weirdest friendship, non-friendship, relationship thing I've ever dealt with. Normal people go on dates. We get in car accidents and then ignore each other for weeks."

He steps closer and I hold out my hands to block him. I need my wits about me if I'm going to make important decisions.

"Maybe I don't know what to do with you," he says, capturing my wrists and gently tugging me closer. "Maybe I've been wondering if it's really best to leave you alone."

His gaze falls to my lips, and I think he's going to kiss me again.

"You shouldn't be showing up here unexpectedly," I say with a weak voice. "You shouldn't be inviting me on a trip, and you definitely shouldn't be sending me flowers!"

He grins, and it's like I'm looking at the devil incarnate. "So they arrived?"

I nod to where they sit on my nightstand. I've cut them and changed the water every day. They're in full bloom now and I know if I stepped a little closer, their fragrance would hit me in full force.

He turns to look at them, and I wonder if it's apparent just how much care and attention I've given the flowers over the last few days. I'm slightly embarrassed until he glances back and says confidently, "Come to Vegas with me."

"The last time you invited me to be your date, I didn't like it," I point out.

"This will be different, I promise."

His voice sounds so earnest that I believe him. Still, I throw my last measly excuse at him. "I'd have to get off work."

He levels me with an amused glare. "Have someone cover your shifts. If not, I'll work it out with Brian."

I'm annoyed that he seems to already know I'll agree to go with him, and I'm confused about why I want to. Nothing has changed between us. Later on, when I'm alone, I'll regret my decision, but right now, he's crowding my space and overriding any sense I might have. My lips still tingle from our kiss, and my heart is still running a marathon.

He's standing a few feet from me, and I'm feeling every bit of his commanding presence. Sure, he's physically intimidating, tall and fit, but it's more in the way he carries himself, an unspoken confidence that makes it difficult to argue with him. A few weeks ago, he said it would be best if we stayed away from each other, and I complied. Now, he's inviting me to Vegas and I'm bending to his will without much of a fight.

That infuriates me.

But not so much that I won't go, because then I'd be punishing myself.

I'll concede, under one condition.

"I'll need my own hotel room."

It's my only way of gaining back some semblance of control.

He barely manages to stifle a laugh. "Did I not make myself clear before? I want you to come to Vegas with me *as my date*."

"Oh, so you expect me to put out?" I quip. "One kiss and now suddenly you think you're Casanova? Maybe I need a little more time before I share a bed with you."

His dark eyes flame with stifled emotion. He steps toward me, advancing until I'm scared we'll be right back where we were a minute ago.

"One room, two beds," he counters.

"Two *rooms*," I insist, straightening my back in the hopes that I look somewhat resolved. "And just to be clear, I'm only going with you because I haven't had a vacation in a while."

His smirk is so damn conceited I want to slap it off his face. "Oh, that's it? Anything else?"

"Yes. I want to lounge by the pool and read a book."

"Uh huh."

"And I want one of those massive volcano drinks."

"Brooke…"

"Oh! And I want to play the slot machines. I love those."

"So you'll come?" he asks, hope brimming in his tone.

Of course I will. The choice was never mine to make.

CHAPTER FIFTEEN

I've never flown private before, but here I am, sipping champagne with raspberries floating in the glass while cuddled under the softest throw blanket I've ever felt. The interior of the plane is the color of wealth: beige and tan with wood trim. Boring and elegant equals money and class, I guess.

James picked me up from the co-op at 4:45 AM looking sharp in jeans and a sweater. I instantly regretted my comfy lounge clothes, but I'm not someone who likes to travel in style. I assumed we would be taking a commercial flight, so I wore yoga pants and a sweatshirt. As we boarded the small plane, the flight attendant made it abundantly clear that she was confused by my attire. Her gaze swooped over me and I was dismissed within a half-second as unworthy of *the* James Ashwood. I don't necessarily disagree, but I'm here, and the champagne tastes amazing, so what do I care?

"A little more, please," I say with a broad smile.

As she tops me off, I think back to how Ellie and Marissa took the news when I told them where I was going. I would rather have kept it a secret, but I needed them to cover my shifts at Twin Oaks for the next three days. Marissa thought I was lying just to get out of work until Ellie corroborated the fact that I've been spending time with James lately.

"YOU LITTLE *MINX*!" were Marissa's exact words.

I smiled and shrugged as she tried to pry details out of me. While I had to tell her about Vegas, there was no reason to go into the complicated dynamic of mine and James' relationship, or lack thereof.

My gaze slides across the aisle to where he's typing away on his laptop. This is a work trip for him. He's made that clear, and I refuse to play the role of whiny brat, so I sip my champagne and try not to bother him. I do, however, take in his profile while I think he's focused on replying to an email. He's clean-shaven, which makes it easier for me to detect the muscles clenching in his jaw as he types away on his computer. Whatever he's dealing with, it's frustrating him. I want to ask about it, but I'm scared he'll shoot me down.

"I can feel you watching me," he says while continuing to type.

I smile and glance away, happy just to be in this environment with him. There've been many nights in the last few weeks where I lay awake wondering what James was up to, what it would feel like to be in his presence again. It's interesting just to see what a day in the life is like for a man like him, someone in charge of an empire.

We've been in the air for an hour, and I don't think his fingers have stopped typing once. It sounds like he's competing in a Mavis Beacon contest. The pitter-patter of the keys becomes white noise as I turn on my Kindle and return to my book.

"What are you reading?" he asks sometime later, and I realize with a start that he's been watching me read.

"Just a bunch of business and finance textbooks," I say with mock seriousness. "I want to be useful on this trip."

"What are you really reading?"

I smile and show him. "It's a book of essays by Samantha Irby."

"They must be funny."

I furrow my brow. "Why do you say that?"

"Because I've been watching you smile to yourself for the last 20 minutes."

I guess two can play the sneaky staring game.

"She's one of the funniest writers I've ever read. It's worth a read when you have the time." His gaze swoops pointedly to his laptop and I chuckle. "Yeah, I guess you probably don't get much reading done."

I think back to the worn paperback sitting on the table back at his house.

"Not much time for fun," he admits.

The flight attendant steps forward from the galley to announce that we're 30 minutes from our destination. James stands and I track his path as he heads back to the small bedroom. When he returns a few minutes later, he's exchanged his jeans and sweater for a fitted black suit. I watch as he pulls a small leather Dopp kit out of his bag. Inside, there's a silver tie clip that he slides across a thin black tie. Cufflinks are added with smooth dexterity. He straightens his collar and folds a pocket square before neatly tucking it into his jacket. Next, he tugs at the bottom of his shirtsleeves, settling the material so it sits a half-inch past his suit jacket. Most of the time with men, especially ones my age, it looks like the suit is wearing them rather than the other way around. That's not the case with James. He seems more comfortable like this than he did in his jeans.

When he finishes, he glances toward me with a quirked eyebrow. I want to pause time and snap a photo of him looking like this, eyeing me with that *exact* look. "How do

I look?"

He knows how he looks. He's likely been told by hundreds of women throughout his life, but he's asking me now, and for some reason I'm scared to inflate his ego any more—probably because I'm still currently sporting a sweatshirt and yoga pants. I curse my laziness. The man is Adonis, and I am Sloth.

I nod curtly. "Looks good. I like the suit."

It's as much as I can do without making a simpering fool of myself.

His smile tells me he sees right through my defenses.

"As soon as we land, I'll need to head straight to the conference. There's a welcome breakfast and then a full day of panels."

"Are you excited?"

He shrugs. "It's rare to have so many tech giants gathered together. I think anyone in the industry would get excited by that amount of brain power in one room, not to mention I went to school with quite a few of them at Caltech. It feels like a college reunion every year."

"Is everyone staying at the same hotel?"

"Unfortunately for you, yes."

I smile. "Why unfortunately?"

His gaze meets mine as he chuckles. "You'll see."

• • •

When we arrive outside the swanky hotel, it's a complete madhouse. Our driver hurries around the back of James' hired car and as soon as we step out, the whispers start. James' name is repeated like a game of telephone so all eyes are on us as we pass through the front doors. Techies overflow every corner of the foyer and lobby, and the line for check-in winds back and forth like a coiled snake. Overheard conversations confirm that they've been waiting there for hours.

The hotel's decor, usually sleek and modern, is hidden behind colorful banners and signs welcoming us to the conference. In fact, the first thing I see as we walk inside is James' headshot waving on a banner overhead.

"You're the keynote speaker?" I ask, pointing up.

He nods and pushes us forward without glancing at it. If I didn't know better, I'd say he's embarrassed to see himself blown up to epic proportions. The concept makes me smile.

A petite redhead comes barreling out of the crowd, beelining straight for us.

"Mr. Ashwood!" she says with a wide smile. A nametag on her black blazer explains that she's the lead coordinator for the conference. "If you'll follow me, we can get you checked in as quickly as possible."

I expected to have to wait in the winding line, but instead, the coordinator leads us to a secluded corner of the lobby hidden behind heavy black drapes. Here, a young man sits behind a computer, typing away. When he sees us walk up, he stops immediately and stands to shake James' hand.

"Good morning, Mr. Ashwood. We have your suite set up exactly as you requested."

James nods. "Good. I'll need you to escort Ms. Davenport there. I don't have time to head up."

The young man turns to me and nods, and just like that, James' power and influence is passed on to me. It's a heady feeling.

"Of course. Let me just get your room keys ready."

I turn to James with a quirked brow. "I didn't think there would be so many people here."

He shrugs. "This is the largest annual tech conference in the United States. SXSW is popular too, but here the events aren't combined with film and music. It's three days focused strictly on innovations in the tech community."

"I saw on that banner back there that your keynote speech will be broadcasted as a TED talk."

He glances over my shoulder and sighs. "Don't remind me. Public speaking isn't my strong suit."

I reach out and squeeze his arm for reassurance. "I think you'll be fine. Did you see the way people reacted to you when we walked in?"

He wraps his hand around my lower back and leans down to press a chaste kiss to my lips. Before he pulls away, he whispers, "No, I didn't notice."

A shiver runs down my spine as he stands back to his full height, and if I wasn't sure of his feelings, they're made perfectly clear by the way he's staring down at me. His dark eyes are unnerving. His hand lingers on my lower back, drawing me closer. I press a hand against the soft material of his suit and offer an easy smile to ease the tension.

"I'm sorry I can't spend the day with you," he says.

"Are you kidding? I'm going to head upstairs and put on a fluffy hotel robe and slippers, maybe order room service."

His half-smile tells me he's imagining me in the fluffy robe.

I flush and look away.

"Brooke," he says, drawing my attention back to him with his soft tone. "I'm glad you came."

I smile. "I am too."

• • •

After the concierge leaves me at the door of our suite, I spend a few minutes snooping around. I can't guess at the square footage, but it's completely ridiculous and has probably housed Beyoncé and Jay-Z at some point. There are two bedrooms off of a main living area. Down one hallway I find a small gym, sauna, and wine room. Down another hallway, there's an office and kitchen. At one point, I GET LOST—that's how big this place is.

I fulfill the promise I made to James by slipping into a fluffy robe and padding around in the hotel slippers. After I unpack my clothes and fall back onto the bed in a heap of comfy pillows and fluffy blankets, I force myself to work out in the gym so I don't feel the least bit guilty about the salted caramel tart I tack on to the end of my room service order.

Later in the afternoon, I start to get ready for the evening, happy to take my time. James and I have plans to meet for dinner at the restaurant on the top floor. Their Asian-fusion cuisine has been touted as the best in Vegas, and I'm giddy to try it out.

I want to make up for my yoga pants and sweatshirt. The flirty dress I borrowed from Ellie is a little too short and a little too red. Back home I would have paired it with a leather jacket to try to tone it down, but this is Vegas— the city of sin. So, I don't think twice when I swipe on an extra coat of mascara and paint my lips in a deep red lipstick appropriately named Candy Apple. With my long black hair and red lips, I look like Snow White's evil twin.

I head to the elevators and check my reflection in the

189

glass. The nude heels were a nice touch, and the dress is a definite head-turner. That's further confirmed when I step on the elevator and two well-dressed men pause their conversation. I turn and face the front, concealing my smile from them. The elevator starts to carry us higher and as we pass floor after floor without stopping, I assume they're also headed to the restaurant.

"Did you catch the panel?" one of them asks.

"Yeah, but I left early. What'd you think of Ashwood?" My ears perk up. "I've always heard he's kind of a prick, but he seemed all right."

"I thought he was pretty good. He was actually a few years ahead of me at Caltech. I didn't think he'd remember me. We only had one class together, but I was able to catch up with him after the panel."

The first guy groans. "Oh c'mon, don't tell me you're another Ashwood sycophant."

I cover up a laugh with a semi-realistic cough. Neither of them notices.

"Name one person here who's accomplished more in less time than he has," the Ashwood sycophant says in his defense. "I don't want to grovel at his feet, but if I get a chance to pick his brain, you better believe I'm going to try."

He snorts. "Keep praying at the altar of BioWear. Meanwhile, Martin Stone is the real tech leader. You know their stock just split again?"

"What has Stone done lately? Come talk to me in five years when Apple is begging to buy out BioWear."

The elevator arrives on the top floor and the doors swoop open. The hostess stand is down a thin hallway, and I make sure both men can hear me as I bend forward and announce that I'm here under a reservation for James

Ashwood.

The hostess beams. "Of course. Right this way."

And just because I can't help it, I turn over my shoulder and soak in the shock on both of their faces. Their jaws are still on the floor when I offer up a sweet smile. "Enjoy your dinner, gentlemen."

The hostess leads me to the back of the restaurant where a small table has been reserved against floor-to-ceiling windows. The Vegas strip spreads out for a mile on either side—twinkling lights, the Bellagio fountains, thousands of tourists snapping photos and strolling from one casino to the next.

A well-dressed waiter arrives and although I'm starving, I don't want to order any food until James arrives. I'm five minutes late, which means James should be here already. I peer around the waiter's shoulder, confirm he isn't in the restaurant, and then settle with water.

15 minutes later, I'm still sitting at the table alone, and I decide to switch to white wine.

"How about something from the kitchen while you wait for your companion?"

I shift awkwardly on my seat, aware that the confidence I felt heading up to the restaurant wanes with each minute I'm forced to sit here and wait on my date. I'm suddenly a member of the Lonely Hearts Club, and I don't like it.

"Ma'am?"

I offer a tight smile. "I'm fine for now. Thank you."

He dips his head and then turns to address the table behind me. I'm aware of the dining room filled with watchful eyes. The restaurant is packed, and no one gets as dolled up as I am to sit alone, sipping wine. I check my phone, assess that James is now over 30 minutes late, and finally decide to give him a ring. I was hesitant to bother him at first in case he's busy at the conference, but he can't expect me to sit here waiting on him all night.

There's no answer. I hang up when his voicemail kicks on and go back to sipping my wine. Laughter and conversations filter toward me as I tap my fingers on the table like I'm strumming the keys on a piano. I swear my phone vibrates with an incoming call, but when I check it, the screen is blank. I'm growing desperate.

Even when I vow to stop checking my phone, the Bellagio fountains force me to acknowledge how long I've been waiting on James. The dancing fountains go off every 15 minutes, in sync with music I can't hear inside the restaurant. So far, I've sat here long enough to see the show six times. My glass of wine has been filled twice, and there's still no sign of James.

"Would you like another refill?"

The waiter feels bad for me. I can tell because both times, he's given me generous pours. I shake my head, incapable of offering him anything more without losing the tight cap on my emotions. I'm done playing the waiting game. James is too busy to let me know he's not coming to dinner, and I've decided I'm too busy to wait for him.

"I'll take the check when you have a moment." Then I think better of it. "Actually, can I just charge this to my room?"

"Of course. I'll just need to see your keycard and ID."

I hand him both and then hold up my finger, scanning the room before landing on a sickeningly adorable couple in their early 20s. They're sharing one entree and sipping on water, likely trying to stretch their Vegas budget as far as possible. "Go ahead and charge me for the bottle and give the rest to that sweet couple over there. There should

192

be enough left for them to each have a glass."

It's hardly a drop in the bucket for James, but it still feels good to jam an expensive bottle of wine into his bill. It's the only form of revenge that's accessible at the moment.

He glances behind him to see where I'm pointing. "Oh, of course. I can do that. Would you like to send them a message along with the drinks?"

"How about, *Enjoy it while it lasts*."

By the time I walk out of the restaurant, I have regrets about skipping out on an appetizer in favor of wine. I'm feeling slightly lightheaded, and while it's probably in my best interest to head up to the hotel room and order food, the thought is too depressing. I've been cooped up in there by myself all day.

I want company. I want James, but he's apparently not available.

The hotel bar is as crowded as I assumed it would be, and every person in the room is wearing a blue lanyard and nametag from the conference. There's no point in trying to find a table—they're all taken—so I head straight for the bar and luck out when a couple stands and vacates their stools soon after I arrive. I steal one of them and wait for the bartender to find me. A few minutes later he heads over.

"What'll you have?"

"Do you serve food here?"

He leans forward and turns his ear in my direction. "Sorry, what was that?"

"Do you serve food here!" I repeat, this time shouting.

"Not right now," he says, indicating to the crowd. "There's a cafe around the corner though."

Just my luck.

"What's your most food-like drink?" I ask. "Anything with, I dunno, a chicken wing sticking out of it?"

The impatient bartender gives me a blank stare.

"She'll have a whiskey ginger."

I turn in time to see a stranger take the barstool beside mine. He's extremely good-looking, blond and tan, a California boy all grown up. He unbuttons his suit jacket and slides an easy smile in my direction. Clearly, he thinks he's here to stay.

I quirk a brow. "I will?"

"Trust me." He nods, turning back to the bartender. "Make it two."

"I don't like ginger ale," I point out.

He chuckles. "See? We're already learning things about each other. I don't like ceviche."

I sigh and turn away, back to staring at the liquor bottles behind the bar. The stranger leans closer to me and I feel him dragging his gaze down my dress and then lower, across my bare legs. Apparently, he enjoys the view.

"Are you here for the conference?"

"No."

He seems to enjoy my one-word response because he leans even closer. "Then why are you in this hotel?"

It's obvious he's not going to leave until I tell him to. I turn and assess him with a cool glance. I hadn't noticed it before, but the lanyard around his neck proclaims him to be Martin Stone. He notices me eyeing it and his smile widens with pride.

"You may have seen my photo in the lobby," he continues.

"Actually, no."

I heard the men on the elevator talking about him, but I don't volunteer that information.

"Are you waiting for someone?" he asks.

"Not anymore," I reply icily.

The bartender slides our drinks across the bar, and Martin picks one up to hand to me. He takes the other and tilts it toward me for a toast. "To meeting new friends."

I clink my glass with his and take a hesitant sip, prepared to hate it. Instead, the sweet and smooth taste of the whiskey pairs well with the spicy notes of ginger.

"What do you think?"

"It's actually not that bad."

He grins and turns toward me, brushing his suit-clad leg against mine. "You know, there are a hundred other hotels on the Vegas strip and they aren't filled with tech nerds. Why are you sitting in this bar all by yourself if you aren't waiting for someone?"

He barely finishes his question before a hand unexpectedly lands on my bare shoulder. I catch a hint of a familiar spiced cologne and turn to find James standing behind me, looking devastatingly handsome in the dim light of the bar.

"Thank you for keeping my date company, Martin."

CHAPTER SIXTEEN

I can only imagine what the scene looks like from James' perspective: he strolled into the crowded bar and found me sipping drinks with another man. Martin's still turned toward me, brushing his leg against mine. I could tell him to back off, but there's no need—he won't do anything now that James is here. As soon as he approached us, I noticed a lull in the conversations around us. Everyone is holding their breath, waiting to see if there's going to be a standoff between James Ashwood and Martin Stone. Every tech blogger in the room has Twitter open and their thumbs at the ready.

Martin sweeps his gaze from James down to me. He's confused, clearly.

"Your date? She just said she wasn't waiting for anyone."

I want to make things perfectly clear. James might have flown me to Vegas, but the second he stood me up at dinner, I stopped being his date. "I'm here alone."

"Brooke—"

"You heard her, James. She's not your date."

James' grip tightens on my shoulder and a shiver escapes down my spine. I don't want him to read my emotions, so I turn back to the bar and take a long sip of my drink, hoping one of them will leave before the situation escalates to a point of no return.

"Plenty of seating over there, James," Martin suggests with a stern tone. He wants to be my knight in shining armor so badly, but unfortunately, he's acting as a pawn in this game I'm playing with James. I should tell him that, but then James steps back and releases my shoulder. I glance up and meet his gaze in the bar's mirrored backsplash. His features are etched in stone, that intimidating jaw is clenched, and while the fury in his eyes should warn me away, I arch a brow and meet it head on. *Your move, buddy.*

Fire blazes between us, and I think he's going to grab Martin by the scruff and yank him off the barstool beside me. He seems angry enough to do it, but then I watch as he slowly overcomes his baser emotions. The tension between his brows eases slightly, his jaw loosens, and I can't be sure, but I think he's trying to fight off a little smile. I narrow my eyes, trying to figure out his game. He tilts his head and waits patiently. He's not going to make a scene, isn't going to explode with jealousy. He's James Ashwood, after all. This isn't his first rodeo.

We're having a fight without words, and Martin is completely oblivious.

"Listen, bud, you look pretty tired. Maybe go rest up for your big keynote?"

James holds my gaze and completely ignores him. I want to squirm in my seat or fan my face, something to ease the tension between us, because I know he won't do that for me. If I want this to end, I have to be the one to speak up.

"Martin, I'm sorry for the confusion."

He rears back, clearly having expected me to side with him after all this.

I reach for my purse. "Let me pay you for the drink."

That makes James laugh under his breath, which only further pisses Martin off. I'd feel really bad for causing so much drama and embarrassing Martin if he wasn't so damn sure of himself. The man's face is hanging on a banner in the lobby—he could use a healthy blow to his ego every now and then.

He refuses the twenty I try to hand him, and when he vacates his seat, he brushes past James with a hard hit to the shoulder. I brace myself for James' reaction, but instead of escalating the situation, he shakes his head and steps forward, claiming Martin's barstool.

The difference between Martin and James is night and day. When Martin sat beside me, I wasn't hyperaware of every move he made. With James, I'm jumpy and nervous, anticipating some kind of consequence even though I did nothing wrong.

We sit side by side for a few minutes without a word. I know he's had a long day, and while I'm annoyed with him for standing me up, I don't necessarily want to talk about it at the moment. Instead, I pass him my drink in silence and he takes a long drag, finishing the last of it.

When the bartender returns, he orders himself a whiskey neat then turns to me.

I shake my head. "Nothing, thanks."

I can't continue drinking without dinner. I'll pass out, or worse, I'll tell James how much I missed him today.

"Have you eaten?" he asks.

"No."

"We'll order something when we go back up to the room."

My stomach dips.

The room. Of course.

It's hard enough sitting beside James in a crowded bar,

let alone following him back up to our suite. I keep my gaze down because it's easier than meeting his eye, but even that isn't safe territory. His strong thighs press against the fabric of his suit pants. His hand bridges the small space between us and grips my leg. Goose bumps bloom across my thigh as he brushes his thumb back and forth along the sensitive skin inside my knee.

"Brooke?"

"Hmm?"

He leans closer when I don't look up. "I like that dress," he says with a whisper against the shell of my ear.

I glance down at my lap and nibble on my bottom lip.

His thumb continues to skim back and forth across my knee, lingering for a moment in the hollow before claiming the bare skin an inch higher up my leg. I like that he can't keep his hands off me. I put thought into my dress, picking the exact silhouette that would make me feel most confident. My hair and makeup are weapons, temporarily forgotten after sitting alone at the restaurant for so long. Now, I remember why I needed them in the first place; I can't keep up with James unarmed.

My fingers ache to reach out and touch his raven-black suit. I want to feel his muscles tighten beneath the soft fabric. Instead, I fist my hands on my lap. James chuckles and turns to accept the drink from the bartender, taking his hands with him. My skin tingles from the ghost of his touch, but I use the moment to regain some ground.

"How was the conference?" I ask, proud that my voice doesn't shake.

He stands and reaches into his wallet for his cash. He only arrived five minutes ago, but apparently he's too anxious to sit at the bar for long. He downs some of his drink and flags down the bartender to pay his tab.

"James?"

He ignores me, tugging a few bills out of his wallet and sliding them across the bar. His hand grips my upper arm and when he turns to walk away, I swivel on my barstool, forced to follow after him or fall flat on my face. His hold on me isn't painful, but there's also not much room for negotiation. He leads us out of the bar and toward the hotel's elevators.

My cheeks flush with embarrassment as people turn and watch us.

"What's wrong? *James*?"

My heels clap against the marble floor as we beeline through the lobby. The doors of the elevator are already open, waiting for us. We step inside and he presses the number for our floor. The doors whoosh closed, we start ascending, and then he turns to me. My pulse jumps.

"I missed you today," he says, his heated gaze lingering on my body.

I step back, and he follows.

He looks like he's cornering his prey.

"Apparently not enough to make it to dinner," I point out icily.

"I called the restaurant and told them I'd be late. Didn't they tell you?"

I cross my arms and glance away.

"Brooke." He steps closer and gently lifts my chin, forcing me to look back at him. "Fight with me tomorrow."

I narrow my eyes, angry with him for shelving this discussion so casually. To him, it doesn't matter that I sat in that restaurant alone, looking like a fool for nearly two hours. He's brushing off my anger, stepping closer and forcing his way past my defenses.

"I think I'd like to talk about it now."

I catch the beginning of a smirk just before he leans in to kiss my cheek.

"Are you sure there isn't anything you'd rather be doing right now?"

He uncrosses my arms and brings them up over his shoulders then steps closer, towering over me. My arms tighten around his neck, but still, I turn away, keeping my mouth from him. His breath hits my neck and he pulls me taut against his hard body, growing more impatient with every moment I try to resist.

"Brooke," he whispers huskily.

My eyes flutter closed as he bends and presses a kiss to my cheek, my chin, then lower, tipping my head back so he can reach the smooth recess at the nape of my neck. I shiver and he groans, obviously aware of what his touch is doing to me.

Torn between wanting to submit to my desire or hold my ground, I turn toward him, and his mouth crashes down on mine without warning. He kisses me mercilessly even as I struggle against him. My hands fight their way between us and I try to shove him off, but his ironclad embrace is too strong for me to break. I know I won't be able to outmaneuver him, so I resist in a simpler fashion by holding completely still. He can force me against him, but I don't have to respond, and I don't have to kiss him back.

My rebellion makes him even more annoyed. His grip bites into my hip and his mouth moves over mine relentlessly. All the while, I ignore the sparks of desire stemming from his touch. I tell myself I would be reacting this way if *any* man kissed me like this, not just James. His kiss turns punishing, and I respond by digging my nails into his suit, hoping to break skin.

We're ascending so quickly. I know any moment the

elevator will ding and announce that we've arrived, but something changes in that short time. His touch turns from brutal to sensuous. His lips move over mine with tenderness. His hand drifts down my back in a slow caress, easing me closer until our bodies are flush. He's rock hard and unyielding. I moan against him and fist my hands into his suit pockets.

The elevator dings and the doors whip open.

I break our kiss and inhale sharply, trying to fill my lungs like a madwoman. James wastes no time hauling me out of the elevator. It's a few feet to the door. He swipes the key and we push inside, halfway through before our mouths collide. He opens his lips against mine and his tongue sweeps into my mouth. My purse is tossed across the room and his jacket follows. I tear at the buttons on his shirt and he reaches around to fumble with the zipper on my dress.

Our passion is fueled by our impatience. The last button springs free and I drag my hands up his toned chest and past his shoulders, taking the fabric with me. It slides down his arms and onto the floor, leaving his toned upper body completely bare. I feel my slip dress starting to slide down my body, but I'm too preoccupied with him, with his powerful, tan shoulders and arms on full display to stop it. I watch the muscles flex and coil as he yanks the garment the remainder of the way off. My strapless bra is already slipping down, halfway concealing my chest. I think he's going to tug it off like he did with my dress, but instead he hauls me up against him and walks us into the suite's living room. I'm a feather in his arms, and then I'm falling through the air, caught suddenly by the couch. He stands over me, his large frame bathed in bright neon light from the Vegas strip. A swath of dark blue darts across his face, and when our eyes meet, it gives him an animalistic glow.

I try to adjust myself to sit up straight on the couch, but before I can, James bends down and grips my thighs. With a hard tug, he drags me to the edge. I prop myself up on my elbows and watch as he steps closer.

His eyes drag down my body. It's a suggestive perusal, as intimate as if his fingertips were following the same trail. I usually don't care what people think of me, but I'm desperate to know his thoughts as he bends down onto his knees and pushes my legs apart so he can fit between them. His eyes are hooded, his touch searing. He drags his fingertips across my thighs and my stomach quivers. Then he grips them and inches them just a little…bit…farther…apart until the backs of my thighs hit the couch. Apparently pleased with my position, he skims his fingers higher across my stomach, and then up and over my bra. There's no rush as he follows the line of the material, dragging his finger pad over each cup. My toes curl. With slow precision, he works the material down, and then my chest is bared for him.

I fight the urge to squirm, instead lying perfectly still as his hungry gaze moves over me.

"*Brooke*," he groans. Then, as if he just can't help himself, he bends low and takes one of my breasts in his mouth. His tongue drags across my nipple and I cry out, arching my back to give him better access. He stays there just a moment, teasing me before he stands back to his full height.

He unbuckles his belt with deft hands. I reach up to replace his fingers with mine and slide it out in one smooth tug. The metal belt buckle hits the ground with an audible *clunk*, highlighting how little sound there is in the hotel suite, nothing but our breaths coming hot and fast. The tension ratchets up another notch as we meet each other's gaze. I can only imagine what he sees in my light eyes— *everything*, no doubt, every ounce of desire surging through me. I blink and cut off the connection, turning instead to the zipper of his suit pants. I tug it down and he pushes the material low before stepping out of them, exposing his long, muscular legs. He obviously spends hours in the gym lifting weights or running or doing some other form of torture that produces results like this. I'm very appreciative, and my sly smirk says so.

James reaches down and strokes across the bottom of my breast, feeling the weight of it in his palm before rolling my nipple between his thumb and index finger. I squeeze my eyes closed, trying to keep my mask of indifference right where it belongs. I've never felt this...this *frenzy* before, this need to get under his skin. The thought scares me and I try to push it aside, but it's like he knows how close I am to begging him for more and wants to stoke the flame.

He bends low and brushes a seductive kiss across my lips before whispering, "You're so beautiful."

His voice is hoarse and raw, so damn sexy that I reach up and grip the back of his neck, tugging him down against me. His hands hit my thighs and he bends low so he's on his knees between my legs. It almost feels like he's submitting to me, but I know better. I doubt this man has submitted to anyone in his entire life.

His hands squeeze my thighs, ensuring that I stay spread eagle on the edge of the couch. My panties are still slightly askew, just enough so that when he tips his head and glances down, I know exactly what he's seeing. A low groan escapes his mouth and I feed on it, letting my legs fall open just a little bit more. His fingers bite into my thighs and I try not to smirk. *Maybe he wasn't submitting to me before, but he is now.*

He loops his strong arms around my legs and tugs me until I'm lying horizontal on the couch, my legs bent up in the air. Before I can process the new position, his mouth hits my inner thigh, close enough to hint at his true destination. Dear god, I'm going to implode the moment his tongue strokes across me there. I try to squirm away, back to sitting up, but he forces my legs apart and pins me down. His finger tugs my panties to the side and I'm utterly exposed with nowhere to go. I'm forced to feel every one of his breaths as it hits the skin of my parted legs. Every instinct in me screams for release, but as soon as his lips descend, I pinch my eyes closed and embrace my lack of control.

I've been here before, but never with someone like James. There's always been a lack of confidence, a grip that's a little too gentle, a hand that's a little too rough. When James sweeps his tongue across me, it's with desire and intent, a hungry sort of lust that fills me with power. I lift my head and watch him between my thighs. His need is obvious in the way he stares, eyes wide and gleaming, like he's a thief who's just found the crown jewels. He dips low and his tongue licks across me slowly, just once before he pulls back and meets my gaze. Tension sizzles between us and he holds eye contact as he bends low again, this time dragging his tongue across me until he lands at the very top, swirling until my hands fist his hair.

I squeeze my eyes closed, let my head tip back, and release his name on an exhale. My voice sounds hoarse.

He picks up the pace, lapping and licking me quickly so there's no time to resist the orgasm building inside of me. The first few waves of passion build and build, and just before they crest, he pulls back, blowing cool air on me until I'm squirming for release. Then he bends low again, kissing and sucking gently until my hips are grinding up to meet his mouth, desperate for him to continue. I'm sweaty and raw, a mess of emotions fully exposed to him. There's no limit to how long he'll drag out this torture. Maybe he really did miss me today, and maybe he really was jealous to find me at the bar with Martin, because right now, he's punishing me for both.

I yank his hair and he growls, finally pinning his mouth on me and licking with enough speed and pressure to build my orgasm to a peak. My back arches off the couch and my head falls back. I see nothing but blackness behind my closed lids as I moan his name again and again.

The climax rushes through me with such force, such power, that I feel invigorated when it's over. It's like a jolt of caffeine to the system, a powerful surge of energy that makes me hungry for more. Without warning, I sit up and leap onto him. We fall back onto the floor of the living room and our nearly naked bodies collide for the first time. Soft curves meet hard muscle. My dark hair fans out around us. He reaches up and cups my breasts, and the feeling is so intoxicating that I give in completely to the kiss he presses against my lips. We're impatient, hot. Weeks and weeks of anticipation built this moment.

His hands grip my ass and he pulls me down hard against him, rolling his hips in a maddening pace. I moan and fist my hands into his hair, hating the fact that our underwear separates us. The friction is teasing and suggestive, but I want to feel his smooth hardness against me, *in* me.

His hands dig into my flesh as his hips roll and grind, teasing me until I'm close to a second orgasm. Just like this, high school-style, over-the-clothes grinding—*no*. I deserve better. I deserve the real thing. I reach down and yank my panties aside, barely noticing the sound of lace gently tearing. He would have to stand to allow me to pull his boxer briefs all the way down, so I make do. I lift my hips just enough and tug until he's exposed enough for me to pull his hard length out of the material. The sound he makes when I sit back down on him, flesh to flesh, is nothing short of a growl.

We are animals.

Hungry.

Impatient.

Wild.

"Brooke," he groans as I roll back and forth across him.

Teasing.

Taunting.

So damn close to letting him slide into me.

I'm reminded of our talk so many weeks ago, and it hits me: we need a condom, NOW. I'm about to tell him that, but he's quicker than me, reaching back for his pants with one hand. He hangs them upside down, shaking them out until his wallet falls to the floor with a heavy *thunk*.

I laugh.

He finds a thin packet, tears it open with his mouth, and then I reluctantly lift off him so he can slide it on with smooth confidence.

My body is shaking with desire and excitement. I know he's going as fast as he possibly can, but it's still not quick enough. My fingers dig into flesh. He groans and rolls the condom all the way down. We don't wait, don't take a breath. I angle him just right with my hand and then he pushes into me with one sumptuous thrust.

"JAMES."

My second orgasm tears through me as I cry out. His mouth covers mine with passionate kisses, and then he picks me up and flips us over so I'm on bottom. The smooth rug cushions me from below as James hovers over me, cast in neon light. God, he's sexy. The way he moves. The way he holds himself up on one arm and stares down at where we're connected, where he drags out of me slowly before thrusting back in. I shudder.

There's too much to focus on: the muscles jumping in his sharp jaw, his abs flexing and straining under the effort when he pulses in and out of me. I reach up and drag my palm across his chest and then I move lower, hooking my hands around his hips and making sure he pushes in as deep as he can possibly go. My eyes squeeze closed as I try to keep up with his unyielding rhythm. He starts moving so fast that pleasure brushes against the boundary of pain.

He tells me he's going to come, and it's such a sexy, bold declaration that I know I'll soon follow. I'm panting. He's groaning. We're so in sync, I feel myself clench around him as his body starts to heave and shake. I look up and watch as his orgasm contorts his features into a mask of ecstasy.

When it's over, he collapses on top of me and I stare up at the ceiling, relishing what it feels like to have his weight stealing my breath. It's just enough to keep me in the present moment, to keep my brain from overthinking every move, every kiss.

"Brooke," he whispers.

I hum.

"I promise I won't miss dinner ever again."

CHAPTER SEVENTEEN

I lie awake in James' bed for hours trying to convince my body to give in to sleep. I should be exhausted after what we've done, but now that the hotel room is quiet and dark, I have nothing to focus on but the sinking feeling in the pit of my stomach. It settled there a few hours ago for no good reason. I can't pin it down to anything said or done. The night went off without a hitch: we had sex (twice) then showered, ordered room service, and eventually succumbed to sleep—or at least James did. I'm wide awake, fruitlessly willing this feeling to fade, and I remain that way until sometime in the early morning hours.

James apparently had to get up at some ungodly hour for the conference because when I jolt awake around 7:00 AM, he's long gone, no trace of him in the suite. I do find some workout clothes in the bathroom, still sweaty, so I guess he found the time to work out before leaving for the day. Meanwhile, I enjoy a quiet breakfast of oatmeal and regret, staring out at the Vegas strip and trying hard not to think of how tightly my stomach is knotted.

I'm not very successful. Every spoonful of oatmeal comes with a healthy dose of reality. To be honest, I didn't go into this trip with the intention of sleeping with James. I can practically hear Ellie in my head: *What else did you think would happen?! You willingly went to Vegas with the man! Did you think you two would be eating platonic dinners and sleeping in platonic rooms and giving each other platonic fist bumps?*

Okay, so a small part of me figured we would be doing some hardcore fondling, but we went beyond that. We had earth-shattering sex—like, slow-jams-in-the-background, candles-burning-the-place-down sex. When I'm midway through my oatmeal, flowers arrive at the suite—a massive bouquet of white garden roses from James. The flowers are so beautiful and so fragrant, I put them in my bathroom and close the door. When that's not enough, I head down to the hotel pool in hopes that a change of scenery will tug me out of my weird funk.

There are three pools at the hotel, each one bigger than the last. All of them are nearly abandoned even though the hot Vegas sun is blazing overhead. I guess techies don't have time for aquatic activities, but I do.

I find a place at the biggest, most luxurious pool and toss my Kindle onto a lounge chair. A cocktail menu is already propped on the small table nearby, so I peruse it thoughtfully. *Is it too early for a piña colada?*

"I'll order one if you do," a voice says beside me.

I turn to find a tall brunette lounging two seats down, eyeing the drink menu I've been hogging for the last several minutes. "Oh, sorry." I lean toward her and pass it over.

"It's okay," she says with a friendly smile. "Do you know what you want?"

I nod and she starts browsing the menu for herself.

Once the waiter comes by and I order, I turn just enough to inspect her out of the corner of my eye. She's very pretty, but it's in a way that's easy to pick apart—she has false eyelashes and a fake tan. Her hair has a healthy dose of extensions and while I came down to the pool with nothing but my Kindle in tow, she has a Chanel pool bag, a Louis Vuitton Neverfull, a stack of magazines, a separate makeup bag, an iPad, and her phone.

Once the waiter strolls away, I move to turn back to the pool, but she glances over and smiles. Maybe she noticed me watching her, or maybe she's just as bored as I am; either way, she strikes up a conversation.

"Here for the conference?"

"Not exactly." I push my sunglasses up to rest on the top of my head. "You?"

She smiles. "My husband is in there giving a speech or something—who knows. It's all pretty boring to me."

I nod and turn away.

"So if you're not here for the conference, what's his name?"

"What?"

"Or *her* name. You must be here for *someone*."

Her question is simple, but for some reason, I'm hesitant to respond, maybe because I don't want to have to explain my situation with James to a perfect stranger.

"I'm here with a date, yeah."

She smiles. "Dave travels here all the time for work and I always join him. I like it because I get to keep tabs on him *and* treat myself to a little rest and relaxation. I swear if I weren't here, he'd get into all sorts of trouble. I'm sure you understand."

I laugh awkwardly. "Oh, yeah, I guess."

She quirks one of her perfectly shaped brows. Clearly she's perplexed by my relaxed tone. "You don't have to keep tabs on your man?"

"It's a new thing," I explain. "Not really a relationship."

Her gaze turns thoughtful as she tilts her head,

studying me. "Is he older?"

I nod.

"Rich?"

I bristle at her line of questioning and fire back, "Why does it matter?"

She laughs. "It doesn't, I just think it's funny that you're sitting there judging me, and I'd bet on my life your situation isn't all that different."

"It is," I insist.

"Oh yeah?" She scans down my bikini-clad body. "Rooms at this hotel start at $1,500 a night. That drink you just ordered? $26.75. You're beautiful and young. Your boyfriend is older and currently working, while you're...what? Waiting for him to finish up so you can be at his beck and call? I bet you've hardly seen him since you arrived."

The knot in my stomach twists tighter.

She turns to the pool and settles back against her lounge chair. "Face it sweetheart, we're not that different."

I don't bother waiting for my piña colada. I leave $30 on my chair (ridiculous) and walk away before Ms. Extensions can keep picking my life apart. How dare she assume I'm anything like her? She might be happy lounging around all day waiting for her husband, but this isn't the sort of life I want. My goal for the next five years hasn't changed.

• • •

James wraps up his day at the conference earlier than I expected, and I'm napping in my room when I hear the door to the suite open and close quietly. He walks in and I listen to his footsteps as they head in the direction of his room, and when he doesn't find me there, they turn toward mine. I keep my eyes pinched shut, pretending to sleep. He opens the door a crack and stops in the doorway, watching me. I'm hyperaware of my breathing, of how bad I am at acting.

Still, he doesn't call my bluff. He pulls off his jacket and tosses it onto the chair in the corner. He circles around the back of the bed, tugs back the covers, and lies down beside me. His cologne washes over me just as his arm wraps around my midsection. With a gentle tug, he pulls me back against him, and I try hard not to make a sound.

"Go back to sleep," he whispers against the back of my neck.

I wonder how he knew I was awake.

We sleep like that for an hour or two, wrapped around one another. I can feel him hard against me, his muscular thighs tight against mine. I know if I gave even the slightest sign that I was in the mood, we would have sex, but I can't. I haven't been able to shake this twisted feeling mounting inside me all day. I'm scared of what will happen if we have sex again, of how much worse it could get.

I push away from him and climb out of bed, anxious for a shower. I turn the water scalding hot and don't step inside until steam is rising up and fogging the bathroom mirrors. I tip my head back and let the water run over my forehead and down my cheeks.

When James speaks, I nearly jump out of my skin.

"I'd like to take you to dinner."

I reach up and try to hide every part of me worth concealing, but it only makes him chuckle under his breath. I guess he's already seen me, but this feels more intimate. I was under the influence of lust and wine last night. Now, I feel vulnerable and raw. I turn over my shoulder and look back to find him leaning against the door, watching me through the fogged glass. Maybe he can see everything, or maybe he has to imagine what I look like in here, but either way, his dark eyes are heated, and I hurry to finish bathing before he can join me.

Apparently, he wants to take me somewhere fancy, so I pull out the other dress I packed for such an occasion. It's black and more modest than the one from last night. The hem hits just above my knees, but the back is low-cut and exposes most of my spine. James takes full advantage of that when we stroll out of the hotel. His palm finds my lower back and he holds it there, leading me toward the waiting car. His touch feels so good that for a moment, I give in to my desire to lean into it. Then I remember the woman from the pool and step away.

"Vue is one of the best restaurants in the world. The chef won the James Beard award last year," James tells me, bringing the back of my hand to his lips and kissing it gently.

I hum in appreciation as I take in the strip whipping by our window. He goes on about the menu and how good the food will be, and I make a point to act like I'm listening. A few minutes later, the car pulls up outside a restaurant that has cars lined up around the curb. A suited attendant runs forward to open doors and glamorous people spill out. It's funny how much I want to stay put and direct the driver to the nearest McDonald's, not because I'd rather stuff my face with a Big Mac, but because maybe then I wouldn't feel so much pressure building in my chest.

When we walk through the restaurant to find our table, I'm aware of the women in the room eyeing James. They just can't help themselves. Tonight, he's wearing another bespoke suit. This one is navy blue, and he's paired it with a white shirt, no tie, the top two buttons undone. The look it supposed to be more casual than what he wears for work, but it's more tantalizing than anything I've seen him in so far. Instead of telling him that, I sip my water.

"Should we get wine?" he asks, perusing the menu.

YES.

Alcohol is really my only hope at the moment. Without it, I won't survive the first course.

The waiter arrives at the side of our table with sparkling water and a snooty French accent. I can tell James is happy to show me off when I rattle off our orders in French. The waiter raises a brow, impressed, before dipping in a short bow and scurrying off toward the kitchen to put our order in with the chef.

"I knew you would like this place," James says with a lazy smile, leaning back in his chair.

He looks like a king surveying his kingdom. I watch as he brings his wine glass to his mouth and takes a small sip. His leg moves beneath the table, sliding between mine so that the silky material of his pants brushes against my bare leg. I clear my throat and sit up straight, but it's no use. We might be in a restaurant with hundreds of people around us, but James is calling the shots, and if he wants to stretch the entire two-hour meal into some form of tortuous foreplay, he will.

"You're quiet tonight," he notes as our appetizers arrive.

I smile softly. "Just thinking about a few things."

"Do you want to share them with me?"

I focus on my plate and shake my head. "Not really."

He nods in understanding. "Tell me about your day instead. Did you use the spa gift certificate I had sent up?"

217

"I didn't find the time."

It came along with the flowers, and when I got back to the room after the pool, I impulsively ripped it into a hundred tiny pieces and flushed it down the toilet.

My answer amuses him. "Oh really? Was your day that busy?"

I know he doesn't mean to make me feel small with his question, but I respond defensively nonetheless. "I worked out and took a nap, went down to the pool…"

I'm aware of how meaningless it sounds. He spent his day with his peers, paving the way for the future tech industry; meanwhile, I sipped on drinks with tiny umbrellas.

"Good. I'm happy you can relax while you're here."

He tries to reach across the table for my hand, but I move it away gently so it looks like a coincidence and not a passive-aggressive act on my part—though it definitely is.

"Do you think your wife will work?"

He pauses with his wine glass halfway to his mouth. Unsurprisingly, my out-of-left-field question catches him off guard. "If she wants to work, she can. I'd imagine it would be difficult though."

"Why's that?"

He sets his glass down and sighs. "Because I live a busy life. If she works long hours as well, we'd hardly see each other."

"So ideally you would want her to stay home and what, raise kids?"

He nods. "I think that'd be easiest. That way she's happy and the children are happy."

I look down at where my finger is turning soft circles on the tablecloth. "What about moms who like to work? Surely you don't think their children are less happy just because they don't spend all day every day with their mothers."

"Brooke, that's not what I—"

"It's good for children to experience things outside their home."

He reaches across the table and catches my hand before I can move it a second time. My circles cease. "I completely agree. You asked a question and I answered it without giving it much thought. If my future wife wants to work, I'll support her."

The sincerity in his voice makes it hard to hold on to my anger. I take a deep breath and turn away, grateful to see our second course making its way toward us from the kitchen.

As we dine on tiny portions of food that cost more per serving than most people make in a week, I mull over all the reasons James and I would be better off staying away from each other. This feels like the beginning of something really serious, and that's not what I want. It's too much too fast. I knew something would happen in Vegas, but with the pace he's setting, by the end of the conference we'll be headed straight for one of those pop-up chapels down the street.

I won't allow James to steamroll over my wants and needs. I'm not ready to play the housewife for him. I'm not ready to be a committee member of the Women's Philanthropic League of Austin by day, mom and wife by night—yeah, no thanks. I'd rather schlep margaritas at Twin Oaks for the next five years.

After dinner, I insist on walking back to the hotel. James points out how impractical my shoes are, but I assure him I'll be fine. I'll do anything to delay our return to that quiet suite.

We walk side by side down the Vegas strip, and he tells me about the conference and what it could mean for his company. He's passionate when he talks about his work, and I admire that. His keynote speech is tomorrow evening, and he tells me the main focus will be on the responsibility of entrepreneurs and inventors to focus on those who can't be their own advocates, that first world progress does not have to come at the expense of third world suffering. He envisions a rising technological tide that lifts all boats, and for him, this means creating smart solutions to prevent and eradicate neglected tropical diseases. He'll be unveiling the prototype for the BioShield, and he expects the press coverage will help bring on new and conscientious investors.

"If there's enough support for it, we can do for health technology what Elon Musk has done for the electric car."

He's almost childlike in his optimism and I have to look away, back down the sidewalk before my heart slips a little more out of my grasp. This is a side of James I wish he wouldn't reveal to me. Beneath the layers of pretension and wealth sits a heart of gold. I doubt many people see this side of him, not because he presents a cold facade to the rest of the world, but because he rarely fills his life with people who take the time to see it. I think of his impersonal, empty house back in Austin, that quiet corner in his living room with the half-read book and the mismatched furniture.

"Do you want to stop in for a drink somewhere?" he asks, reaching out for my hand.

His palm covers mine so easily that for a moment I forget about my niggling doubts. I think we *should* stop and get a drink, and after, when I'm just a little bit tipsy and we've made out like two teenagers on the side of the street, we should head back to the hotel and have a repeat of last night. It would feel good to forget about better judgment for another few hours. Maybe that's exactly what I would have done, but then we walk past the Paris hotel and it jogs his memory.

"Oh, remind me when we get back to Austin," James says, "there's a restaurant I want us to try, Détour. It's a bistro, romantic and small, not the kind of place you go to unless you're there with someone special."

I stiffen, aware of the meaning dripping from that sentence. First, I'm that someone special for James. Second, it's the first time either of us has brought up the idea of continuing this once we're back in Austin.

"Have you heard of it?" he continues, oblivious to the fact that I'm minutes away from a panic attack.

I nod and continue walking, all but pulling him in my wake.

"Hey, slow down. There's no rush."

His imperturbable calm finally does it. I can't keep the lid on my emotions for another second.

"Yes, there is!" I explode, tearing my hand away from his and spinning around to face him on the sidewalk. "What are we doing? What is this?"

We're blocking the flow of traffic, forcing tourists to weave around us.

"What do you mean?" he asks, wearing a mask of perfect confusion.

It makes me absolutely furious. He doesn't get to suddenly feign amnesia. We both went into this with eyes wide open, but ever since we arrived in Vegas, James has acted like the two of us could actually be something, like this is a real thing forming here.

"Why'd you bring me here?" I shout over the noise of the crowd.

"Because I wanted to," he answers simply.

I shake my head, angered by his answer. "No, why did you *really* bring me here?"

He looks away, tugs his hand through his hair, and then finally looks back. His eyes are different, the hopeful gleam gone. "Because this is pointless, us trying to stay away from each other. *Why*? For what? Because you don't want to get married? Great!" He throws his hands in the air. "We won't get married!"

"It's more than that!" I cry.

"Fine. C'mon." He steps closer and reaches for me, tugging me against him so I have to lean my head back to look up at him. "Tell me all the reasons we shouldn't be together. You're too young? You want to travel? You have a million excuses you've built up against me, haven't you?"

"Excuses?!" I'm furious at the fact that he's trying to belittle my goals, my *life*.

"Yeah," he says, dropping my arms. "You think I haven't noticed how distant you've been today? When I reached for your hand at dinner and you pulled it away? I got it, Brooke. Loud and clear."

Unshed tears burn the backs of my eyes. "Why did you have to put so much pressure on this, on us, right from the beginning? *I'm looking for a wife and kids*—who says that to someone they just met? Haven't you ever heard of the whole boiling frog thing?"

"What are you talking about?"

I'm annoyed that I have to explain it.

"If you throw a frog into a pot of boiling water, it's going to panic and jump out. But, if you put the frog in cool water then slowly heat it up, it won't even notice the temperature rising."

"So you want to be a dead frog?"

He's being obtuse on purpose.

I sigh, exasperated. "The point is, with us, the water started too hot."

He shakes his head, visibly frustrated. "Don't paint me out to be the bad guy. I was honest with you—don't throw that back in my face."

By now, it's abundantly clear that we're causing a scene in the middle of the sidewalk. Pedestrians loiter around us, probably unsure whether or not we're street performers.

I want to shout at them to keep it moving, but I can't turn my focus away from James. I'm heaving in big gulps of air and trying to make sense of the last few minutes. My whole body is shaking with pent-up anger—at him, at me, at the unfairness of the situation we've found ourselves in.

"What do you want to do, Brooke?"

"I don't know."

He looks down at his shoes and shakes his head. A sad laugh spills out of him before he glances back up and meets my gaze. "Yes you do. Say it."

He's forcing an answer out of me, but he already knows what it is.

"James, you can't tell me on day one that you want a wife because then when you try to take it back and make things more casual between us, it's not believable. Even if it's not your true intention, I feel like all this—the flowers, the fancy dinners, the amazing suite—it's like you're inviting me into your delusion."

"Oh come on, Brooke! I'm sorry I'm not some stoner at your co-op who shows his interest with a joint and a Hot Pocket," he rasps, dragging his hands through his hair angrily. "I wanted to show you I'm interested in seeing where this goes, nothing more. That's what the flowers are.

That's what this trip is." He turns away and takes a deep breath before continuing, "It's fucking impossible to navigate the emotional minefield of a 25-year-old. Anything I do to show you I care just freaks you out, but if I back off, it's even worse. You'll assume I'm uninterested, and then there's no hope that the relationship will progress naturally. It's a lose-lose. All I can do is keep trying or walk away, and I think it's worth it to keeping trying."

And I think it's time to walk away.

I don't have the guts to say that though, so I sugarcoat it.

"There's no point in continuing this," I whisper, wiping hard at the tears spilling down my cheeks. "We're only going to end up hurting each other even more. Don't you see that?"

"No," he says, calm and resolute. "I don't."

His admission stuns me into silence, and it's clear we're at a stalemate. James wants something from me that I'm not ready to give.

"I'll see you back at the hotel," he says, stepping forward to move around me.

My hand reaches out for his and I squeeze his wrist. "Please don't go, not like this…"

My voice trails off when he jerks out of my hold and continues on down the sidewalk.

"James!" I turn and cry out after him but he doesn't stop, and it only takes a few seconds for the crowd to swallow him up.

• • •

On the Vegas strip, hundreds of tourists fill the sidewalk,

dressed up for the evening. I fight against the flow of pedestrian traffic, annoyed as their chatter invades my depressed fog. *What the hell are they so happy about?* I tuck my arms around my middle and pick up my pace, nearly stumbling right into an animated street performer dressed like Elvis. When he leaps back in front of me and offers a trademark, "*Thank you, thank you very much*," I tell him to go die on a toilet.

I have no clue what I'll say to James when I see him. My only hope is that he has calmed down and is willing to talk. I need to apologize for the way I treated him. I want to explain my side, the panic that was gripping my thoughts all day. I don't expect him to forgive me yet, but at least we can come to an understanding. Unfortunately, the hotel room is pitch black when I arrive. I flip on the light and find the suit jacket he was wearing at dinner sitting on the back of a chair in the living room. He came back to the hotel after our fight, but he's not here now. I check his room, just to confirm, but it's empty and quiet.

I sit in the living room and wait for almost an hour—I know because I look down and check my watch every 10 minutes. I wait in silence, willing the door to swing open. At this point, I'd willingly accept his anger if it meant he would return. Somehow, his absence is worse. It means he's unwilling to fight. He wants distance, and more than likely, he wants me gone. When the hour strikes, I stand and head for my room. It only takes a few minutes to pack my bags. Usually I scatter my things all over a hotel room, but since my arrival in Vegas, I kept everything neat and organized, almost like I always knew I'd be making a quick exit.

After I've gathered everything, I grab a cocktail napkin from the bar and jot down an apology, just *I'm sorry*, but for some reason, it seems worse than leaving nothing at all. I crumble it into a ball and toss in the wastebasket before walking out the door.

It's late, but I'm hoping there's still a flight or two leaving Vegas headed to Texas. If not, I'll sleep in the airport and leave on the first flight out in the morning. Anything is better than staying here and waiting for the other shoe to drop.

On the way down, I can't meet my reflection in the mirrored elevator. Shame is a heavy burden, and one I'll probably carry for a long time. I should have been honest with James earlier. I should have told him I deserve at least half the blame for whatever panic I was feeling.

If I could go back in time, I never would have come to Vegas. I knew it would make things more complicated, but I ignored my intuition and boarded that plane anyway. The only thing I can do now is leave before I make things even worse.

The elevator dings, the doors slide open, and I roll my suitcase out behind me. My heels clap against the lobby floor, and I realize that in my rush to pack, I forgot to change. I should have swapped my dress for jeans and my heels for sneakers. As a compromise, I pause in the lobby and unzip my suitcase to grab a thick, long sweater. I slip my arms in and wrap it around myself. When I stand again, I find I'm paused directly in front of the lobby bar—and a few yards away, James sits alone, nursing a drink.

Even with his profile to me, I see how dejected he is. His broad shoulders are slumped forward as he rests his elbows on the bar, his head hanging low. I wonder if he's waiting for me. The bartender says something that catches his attention. He looks up, shakes his head, and then takes a long sip of his drink. I should turn and continue through the lobby, but I stand immobile for another second. I thought I would leave Vegas without seeing him. This is a gift, one last chance to make things right between us.

I take a step toward the bar and he turns. My stomach dips as his warm brown eyes meet mine. They're so sad and heavy that I can barely stand their weight. He scans down to where my suitcase sits beside me and his brows arch in surprise as he registers the fact that I'm leaving. Hope explodes inside of me—*STOP ME, PLEASE*—but when he glances back up, the emotion in his eyes is gone, erased in the blink of eye. Now, he looks right through me. To him, I'm already gone. Then, to nail home that fact, he turns away. No nod, no wave goodbye.

I stand there immobile for a few seconds and then, when I realize how pathetic I look, I reach for the handle of my suitcase with a shaky hand and nearly sprint out of the lobby. As soon as I slide into the back of the taxi, the tears start to flow. The old cabbie is at a complete loss for what to do with me.

"All right, there, there. Where to?"

I tell him.

"Aww c'mon, lady. I can't hear you with all that blubbering."

I cry harder.

"Jesus. Why do I always get the basket cases?"

He sighs and tosses back a couple of crumpled Subway napkins for me to use to blow my nose. They smell like roast beef.

"Listen, okay, I'm no Sherlock, but you've got a suitcase, so I'm going to head to the airport."

"Th-Thank you."

"Yeah, yeah," he grumbles, pulling away from the hotel. "Looks like Vegas bagged another one."

CHAPTER EIGHTEEN

There's no way James hates me more than I hate myself, but it's probably pretty close. Things between us were always going to end—we both knew that. I'm not going to forfeit my dream of living abroad and traveling, and he shouldn't give up the hope of finding someone who's ready to take a leap. He doesn't have time to reassure the scared girl tiptoeing backward off the high dive.

Since Vegas, nothing has changed, and nothing will change, which unfortunately means there's no point in trying to reach out to him. Still, that doesn't mean I don't want to.

Instead, every day since I returned follows one of two patterns. If I have a shift at the country club, I roll out of bed, eat soggy leftovers, slip into my Twin Oaks uniform, and sit in front of the mirror to practice my fake smile. If it's my day off, I stay in bed, job hunting until my fingers are numb from filling out questionnaires and typing emails and letters of intent. The agency says they have a few leads for me, but I don't believe them. I've taken matters into my own hands, searching message boards and au pair websites for active listings. At this point, I'll take a job tutoring kids in Siberia if it means I can leave Twin Oaks.

I even contemplate leaving my job before I find a position. I have some money in savings, and I figure if I use it wisely, I could go four or five months before it's completely depleted. It's a tempting option, but I won't do it. I put that money aside for travel and I refuse to use it now, for this. I can endure a few more weeks at the country club, especially considering I've already gone five whole shifts without coming in contact with James. According to Ellie and Marissa, they haven't seen him around either.

I don't know how I feel about that. He could be staying away because he can't stand the sight of me, or he could be staying away because he actually doesn't care to see me. Or, worst of all, he could be going about his life with no thought of me at all.

It's been eight days since Vegas.

By now, I expected to be well into phase two of Operation Get Over James, but I'm still held up in phase one: Stop Thinking About Him Every Minute of Every Damn Day. It doesn't help that his company has been all over the news. Apparently his TED talk at the conference went really well. I broke down and watched it one night in an incognito browser tab, like maybe that way I wouldn't have to acknowledge what I was doing. I wanted to see some hint of emotion in his eyes, but he was nothing but professional, not even a hint of bags under his eyes. I made it through the entire speech, filled with pride for how eloquently he spoke, and then I promptly slammed my laptop closed and tossed it aside.

Early the next morning I saw an article on the front page of the Texas Monthly website highlighting a union between BioWear and a large foreign tech NGO based in London. Apparently, they were also in attendance at the conference in Vegas and James' presentation piqued their interest. Their focus is on creating technology for underserved populations, and they're equally motivated to develop the BioShield. The article predicted that with the new infusion of capital, BioShield could be ready for trial deployment within the next few years.

I'm ecstatic for him, and I want him to know that.

BROOKE: I   heard   about   the   deal. Congratulations. I know how excited you must be to see your dream get one step closer to reality.

After I send it, I keep my phone near me at all times, checking it every few minutes to see if a reply has come through. After two days, I decide he's probably not going to respond.

Still, I don't regret sending it.

I try to distract myself with more job searching, and I finally catch my first lucky break a few days after I read the article about the merger. My agency calls to notify me of a family looking to hire an au pair. It's exactly what I've been looking for since I lost my last position. The couple, Diego and Nicolás, are moving back to Spain at the end of the summer and would like to bring an American tutor back with them. Their two adopted daughters have been learning English while in the United States, and Diego and Nicolás are anxious to continue their education in Spain.

"You're one of only a handful of our tutors who are willing to relocate," the head of the agency points out. Yes, technically that's true. When I first put in my application, I made myself completely available for travel around the United States or abroad. "Frankly, you're not going to get another opportunity like this," she insists. "We've had a hard time placing you, and this position is perfect. The children are young and according to their fathers, they're eager to learn."

I ask for a few days to think about it, which she grudgingly gives me, along with a harsh warning about the job slipping through my fingers if I'm not careful.

I've been job hunting like crazy, so I should be thrilled by the prospect of starting a new position with a family, but my fight with James and our subsequent falling out means I can barely work up the shadow of joy.

I'm distracted as I get ready for work and bike to Twin Oaks. I've always wanted to travel as much as I can while I'm young, so it's slightly unsettling that I'm not jumping at the opportunity to move to Spain. There's a good reason for my hesitation, but I don't let it surface. Instead, I lock my bike up and head inside.

"Guess who's finally showing his face," Ellie says, dipping her head into the employee locker room.

I stiffen and focus intently on the contents of my locker. When I'm sure my voice won't break, I finally answer. "Oh yeah?"

"Yup. He's in the dining room. There's a luncheon benefitting the less fortunate."

"Is he alone?"

She hesitates before she replies, "No."

Just past the swinging door that divides the kitchen from the dining room, there's a small dark alcove where servers use a mounted tablet to put in orders with the chef. I stand there, half hidden behind the wall, spying on James as he enjoys lunch with Lacy Nichols. They've been placed at one of the tables near the fireplace, slightly secluded from the crowded charity luncheon taking place around them. They're in profile, which affords me the perfect vantage point. Lacy looks radiant in a fitted light pink wrap dress, and her blonde hair tumbles down her back in old Hollywood curls. I reach up and self-consciously touch my messy bun.

James is wearing a charcoal gray suit. I wonder if he just came from the office or if maybe he took the day off to spend it at the event with Lacy.

"Spying on them?" a server asks behind me.

"Who?" I ask innocently, my gaze on James and Lacy unwavering.

He chuckles and brushes past me to deliver food. "The fortunate ones."

Just then, Lacy leans forward and wraps her hand around James' on top of the pristine white tablecloth. The swinging door behind me whips open and a commotion draws my attention away from their locked hands. Three servers follow after the head chef, a stout, angry man I've only had the displeasure of being around a handful of times. Apparently the club poached him from a Michelin-starred restaurant, and he has the ego to prove it.

I watch as he orders the servers to straighten their shoulders and "act like you've been here before. Jesus."

"Yes, Chef," they reply with clipped, respectful tones.

With impatience, the chef steps forward and points to each dish, reminding them of what they're holding on their trays. "Bouillabaisse with poached lobster. Crispy oysters with vegetable salad and citrus mayonnaise. Sea bass with prawn tortellini, fennel purée, and white wine sauce. Serve Ms. Nichols first, and then Mr. Ashwood. If they ask about a dish and you don't know the answer, for the love of god, keep your mouth shut."

Then he turns and finally sees me standing there, watching. "You," he says, pointing to me. "Come help serve."

I pale. "Oh, I can't. I'm stationed at the cabana."

He's taken aback at my audacity, his oily face turning

bright red with anger. "I didn't study at Hyde Park to be refused by a fucking *cabana* girl."

He shoves a small tray at me and releases it, so I have no choice but to grasp it tightly or let it crash down to the floor. The servers eye me with mild curiosity as they pass and then I fall in line, using the last server as a shield between me and our final destination. I could bolt at any moment, but it doesn't seem worth it; I don't want to incur the wrath of Mr. Michelin Star.

We descend upon James and Lacy, and I hover in the back, behind the servers and the chef. I can barely see James, which means he can't see me. *Thank goodness.*

The chef steps forward and addresses them. I'm shocked at how quickly he can change his tone. Out here, he sounds gentle and kind. "As promised, we have the next round of courses for you both to sample."

Lacy claps gleefully. "Oh wonderful! It looks amazing."

"Yes, we'll just clear these dishes off for you. I'm sorry, that should have been done already. Let me just—"

He turns and peers around the servers, pushing one of them aside until he finally gets to me.

"You," he clips out impatiently. "Come clear these."

Another server steps to the side and my cover is blown. There I stand, a few feet from James and his date, wearing my pleated skirt and Twin Oaks Polo. I know how I look: bags under my eyes, messy hair, slightly skinnier than I was a few weeks ago. Still, I try to lift my chin as I step forward and reach for the empty plate in front of James. He's so close I can smell his cologne, and yet he doesn't say a word. Maybe he's shocked to find me here suddenly, but then again, so am I.

My hand shakes as I clear the dishes out from in front

234

of him, and I come an inch away from toppling his wine glass. He reaches out to steady it, for which I am eternally grateful. I'm pretty sure the chef would flay me right here if I spilled wine on James Ashwood.

"Thank you," he says with quiet formality as I stand and turn to Lacy.

Our eyes lock, and she tilts her head in recognition.

I hurry and collect the few dishes in front of her, but before I can turn and scurry away, she leans forward.

"You're Martha's stepdaughter aren't you? Ellie? I'm Lacy, I'm a member of the Philanthropic League with her."

I smile tightly. "Ellie is my sister. I'm Brooke."

"Of course." She drags her gaze down me in assessment and then smiles. "Martha mentioned you both work here." She eyes my uniform and her nose twitches almost imperceptibly. It's like she's allergic to starched polos. "How fun, it's almost a family business."

I wait for James to chime in and announce that he knows me as well, but his imposing silence is worse. I've been wondering what it would be like when we finally came face to face, and now that it's happening, all of my worst fears are coming true. He's still holding on to the anger. I hurt him in Vegas, and for that, I'm sorry. I need him to know that.

"James, how are you?" I ask, peering over at him beneath my lashes.

Look at me, I beg. *Look at me so you can see how sorry I am.*

"Fine," he replies with a bored dismissal.

"*James?*" Lacy asks. "Do you two know each other?"

"We're friends," I reply with a small smile.

"Is that so?" Lacy asks, her perfectly manicured brow arching in surprise. Her gaze scans back and forth between us, alight with cunning mischief. "I would have thought it was frowned upon for employees to befriend club members."

Just then her hand shifts so quickly and so deftly that I know I'm the only one who sees it, and then her napkin goes tumbling to the ground. She claps her hand to her chest. "Oh, goodness, I'm so clumsy today!"

She apologizes, but she makes no move to retrieve it. We all freeze there for a long moment before it becomes clear that she expects me to bend down and pick it up.

"Allow me to get you a clean napkin," I suggest as my mind races to find an escape from the humiliation.

"Don't bother, this one is just fine!" she insists.

Her message is received loud and clear: it's not about the napkin, it's symbolic. In this moment, I'm *the help*. I've never felt so degraded, and a part of me wants to leave right here and now, but the chef clears his throat and I know I have no choice. I bend slowly, cheeks flushed with embarrassment. I wrap my hand around the napkin just as Lacy's heel shifts one inch to the right, pinning it to the ground. I tug it once, and when she doesn't release it, I tug again, harder this time. Her heel lifts at the last second, taking the resistance with it. My momentum carries me back and I land on my ass, the dishes sliding off my tray in a mess of crashing porcelain and leftover food.

Some kind of disgusting green goop flies up and blankets my hair, and the edge of the heavy tray drops heavily onto my ribs. James leaps to his feet to help, and as he hooks his hands under my arms and lifts me up, more dishes clatter to the ground.

I aim a furious glance at Lacy, but she's wearing a perfect mask of shock and concern.

"Oh my gosh, you poor thing! Are you okay?" she

asks. "My clumsiness must be contagious."

James brushes bits of food off my shirt and skirt before I realize what he's doing. When I do, I yank my arm away from him and take a step back. By this point, the chef has gone completely apoplectic. He flits around me, yelling obscenities and calling me a "stupid philistine". In a last-ditch effort to preserve a modicum of dignity, I fling as much food off my body as I can and then storm out of the dining room. I'm still due to start my shift in the cabana any minute now, but I could not care less. Right now, I have a job offer to accept.

CHAPTER NINETEEN

Diego and Nicolás sit across from me at Starbucks, smiling as I fill them in on my resume and experience. They're both in their mid 40s, well-dressed artist types. Diego wears clear-framed circular glasses and Nicolás has long blond hair that could rival James'. I decide there's no point in leaving out the details of why I left my former position as a tutor. Fortunately, they find the whole ordeal amusing rather than concerning.

"She thought you'd sleep with her new husband?" Nicolás asks with wide eyes.

I shrug. "She never said those exact words…"

"Well fortunately Nicolás prefers blonds, so I think we'll be fine—oh, and men, in case you hadn't guessed!"

There's half a moment of hesitation before we all crack up laughing.

For the next hour, we get to know each other better. They tell me all about their daughters, Olive and Luciana, bragging about their Spanish and English skills.

"We've been here in the United States for a few years," Diego explains, "so they've picked up quite a bit, but it's important to us that they continue speaking English once we return to España."

I nod. "Of course."

After that, they outline what they're looking for in an au pair. They don't expect me to be at their beck and call, and more importantly, I wouldn't be viewed as the help. They want me to feel like I'm part of the family. I'd only work on the weekdays, and I'd get plenty of time off to travel. Diego will begin his position as a professor at the University of Barcelona in two weeks, so he's flying out in a few days. Nicolás and the girls will join him soon after.

"Obviously we'd like you to come with us if you accept the position. It might be nice to have another adult to make the trip overseas more bearable," Nicolás admits.

"Right. Of course." I smile and nod, trying to ignore how wrong this all feels. It's one thing to talk about leaving, but now that I have a real job lined up, I'm not sure I should take it.

The next day they arrange a meeting to introduce me to Olive and Luciana, and I try hard not to like them. If they were two snotty teenagers, I'd turn down the job in a heartbeat. Unfortunately, they're both adorable and well mannered. Olive is older, nearly twelve, and Luciana is nine. Because Diego and Nicolás don't keep televisions in the house, they both tell me their favorite hobby is reading—READING—not to mention, Olive pulls out a tube of strawberry Lip Smacker and NOT a Kylie Lip Kit like every other tween in the continental United States. Their innocence is infectious, and I know I'd enjoy teaching them.

The girls apparently give me the thumbs up because the next day, Diego calls to formally offer me the position. I let his call go to voicemail so I don't have to give an answer on the spot, though I know they need to hear from me in a day or two so they'll have enough time to scramble and find someone else. I don't want to put them in that position, but I also want to postpone the decision in front of me: move to Spain and leave James for good, or stay at the cost of this once-in-a-lifetime opportunity.

This position with Diego and Nicolás is what I've been holding out for these last few months, and the fact that I'm wavering about it only makes me hate myself more.

The problem I have with life-changing decisions is my imagination. I'm way too adept at projecting out all the different timelines, imagining the many lives I stand to unlock and the ones I'm leaving behind forever. When you're young, life stretches out in front of you like a train track. Grade school, high school, college—every new stage is designed to feel like some pre-ordained leveling up, but then suddenly you're thrust into the Grand Central Station of your mid-twenties with just enough pocket change to buy a one-way ticket. There are no maps with warnings of *heartbreak ahead*, no guideposts to direct you on the path to happiness, just a churning sea of doubt, and with enough time, regret.

Not two weeks ago, I was in Vegas with James, sick to my stomach over how fast things were progressing with us. I wanted an out and I got it, and now that I have the potential to leave Twin Oaks and start my dream job in Europe, I should be ecstatic.

But I'm not.

My indecisiveness is so frustrating that I sit in my room staring down at a coin, debating whether or not I should just flip it and let fate decide my next step. Heads, I stay. Tails, I leave. At least that way I will have something else to blame for any ill that comes of it. Then I think about James, and how I would feel if I knew he was letting a coin decide whether or not he wanted to be with me. I toss the coin aside quickly, embarrassed that I even came close to using it.

Even though I'm still debating what I'm going to do, I

decide to submit my two weeks notice at Twin Oaks. Whether or not I'm leaving for Spain, I can't stomach working there another day. Brian doesn't even feign surprise.

"I heard what happened the other day in the dining room," he says, reclining in his chair.

He's referring to when I spilled green sludge all over myself in front of James and Lacy.

I glance down. "Yeah, sorry I left before my shift. I wasn't really in the right state of mind."

"Our chef demanded that I fire you."

I glance back up and smile when I see the amusement on his face. "Guess I'm saving you the trouble."

He nods with a small, sad smile. "It'll make my life easier."

Later that night, I join Ellie, Martha, and my dad for dinner and decide to broach the subject of my potential move. Ellie already knows about it (she's furious), but I fill my dad in over the first course.

"Spain, huh?"

I nod.

"I guess there's no talking you out of it?"

I focus on my plate so he can't see just how close I *am* to being talked out of it. A soft breeze could keep me from Spain at this point.

"She's already put in her two weeks at the club," Ellie announces right before she jabs her heel into my foot under the table.

"Ow!"

"That's what you get for leaving me."

Like I said, she isn't coping with the news well.

I meet her gaze across the table. "I was never going to stay at Twin Oaks, you know that."

"Aren't there tutoring positions in Austin?" Martha asks.

"She's just like her mother," my dad says.

My fork clatters down onto my plate and I whip my gaze up to meet his. "What's that supposed to mean?"

His blue eyes widen with understanding. "No! Sweetie, I meant your wanderlust!"

"He didn't mean it like *that*, Brooke," Ellie insists, coming to his defense.

"Getting a job that doesn't make me want to kill myself isn't the same as abandoning my family," I point out harshly.

My dad reaches out to grip my hand on the table and squeezes gently. "I know that, Brooke. I'm sorry, I shouldn't have said that."

The silence around the table is fraught, and my dad tries hard to salvage the rest of dinner by asking us how our days went. Ellie offers a quick reply and I stay silent, so it's up to Martha. Fortunately, she can talk enough for all of us.

"Oh, it was fine. I had lunch with Lacy and Jillian to go over final plans for the fall fundraiser. It's going to be sensational. We've got everything booked at the Driskill. Bob Schneider has agreed to perform, and you won't believe this, but apparently Lacy was able to get quite a large sponsorship from BioWear." She turns to address me. "You know James don't you, honey?"

The hairs on the back of my neck stand on end. Ellie tries to meet my eye, but I keep my gaze on my lap.

"Apparently they're dating! Can you believe it? You know how much I love Lacy. She's done so much for the League, and I'd be so happy to see her land someone like James. He's quite a catch."

"H—" I try to speak, but my throat is so tight I can

243

barely get the words out. I clear it and try again. "How do you know they're dating?"

She beams. "She told me so herself. She thinks they're on the fast track to marriage."

"How is that possible?" Ellie asks on my behalf. "They just started dating."

Martha casts a loving glance toward my father. "Sometimes when you know, you know."

Shockingly, I'm not able to force down the rest of dinner. I ask to be excused before dessert and storm straight up to my old bedroom. Once the door's locked, I dial James' number. He doesn't answer, but I call again. Still...nothing. I wait for his voicemail to click on and ignore how chipper his voice sounds as he politely asks me to leave a message. I have a scathing monologue prepared in my head all about his so-called feelings for me, but the moment the beep sounds, I pull the phone away and quickly stab my finger at the end button before the message starts recording.

Later, back in my room at the co-op, Ellie points out the obvious. "Why is this bothering you so much? You don't want to be with him, remember?"

"Don't really wanna talk about it, Ellie."

"You should be happy he's with Lacy."

I yank a dress out of my closet and toss it on the ground. I'm creating three piles: clothes for Spain, clothes for Ellie, and clothes for Goodwill.

"She's horrible."

"Ohhhh, so you're upset because you don't think she's good enough for him?"

"Exactly."

She grunts in disbelief. "You're delusional."

I ignore her and go back to sorting clothes. When I

come across the slinky flapper dress from the speakeasy party, I toss it into the Goodwill pile without a second thought.

"Whoa!" Ellie leaps up off the bed to rescue it. "Why are you donating this?"

"Want it? It's yours."

"It looks expensive."

"It was."

She holds it up and admires it with a greedy smile. "Well if there's anything else like this, I want it."

I nod and get back to work, but clearly Ellie isn't done. A few minutes later, she decides to pry a little deeper into my life. "Tell me again why you're doing this?"

"Moving to Spain?" I ask, keeping my back to her as I file through my t-shirts. It's easiest to hide my cards if I don't have to look her in the eye.

"No, leaving when you're clearly in love with this great guy."

My back stiffens. "I've told you, it just isn't good timing."

"This is about Mom, isn't it?"

I throw up my hands in defeat and glare at her over my shoulder. "Stop asking me questions if you think you have all the answers!"

"Right, okay, he's older. I'll give you that, but that's not why you're doing this. Mom really did a number on you, didn't she?"

I purposely delay answering. Instead, I yank a shirt out of my drawer and start to fold it into a tiny square so it can fit snugly in my suitcase—a suitcase I'm packing for a position I have yet to officially accept.

"It's not your fault she left Dad," she affirms, her voice clear and gentle.

I pick at a nonexistent piece of lint on my shirt. "I know that."

"So then talk to me. What's the real problem?"

She's relentless. I could kick her out of my room, but being Ellie, she'd probably just slither right back in. So, I give her honesty in the hopes that this conversation will end soon.

"James made his intentions perfectly clear from the beginning: he wants a wife and kids. After I pressured him to just go with the flow, he claimed to have cast those goals to the wind."

"And you don't believe him?"

"It's not that I don't believe he's trying, I just…" I struggle to find the words. "I just don't think it's that easy to change. I couldn't help but see a deeper motive in all the sweet, innocuous things he did. I felt like Hansel and Gretel—on the surface, I was just eating cake, but really I was being fattened up."

"But you love cake!" she teases, trying to lighten my mood.

I smile and shrug. "Exactly. I had to get away before I lost my ability to resist and ended up as someone's wife and someone's mother."

"Why is that a bad thing? Don't you want kids?"

"Eventually, but not like *tomorrow*!"

My shouting stuns her for a few minutes, and I relish the silence. My suitcase is half packed for Spain, and my Goodwill pile is growing taller by the minute.

"You know Mom had me when she was only 21?" Ellie offers thoughtfully. "She had one year left at St. Edward's, but she couldn't finish her degree, and I think she always resented Dad a little bit for that. He was able to finish college and find a solid career. I think Mom wanted to do the same."

I didn't know that.

"She could have gone back when we were older," I point out.

She shrugs. "She probably would have if she hadn't found Jorge. He fulfilled something in her that Dad never could."

I know what she means. With my dad, she was only ever a stay-at-home mom and a doting wife. He thought her time was best spent rearing children and cleaning house. Jorge tore her from that world and flipped her entire script. Together, they travel the world, working as partners in the Peace Corps. I don't have to like the fact that she left to understand why she did, which is the exact reason I decide I don't have to like that I'm going to Spain. I just have to do it.

● ● ●

The shitty thing about putting in my two weeks notice is that I don't get to go out in a blaze of glory. I have eight more shifts to get through in the next two weeks, and as much as I'd like to blow them off, I could actually use the money. There are a few last-minute things I need to buy before I head to Spain, not to mention, I have to pay off the rest of my lease agreement at the co-op. For free-loving hippie types, they sure made a show of squeezing every last dime out of me.

The country club is quiet during my shift on Monday. Summer is winding down and school is starting soon. Now, midday, there are only a few families at the pool, and they've been here all morning. I've offered them enough beverages and food to hold them over for the next hour, which means I have nothing to do but stand in the shade near the bar and focus on the rippling water of the pool. I wonder if Spain will be this hot when I arrive, if the cicadas will chirp as loud there as they do here.

One of the mothers near the kiddie pool waves me over and asks for a few extra napkins. I take my time with the task, trying to ignore the fact that I still have another few hours of this. By the time I hand her a half-dozen, I'm hopeful they'll need something else, but she dismisses me and I'm back to moseying around the pool. I've already swept out the bathroom and restocked the toilet paper. The cooking staff takes care of everything inside the cabana kitchen, but I ask them if they need any help restocking. Unfortunately, they have everything covered. I frown and head back out to stand by the pool, wondering if I actually see a black Porsche driving down the tree-lined drive or if it's a figment of my imagination.

It winds slowly toward the parking lot and then takes a sharp left and a right before stopping in James' parking spot. He could see me from where he is, though thanks to the tinted windows, I have no way of knowing if he's looking or not. Either way, I jump at the opportunity.

"I'm taking my break!" I shout to the cooks inside the cabana, though they're too busy watching a soccer game to do much more than grunt in response.

By the time I make it out of the pool gate and down the path toward the parking lot, James is getting out of his car and glancing my way. Fortunately, there's no one with him. If Lacy had slid out of the passenger side, I'm not sure I would have had the courage to approach him. Even still, it's hard to continue considering James doesn't seem all that enthused to see me walking toward him. At least he doesn't turn and walk away as I approach. He toys with his keys as I come to a stop a few feet away from him.

"Hey, do you have a second to talk?" I ask, hopeful.

He nods toward the main clubhouse. "I have a lunch meeting in a few minutes."

I wring out my hands in front of me and nod. "Right, yeah. Okay, I just really think you and I need to clear the air after what happened in Vegas." I look down at my feet. "I don't want to leave things...the way they are."

"I appreciate it." I look back up in time to see him cross his arms and glance away, thoughtfully staring off into the distance for a moment before he turns back to me. His features hardened in those few moments, and now he appears every bit the cavalier businessman I used to assume he was. "But I don't think it's necessary. I was 25 once. I understand where you're coming from. Maybe I pushed too hard, or maybe it never would have worked. Either way, you don't need me chasing after you to figure things out. If my experience counts for anything, you just need time."

I didn't expect him to be so diplomatic about the whole thing. The way he speaks, I can tell he's thought long and hard about saying exactly this, but there's no conviction behind his words at all.

"I still want to apologize."

He shrugs. "Consider it done."

His words are infused with arrogance I don't recognize, and though I should walk away and finish what I started, I can't help but fire back.

"So Lacy is probably a nice change of pace right? I've heard y'all are on the, quote, *fast track to marriage*?"

His eyes narrow. "If we are, you should be happy for me."

I look away, angry that he didn't outright deny it.

"That didn't take long. Weren't we in Vegas just a few weeks ago?"

"A lot has happened since then."

I think of Spain and the job I've accepted; obviously he's somehow heard about it through the grapevine. "I guess you're right." I step back toward the cabana. "I'll see you, James."

I'm more angry with the situation now than I was before. I wanted to apologize and then tuck James into a clean little box, but he isn't making it that easy. Now, I have two weeks left until I move to Spain, and I still feel like he and I have unfinished business—starting with the bike he gifted me.

I plan to return it later that night because I can't stand the idea of hanging on to it any longer. Sure, public transportation will take longer to get around on, but I'd rather sit on a thousand urine-soaked bus seats than spend one more minute on that sunflower-yellow reminder. I wonder if he's purchased anything to consummate his relationship with Lacy yet. Maybe he's gotten her a bike as well and had a local artist paint it shit brown to match her soul.

After a lonely dinner back at the co-op, I pedal as hard as I can toward Mount Bonnell Road, sticky with sweat by the time I pull up in front of his neighborhood's private gate. I forgot about this part. I don't know the code, and I'm not about to call James and ask for it. Part of me wants to just sling the bike up and over the gate and let him deal with the aftermath, but I won't. Instead, I lurk in the bushes like a creepo until a car pulls up and the heavy iron bars swing open. I wait a few seconds so they can pass and turn down a side street and then I race through the gate before it squashes me like a bug.

I have a hard time finding James' house once I'm inside the neighborhood. It didn't seem all that complicated the last time I was here, but then again, I was frazzled from our crash and didn't really pay much attention. I do find it eventually, but not until I'm coated in a new, second layer of sweat and more annoyed than ever. I want to drop the bike at the curb and bolt, but better judgment warns me against it. So, I take a deep breath and head for the front entrance of his property. Fortunately, the pedestrian gate is unlocked, and I start to walk up his front path. His Porsche is in the driveway and there are lights on inside, but I don't see any movement behind the floor-to-ceiling windows along the front of the house. I pick up the pace and hustle, scurrying up before he walks by and sees me in all my sweaty glory.

I leave the bike just outside his front door with a note I painstakingly drafted before I left the co-op. There were half a dozen different iterations, but this one is the most simple.

Thank you for the bike, but I won't be needing it in Spain.
All the best,
Brooke

I think it sounds mature. Ellie thought it sounded slightly bratty when I texted a photo of it to her. Obviously, I ignore her advice and leave it anyway, angling it so it sits centered on the bike seat. That way, there's no way he'll miss it.

"Brooke?"

"JESUS, MARY, AND JOSEPH!" I scream and slap my hand to my chest like I'm trying to stop myself from having a heart attack. When I spin on my heel, I find James

standing a few yards down his driveway, and I think maybe
I will have that heart attack after all.

CHAPTER TWENTY

Can't a girl break into a neighborhood, sneak onto someone's property, and leave a gift without being noticed? Isn't that Santa's entire MO?

"Brooke?" James asks again, clearly confused as to why I'm currently frozen in place on his front porch, sweaty and wide-eyed.

The note I left on the bike seat goes sailing toward the ground before I can speak. We both glance down at it and I reach for it quickly, snatching it up before he can. When I straighten, he's only a few feet away, dressed in a black t-shirt, shorts, and Nike sneakers, as if he's just returning from an evening run. He's sweaty (almost as much as I am) and breathing hard, and I could be imagining it, but his tall frame seems more imposing than usual. It's probably just because he caught me off guard.

"Oh, hey. I was just returning this," I say, pointing back at where the bike rests on its kickstand. I took the time to clean it before I rode over, and it looks every bit as new as it did the first day he had it delivered. My heart aches at having to give it back; I probably won't ever get another one like it.

"It wasn't on loan," he points out with a biting tone. "It was a gift."

"I shouldn't have ever accepted it, but I don't need it anymore."

He looks stricken. "Did you get a new one?"

"No," I say quietly. "I'll wait and get one in Spain."

His rears back and frowns darkly. "Spain?"

My mouth drops open. I'm confused. I thought he knew, but now that I think about it, how would he have?

"I'm moving." When recognition doesn't dawn in his eyes, I continue, "I found an au pair position. Didn't you know?"

He steps forward and snatches the note out of my hand, the note I now agree sounds slightly bratty. He reads it and then shakes his head. With a sad laugh, he moves around me and unlocks his front door.

"No, I didn't know."

I turn over my shoulder. "Earlier at the club, it seemed like—" I shake my head. "It doesn't matter. I finally found a new tutoring position with a family that's moving to Spain, and they've offered to bring me along."

"Congratulations. It's what you've been searching for."

He doesn't sound like he's congratulating me. In fact, he doesn't even glance up as he takes the bike and wheels it into the front foyer of his house.

"You really should be happy for me!" I call out after him. "Especially after what happened in the dining room the other day!"

He laughs like I've just proposed something absolutely ludicrous. Then, finally, he glances up and meets my eyes with enough emotion and anger that it feels like a direct punch to the chest.

"I guess you should be happy for me that I've found someone like Lacy. Is that how this works? We're just supposed to be happy for each other?"

"Yes. That's the mature thing."

"Please don't lecture me on maturity," he snaps back.

We're both sweaty, our hearts racing from physical exertion and the heat of this encounter. He's provoking me into a fight, and after my annoying bike ride and my 30-minute trek through this stupid rich neighborhood, I don't have the patience to take the high road. So, instead, I go in head first. *BRING IT ON.*

"You know what?!" I say, stepping past his doorstep. "If we're being honest, I think Lacy sucks! You saw how she treated me the other day—how do you think a person like that is going to treat those kids you want so badly?"

He turns and marches off down the hallway. If I want a fight, I'll have to follow him. That's fine by me, because I'm just getting started.

He walks straight into his kitchen and yanks open his refrigerator, withdrawing a single bottle of water for himself without bothering to offer me one even though I'm clearly a panting mess. I stare at him over the kitchen island with simmering rage as he slowly lifts it to his mouth and takes a long sip. His gaze is locked with mine. We're cursing each other to hell without words, and then finally, after he's drained nearly half the bottle, he sighs and drops it down onto the island. His thirst is quenched, and mine just got 10 times worse.

"I thought I had gotten to know the real you, but if you're actually choosing to be with someone like Lacy, I don't know what to believe."

He leans forward so there's no chance I miss his next words. "You know what I don't believe? I don't believe you want to go to Spain half as badly as you say you do."

"Are you really with her?"

"Are you really moving to Spain? The thing is, I don't think this is about Lacy or Spain. I think you came here looking for a fight." Then he goes one step further. "I think

255

you like it."

"I don't need you playing shrink," I groan, turning away and breaking eye contact. It feels good to regain some composure, though it doesn't last long.

"You're the one who came to my house," he points out with a haughty tone.

"To drop off the bike!"

"Yeah, that's done," he tells me with a knowing gleam in his eyes. It's like he sees right through my motives, which is infuriating considering I can hardly see them for myself. "So why are you still standing here?"

"Because you're pissing me off," I reply without missing a beat.

A slow-spreading smirk transforms his steely features.

"Then it's probably best that you go," he says, rounding the side of the island toward me. "I'm sure you have a lot of packing to do."

HE'S KICKING ME OUT!

I straighten my shoulders and lift my chin in self-preservation. "Yes, as a matter of fact, *I do*. Looks like I'll be going to Spain with a shitload of baggage."

"Good. I'll walk you out," he says, wrapping his hand around my elbow in an unyielding grip and all but dragging me down the hallway after him. I try to yank my arm away but he's doesn't budge.

"I can walk out by myself!"

And to think I actually once *liked* this man.

At the door, he holds my handwritten note out for me. "Don't forget this."

I snatch it out of his hand and crinkle it into a tiny ball. "I can't stand you."

"Good." My angry outburst bounces off him. "How are you getting home?"

"I'll walk," I snap.

"Right, well make sure to take main roads," he says with a tone of bored disinterest.

It's the last straw. I curse under my breath and turn to perform a frustrated walk-run down his front path. I have visions of inflicting property damage on the way out, maybe dropkicking the mailbox or shredding a few of his precious hedges. I'm halfway to the road when he reaches me with his long strides. I'm not even aware he's chasing after me until he spins me around and captures my wrists in a vice-like grip. With one hard tug, he draws me against him until our bodies are flush.

My mouth is open to shout at him yet again, but his lips crash down against mine in a punishing kiss. I struggle against him and his mouth turns merciless. I'm angry— livid, in fact. Tears of exhaustion and rage slide down my cheeks. I want my freedom, and I'm prepared to get it by any means possible. I even try one well-placed stomp on his foot, but he evades my assault and I grow still, defeated, allowing his lips to move over mine with fierce tenderness. Eventually, sick of my games, he pulls back and cradles my face between his hands. I'm trembling, and his stormy eyes are seeking honesty in mine. I refuse to give it to him. My gaze narrows, focusing all the anger my mouth refuses to produce.

His mouth descends toward mine again, and this time, he kisses me with such gentle affection that I can feel my heart breaking. My competing emotions riot inside of me at the precise moment he coaxes my lips apart. Wild sparks jolt through my body as his tongue slides over mine, forcing me into perfect compliance for fear that he'll pull back and end the kiss at any moment.

He doesn't drag me back inside, but I wish he had,

because when the front door closes behind me, I have no one to blame but myself.

James takes my hand and leads me wordlessly through his house. We pass empty room after empty room, and then we step into his bedroom and he lets go of my hand to close the door behind us. It feels like a pointed move on his part, as if by shutting the door, he might be able to block out the problems of the past and future for just a little longer. In this room, it's just him and me, just now.

I'm shocked to see furniture in this room—well, just a bed, but it's better than nothing. I wouldn't put it past James to sleep on a mattress he tossed onto the ground in his palatial mansion.

Sitting in the center of the large room, there's a dark four-poster bed with a fluffy white duvet cover that sits slightly askew. I can't help but laugh.

"Another surprise—I would have pegged you as a bed-maker."

He strolls past to stand in front of me, blocking my view with his broad chest. I glance up to his face just as he reaches to skim his fingers up my arms. He caresses my forearms, biceps, shoulders, and then higher until he's cradled my head so I can't turn away. His fingers wind through my hair, and I'm reminded of how sticky and sweaty we both are. When I mention it, he doesn't care.

"It's fitting. I'll burn the sheets," he promises before tugging my head back and giving himself better access to my soft lips. I smile as he bends low and hovers his mouth over mine. My breath catches in my throat. Outside, he kissed me passionately, *forcefully*, but it's clear that in here, he's not going to take anything I'm not willing to give. I reach up and wrap my hands around his forearms before tipping my head back just another inch. It's a silent plea, a *kiss me, you fool.*

He smiles and bends low, skimming his lips gently across mine. My eyes flutter closed and I let out a low moan as our lips slide open. Our tongues touch and desire builds low between my legs. He moves to grasp my waist and then he starts to work my t-shirt up. It's gone, slipping down to the floor behind me. My sports bra is next, and then his big, masculine hand drags up from my navel to skim along the bottom of my ribcage, up to the underside of my left breast. His touch is sweet as he caresses my skin. He takes turns holding each breast in his palm, kneading the soft flesh. When I'm close to melting on the spot, he finally, *finally* skims his palm across my nipple. A thousand shockwaves move through me and I moan for more. He obliges, dipping down and replacing his hand with his mouth. His tongue is rough yet tender, a reminder of what he did to me back in that hotel room in Vegas.

Just when I think I can't take another second, his fingers skim down, dragging along the top of my shorts. He dips down beneath the elastic band, sliding lower until his fingers brush across my center. My head tips back on a moan. It's a slow give and take. His finger pads tease me with gentle kisses until I'm so hungry for more that I reach down and hold his hand still, willing him to touch where I need it most.

What are we doing? Why am I letting this happen? The rational part of my brain vies for the controls to my body, but the mutiny doesn't last long.

When he brushes across my tight bundle of nerves, I lose my footing. If he keeps it up, I won't be able to stand at all. I blink my eyes open to find him staring down at me with undisguised emotion—in fact, he's looking at me as if I'm the most beautiful thing he's ever seen, and it's too much. I clamp my eyes shut again and swear to keep them closed until it's over, until I can regain some semblance of my sanity.

"Brooke," he groans as his finger dips into me.

I squeeze his shoulders in response, showing him how much I like his touch, the feel of him inside me. His mouth lifts back up to my neck and he presses a kiss there, whispering something against my skin. I ask him to repeat it, but he ignores me and backs us up to the bed instead. I know where we're headed. In a few minutes, we'll both be stripped down, our workout clothes tossed to the floor and forgotten. He'll guide me backward until my bare thighs hit his cool sheets, the sheets that smell like his spiced cologne, the sheets he sleeps on every night. This is his private sanctuary, the place where he rests after a long day, and probably the last place we'll ever see each other. He's wrapping me up in his bed and covering me with his body.

"I accused you of wanting to fight, of liking it," he whispers. "I guess I like it too."

● ● ●

I'm grateful that James doesn't ask me to stay the night. It's 12:45 AM when I summon an Uber, and I have just enough time to rinse off in his shower before it arrives. He hands me a set of clean clothes when I step out and wrap a towel around myself. They're his clothes: a white Caltech t-shirt I haven't seen before and some workout shorts that hang loose around my hips. I make an empty promise about mailing them back, but I know I won't. Unlike the bike, these clothes are a gift I won't be returning. They're a little piece of him I'm going to keep no matter what.

He walks me to the street and opens the back door of the Uber for me. We forgot to kiss goodbye at the door, which means anything we do here is under the careful supervision of the woman in the driver's seat.

I turn to him and aim my focus somewhere near his heart.

"When do you leave?" he asks, and I'm surprised to find that his tone is completely neutral, not hopeful or angry, just...curious.

I shake my head and glance down his street. "I'm not sure. Soon."

I can't give him any more details than that. I can't tell him that as of this moment, I can't imagine leaving at all, much less in a few days. I can't tell him I've already agreed to take the job. Diego and Nicolás are counting on me, and if I pass up the opportunity, who knows when the agency will find another position for me. It's not something I can dismiss lightly. I didn't bust my butt through college to spend the rest of my 20s peddling Mai Tais around the pool at Twin Oaks.

I think we both know that, and I think that's why he doesn't ask me to stay. He dips down and presses a kiss to my cheek. I inhale as long as I can, holding his scent with me even after the driver pulls away from his curb.

# CHAPTER TWENTY-ONE

Diego and Nicolás had me sign and fax over a contract when I agreed to take the position, and though it's non-binding, it feels like it is. I refuse to entertain the idea of staying behind. I've agreed to work for them, and I won't give up the opportunity. The pay is insane, Barcelona is beautiful, and most importantly, I will never have to don this Twin Oaks uniform ever again. Every day brings me closer to freedom, and every day the polo shirt feels slightly more constricting than the day before, almost like it knows I'm trying to leave. I tug at the collar and try to adjust my skirt so it covers up a few more inches of my thighs.

Brian is training my replacement in the cabana, some overeager UT student. In the five minutes I was around her, she kept going on and on about how Matthew McConaughey is a member here. Then she looked me dead in the eye and asked if I'd ever seen him. Once with Andy Roddick and Brooklyn Decker, I tell her, and yes, they're all beautiful in real life.

I think Brian could tell she was annoying me because he sent me back into the main clubhouse to roll silverware. They have the assembly line set up in the employee break room, where a small flat-screen plays daytime soaps. I tune it out and focus on the forks and knives in front of me. Maybe if I roll them fast enough, Brian will let me go early.

"Knock knock," Ellie says, tapping her knuckles on the doorframe.

I glance up but don't stop rolling. "What's up? I thought you were on hostess duty."

"I am," she says before nodding her head behind her and flashing me one of her trademark *don't hate me* smiles. They're usually reserved for when she admits she lost a piece of borrowed clothing. I mentally prepare myself to hear her tell me she ruined my favorite pair of Madewell jeans, and then James steps into the doorway behind her. My heart soars and my stomach tightens into a ball of anxiety. I don't know what he's doing here; we haven't talked since I left his house the other night. I've actually appreciated the fact that we haven't run into each other at the club, and it takes me a second to remember that he shouldn't be back here. This area is employees only.

Ellie turns and pats James' shoulder.

"Pay up, moneybags."

He casts an amused glance down at her as he pulls his wallet out and produces a crisp hundred-dollar bill. She pops it out of his hand with her thumb and forefinger and walks away, snapping it a few times for emphasis.

"'Preciate ya!"

I can't help but smile. "Did you just bribe my sister?"

He leans against the doorframe, crossing his arms over his broad chest. The employee break room is small to begin with, but with him looming there, surveying the space, it becomes stifling. "I offered a twenty, but she's a good negotiator. I might hire her."

I shake my head, turning back to my silverware. "Good to know the value of a conversation with me. My normal rate is $600 an hour, so you have 10 minutes." I snort.

"Are you busy?" he asks, no hint of amusement in his

tone. "Can you talk?"

Talk.

The most terrible word in the English language.

I wave my hand across the mess of silverware spread out on the table before me. "As you can see, I have my hands full."

"Brooke," he says with calm emphasis.

His heavy tone is enough to convince me to take him seriously. If he wants to talk here, fine—it's not like they're going to fire me—but if he wants to come to the workers' quarters, I'm going to put him to work.

I push my current set of silverware toward him. "Get to rollin'."

He steps into the small room and closes the door behind him. The soap opera on the TV plays out in the background. A woman is shouting at a man about sleeping with her business partner. It's all very dramatic compared to the atmosphere in here.

I peer up at James from beneath my lashes, trying to get a sense of how he feels. Is he upset about what happened the other night? Terrified of losing me?

He remains a few feet from me, studying my face in thoughtful silence. Apparently, we're both at a loss for words, but I manage to speak first.

"I want to clear the air once and for all," I say, playing with a stray thread on the linen napkin in my hand. "I didn't mean to shout at you the way I did the other night. That was…that's not how I want to conduct myself in the future."

"You don't have to apologize," he replies with quiet solemnity.

If he's not here to demand an apology and he's not here to fight, then there's only one other option.

I shoot to my feet. "James, I really need to—"

He steps forward and cuts me off. "Should I ask you to stay?"

His resolved tone hints that he already knows the answer.

"Please don't," I beg with a pleading glance, desperate to end this conversation before it even starts. "I've already committed to this. It's what I want."

"How long will you be gone?"

I choose complete honesty in my response. "Indefinitely."

The word is a nail in our coffin. Indefinitely means there's no point in waiting for me to come back.

He drags his hand through his hair in a stressful tug then turns and paces back and forth in the small space. As the owner of a company, he's probably used to solving problems and putting out fires. I know his brain is working overtime to come up with a solution for this, but there really isn't one.

"Foundations like ours don't really lend themselves to a long-distance thing," I joke sadly.

"And that's not what either of us wants," he says.

No, it's not. It would be an ill-fated compromise that would only make things worse. How long would James put up with me being in Spain when what he really wants—really *needs*—is a partner here, now.

"Maybe if…" My voice trails off.

What, Brooke? What could you two be? Pen pals?

"What?" he asks hopefully.

His tone is enough to tear down my calm resolve, because while I can handle us fighting up until the day I leave, I can't handle his kindness, his ability to bring softness to a situation that really sucks.

He rushes toward me to wipe my cheeks with the pads of his thumbs. "Please don't cry."

How can I not?

"Why does this feel like our 100th breakup?" I ask with a pitiful little hiccup.

"Because it is."

Sadness ripples through me and the tears start coming a little faster.

His admission breaks the floodgates. I'm a blubbering mess thinking about him alone in his house, working long hours, wishing he had someone to come home to at the end of the day.

"Do me a favor, okay? Just forget about me. Move on."

It's not that I thought he would ever wait for me, but it bears saying just in case. The thought of him spending another day alone makes my stomach ache and tears burn the backs of my eyes. I want him to find happiness. I want to think of him with a wife and children, completely fulfilled.

He turns his profile to me, narrowing his eyes at some point on the wall beside us. Maybe he's collecting his thoughts or trying to keep his emotions at bay, but when he finally turns back to me, I can see he wasn't successful. Big, sorrowful brown eyes implore me to change my mind, to stay for him, and for a moment, I cave.

"This doesn't feel right," I whisper.

"I agree." He pulls me closer so my hips touch his and then he tips my chin up. From this angle, I can see every strand of his dark, sooty lashes, every shade of brown in his eyes. "You should stay."

"You said you weren't going to ask me!" I cry.

"*Stay*."

Tears cloud my eyes and I wipe at them, angry with

myself for not keeping it together. "James."

His name is a plea. If he keeps asking me to stay, I just might, and I firmly believe it would be the wrong decision. I'd be staying on a sinking ship.

A knock sounds on the break room door, and then Ellie's voice cuts through our private moment. "Hey, Brooke. Sorry to interrupt, but Brian is looking for you. I think he wants to know where you want him to mail your final paycheck."

I wipe at my eyes, trying to quickly put myself together before Ellie whips the door open and sees me having an emotional breakdown. "Yup. Got it!" I call back. "I'll be right there."

The conversation doesn't feel over between us, but what's left to say? We could go around in circles all day, crying and slowly tearing each other down until one of us caves, and it would have to be me. I'd have to give up the opportunity in Spain, and I can't do it. It's better that he came to see me at work, in this cold, sterile room where there's no chance of us forgetting ourselves. I've been given an opportunity to leave this hellhole, to do what I love most, and he knows that.

I step back out of James' arms and try a timid smile on for size. It feels tight and fake, but I hope he doesn't notice. One of us has to be strong, and if he thinks I'm doing the right thing, he won't try to stop me. My mask of resolve doesn't have to be perfect, it just has to be enough.

His pointer finger hooks beneath my chin and he lifts gently until our gazes clash in an unspoken goodbye. The tears I'd momentarily capped start to spill down my cheeks again. James doesn't wipe them away. Instead, he bends down and presses a soft kiss to my lips. It's the only farewell he gives before he turns and opens the door. Ellie nearly topples into the space, most likely having been listening with one ear pressed to the door. James steps around her and turns down the corridor.

It's the last time I'll see him before I leave.

Had I known it at the time, maybe I would have done things differently. Maybe I wouldn't have stood immobile in that shitty employee lounge, looking to Ellie to wipe my tears and solve my problems. She wraps me in her arms and I bury my face against her shoulder. I cry at the unfairness of it all, the choice that was forced out of me and the lesson that's getting hammered home in the most unforgiving way: you can't have it all.

James once asked me where I want to be in five years. Wherever I am, I hope I'm not looking back on this day, wishing I'd done something different, because if I had run after James and caught up with him before he left, if I'd jumped into his arms and told him I'd stay, maybe I wouldn't have regretted it.

I'll never know, and that's what makes life worth living.

CHAPTER TWENTY-TWO

Spain is beautiful, hot, and sunny—the antithesis of how I feel inside.

It's basically that annoyingly upbeat friend you want to deck in the face every time she comes around. To her, everything is great and carbs don't matter.

I am not in the mood.

I arrive at the tail end of summer, when the days stretch out long and tourists are deployed in full force. I suppose I'm one of them, another newbie trying to learn the layout of the city as quickly as possible. Public transportation takes some getting used to, and I hate having to use my GPS to find my way. In those first few days, I get lost so many times that I vow to never leave the safety of Nicolás and Diego's apartment until I have all the city blocks memorized 10 times over.

The culture shock is hard to overcome. Though I speak the language, Barcelona still takes some getting used to. There's no Ellie to decompress with at the end of a long day, and even though we FaceTime each other constantly, it's not the same.

I'm homesick and filled with niggling doubt over my decision to come, though I try to separate the two from each other. Even without James, moving to a new country would have still been a major adjustment. I try to give myself enough space to feel sad without allowing myself to get lost in the what-ifs.

I'm here now, and it's time to get used to it.

The usual loneliness that settles in while traveling alone is relieved by the fact that I'm living with Diego, Nicolás, and the girls. We live in a three-story townhouse in the heart of the city, and I have the entire top floor to myself: a small bedroom, bathroom, and sitting area with a huge picture window. Most nights, Olive and Luciana wander up to see what I'm doing, even though their fathers implore them to give me private time. I don't mind it though. I crave the company, and since they love to read so much, I try to join them whenever possible. We tear through books together, all of us a little intimidated by our new surroundings. They'll be starting at a new school soon, and Luciana is worried she won't be able to make friends. Olive is more concerned that she might have fallen behind other students in her class, so I asked her dads to pick up some workbooks early. Now, we work ahead together in the evenings to ensure she'll feel extra prepared for the first day of school. Luciana, on the other hand, insists on taking "full advantage of the summer holiday", which means anything but homework.

Honestly, in those early weeks, I use the two of them as a shield against the homesickness. As long as I'm focused on Olive and Luciana's troubles, mine can take a back seat, and maybe if I can stay distracted long enough, they might eventually disappear altogether.

If my sadness is obvious to others, Diego and Nicolás do a good job of respecting my privacy. It's not until one night over dinner, a few weeks after our arrival, that Diego asks me point blank if I've left someone behind in the United States. I shake my head hard, trying to keep my focus down on my lap. They don't push the subject, instead quickly shifting to discuss some presentation Diego has coming up at the university. I finish my food quickly, push away from the table, and escape to the third floor.

Luciana finds me sitting on the foot of my bed, staring out the window that faces the market across the street. Even at night, it's packed to the gills with tourists and locals browsing the various stalls.

She stands at the door, toeing the threshold, too scared to invade my space until I give a silent nod of approval. She runs over and leaps onto the bed, scooting close until her hip presses against mine. Her short legs can't reach the floor and I glance down, admiring her glittery Toms.

When she speaks, I'm surprised to hear such profound sadness in her tone. "You know, I miss *my* boyfriend too."

Her admission catches me so off guard that I'm helpless to quell the burst of laughter that spills out of me.

She shoots me a death stare. "What's funny?"

"No." I wipe the smile off my face. "Nothing."

It's not. Luciana might be young, but she's perceptive and thoughtful. If she cared about a boy back in the United States, she likely carried those feelings across the ocean with us.

"Tell me about him," I ask, tapping my shoulder against hers.

For half an hour, she goes on and on about a boy named Collin who was the nicest person in her class back home. Her dads don't want her dating yet, of course, BECAUSE SHE'S NINE, so she and Collin had to "just be friends at school". I expected her relationship obstacles to pale in comparison to what I'm dealing with, but to hear her tell it, it's pretty close.

"My friend Valerie likes him too, and the day I left, she told me she was going to marry him."

Damn, nine-year-olds are savages.

"What did you tell her?"

She shrugs. "That it was Collin's choice to make. If he wants to marry her, then that would be okay. As long as he's happy."

"Even if that means you lose him?" I push.

She looks up at me like I'm an idiot. "Ms. Brooke, I can't expect him to wait around for me forever. I mean, we're almost 10 years old."

Touché.

"Do you want to talk about what's going on with you now?" she asks with kind, gentle eyes. "Maybe I can help."

Though my usual emotional support system has not included girls that still use a Barbie toothbrush, I'm tempted by her offer. Ellie is exhausted with hearing me talk about James and how much I miss him, and nobody else knows about the things we've gone through.

I don't go into any of the PG-13 details with Luciana, but I tell her enough to make her nod sympathetically.

"Star-crossed lovers," she concludes with a long sigh. Then she taps her chin like a thoughtful psychologist. "I know you're really sad, but Olive and I think it's boring when you're sad. So you should just stop."

"What?"

"Stop being sad."

Oh, okay. I hadn't realized it was that easy.

"I miss Collin too, but I don't let it ruin my day. I still play with Olive and smile and stuff. And I can still read. You just *pretend* to read."

I thought I was being more convincing with that...

"What do you think I should do?"

I tell myself I'm humoring her, when really she's giving me the best advice of my life.

"Just smile."

"Smile?"

"Yeah, even when you don't feel like it. My dad says smiling is infectious. It'll make you feel better."

I spread my lips, straining my face into an odd caricature of a smile.

She erupts into a fit of giggles. "No! Not like that!"

I contort my features into another silly face. "How about this? Am I doing it now?"

She claps her hands over her face and shakes her head fervently. "Ugh! That's not even close!"

"No, no." I reach for her hands to pull them away from her eyes. "I got it now. Look."

• • •

It takes me a long time to get my genuine smile back. For weeks, I wallow in regret, scared to admit to myself that I might have made a mistake in coming to Spain. The thought keeps me up at night, long after the rest of the house has gone to bed. I lie awake, listening to the sounds of Barcelona outside my window, imagining what my life might have been like if I'd stayed back home in Austin. It's a painful game to play, and some nights, I come close to calling James. I pull up his contact, hover over the green button, and my heart starts to pound in anticipation. I think he will answer, especially in those early weeks when our heartbreak is fresh and the possibility of reconciliation within reach.

There's one incident, a night that starts with pure intentions. Diego finds a few bottles of wine at the market on his way home from work. It's apparently a steal, some really fancy shit he scores at a bargain price. He wants to celebrate, so after the girls go to sleep, we stay up watching bad TV and guzzling down glasses like there's no tomorrow. We finish off the good stuff and then dip into the cheap bottles. Honestly, it all tastes the same to me.

Bad TV gets boring, and they decide they want to relive their teenage years with a game of truth or dare.

I go first and choose dare.

They dare me to call the guy I've been so mopey about.

"No," I insist, suddenly feeling the wine churn in my stomach.

Nicolás reaches for my phone on the coffee table and slaps it into my palm. "A dare is a dare!"

I shake my head. "Something else. Anything."

I look to Diego for a lifeline, but he's giddy from the wine and can't stop laughing long enough to come to my aid.

"Fine."

I pull up James' number, trying to ignore my shaking hand. I'm pretending this is a huge inconvenience, something I'd rather not do, but deep down I've been wanting to do it for months. I want to hear his voice and listen to him tell me to come home. I've replayed our last conversation at Twin Oaks so many times that it's like an old record, warped and distorted. Did he really ask me to stay, or have I imagined he did so many times that now I think it's reality?

"CALL!" Nicolás says, punching the button for me.

It starts to ring, and it feels like I just leapt out of an airplane. My heart beats wildly. My stomach flips and then clenches tight.

"Speaker, speaker!" Diego insists.

I oblige, and the last two rings reverberate loudly across their small living room.

My palms are sweaty. For that matter, so are my pits.

Finally, the call clicks on and a soft, feminine voice starts to talk.

"Hey! Brooke! Is that—"

I don't hear the rest of the sentence because I press the red end button so fast and so hard, I nearly crack my phone's screen.

Diego and Nicolás both groan in protest.

"*Come on*!" Diego says. "Why'd you hang up?!"

"Because some woman answered!"

My phone vibrates in my hand and I look down. James is calling back, or at least his phone is calling me back. It's probably the woman. His wife? Girlfriend? I'm not in the right state of mind to handle this. I'm going to spew wine all over their distressed leather couch. Shows them for getting me drunk—they had it coming.

"Answer it!" Nicolás shouts.

I do, holding the phone to my ear with a shaky hand.

"Brooke?" the woman asks.

It's the same voice from a second ago.

"Uhh, yes?" I answer hesitantly.

"This is Beth, James' assistant?"

Relief floods my veins and I sag against the couch.

"Oh, right. Of course."

Makes sense, I guess. Americans are still at work at this time.

"James is in a meeting at the moment so he redirected his personal calls to me. Would you like me take a message and have him call you back?"

A message?! How mortifying.

"Oh! Dear god no."

I think I hear her chuckle, but I can't be sure.

"Brooke, I think he'd be happy to hear from you."

How would she know that? And what would I even say if I *did* leave him a message?

Nothing poetic comes to mind, just a lot of drunk rambling about the potential for love and maybe a possible reconciliation. She hangs there in silence for a few seconds as I ponder an impromptu proposal. No. *Hell no.*

Then it gets worse, because I hear James' voice in the background. He's bidding someone farewell, and then his attention turns to Beth.

"Who's on the line?" he asks.

I pinch my eyes closed and try to keep my calm. His voice is just like I remember: confident and hard, all business. I leap into action when Beth stammers, "Oh, umm…"

"No message!" I plead, "and Beth, please, *please* don't tell him it's me."

Then I hang up and toss my phone across the couch like it's on fire.

I was so close to talking to him that my body shakes with an embarrassing amount of adrenaline.

Diego and Nicolás sit there staring at me in shocked silence. Their eyes are wide and their mouths are hanging open. Diego pushes his glasses higher on the bridge of his nose. Nicolás clears his throat. Sounds from the street drift in through the open window.

"Happy?" I ask, reaching for my wine glass and polishing off the last few ounces in the hopes that it'll calm me down.

"Oh my god. That was…something. Are you still in love with him?" Diego asks gently.

"No!" I insist with a hard shake of my head, and then I

emphasize, "I never was, I don't think."

He tilts his head, studying me thoughtfully.

"I wasn't! Probably!"

His eyes widen in a mixture of fear and shock, and then he holds up his hands in innocence. "Of course. Right. Whose turn is it?"

I exact retribution by forcing Diego to drink a jar of pickle juice, and I force out hearty laughter while he does it. In reality, I'm seconds away from losing my shit. This distance I've put between James and myself has been a safeguard against my feelings, and calling him was a terrible idea. It's like I opened Pandora's box, and though I may try to cram all my half-baked feelings back inside, they don't quite fit. The box is lumpy and straining at the seams. Mentally, I try sitting on it like an overstuffed piece of carry-on luggage, but it doesn't work. That night when I go upstairs, I pull James' Caltech t-shirt and gym shorts out of their spot in the top drawer of my dresser and slip them on. I don't wear them often, fearful that the cotton will get too worn. In the beginning, they still smelled like him, but the scent is fading.

I crawl into bed and focus on how the soft cotton feels against my bare skin. It's like I'm poking a bruise over and over again, but I can't stop. In some sad way, the pain feels like my only connection left to him.

After that, I never call again, and the days add together to form weeks, and then months start to divide now and the moment when we last spoke. It finally gets to a point where it would be really awkward to reach out again, and that moment brings with it a fresh wave of heartache, almost like I know I'm crossing the finish line, and once I do, there's no going back. Luciana is perceptive during those weeks, doing her best to distract me.

We explore the city together after I pick the girls up from school each day. On weekends, we set our sights on a new destination, either a museum or a park. We love to bring a blanket and lie outside in the early afternoon. We all get tan from walking around outside so much, and the girls tell me I'm "prettier than I've ever been". It's a sweet compliment to hear from two preteen girls, considering they're the most brutally honest focus group demographic in existence. For instance, they once told me I should never wear pale yellow. "It makes you look like rotten milk." Alrighty then.

The weather turns chilly, and I'm supposed to go home for the holidays. My family misses me—Ellie most of all—but I beg out of it. I'm not ready to leave Spain; I've put so much work into forming a life here, but it's so tenuous. Stepping back into my old life, even for a few weeks, feels like it would be a major setback. So, instead, I stay and celebrate the holidays with Diego and Nicolás and the girls. Those weeks are extra special. We decorate a tree in early December and sip hot chocolate every night after dinner. It gets to the point where I can't stand the sight of a mini marshmallow, which, for me, is saying something. On Christmas morning, they surprise the girls and me with matching aquamarine bikes, and we make promises to use them every day this spring. I have visions of exploring the city on two wheels, and I'm giddy thinking about it.

During the coldest nights, Luciana sneaks up to sleep in my bed with me. Her dads want me to set boundaries with her, but I can't work up the nerve to do it. She's the absolute worst person to share a bed with—her feet end up near my face more nights than not—but nights are the loneliest for me, and with her there, it's easy to forget that.

 **CHAPTER TWENTY-THREE**

When I first moved to Spain, I toyed with the idea of inviting my mom to visit. Honestly, I didn't expect her to actually take me up on it, but in that first year, she visits me three times. I even take a month off and we travel through Europe together, just the two of us. It's painfully awkward for the first few days as we readjust to being around one another 24/7. I feel like I'm walking on eggshells, careful not to talk too much or too little. At dinner, when I want red wine but she wants white, I acquiesce. When she wants to tour the Parthenon but I want to head back to the hotel for an afternoon nap, I down an espresso and brave the crowds for her. I'm aware of how much shampoo I use when I shower. I deliberately let her take the side of the bed she prefers. It's exhausting and draining, and after the first week, I think I'm going to have a nervous breakdown, but each day, I grow a little more comfortable in my own skin. I push back and assert myself more and more, testing the limits of our reconstructed relationship.

By the time we're a few weeks into the trip, I finally realize she isn't going to ditch me just because I'd rather eat pasta than share salmon with her. It's a good revelation to come to because if I have to stuff another bite of bland fish into my mouth, I'm going to barf. After that, the trip really settles into place. We spend long evenings chatting at small cafes, people watching in between our conversations.

Sometimes we talk about the past, a little at a time, until one evening, after a few glasses of wine, I work up the courage to ask her if she ever regretted leaving us.

She frowns, seemingly confused by the question. "I never thought of it like that, like I was leaving you."

I laugh awkwardly. "Well…you did."

Her shoulders droop as she tilts her head, her light brown eyes studying me sadly. "I gave you and your sister a choice. I wanted you to come with me."

I shake my head. I don't remember that.

"Obviously your father and I couldn't stay together after I had the affair with Jorge. I moved out of the house and asked you if you wanted to come with me."

"Yeah, once."

And I obviously turned her down. In those early days, Ellie and I resented her for tearing our family apart.

"No. I asked you over and over again if you were sure you wanted to live with your father. You and Ellie insisted, so I lived with Jorge in Austin for two years, hoping the two of you would come around once you were ready to talk."

"I don't remember this," I say on a weak whisper.

She sighs and glances away. "You were young."

"I thought you left us and went straight into the Peace Corps."

"No, we didn't leave until you were in high school."

"What?!"

How has time twisted so much of my memory? I always remember her leaving when I was younger, or maybe I just assumed she did.

I always think back on that time in my life with resentment. I carried a bitterness about the fact that she could pick up and leave us so quickly. She tells me she wanted to take me along with her during her first Peace Corps assignment, but my father thought it would be better for Ellie and me to stay in Austin and finish school the normal way.

I'm shocked into silence, my brain working overtime to try to reconcile my memories with reality. I decide to push a little further and ask if she ever resented us, if maybe she would have preferred a life with no children. At that, she reaches across the table for my hands and squeezes them tightly, imploring me to listen to her.

"I love you and Ellie so much. I wanted you from the very first moment I found out I was pregnant." She leans forward and levels her gaze with me to ensure that I'm listening. "Do you hear me?"

My throat is too tight to speak, so I nod.

"My affair with Jorge was terrible and I regret hurting you and your father, but you have to know it had nothing to do with you or Ellie." She smiles and quickly wipes the tear rolling down her cheek. "I love being your mom, and I know there are times where I've really sucked at it. I'm still learning, but I want you to know that you've always been first in my heart. Always."

It's the longest, most exhausting night of my life. The conversation ends with me crying against her shoulder, accepting her apologies and promising to leave the past in the past. When we leave the restaurant with her arm slung around my shoulder, it really feels like we're turning over a new leaf.

The last week of our trip, Ellie flies over to join us. We spread those seven days out along the Amalfi Coast, lounging on the beach and eating enough pasta that we all have to casually unzip our jeans beneath the table. It's a healing and bonding trip, one that will undoubtedly change everything that comes after it.

I return to Spain invigorated and ready to jump back into work. It's been almost a year and a half since I first left Austin, and I've never felt more in control of my life and destiny. I have goals for the next few months. Fall is upon us, and I remember how nice it was this time last year. Luciana, Olive, and I sit up in my room, mapping out new destinations around the city. I don't let them use Google Maps to figure out how to get around—sometimes, all we take is a handful of jotted notes, a compass, and a sense of adventure. The weather has already turned too cold for the beaches, but that won't stop us from taking our bikes out nearly every day. I want to take in more of the architecture and Olive agrees, but Luciana would rather eat her way through the city one deep fried pastry at a time. I'm willing to oblige them both.

We settle on taking a cooking class together every Friday night for a few months. The girls manage to make fancy Spanish cuisine without causing permanent property or bodily damage; this constitutes success in my book. As for me, I manage to catch the attention of the very single, very flirty cooking instructor. He tastes my food and tells me enthusiastically that I'm the best student in the class. There's an actual chef in the class, so I know he's flirting, not to mention I burn half of my dishes while trying to keep Olive's pyrotechnic proclivities at bay. Once, when I turned my back for one second, she piped the flame on her classroom stove as high as it would go. The only casualty was Luciana's right eyebrow, which I proceeded to recreate with a brow pencil for two months until the hairs regrew. By the end, when Diego and Nicolás are none the wiser, I reflect on how frightening it is that these little girls can keep a secret of that magnitude. God help their future husbands.

On the last day of our class, the instructor asks me out on a date. He says he's been wanting to ask me for months, but he didn't want to break the student-teacher code of ethics. I didn't think there was such a thing in a non-graded community cooking course, but maybe things are different in Spain.

Olive and Luciana make kissing faces in the background as I try to think of the most polite way to turn him down. There's a lot of "it's not a good time for me" and "I don't want to lead you on" before he finally has to cut me off with a tight, awkward smile. He tells me he understands, says he just got out a relationship himself. The entire way home, the girls tease me about what my life could have been like if only I'd said yes.

"You could have been his sous chef!" Olive exclaims, like this is a plausible turn my life could take.

I dismiss her suggestion with a shrug. "Ugh, and wear that dumb chef's hat all day? No thanks. Luciana, stop touching your face! You're wiping away your eyebrow."

• • •

The cooking instructor isn't the first man to pursue me in Spain. Don't get me wrong, I don't keep a harem, but for a woman who spends most of her time holed up tutoring young girls, I deflect a fair number of suitors. There's a barista that works at a cafe down the road from where we live. He's there every morning when I stroll in after dropping the girls at school and knows my usual order, but most of the time he throws in a fluffy croissant or pastry for free. I should probably stop leading him on, but...they happen to be really good pastries.

Diego and Nicolás are perceptive. They ask me about my personal life every now and then, focusing on the details of my love life (or lack thereof). When we first moved to Spain, I told them I wasn't interested in dating, said I wanted to soak in everything Spain has to offer on my own. They bought that response for a while, but now, they grow more skeptical with each weekend I spend with the girls instead of going out. I'm supposed to have the weekends off. They want me to go out on dates and meet friends, but I'd rather just stay in, eat dates, and watch *Friends*.

Right around the time our cooking class ends that fall, I nestle into a comfortable realization. I come to the conclusion that there are no mistakes in life, just decisions. I chose to come to Spain and here I am, finding my footing. I had a goal of succeeding as a tutor and exploring the world, and that's just what I've gotten to do. There's a sense of accomplishment that comes with that, and a reminder that whoever came up with "This too shall pass" really knew what they were talking about. Sometimes things pass like giant, painful kidney stones, but in the end, they pass.

When I first left Austin, the future looked bleak. My heart was broken, my world flipped on its head. Now, looking back, it's hard to regret my decision. In fact, I conclude that there was never a right or wrong decision at all. I didn't make a mistake in leaving the States, just like I wouldn't have been making a mistake in staying behind for James. I still miss him—of course I do. Maybe I always will. Maybe that's part of the lesson I've learned here: some people carve their initials so deeply into your heart, they'll always be a part of you. James and I had a tumultuous few months, and I felt more for him than I've felt about any man I've ever met. Even now, his old clothes are still the most comfortable pajamas in my dresser, and I wear them to sleep a few times a month. I sometimes scour the internet for news about him or his company, but only late at night, and only after I've had a little bit of wine.

During the day, when I'm busy and enjoying life, I feel whole and normal again. I'm more excited for the future than reminiscent about the past. I think Diego and Nicolás can see that, because it's right around this time that Diego announces he's bringing a friend for dinner—a young, handsome colleague named Alejandro.

 **CHAPTER TWENTY-FOUR**

"*That's* what you're wearing?" Luciana asks, eyeing my dress from her perch on my bed and scrunching her nose in distaste.

"What's wrong with this?" I ask, spinning in a circle to take myself in from all angles in the small full-length mirror mounted on the back of my door. I'm wearing a simple white sundress. I've worn it a hundred times before, and she's never said anything about it.

"It's fine for any other night but...Alejandro is coming to dinner tonight!"

I nod. "And?"

"So maybe you should put something else on," she says with a pointed glare. When I don't make a move to change, she hops up off my bed and starts rifling through my closet until she comes back out with a slinky black dress I packed on a whim and have not worn, or even entertained the idea of wearing, even once.

"This!" she says, her eyes wide with wonder. "It looks like something a lady of the night would wear!"

I laugh and yank it out of her hand, hanging it back up where it belongs. "That dress isn't appropriate. Also, that phrase doesn't mean what you think it does."

She frowns. "Fine, but the dress you have on makes you look frumpy."

"What? No way." I reach down to lovingly smooth out

the faithful cotton fabric. "This dress is a classic."

"Exactly," she stresses with every ounce of preteen attitude roiling inside her tiny frame. "And it shows. There are...one...two...three gelato stains down the front."

Oh, well, yeah. I try in vain to clear the most noticeable stain with the pad of my thumb. It's there to stay, but it's tiny, hardly visible at all really. I ignore her remaining reasons for why I should change and instead reach for the hair tie around my wrist and twist my hair into a low ponytail at the nape of my neck.

"Yeah, of course! Why wear your hair down, how it looks the *prettiest*, when you can just throw it up in a ponytail!" She throws her hands up in defeat. "You know where a pony's tail is, right? *On its butt!*"

"Audrey Hepburn wore a ponytail," I remind her.

"Yeah, but Audrey Hepburn also probably went on tons of dates! You haven't had a single date since we've been here!"

It's true, not a one. I've been a lone wolf since arriving in Spain and that's the way I'd like to keep it, hence the dress and the ponytail.

I pat her on the head (which she hates) and then pass her up to start down the stairs toward the kitchen. I can hear Olive down there helping her dads prep for dinner. Luciana begrudgingly follows behind me, grumbling under her breath about my "undateable" hair.

When we step into the kitchen, Olive looks up and smiles timidly at me. "I like your dress, Ms. Brooke."

I thank her while aiming an I-told-you-so grin at Luciana. She sticks her tongue out at me and winds around the back of the kitchen island to steal a piece of bread Diego just took out of the oven. He shoos her away, lest she ruin her appetite before dinner even starts.

My eyes widen as I scan the kitchen. Diego and Nicolás have gone all out for the occasion. The large, antique dining table is already covered in appetizers and wine. Nicolás hurries over, asking me if I'm excited to meet Alejandro.

"I'm sure if he's a friend of yours he can't be too bad," I say with a casual shrug.

He steps closer and drops his voice to a whisper. "Diego tells me half the women at the university have eyes for him."

I hum in mock interest. "Sounds like he must be one hell of a professor."

He throws up his hands, exasperated by my lack of enthusiasm. "Forgive me for the intrusion, but you aren't still interested in that man back home, are you?" He turns to Diego. "What was his name?"

"James, I think," Diego supplies.

My heart leaps at the mention of his name. "Nope. Thanks for asking though," I add with a quick, easy smile.

He narrows his eyes in disbelief then quickly changes tactics. "Right. Good." Then his gaze drops slightly. "Hey, it's the gelato dress!"

Luciana claps across the room. "Ha! SEE?!"

Jesus! What is it with this family and my clothes?!

"All right, if you guys want me to change, I'll—"

There's a knock on the front door, and all four of them freeze in panic then turn to me.

Diego drops his salad tongs and wipes his hands on the front of his apron. "No, no. The dress is fine—endearing even. Anyway, it's too late to change." Without warning, he rounds the island and beelines for me. Then he reaches up and tugs the ponytail out of my hair. My long, thick black hair tumbles down my back, and he smiles in appreciation. "Much better. Now, could you please answer the door?"

I get it. This dinner is a setup. They feel bad for my lonely heart, and they want to set me up with a nice, handsome man. I don't even have the energy to be angry with them. A part of me is curious to see if this mythic Alejandro can stir something within me that other men in Spain have yet to evoke. I've seen enough men to write a Dr. Suess book about it: tall men, short men, rich men, poor men...clergymen, firemen, postmen, doormen. None of them have made me feel even a sliver of what I still feel for James.

I curse, angry that I'm still playing this game with myself. James isn't in Spain. He's in Austin, and likely married now. My stomach twists at the thought of Lacy. It'd be easy to figure out if they were together. Ellie asks periodically if I want an update about him, and I always, *always* turn her down. It's a slippery slope, and we both agreed early on that it was best if she stopped telling me what she knows about him.

So far, it's proven successful, because if I don't know whether or not he's married, I don't have to come to grips with the fact that I'm just as hopelessly lovesick over him as I was when I first left.

I take a deep breath and open the door.

Alejandro stands on the doorstep with a bottle of cava in one hand and flowers in the other. They're sunflowers wrapped in butcher paper with a thin ribbon tied around the middle. When he sees me standing on the doorway, his brows rise in shock. Apparently, I'm not the only one who's being set up.

In the two seconds I stand there before I greet him, I come to the conclusion that he is indeed the most handsome man I've seen since arriving in this country. He's everything you'd want in a Latin lover: thick hair; dark, smoldering eyes; olive skin; a strong, muscular frame; and a smile that widens as he watches me assess him. He's wearing a black leather jacket and nice-fitting jeans with boots that look entirely too stylish for most men to pull off. He's a danger to all womankind.

I reach out my hand in a friendly greeting. *"Hi, I'm Brooke,"* I say in Spanish.

He accepts my handshake with a firm grip and I wait for the butterflies to kick in. "I'm Alejandro, but my friends call me Alex."

"Ah, you speak English?"

He nods and releases my hand. "I do, but my accent could use some work."

It's true. He speaks well, but it's clear it's not his native tongue. As I lead him through the entry and toward the kitchen, he explains that he's spoken the language for a few years, but he doesn't have many people he can practice with here in Spain. Once we join the others, Diego rushes forward to accept the flowers and wine, promising him I am the perfect person for the job.

"She's been helping our girls keep up with their English and has even started to teach them French!"

As proof, Luciana, who is sitting at the table, groaning in protest at having to wait before starting appetizers, says, *"J'ai tellement faim. Ils m'affament ici."*

Translation: I'm so hungry. They starve me here.

I smile innocently and turn to the adults. "She means to say she's pleased to meet you."

Alejandro smiles appreciatively at Luciana, and then Nicolás ushers us all to the table. A large glass of wine is placed in my hand just before I'm pushed into the chair

293

beside Alejandro. I feel like a marionette.

I shoot him a death stare over my shoulder, but he's oblivious, too focused on his crusade to make Alejandro fall in love with me. As they start doling out appetizers, I'm forced to sit as Nicolás performs the role of a mother in the 1800s trying to marry off her eldest daughter.

"Did you know, Alejandro, that our Brooke is an excellent chef? She just recently took a class with the girls."

I smile sheepishly. "Chef is a strong word."

Diego leans forward. "And she's very accomplished in languages. She speaks English, Spanish, and French fluently."

Alejandro nods at me, impressed.

"Not to mention," Nicolás adds impatiently, "she's an *angel* with our girls. I mean, they're impossible to handle on a good day—"

"HEY!" Luciana cuts in.

"But Brooke quells their worst tantrums with great aplomb."

Alejandro's smile fades gently. "Aplomb?"

Nicolás waves away the language barrier. "Oh, it just means she's calm in tough situations."

"Oh." Alejandro's gaze cuts to me as he nods and smiles tightly. "Okay."

They take his lackluster response to mean they haven't played up my attributes enough, so for another 10 minutes, I sit in silence as they continue to regale Alejandro with all of my talents and skills. Apparently I am "an avid reader", "a world traveler", and "a laundry expert", and when that's still not enough to convince him, they turn to a cheap tactic: outright talking about my looks.

"I mean, she's beautiful, isn't she?" Diego says.

"Not many women like her," Nicolás adds. "Look at those sapphire eyes!"

Luciana crosses her arms and furrows her brows, announcing, "You guys are being really weird."

Olive agrees. "It's like you're trying to sell Ms. Brooke off or something."

A laugh bursts out of me before I can stop it, and then I slap my hand over my mouth, trying to salvage the moment. Diego aims a hard stare at me, probably annoyed that I'm not doing more to sell myself. I shrug and sip my wine, glad Alejandro isn't making the situation any worse. He's staring down at the table, probably too embarrassed to meet my eye at this point. I'm not sure what they told him to convince him to come to dinner, but I doubt it involved anything close to the truth.

Before we're done with appetizers, I've drained my wine and am in desperate need of a refill.

I push my chair back and ask if I can get anyone else anything while I'm up. Alejandro stands and accompanies me over to the kitchen, insisting that he'd like to help me. I can feel Diego and Nicolás staring us down as we walk away. They probably think we're going to sneak off and make out, but the moment we're out of earshot of the table, I turn to Alejandro.

"I think there's been a misunderstanding."

"A misunderstanding?"

His Spanish accent is so damn adorable that for a moment, I try very hard to feel something for him...anything. God, it would be fun to love a man like Alejandro, but then I'm reminded of another pair of dark eyes back home in Austin and I turn away.

"Yes." I smile tightly and point between us. "I think Diego and Nicolás want us to date."

He looks down at his shoes and sighs before addressing me. "Brooke, I'm not really...er, well, you're beautiful, of course...but this isn't a good time for me."

Though he's struggling to come up with the right words, it's clear what he's trying to say.

"No. Don't worry," I tell him, meeting his eyes with a bright, honest smile. "They're just convinced I need to be set up with a nice guy and you fit the bill. Consider it a compliment."

His brown eyes light up with amusement. "But you don't want that? To be set up?"

I refill our wine glasses before I work up the nerve to answer honestly. "No. I don't want that."

He smiles, visibly relieved. "Then here." He holds his glass up for a toast. "To new friends."

His emphasis on the word ensures that we're both on the same page. When we return to the table, shoulder to shoulder, the family's faces light up expectantly. I let the illusion linger for a moment before proudly announcing that Alejandro and I are not going on a date.

"Okay," Luciana says, sitting up straight and pointing her fork at Alejandro. "So does that mean he's up for grabs?"

CHAPTER TWENTY-FIVE

My family has finally convinced me to come home for a visit. It's mid-December, and ever since I skipped out on the holidays last year, my dad has made it a point to guilt me into returning home this year. He bought my ticket *last* December just so I couldn't back out. That's a year of planning, friends. Now, I'm not sure how I feel about it. I'm excited to see him and Ellie, and—*dare I say*—even Martha. All these months apart have actually helped me to see how much I genuinely care for her. I know, shocking. I'll probably promptly renew my annoyance with her upon my arrival, but those first few moments of our reunion will be wholesome and Hallmark-y.

Diego and Nicolás are happy that I'm going home, but Luciana has been moody for the last two weeks, punishing me for having the audacity to leave her. Last week, she tried to hide my laptop in the hopes that I couldn't go home without it. I found it under her mattress, unharmed except for the ominous record of transatlantic flight crashes on Wikipedia that she left open as a warning. This week, she's subjected me to the silent treatment. Not a peep has left her mouth in over 72 hours, and I haven't decided if I should be annoyed or impressed by her resolution. Even now, as I finish packing up my suitcase, she sits on the edge of my bed, aiming her best death glare at me.

"Is there something you'd like to say, Luce?" I ask,

amused.

She zips her lips with her thumb and forefinger, proving just how far she's willing to go to prove her point.

"Now I wish I had taught you sign language! I'm going to miss you when I'm gone," I say, knowing that's what she needs to hear most. "And if you tell me what you want, I'll bring back some good stuff from the States. You know those Central Market chocolate truffles you always talk about missing? Maybe if you speak up, I'll bring some back."

She fidgets and her face reddens, as if the strain of staying silent is starting to take its toll.

"Oh, I wonder if a cupcake from Sugar Mama's would travel well?" I ask, sounding casual and aloof.

She stifles a groan.

"No, you're right, probably not."

That does it.

With an explosive exhale, she leaps off the bed and grabs my forearms. "PLEASE BRING ME BACK A CUPCAKE!"

I smile, proud of my hard-won victory. "I'll see what I can do."

She sneers and tosses my arms away, returning to her perch on my bed. "Are you *sure* you want to go? It's such a long way."

"I want to see my family."

"But you FaceTime with Ellie like every day. What's the difference?"

"Luce, c'mon. Think of how much you would miss Olive if she was halfway around the world."

She shrugs, staring down at her nails, completely unbothered by the concept. "Sometimes I wish she was on another world entirely." I glare at her until she relents.

"Fine, sure, I guess I'd miss her a little."

I throw a cardigan into my carry-on. "You weren't like this when I left for that trip with my mom last year. How is this any different?"

She looks down at her dangling feet as they sway back and forth off the side of my bed. "Because it feels different."

"How?"

"Because...I don't know. My dad said something the other day..."

She still won't look up and answer me, but I know exactly what she's referencing. I had a conversation with Diego a few nights ago. I was in the kitchen, enjoying a bowl of cereal as a midnight snack when he walked in and took a seat beside me at the island. I'd already gathered a bowl and spoon for him, so he poured himself some cereal and together, we ate in silence.

It's a nightly ritual for us because I'm a night owl and he's an insomniac. Sometimes we talk, but that night, we enjoyed the quiet cadence of spoons clinking against bowls and teeth munching on cereal. I was halfway finished when he finally spoke up, catching me off guard with his topic of choice: "I'm glad you're going home."

"Oh..." I glanced over at him. "Yeah, I am too."

He aimed his furrowed brows down at his cereal bowl. "I know when you first started, we didn't put an end date in your contract."

"Right."

"But, I think that was a mistake."

I dropped my spoon into my bowl with a loud *CLINK* and turned to him, stricken by the idea that I was being let go.

"Have I done something wrong?"

He smiled and shook his head. "No, of course not, and I'm not firing you, Brooke," he said with a low chuckle. "You've been wonderful, and I want you to stay with us until I'm 80. God, Luciana would love it."

I frowned, confused by where the conversation was headed.

"But I don't think that's what *you* need. By not setting an end date, I feel like we're enabling you in running away from something."

"I love this job," I insisted.

He nodded. "And we love having you here."

"So then there's nothing to discuss," I declared, turning back to my cereal and attempting to put the kibosh on the whole conversation. He let me have silence for a few minutes before he launched back into the topic at hand.

"Tell me, have you made a single friend since you've been here? Have you tried to make it your home?"

I thought back to the few people I encountered in my daily life. There was the teacher at the girls' school who waved at me when I dropped them off and picked them up. There was the nice old lady who kept the bookshop a few blocks down. Sometimes she talked to me about books, but she also talked to her cat about books, so I didn't think I was special in that regard. There was the chef I turned down for a date, and of course, Alejandro. Other than that...

I sighed. "No, I guess not."

"Why do you think that is?"

"Because I like hanging out with you guys and Luciana and Olive." *Never mind that they're half my age.*

He nodded and stared down thoughtfully at his cereal bowl. "I think you're leaving out the most important reason."

There was no other reason, at least not one I had thought of, but he disagreed.

"You haven't put down roots here because you know it's not where you want to be."

Well that's some psychobabble if I've ever heard it.

I scooted my stool away from the island and stood to deposit my bowl in the sink.

"Of course I want to be here."

He laughed wistfully. "Brooke, when we met you in Austin, you reached for this job like it was a lifeline."

I snorted. "Because it was one! I hated that stupid job at that country club. Of course I was anxious to leave. Do you know how annoying it is to serve margaritas to snooty assholes?"

He nodded in understanding and then stood to join me at the sink. "I'm worried you still don't see it."

"Don't see what?" I asked, stepping back.

He looked at me out of the corner of his eye. "Why are you really here, Brooke?"

I gave him the most basic answer, the answer I'd clung to for the last year and a half. "Because I want to tutor your girls."

"*Why* are you *here*?" he repeated with emphasis.

"Because…" I grappled for another response. "I want to travel…I want to see the world."

"You have," he pointed out. "You've seen more of the world than most people will see in their entire lifetime. Do you feel any more fulfilled?" I narrowed my eyes, not liking where the conversation was going. Maybe he could tell I'd reached my limit because he stepped back and held up his hands in surrender. "I won't keep pushing you. The point of all of this was…I don't know…to let you know that if you head home and find that you'd like to stay, we'll be happy for you."

I frowned. "What about the girls?"

He smiled softly. "You've given them so much, but I think you might need them more than they need you."

Even days later, that conversation is still nagging at me. I know he was trying to give me an out if I wanted it, and though I appreciate his concern, I don't need it. I'll be returning to Spain in two weeks no matter what.

CHAPTER TWENTY-SIX

I dip toward the air-conditioning vent and close my eyes, sighing as the cold air blasts my face. It's two weeks until Christmas and Texas is unseasonably warm—we're talking low 90s. Poor Santa Claus is going to be a sweaty mess in that sleigh of his. I want to shred my bulky knit sweater like I'm the Hulk, but then Ellie would see that I stole her lacy bralette before I left for Spain, so instead, I suffer in silence.

"Jesus, how much stuff did you bring home for two weeks?!" Ellie groans before she slams the trunk.

I shrug. "Winter clothes are heavy."

"Yeah, and you don't even need them," she says, slipping into the driver's seat and buckling her seatbelt. "You should have brought flip-flops and a bikini."

I grin. "I did, *along* with my winter clothes. Why do you think my luggage is so heavy?"

She rolls her eyes and puts the car in drive.

It's been months since I've seen her and though I've already pissed her off, I know it's all for show. She's missed me as much as I've missed her, and if she wasn't currently hurtling down a highway at 80 MPH, I'd reach across the console and squeeze her as tight as I could. She'd hate it, which only makes me want to do it more.

I just finished nearly 17 hours of travel and smell like an old boot. By contrast, Ellie smells like an Herbal

Essences commercial and looks like she could star in one too. She's wearing cutoff jean shorts and a tank top. Her long blonde hair is braided down her back, loose and simple. I would tell her how pretty she looks, but her head is already big enough to fit on Mt. Rushmore, so I just keep it to myself.

It's a short drive to Westlake Hills, and while Ellie fills me in on all the drama that's been going on at Twin Oaks since we last spoke, I stare out the window trying to place the odd sense of foreboding that settled in my stomach the second my plane touched down on the tarmac.

I know it has to do with James and whether or not we'll cross paths while I'm in town. Austin is a big enough place that the odds of us bumping into each other randomly are slim to none. The only place I could possibly see him would be at Twin Oaks, and I have no plans to go there. Therefore, I shouldn't be worried. I won't see him. I'll stay for two weeks, hang out with family, and catch my flight back to Spain.

"—wait for the winter gala to be done! Martha has cranked up her annoying tendencies tenfold in the last few weeks."

The tail end of Ellie's rant catches my attention.

"Winter gala? For the Philanthropic League?"

"*Yes*," she stresses with a harsh scowl. "Have you not been listening?"

"Sorry. I zoned out." My apologetic half-smile doesn't work, so I add, "It's like 3 AM my time!"

"Yeah, yeah. Whatever."

She turns back to the road and starts to launch back into her rambling, but I'm curious. "When's the fundraiser?"

"Next week."

I brace myself for the worst possible news. "Are you going?"

Her amused smirk is enough of an answer on its own, but then she adds, "We both are."

No. I have the perfect out because like most normal adults, I don't travel with layers of taffeta stuffed next to my socks. No dress, no gala. I think this will be enough of an out on its own, but the second we arrive home, I suspect I'm wrong. My dad hugs me hard, telling me how happy he is to have me home. Martha stands to the side, wringing her hands out excitedly. She looks like she's about to combust, and I know, before she even tells me, that she already has a dress waiting for me.

How convenient.

She leads me upstairs to my room, where a large garment bag hangs on the front of my closet door.

"Open it!" she urges, pushing me forward.

"How did you know my size?" I ask, clinging to a final sliver of hope that it doesn't fit.

Her gaze flickers to Ellie just long enough to throw my dear sister under the bus.

Ellie snorts. "Cool your jets. I told her your size because she was going to get you a dress no matter what. This way, you won't look like a fuckin' lump."

"Ellie," Martha hisses at Ellie's use of a curse word.

I expect to find something stuffy and pink (like most of the clothes in Martha's closet) but when I unzip the bag and step back, I'm surprised to find an understated velvet gown such a dark shade of emerald green that it's almost black. When I try it on, at their urging, it fits like a glove. The long sleeves are snug around my arms, the top is tight around my hips and waist, and the skirt flares out gently before it reaches the ground. The high waist and V neckline bring an element of sexiness I'm surprised to find in such a simple design.

"And there's a slit," Ellie says, pointing to where a hint of my tan leg peeks through.

"It's gorgeous," I relent.

Martha claps excitedly. "YAY! So then you'll come?"

My mouth is open and a refusal is formed on the tip of my tongue, but then I meet Ellie's stare behind Martha's back and she shakes her head once then slices her finger across her neck in a threatening gesture.

Jesus, fine!

"I'll go."

• • •

The week before the gala passes more quickly than I would have liked. Since I'm not working, Martha enlists me to help her with last-minute things. Together, we drive around Austin, stopping off at high-end boutiques and designer showrooms. She's somehow managed to finagle a donation for the silent auction from every shop in the city, or so it seems. The day before the gala, the back of her Range Rover is packed to the gills with Louis Vuitton purses and spa goodie bags. There are Hermès bracelets and a few pairs of those Gucci loafers everyone and their dog is wearing these days.

We stop at florists and bakeries, confirming all the final details. She doesn't need me. I basically just sit quietly in the background, wondering if the cake they have displayed in the center of the table is edible or just for show. When I ask at the end of the meeting, they laugh politely before asking me to leave.

I'm technically supposed to be on vacation, but apparently, Martha has a rule against letting people relax. I haven't had a single day to sleep in and lounge around except for the morning of the gala, and I use it to my advantage. I'm knee-deep into a Bravo marathon when Martha finds me splayed out on the couch with coffee-stained pajamas and bedhead.

"Let's go! We're getting our hair done today," she sings with a chipper tone before reaching for the remote and turning off the TV mid-catfight.

"I'm all set," I tell her, pointing to the mess on top of my head.

She grimaces. "It needs a trim." Then she sniffs the air and scrunches her nose when she finds my aroma distasteful. "Probably a couple rounds of shampoo too."

Oh okay, MARTHA.

I heave my body off the couch with a groan and force my limbs into normal clothes. It's not that I don't love having someone else wash my hair, I just need a major break from Martha. Ellie and my dad have been working this week, which means all of Martha's cheeriness has been focused on me like a death ray. Even worse, her favorite topic of choice has been Lacy Nichols. She won't stop going on and on about how helpful she's been for the fundraiser.

"She's my co-chair," she tells me for the 67th time as we get our hair cut side by side.

"That's great," I deadpan.

"*And* she works part-time to help coordinate volunteers at the children's hospital. I don't know how the girl finds the time."

One time I stopped and helped a turtle cross the road, but you don't see me bragging about it.

I'm relieved when the stylist flips on the hair dryer. Martha jabbers on, but I get to point up to my ears and mouth, *Sorry. Can't hear you!* Even though I can. My brain sends a smirk emoji to itself.

I feel terrible about harboring such strong feelings of annoyance with Martha when the hair stylist whirls my chair around and I'm presented with a *Princess Diaries* moment. I didn't touch my hair in Spain, opting for the very cheap, very hip option of letting it grow out with no maintenance whatsoever, so obviously it needed some major cleanup. The stylist left most of the length, but she trimmed the ends and added a few layers for volume and depth. She even did some of those lustrous beachy waves in preparation for the big event. I hate to admit to Martha how good it looks.

Ellie meets up with us for the next phase of our prep: makeup. I put up a small fight, trying to insist that I can apply my own. My eye shadow will be basic, probably consisting of a vague brown color, and my lips will be covered with chapstick—the belle of the ball, for sure. Martha isn't convinced. She plops me down in the chair and holds up a photo of my dress for the makeup artist. He taps his finger on his chin, thinking, and then his eyes light up and he grins. "I have the *perfect* shadow for you."

It turns out, he does. It's gold and shimmery, and when I put on my dark green velvet dress back at home, I look like Holiday Barbie.

Ellie, not one to be outdone, looks ridiculously gorgeous in a dark red silk gown. The neckline falls just across her collarbones, but the back dips dangerously low. It's equally as understated as my gown, and apparently, they're from the same designer. Our coordination efforts pay off when we stroll into the W Hotel later that night and

I catch our reflection in a floor-length mirror.

Damn.

"I bet this is what Gigi and Bella feel like 24/7."

She grins and hooks her arm through mine. With her by my side, I feel confident as we enter the ballroom. Martha and the rest of the event organizers clearly ran away with the theme. It looks like they hired Elsa to turn the whole room into a winter wonderland. Icicles hang from the ceiling in densely packed clusters, and flocked Christmas trees line the perimeter, filling the air with a soft aroma of spruce and pine. Beneath them, fake snow covers the floor. Special lighting casts everyone in an icy blue glow, and either winter has finally arrived or they cranked the A/C because it's freezing in here. I'm grateful for my long-sleeved gown as Ellie and I reach for flutes of champagne from a passing waiter.

We meet each other's eyes and clink glasses.

"Here's to hashtag dat gala lyfe," she says with an arched brow.

I laugh and we turn to peruse the ballroom. Martha is greeting guests a few yards away. I know for a fact she's been busting her butt putting the finishing the touches on the event all week, but it looks as if she's just returned from an extended stay on some tropical island. Her blonde hair is swept up in an elegant French twist, her makeup is impeccable, and she's wearing a dark navy gown that sparkles every time she moves. My dad is by her side, helping her with her hosting duties, looking very dapper in a fitted tuxedo. Side by side, they look like they were born for this role, and I can't help but smile thinking about my mom off in the middle of a Peace Corps assignment with Jorge. *To each their own.*

We head in their direction to compliment Martha on a

beautiful event, but I stop dead in my tracks when the crowd shifts and I spot Lacy just on the other side of her. Of course, as co-chairs, they would be greeting guests together.

I ask Ellie to assess how she looks since *obviously* I can't objectively judge her outfit.

"Like a shitty Christmas ornament some kid make in art class," Ellie says, surreptitiously studying her over her glass as we approach. "Her gown is hot pink and she's wearing dangling earrings stuffed with so many diamonds that her earlobes are probably insured for the night."

Everything she's said so far is true, but the ensemble doesn't stop there. Around Lacy's shoulders is an over-the-top white fur wrap. Her blonde hair is curled in soft waves reminiscent of the 1920s. Her makeup looks like it's been airbrushed on, making her complexion smooth and flawless.

"She doesn't even look real," Ellie points out before quickly adding, "and that's not a good thing."

My dad spots us just before we reach the small group and waves us over with a wide, proud smile. I dutifully oblige, though I'd be equally happy to run in the exact opposite direction. At least my dad has the decency to lay the compliments on thick.

"You both look absolutely *stunning*," Martha adds, beaming. She turns to a few of her friends and proudly introduces us as her stepdaughters. Lacy's gaze finds me and when I meet her eyes, she produces a villainous smile—at least that's what it looks like to me. To the rest of the group, I'm sure it appears perfectly cordial.

"Hello Ellie."

I smile sweetly. "It's Brooke."

She presses her hand to her chest in feigned

embarrassment. "Of course, *Brooke*."

"I'm Ellie," my sister says, stepping forward and extending her hand to Lacy. "You must be Lacy, I've heard so much about you."

Lacy arches a brow. "Have you now?"

Ellie beams, and I'm nearly struck silent by my sister's beauty. She's everything women like Lacy strive to be, and it feels good to have her by my side. "Yes. Brooke has told me everything."

Lacy connects the dots quickly and realizes she has two adversaries before her. She gathers her dress in one hand and clutches her champagne flute in the other, presumably preparing to bolt, but then her gaze shifts just over Ellie's shoulder and her eyes light up. I watch as her smile turns from sour to sweet. A candy coating oozes from her pores, and I realize a moment too late that there's only one person who would elicit that sort of reaction from Lacy.

I hear his deep voice before I see him.

"Martha, you've really outdone yourself with this event."

I watch Martha blush a perfectly adorable shade of pink. My skin tingles, and I inhale a deep breath before I glance over my shoulder and find James standing only a few feet away. My heart comes to a screeching halt, plummets, and then starts to race. I quickly blink twice, trying to reconcile the idea that he's here, standing so near after so many months apart. He looks the exact same as the last time I saw him, except his hair is shorter, trimmed in a way that emphasizes his handsome features even more.

I must say his name because his gaze whips to me and his smile falters. His eyes widen in shock and his body visibly stiffens.

"Brooke."

It's a statement and a question. He clearly wasn't expecting to see me here.

"Hi," I say, sounding breathy and flustered. "I didn't know you'd be here."

It's the truth, and yet as soon as the words leave my lips, I wish I could reach out and steal them back.

He tilts his head down and frowns, and when he glances back up, his expression is stony and closed off. Then, I watch as a bitter smile spreads across his features.

"Apparently you haven't looked up."

I glance to where he's pointing and see a large banner hanging there. In scrolling font it reads: *Austin Philanthropic League 78th Annual Winter Gala*. Beneath that is the BioWear logo. Now that I'm aware of it, I see it plastered on all the signage around the room. Apparently, his company is the event's official sponsor.

Of course. Funny how Ellie conveniently left that part out when she first told me about the gala. I glare at her, but a deep frown and quick shake of her head says she didn't know. Well then. I have no one to blame for this series of events, but it's clear when I turn back to James and find his features haven't softened that neither of us knows how to proceed from here. I'm attending the event to support Martha. He's here because his company is a sponsor. This isn't a planned reunion or reconciliation on either of our parts, and yet my body is humming with anticipation like maybe…it could be. I grip my hands into fists by my sides, trying to keep them from shaking too violently. I might as well be on the starting line of a race with the way my heart is pounding in my chest.

I open my mouth then close it again, at a complete loss for words.

Unfortunately, Lacy isn't.

"James, you look so handsome! I told you a traditional tuxedo would look best."

His steely brown eyes shift to her, and he manages a small smile.

"Will you come with me to get some champagne?" she asks with a pleading glance. "I've been greeting people for *hours* and I could really use a break."

With all of us standing there watching him, he can't very well turn her down. He nods gently and steps back with his arm outstretched, making way for her to join him. I shiver as she slithers past me. Her tactics are underhanded, but her point is clear: James belongs to her.

Martha nails that point home further when she chuckles in amusement. "God those two have been circling each other for years now. When will that man finally get some sense and marry the poor girl already?"

The other women in the group nod emphatically, clearly all t-shirt-wearing members of Team James and Lacy—Team Jamy, or maybe Team Lames. I prefer the latter.

Then Ellie speaks up. "If you ask me, I don't think he's all that into her."

All eyes in the group whip to her in shock. Clearly, very few people have had the audacity to speak out against Lacy.

"Why do you say that?" Martha asks, sounding truly troubled by the idea.

Ellie grins and turns to me with a proud gleam in her eye. "Duh! Because he's still in love with Brooke."

CHAPTER TWENTY-SEVEN

James looks like The Bachelor right before a rose ceremony. There has been a constant stream of women grouped around him from the time Lacy led him away to get a drink until now. As soon as one woman manages to claim his attention, another one works up the courage to whisk him away. I watch the scene unfold from afar, sipping on my second flute of champagne and pretending to bid on silent auction items with Ellie.

"Do you think I should bid on this purse?" she asks, testing whether or not I've been listening to her.

I say yes without looking at it. I'm too busy narrowing my eyes as yet another woman in a clingy gown touches James' arm and titters like a little schoolgirl. I recognize her. I'm pretty sure she's a news reporter—yes, a local weather girl. *Shouldn't she be off chasing a storm or something?*

"But the bidding is already up to $85,000," Ellie points out.

"Oh, crazy," I say, sounding about two percent interested.

The weathergirl inches closer and drapes her hand casually on his arm. In doing so, she manages to edge a few women out of the group, and I start to see red. Clearly James hasn't been lacking for company since I left for Spain. If this is any indication of how he's spent the last

315

year and a half, I'm surprised he even still remembers my name.

"I've got a forecast for you: cloudy with a chance of *skanks*," I mumble grumpily.

"What was that?" Ellie asks.

I turn my back to him. "Nothing."

She smiles, clearly pleased with her role as firsthand witness to my outrage. "You should just go talk to him."

"Oh okay, Ellie. What a good idea. Do you think I should just get in line behind the blonde? Or how about the curvy brunette that could balance a champagne glass on her ass *à la* Kim K?"

She wraps her arm around my shoulder and tugs me into her side. "I wasn't kidding about what I said earlier. He still loves you. He asks me about you all the time."

I jerk away in surprise. "What do you mean?"

She shrugs and continues down the line of auction items. "Every time our paths cross at Twin Oaks, he asks how you're liking Spain, if you'll be returning to the States any time soon, that sort of thing."

This is news to me. I told Ellie I didn't want any James updates, but this is different. This is something she should have told me!

"*AND*," I stress. "What do you say?!"

She leans down and studies a diamond ring that is currently going for $74,000, staring intently like she's actually going to bid on the thing.

"Ellie!"

She stands and waves away my obvious panic. "Oh, right. I tell him you're loving life over there and you never want to come home."

I straighten my shoulders. "Good. Yeah, that's what you should tell him."

"I even tell him about all the Spanish men you have after you."

I reach out and grip her shoulders, spinning her around until she's facing me. "Why would you say that?!"

Her blue eyes, a pair that match my own, are so large and vulnerable that for a second, I forget I'm supposed to be mad at her.

"Because it's the truth," she says defensively.

Still, she had no business telling him that. I just assumed that since she wasn't giving me updates about James, she wasn't giving him updates about me either. Clearly, I was wrong.

Her eyes narrow at a sight just behind me before she unravels a conspiratorial smile. "Come on, sis. I'm thirsty."

We both have champagne, and I point that out as she drags me after her, but that doesn't stop her from leading us to the bar where James is currently waiting in line. There are half a dozen other bars in the ballroom, two of which were in between where we stood at the silent auction and this one. To anyone watching, it's obvious that we darted across to room to get in line behind him, but hopefully no one is studying our actions that closely. If they are, they probably also saw me pick some spinach out of my teeth using my phone's camera five minutes ago.

James isn't alone; Weathergirl still clings to his side like a low-pressure storm system. Lacy is probably seething with jealousy. Me, on the other hand? I'm busy coming up with more weather-based insults in my head.

"James," Ellie says, tapping him on the shoulder and drawing his attention so he turns and finds us standing there. "So good to see you. I didn't get the chance to say hi earlier before Lacy started ordering you around. Boy, she can be a real bear sometimes, right?"

With her tone, she makes it seem like it was a happy coincidence that we got in line behind him, but James is too smart for that. He drags his gaze from Ellie to me, and there's an extra little spark of something that wasn't there before. Anger? Annoyance?

"When did you return to Austin?"

Yeah, it's anger. Definitely anger.

"A week ago."

"And I assume it's—"

"Temporary, yes."

"And when do you leave?"

"In a few days."

He nods in understanding. "Enjoy your trip."

Then he turns and picks up his conversation with the weathergirl like I'm not even there. I've been dismissed.

OH OKAY. Good to see you for the first time in years too.

I should follow his lead and turn away, mind my own business and finish the gala on a high note. This is a conversation best done in private, but instead, I tap his shoulder and interrupt him midsentence.

"I'm sorry, but did I do something wrong?"

My tone isn't so gentle now that he's pissed me off.

His gaze spits fire when he replies, "Not a thing."

The woman at his side wraps a possessive hand around his forearm, and I've had enough. I'm about to walk away, but then Ellie pushes me toward him.

"Brooke was actually just telling me she'd love to dance, and I'm sure you two have so much to catch up on."

Dance?!

No.

While there *is* a dance floor, it's currently occupied by only three couples, and each person is upwards of 80.

They're just sort of shuffling around while they lean on each other. James and I would stick out like sore thumbs.

He smiles tightly and extends his arm to encompass the room. "I'm sure there are plenty of men who would be more than willing to oblige."

My cheeks flush with embarrassment. Not only did he turn me down, he did it in front of the weathergirl, and when she snickers and tries to hide it behind her hand, I've had enough for one night. Martha will have to understand. I'm leaving early.

I turn on my heel, prepared to beeline for the exit, but Ellie's hand digs into my back and she pushes me toward him.

"Plenty of men, sure, but you're the closest!"

Cupid had enough tact to use arrows in his matchmaking. Ellie, on the other hand, seems to have chosen a hatchet.

I'm not sure if I'm angrier with her for throwing me at James or with James for standing there, actually contemplating turning me down a second time. I narrow my eyes, *daring* him to do it. He meets my gaze head on, and a muscle in his jaw twitches as he tries to grind his teeth to dust. It feels like I'm winning even though his searing gaze is hot enough to burn through flesh.

Finally, with a heavy sigh, he grabs my hand and turns to lead me toward the dance floor, or at the very least, away from Ellie. For all I know, he could be on his way to depositing my body outside in the dumpster. I'm sure that's what he'd like to do, though I have no clue why. When we last spoke in Austin, we left things on good terms. Our breakup was mutual and healthy—adult, even. Now he's suddenly acting like some scorned lover. He's holding my hand in a punishing grip I don't particularly enjoy, so I tug hard to extract it, right in time to nearly trip into an ambitious waiter holding a massive tray of hors d'oeuvres. James' hand settles around my waist as he gently pulls me against him, saving me and the poor server in the nick of time. I stiffen at the familiar warmth that radiates from his touch. He squeezes my waist and then quickly releases me, taking a step away as if he's trying to put a healthy distance between us. I glance down at the offending hand in time to see him clench it into a tight fist.

"The dance floor is that way," he says with a cold, distant tone.

I whip my gaze to his face and for one wild moment, I contemplate leaving him right then and there. I spy an exit a few yards away; I could be outside in a minute, two tops. He sees where I'm looking and shakes his head with a quiet reprimand. "Don't."

I lift my chin and walk purposefully toward the dance floor, stopping at the very edge. James' hand hits the small of my back and he continues forward, sweeping me into his arms. One of my hands rests delicately on his shoulder while he grips the other one tightly. His touch is exciting, and strangely familiar after so much time. The band is playing Nat King Cole's "L-O-V-E" and the upbeat jazz song is no trouble for James, who's clearly spent time learning how to lead a woman around a dance floor. He's not making it easy for me though. I'm sure he'd love for me to stumble in front of everyone—and I do mean *everyone*—but too bad for him, Martha enrolled Ellie and me in a few months of ballroom dance lessons when we were teenagers. I hated every second of it, but now I can foxtrot with the best of them—that is, until James picks up the pace, spinning me out and back in with a hard tug. I collide with his chest and manage to step on his foot. He smirks and I resolve to stomp harder next time.

There's no time to try to plan ahead for another opportunity to maim him. With James at the helm, towering over me in his midnight black tuxedo, we breeze across the dance floor so quickly that all my focus goes to trying to keep up with his long strides. The song hits a crescendo, and the trumpet player takes a solo. James uses the opportunity to toss me out and roll my body back into him before he dips me sharply toward the ground. I squeeze my eyes closed, bracing for impact, but then he pulls me back up and swings us back into the rhythm of the song with confident ease. There are whistles and claps from the crowd of onlookers. Thanks to James' moves, I doubt there's a guest in attendance who isn't watching us. I hope Ellie is happy. In fact, I *know* she is.

Together we move to the beat, our feet in perfect sync. I'm actually enjoying the pace of the dance. It's thrilling to be led by someone like him, right up until he opens his mouth.

"If you wanted to talk to me so badly, you could have just asked. You didn't have to use your sister."

His smugness rubs me the wrong way. I tilt my head back to meet his gaze and reply coldly, "I didn't put her up to it. She's convinced we have some unfinished business."

He grunts as if he was expecting nothing less. "Do we?"

I ignore his question. "Y'know, you admitted yourself that I've done nothing wrong. Why are you treating me like this?"

He turns away, granting me a reprieve from his intense gaze, though his profile isn't much better. His smooth jaw and sharp features are just as tantalizing as I remember, maybe more so now that I've had so many long nights to fantasize about them.

When he finally glances back to me, he's removed the emotion in his eyes. He's a cold, unfeeling blank slate as he tips his head and studies me. "What did you call it once? *Self-preservation?*"

I flinch. His honesty catches me off guard. I was prepared to deflect another harsh comment from his barbed tongue.

"James." My shaky voice only further angers him. Clearly, he doesn't want my sympathy. "You don't have to be like this. Soon enough, I'll be gone again."

He furrows his brows angrily. "How would you like me to be? Polite? Talkative?"

"It'd be a good start."

"Ellie tells me you're popular in Barcelona," he says acerbically.

I flush, aware of what he's insinuating. "Ellie was exaggerating."

"Rest assured, Brooke, I realized you'd moved on the day you boarded that flight to Spain. You didn't need to have your sister rub salt in my wound."

I stiffen, finally aware of the barely concealed pain emanating from him. The song fades and he tries to step away, but I tighten my hand on his shoulder. "James."

A soft piano starts to play, introducing the next song, and I pray he won't leave me out here alone, not when I have so much I need to tell him. My fingers dig into his tuxedo jacket and I plead with him to turn and look at me.

"You have it all wrong."

"How?" he asks harshly. "Please, enlighten me."

I can't stand this version of him, the unyielding jerk who makes my legs shake and my lip quiver. I look away and try to inhale deeply so when I speak again, my voice doesn't sound so small. "I didn't ask her to give you updates about my time in Spain. That was her...sisterly way of trying to make you jealous."

"Why?"

I nearly laugh. "You expect me to know what motivates Ellie?" I shake my head as we move slowly around the dance floor, and I can't meet his eyes when I offer him the whole truth. Instead, I focus on a point just over his shoulder.

"She thinks you're in love with me, and I suppose she thought it might spur you into action or something."

I expect him to flinch or sigh or give me some kind of sign to prove or disprove Ellie's hypothesis, but James is first and foremost a savvy businessman. His poker face betrays nothing. If I want to know the answer to that burning question, I'll have to ask him outright. At the moment, I'm scared his reply will be colored by misconception and hurt. I wonder just how hyperbolic Ellie's tales of my time in Barcelona actually were. Sure, I got asked out a time or two, and I had a pretty good setup with those free croissants for a while, but there weren't men sweeping me off my feet right and left. In fact, there was no sweeping, whatsoever. For the last year and a half, I've been singularly focused on the man I left behind, the man currently doing his best to slice me in half with his gaze. Still, I trudge on, offering him a bit of honesty in the hopes that it will melt his hard exterior just a little bit.

"I would never play games with you after how we left things," I say earnestly. "If I'd known Ellie was doing that, I would have insisted she stop, believe me. I couldn't even handle her giving me updates about you. For the last year, she never once mentioned your name because she knew how I felt...how much it would upset me."

His dark brown eyes widen and then quickly narrow, as if he's trying to pick apart my words and find the deceit in between the syllables. His hand tightens around my waist and the animosity between us starts to fade, slowly, *faintly*, but I feel it in the way he holds me. There's no longer malice in his grip. He presses me against him, not so he can try to outmaneuver me on the dance floor but because maybe, *hopefully*, that's how close he wants me.

For a few minutes, he leads me in silence as I try to come up with some way to convince him of the truth. I could drag Ellie out here and force her to redact her wild stories, but even if he does believe my time in Spain was spent largely thinking of him, wondering whether or not he'd moved on, would it even matter? As the second song fades, so does my hope of reconciliation. He leads me to the side of the dance floor and I grasp for something to say, some way to keep him here with me.

"James—"

He shakes his head and speaks with a dejected tone. "I thought about what it would be like when you came back," he admits with sad eyes. "And not once did I think you'd show up like this."

"Well I'm here now," I say, my voice brimming over with hope.

"Temporarily," he points out bitterly.

Of course. That's when reality hits me like a ton of bricks. This isn't some grand gesture. I didn't fly back from Spain with the hopes of reconnecting with James. I came here for a quick visit to see my family. I'm at the event because of Martha, not in the hopes of running into him, and he knows it. It was the very first thing I said to him. *Oh, I didn't know you'd be here*—how's that for love? Any attempt I make to explain myself here will seem half-assed and coincidental. *Oh yes, sorry about all the trouble I put you through all those months ago. See you around!*

He turns to walk away and my hand shoots out to stop him. "If you wanted me to come back, you could have reached out, or..."

My voice fades when he laughs incredulously. It's a sad, pitiful sound that splinters my heart.

"I already asked you to stay once."

I get it—once bruised, a man's ego isn't so easily healed, especially a man like James.

As I watch him walk away, clarity sets in like a shiver up my spine: I want a second chance with James, a chance to make things right between us now. Even though every decision I've made in the past year and a half has opened up millions of potential paths and parallel universes away from him, there's nothing stopping me from turning around and retracing my footsteps back to the point where they all meet. It's true that every time a door closes, a window opens, but that doesn't mean the door just disappears. Hell, it's just a closed door, and no matter if it's jammed, locked, or broken, there will probably come a time when you can break the rusted hinges and fight your way back in.

If you truly want to.

Walking backward should feel like a retreat, but it doesn't feel that way for me, because all that time marching forward has changed me from the person I *was* into the person I *am*. I traveled, explored, and got myself lost more times than I can count. I wallowed in heartbreak over James, but I also learned that I could find my smile again, even on my own. I think that lesson was the hardest to learn, but ultimately, it's what matters most. I don't *need* James to survive; *I want him*. When I dig deep for my old insecurities, they aren't there anymore.

Now, the idea of marrying James fills me with hope, not dread. I want to share my life with him and I need him to know that, but I know it won't be easy to convince him.

Looking at things from his perspective, his behavior tonight makes perfect sense. He doesn't owe me kindness. He surrendered his pride and begged me to stay in Austin, and I still went to Spain. Then, thanks to Ellie's well-intentioned storytelling, he assumed I humped around Europe without a care in the world. He must think I'm the most callous, unfeeling person on the face of the planet. Why would he believe me if I told him I want a second chance now? What have I done to try to restore things between us?

Nothing. The door is still closed, dead-bolted, and rusted over.

Welp, looks I'm going to need a crowbar.

CHAPTER TWENTY-EIGHT

"Oh my god, Ellie, I'm such a cliché! James Ashwood wanted me and I tossed him away like yesterday's garbage—for what?! A few sunny months in España!?"

She hums thoughtfully, doing her best rendition of Bored Sister #1 as she reclines on my bed and scrolls through her Instagram feed. I'm glad she can relax at a time like this. I didn't sleep at all after the gala, partly because I'm still recovering from jet lag, and partly because my life just took a sharp right turn off its charted course. I feel sick. I think I'm having a heart attack, and I've forced Ellie to check my symptoms on WebMD three times already.

"It's says you're probably just having a garden-variety psychotic break," she reassures me.

"I think I'm going to go to his house," I exclaim, turning for my closet.

I'm a ball of anxiety and emotions. It's the morning after the gala, and I need to act—NOW. I've thought about nothing but James all night, of how I could possibly convince him I'm sorry and deserve a second chance. I want to throw on sneakers and run to his house. I want to press play on a boombox beneath his bedroom window and light a million candles and ride up in a limo, dangling out of it precariously with a red rose stuck between my teeth. I need a grand gesture, and I need it yesterday!

"Slow down, mental case! What are you talking

about?"

Oh, *now* she closes Instagram.

"James," I say, flinging shoes out of my closet in my quest to find a pair of running shoes that still fit me. I haven't lived at my dad's house in a while, and the selection in my closet is pretty slim. Stuffed in the back, I find a pair of hiking boots and decide they'll do. "I have to get him back."

"Since when?"

"Since always!" I shout, annoyed with her for not keeping up. "I was just too stupid to see it before."

"Oh," she grimaces. "That's pretty inconvenient considering he hates your guts."

"Yeah, no thanks to you," I throw back heatedly. "Really good job, by the way. I think he assumes I slept with half of the European Union."

"No, just half of Spain," she clarifies with an utter lack of concern for her misdeeds.

I want to throw one of my chunky hiking boots at her head, but I'm scared it'll cause permanent damage. Besides, I need them. I plop down in the center of my room and start working on lacing them up. Ellie is trying to get my attention, but I can't get distracted now. I have too much pent-up energy exploding inside of me. I'm jittery, and I don't know what to do. I was perfectly fine yesterday before the gala, but seeing James and twirling around in his arms like some kind of fairy princess was like pouring lighter fluid on a slow-burning fire. I knew I still had feelings for him, but not like this. This is terrible! It hurts! See: heart attack. *Speaking of...*

I glance up when I'm midway through lacing up the first boot. "Are you sure I shouldn't go to the hospital? I think I'm having pain in my left arm."

Ellie leans down and catches my shoulders in her palms. Then she levels her gaze with mine and inhales deeply.

"Do it with me," she says.

I breathe.

It only makes things worse. *I don't have time to breathe! I'm supposed to go back to Spain in six days! How am I supposed to convince James I love him in six days?!*

It's obvious.

"Oh my god, Ellie. I can't go back to Spain!" I exclaim.

She smiles. "Duh."

I reach for my phone. "This is an actual emergency!"

"Don't tell me you're calling an ambulance," Ellie says, rolling her eyes.

I settle for the second best option: the cookie delivery place down the street.

CHAPTER TWENTY-NINE

Ellie locks me in my room and makes me promise I won't go see James on a whim. She thinks I need to be armed with a thoughtful speech, a sexy outfit, and at least half a Xanax before I attempt whatever it is I think I'll be attempting. I think she's being ridiculous, so I spend upwards of two hours trying to knot my bed sheets together to make an escape ladder. It doesn't work. I grow weary, lie down on my floor, and crash hard for a solid 12 hours. *Huh.* Turns out, I was pretty exhausted. Something about travel, galas, and massive life decisions really conks you out.

The first thing I do when I wake up is FaceTime Diego and Nicolás. I've had time to consider my options, and now that I'm well rested, I still agree with the decision I came to in the midst of my mania. If I want James to take me seriously when I ask for a second chance, I have to tell him I'm moving back to the States.

FaceTime connects right away and Diego leans forward, scrunching his nose and studying me.

"What's that on your face?" he asks in lieu of a greeting.

"Oh, nothing, just indentations from sleeping face down on the carpet. Anyway, I have news…about what Diego and I talked about the other night."

Diego claps gleefully and turns to Nicolás. "I told you

so!"

"I should have never taken that bet!" Nicolás replies with an eye roll.

"Well you did, and I won, so pay up."

Nicolás turns back to the phone. "Wait, Brooke, are you staying for the guy?"

I nod.

"Sí! SEE!" Diego shouts triumphantly.

After Diego is done gloating, I try to turn the conversation back to a more professional topic: my resignation.

Nicolás laughs. "Wait, let me get this straight: you're putting in your two weeks notice with one week of vacation left? What does that even mean? You're going to fly back here for a week and then fly home?"

It makes sense to me. "I need to get my stuff and say goodbye to the girls."

Diego shakes his head. "No, no. While we'd love to see you once more before you move back to the States for good, why don't we just ship your stuff back to you?" He glances toward Nicolás, who's nodding in agreement. "No sense in wasting a couple grand on flights if you don't have to."

I laugh at how naïve they're being. "Olive wouldn't mind so much, but Luciana will never forgive me if I don't come back to say goodbye to her."

Diego rolls his eyes. "Don't worry about that. Luce will understand if we frame it as a love story: your clock struck midnight and you had to rush home from the ball. Now all you need is to find your prince."

I'm glad they seem to think that, because when they hand the phone over to her during the FaceTime call and I begin to explain the situation, she hangs up on me midsentence, and not by accident. I call again. She answers, and HANGS UP AGAIN.

Diego shoots me a quick text.

Diego: Okay, she's taking it slightly harder than expected, but there is still no reason for you to come back to Spain just to get your stuff. Luciana will calm down. Also, when did she get too old for fairy tales?

Olive, bless her, doesn't give a shit that I'm leaving. She sends me a thoughtful, quick text message thanking me for being her tutor and wishing me well in the future. By contrast, Luciana texts me 15 skull emojis paired with an adorably incorrect English idiom.

Luciana: Sorry, can't talk—too busy pulling this fork out of my back!

I hate the fact that I'm hurting her, especially because I know what it feels like to be left at her age. It's not like Luciana expected me to stay with her and her dads forever—we even joked about how terrible her next tutor would be compared to me—but this abrupt exit isn't ideal. If I could explain my reasons to her, I know she'd understand. After all, she knew how I felt about James.

I try to call her several more times, but she's obviously not ready to talk. Eventually, she blocks my number, and Diego tells me to give it time. She'll cool down, he assures me, though I fear that's not the case. Luciana is headstrong and stubborn. All I can do is hope that one day she'll understand my decision to stay in Texas.

CHAPTER THIRTY

Against Ellie's advice, I try to call James first thing the next day. I'm sitting on the floor in my room with sticky notes spread out around me.

The green ones are covered with all the things I want to say to him:

I'm sorry!!!!

I'm not going back to Spain!

Our timing sucked, but I want a second chance!

Please, let's sit down and talk.

The red ones are covered in the things I absolutely mustn't say to him:

How many times did you and Lacy bang??

Was she good? Better than me?

When do you want to get married? What should we name our kids?

Finally, on a small note near my foot, there are three words I'm not sure I'm ready to say, but they're there, just in case.

The sticky notes are necessary because I'm scared that once the call clicks on and his deep voice filters over the line, I'll lose my cool. I want to be prepared. I want to sound eloquent and sure of myself. The rings drone on and on, and I unconsciously start to crumple one of the sticky notes. I freak and try to flatten it again, but my sweaty palm smears the pen. *I'm sorry* now looks like a jumbled mess of gibberish. The call rings one final time and then jumps to voicemail.

BEEP

"James! Hi! It's Brooke calling again. I was hoping to reach you so we could set up a time soon to sit down and talk." My sticky notes jump out at me. "I'm sorry! And I'm not going back to Spain! And I would really like a second chance! Did I already say this is Brooke? I can't remem—"

The voicemail cuts off and when the little automated voice asks me if I'd like to rerecord my message, I jump at the opportunity and just delete it all together. So much for my sticky notes helping me sound eloquent.

I try his phone twice the following day, but the calls go straight to voicemail. He's ignoring me on purpose, just like Luciana. They should probably start an I Hate Brooke fan club.

I'm now up to four unanswered phone calls, and as the number grows, it sounds more and more pathetic. Even Ellie agrees, but I can't give up; I just need to change my tactic.

I come up with a diabolical plan while I'm shampooing my hair later that night, and I shout for Ellie to come in so I can relay it her.

"Did you get it?" I ask over the sound of the shower.

"Yeah, it isn't that complicated," she says, sounding less than impressed.

"Who cares?!" I say as I rinse my scalp. "Diabolical plans don't have to be complicated, they just have to work."

"Yeah, no shit. I'm just saying, why did I have to come in here and see your naked butt just to jot this down? You could have remembered it."

No. It's a universal truth that all good ideas generated

in the shower are forgotten as soon as the water cuts off.

"Do you think it'll work?" I ask hopefully.

"Sure thing," she says, appeasing me. "But just in case, use some of that deep conditioner I have in there. That way, when this doesn't work and he rejects you, at least your hair won't lose volume like your heart will."

She's wrong. It will work, as long as Beth is willing to play her part. I call her first thing the following morning.

"Good morning, you've reached BioWear. This is Beth speaking."

Her voice is chipper and upbeat. It fills me with hope for what I'm about to ask of her.

"Beth, hi! It's Brooke."

"Brooke Davenport?" She sounds surprised, and I guess she probably should be considering how awkward our last exchange was.

"Yes, *that* Brooke. How have you been?"

"I'm good, thanks for asking," she answers tentatively. "James isn't in the office yet, if that's—"

"No, no. Actually, I called to talk to you."

"Oh, okay." Her voice sounds hesitant. "What can I do for you?"

I take a deep breath before laying out my plan to her. It doesn't take long, and I try to speak quickly considering she probably has a busy schedule that doesn't include scheming behind her boss' back.

"Are you sure you want to do this?" she asks after I finish. "Why don't you just try calling him?"

"I *have* tried, but he won't answer."

She hums in sympathy. "Yeah, he can be pretty stubborn when he wants to be."

"That's why I need your help."

"You know this could get me fired," she points out.

I cringe, feeling terrible for putting her in this position in the first place. "I completely understand if you don't want to be part of it."

"I didn't say that," she says quickly, then after a long, strained pause, she sighs. "Fine. Tomorrow. I'll put it on the schedule, but you're taking the fall if this turns out badly."

"Thank you, thank you, thank you! I owe you, Beth, and if he gets mad, you can tell him I threatened your life!"

"I'm doing this for him," she clarifies, ensuring I know where her loyalties lie. "Last year, when you begged me not to tell him you called, I felt terrible keeping that secret for you. For months after you left, he moped around this office. I thought he was never going to break out of that fog, and...well, he never really did, but things got a little better, manageable—but Brooke, if you're here now to just stir the pot again, you need to spare him the trouble. He puts up a good front, but he's one of the most sensitive men you'll ever meet."

I don't take her warning lightly.

"I promise I won't screw it up again."

At least, that's not part of my diabolical plan.

• • •

The following night, I pause outside the front entrance to Twin Oaks Country Club. The ornate front doors are made of solid wood and carved with incredible attention to detail. They're designed to feel imposing, and it works. I know it's a trick, and yet I can't seem to make myself step past them. Inside, James sits in the main dining room, waiting for a business associate who will never come so he can have a meeting that was never real. It's a trick, and a weak one at that, but it's the only way I could ensure he would be here, alone, and hopefully ready to listen.

I take a deep breath and finally enter. It's very strange to walk through a place you used to work as a civilian. Dinner service is in full swing, and I have the irrational fear that Brian is going to throw a polo at me and tell me to refill waters. Ellie's manning the hostess stand, and when she sees me arrive, she nods her head toward the dining room and mouths, *Good luck.* I turn and my stomach flips when I see James sitting alone at a table for two near the fireplace. A part of me feared he wouldn't show up, even under the guise of a pretend meeting, but there he is wearing an impeccable navy blue suit. He's added all the required accouterments—pocket square, tie clip, watch— and he's never looked more handsome or more unattainable. It's enough to make me want to turn around and run back home. He's going to be a formidable opponent, and maybe I'm not quite ready to face him yet. I glance down and reassess my outfit. Nothing in my suitcase was nice enough, so I raided Ellie's closet. Her flirty blue dress and nude, strappy heels are sexy, but are they enough?

I look back up to find James checking his watch, and his handsome features contort into a frustrated scowl. I'm late thanks to Austin traffic, and it doesn't help that half of the wait staff recognizes me as I begin to weave through the dining room. They want me to stop and chat, but I smile politely and keep it moving.

I'm a few feet away from stepping into his line of sight when another member of the club—an older, well-dressed man—walks up to James' table and claps him on the shoulder. James glances up and smiles, offering a handshake and a few words I can't hear. I falter, unsure if I should proceed or not. I don't really want an audience for this conversation, but I can't delay any longer. I don't want him to use my tardiness against me.

I have no choice but to continue.

"I hear you've been working on your short game," the older man says.

James chuckles. "If only to distract from how I've been slicing it off the tee the past few—"

I step up to the table, drawing James' brown eyes to me midsentence. His friend turns as well, and their reactions are polar opposite. I get a warm, welcoming smile from the older man and a confused, angry scowl from James. His hard gaze rakes over me, and my knees actually quiver.

"What are you doing here?"

I swallow and speak up in a barely audible whisper. "I came to see you."

His friend clears his throat and extends his hand out to me. "I'm Leonard West. Pleased to meet you."

"Brooke Davenport."

His eyes light up. "Ah, are you Brad's daughter?"

I nod, too caught up in the moment to manage a smile.

He scans back and forth between James and me. "And you're a friend of James?"

"Yes," I reply cautiously.

When James doesn't speak up to confirm that fact, I add, "Well, I think I am."

Leonard chuckles good-naturedly. James exhales a long, defeated sigh, obviously too much of a gentleman to toss me aside in front of an audience. He tells Leonard he'll catch him on the links sometime soon. When we're alone, I glance at the empty seat, wondering if it's still a good idea to sit down.

James, having followed my gaze, hardens his own and shakes his head. "I'm afraid our reunion will have to wait. I have a business meeting."

I draw in a tortured breath before working up the nerve to reply, "Exactly. Let's talk business—*unfinished business.*"

He leans back in his chair, surveying me with a bemused scowl. "What do you mean?" He connects the dots before I can explain, shaking his head and waving away his question. "Beth."

He tosses his napkin on the table and surges to his feet, prepared to leave after all the work I did to get him here.

"James! *Please*...please hear me out."

I wish so badly that we were in private. I'm aware of the other diners around us, and now I wish I'd concocted some way to have this meeting somewhere else, but it's too late now. This is the opportunity I've been given, and I won't let it go to waste.

A muscle in his taut jaw shifts as he clenches down, no doubt trying to keep his temper in check.

I knew he wouldn't like being tricked, but what choice did he give me? The only other option was to camp out at his house until he finally showed his face. This, while unbearably awkward, is at least efficient. By the time we walk out of this dining room, I'll have my answer about how he feels for me one way or another. He'll either give me a second chance or he won't.

His gaze shifts to the door and my heart drops. *He's actually going to leave.* He takes his first step just as Marissa strolls up with a small notepad in hand. She's been assigned as our waitress, no doubt on purpose.

"Good evening!" she announces cheerfully. "My name

is Marissa and I'll be taking care of you tonight." If she thinks it's weird that we're both hovering beside our chairs instead of sitting at the table, she doesn't let on. "Can I get either of you a glass of wine? We have some excellent new appetizers."

James shakes his head sharply. "I won't be staying for dinner."

Marissa beams, unbothered by his sharp tone. "Then wine it is. Red or white?"

"White," I snap quickly, hoping he'll feel compelled to stay if I order us a drink.

We both turn to him and wait on baited breath to see what he'll do. He doesn't nod or agree, but he does yank his chair out and take a seat. I let out a relieved sigh and follow suit. We sit across from each other in tense silence as Marissa sprints off for the wine and returns in record time.

"I know you mentioned you wouldn't be staying for dinner, but our chef would love your opinion on some new starters, Mr. Ashwood. I'll bring them out, courtesy of the club, of course."

He isn't amused by her meddling, but I love her for it. She pours our wine quickly and then dips in a little bow before leaving us alone to talk.

I reach for my glass of wine and realize a moment too late that my hand is shaking. It's evident to the both of us, so I clench it back and hide it beneath the table. I don't need wine that badly anyway.

"I'll give you until the food arrives to explain the purpose of all this cloak and dagger," he announces sharply.

Jesus, an elevator pitch. I'd hate to face him in a conference room.

"Oh! Right. Um, well you s-see…" I stumble over my words in my effort to explain myself before Marissa returns. The appetizers won't take long, especially if the kitchen knows they're going to Mr. Ashwood's table. I fight back a cringe. It's not nearly enough time to vindicate myself. This could take all night, but his rigid expression and hard frown prove he intends to keep his word. "I br-brought you here because I wanted to let you know I'm not going back to Spain."

He arches a brow. "I'm sure your family is happy about that."

He doesn't seem that enthused, and I realize I'm going out of order. My well-planned speech has turned to scramble in my brain.

"Oh no! You see—well, that is, I'm not going back to Spain because I want to give us a second chance." Wrong, unfiltered words spill out of my mouth as quickly as they come to mind. I feel like I'm going to explode in my attempt to gain his forgiveness before he leaves. "I should have never left like I did. When you asked me to stay, that was—that took bravery, and I was so stubborn and set on the idea of leaving."

His gaze flicks over my shoulder and my heart rate kicks up—surely the appetizers aren't already on their way?

"There's Marissa now—"

I lean forward over the table. "James! Please!" I cry desperately. This is ridiculous. If he really intends to get up and leave the second the food hits the table, I won't let it arrive. I'll fling it out of Marissa's hands before she has the chance to put it down in front of us. "Honestly, we can't keep doing this to each other! For once we both need to put our pride away at the same time. I just want you to see that

I still care and I know you do too! Do you really have no interest in giving this a second try?"

"Why should I? What's changed from when you left?"

"Everything!" I insist, pleading. "*Everything*. I left you last year in such a terrible way, but in the long run, I think it was for the best. I had growing up to do. Can't you understand that? At times it was unbearable being apart from you, but it brought me so much clarity about my life, about my mom, about where I want to be in five years." When he doesn't make a move to respond, I continue, breathless. "You asked me that once, where I want to be in five years. Don't you remember?"

His eyes soften and he nods, just once.

"Well my answer has changed. I don't really care where I am or what I'm doing, as long as I'm with you. Surely you still have feelings for me deep down in there somewhere. You've just covered it up with all this—" I fling my hands in the air. "This pain."

I heave a heavy sigh and wait for his response. After all that, he must have one, but he sits in silence, gazing at me intently as if working something out in his mind. It doesn't look like a good sign.

I clench my fists, digging my nails into my palms as I try to stave off defeat. He wants to push me away for good because that's easier than forgiveness, but I won't let him do it. My voice shakes when I say, "I came here today with my heart in my hand. I came here because I think I'm in love with you, and I won't leave until—"

"You think?" he asks curiously.

"What?" I blink, shocked that he's finally speaking.

"You *think* you're in love with me?" he asks again, leaning forward across the table, not mincing his next words one bit. "Because I know I'm in love with you."

His words, spoken so clearly and matter-of-factly, are enough to strike me silent. I sit across from him with my mouth gaping open. Then, realizing I probably look like a largemouth bass, I clench it closed again.

I can't...He can't...

"Here we are!" Marissa announces cheerfully, striding up to the table with a tray full of fragrant food. The appetizers have arrived, and I'm too stunned by his declaration to remember that I was supposed to flip her tray and spill them before she could set them on the table. I sit perfectly still, paralyzed by fear as I wait for him to shoot to his feet and leave. Instead, he closes his eyes and leans back in his chair, seemingly exhausted.

Marissa is completely oblivious to the scene she's witnessing. She arranges four different appetizers on our table with careful dexterity, all the while explaining each one in excruciating detail. James opens his eyes and meets my gaze, and I'm surprised to find his expression has softened to one of what I'm really hoping is forgiveness. My heart leaps in my chest.

"So you're going to want to dip those in the spicy mango salsa," Marissa explains. "It has a kick to it thanks to the jalapeños, but it is *literally* to die for."

"Marissa," I say, cutting her off while maintaining eye contact with James.

"Yes?"

"We got it, thanks."

She beams. "Sure thing. Let me know if you need anything else."

She waltzes away with a pep in her step, probably aware that her work here is done. When she's out of earshot, I lean forward.

"*Love?*" I ask, my voice shaky and fragile.

His warm brown eyes scan my face before a slow-spreading smile overtakes his handsome features.

"Love," he agrees.

I exhale the breath I've been holding for the past 10 minutes and then sag back against my chair. The range of emotions I've felt in the last few days is enough to send anyone over the edge, but now I sit here across from James, contemplating love—LOVE, of all things! I thought I'd be leaving the club in a body bag, stricken dead from a broken heart.

He's studying me thoughtfully, probably wondering the same thing I am: what happens next?

I reach my hand out for his, face up across the table. It's a vulnerable act, especially in the middle of the club's dining room, but James doesn't hesitate before he takes it. His hand envelops mine, and somehow it's the most intimate way we've ever touched, palm to palm, heart to heart. I want more—a passionate kiss, a long embrace. Hell, I'd shove the appetizers to the floor and crawl across the tablecloth to get to him, but I'm not trying to send any of these old fogies around us to the hospital.

"I missed you," he admits, stroking his thumb across my knuckles.

I still don't trust my voice, so I squeeze my lips together and nod.

"I want to hear about your travels."

There's so much to catch him up on, and I do, over dinner. We start with the appetizers, and yes, the spicy mango salsa does strike me dead. I tell him about Diego and Nicolás and the girls. I scroll through my iPhone camera roll to show him the highlights of my time abroad and am embarrassed by the utter lack of photos of architecture or landscape. *Surely I visited something that makes me look worldly? A cathedral? A statue?* Instead, my phone is jam-packed with photos of Luciana making faces, Luciana waving to me on a playground, Luciana posing in front of an ice cream shop with a massive melting cone, Luciana and me with our cheeks smashed together as we test out various Snapchat filters. My heart aches knowing she's still upset with me.

"She'll come around," James promises once I fill him in on the situation, and I hope he's right.

After five courses and a delicious fruit tart, we walk out of the club hand in hand. He hasn't invited me back to his house yet, but I'm hopeful that he will. I'm hesitant to leave him. It took so long for us to get to this moment, and we still have so much to clear up. I fear if we leave separately, he'll go home and think over what I've told him then change his mind about us.

We're standing beneath the porte cochère when he brings the back of my hands to his lips for a kiss.

"That's all I get?" I tease.

He smirks before he tugs me closer and grips my chin between his fingers. With a subtle tilt, he tips my head back and kisses me gently. My eyes flutter closed as I wrap my arms around his neck and press up onto my toes. A groan ripples through me as he tightens his possessive hold, gathering me close. Our chests brush and he urges my mouth open so his tongue can skim across mine. A shudder runs down my spine as the kiss turns urgent, *hungry*. His hand fists my dress at the base of my back and my nails dig into his shoulders.

"*Ahem.*"

A voice clears comically behind us, and James breaks the kiss. We turn in sync to find Ellie standing with her hands on her hips. She's wearing a smug smile as she asks,

347

"Isn't PDA against club rules?"

James smiles. "Since when do any of us follow the rules?"

She delivers an exaggerated eye roll before stepping forward and holding up her keys. "Brooke, if you're coming home with me, I'm leaving."

"Oh, right. Yeah…" I look back at James. "I should probably go with her, right?" I ask.

"Probably," he answers with a telling smile. "But I'd rather you didn't."

That smile is *dangerous*. A girl could be convinced to do just about anything with a smile like that.

"I don't have any of my stuff," I point out.

"You have everything you need," he responds with a telling smile while his fingers trace slow circles along my spine.

"Yoohoooo, can you two freaks work this out later?" Ellie asks, interrupting our moment. "My shift is over and I want to get the hell out of here."

I pinch my eyes closed and try to stifle a laugh. "I can't believe I'm saying this right now, but—I'm going to go home with Ellie. It's been a wild few days—I've barely slept, and I've been on a rollercoaster ride of emotions. I need a moment to catch my breath. I'm so happy and excited and grateful and I just want to make sure we don't screw this up and Iwantyoutoknowthatiwanttogo homewithyousobadbut—"

"Slow down, Brooke," he says, putting a finger up to my lips with a laugh. "Let's get lunch tomorrow."

I smile and step back. "Okay. It's a date."

• • •

348

James insists that he wants to eat at home the next day, and anyone with half a brain could guess his motive. Why doesn't he just say he wants to eat lunch in his bed, under the covers, naked? Cut out all the pretense, right? Beth clears his schedule for the rest of the afternoon, and I arrive at his house by Uber at noon on the dot. When he sweeps the door open, he's wearing jeans and a soft cotton t-shirt. The look is so simple and sexy that I nearly melt. Instead, I hold out the loaf of banana bread I baked with Martha this morning. He glances down at it and groans in appreciation.

"It's her secret recipe," I brag as he drags me inside by my hips. "She adds canned pineapple, which sounds odd, but I swear it's the best thing you'll ever taste!"

He takes it out of my hand, sets it on the side table beside the door, and yanks me against him.

"I guess you really like banana bread?" I tease before he tilts his head down and steals a kiss.

I close my eyes and let myself revel in the feeling of being in his arms again. I wasn't sure if I'd played up how good of a kisser he was in my mind over the last year and a half, but now I know for a fact his skills weren't embellished by time and distance. The man is lethal. He sweeps me up and kisses me so passionately I become a mess of aching desire, half-convinced we should just get it on right here—his scratchy welcome mat is as good a place as any. Then something familiar catches my attention over his shoulder and I tear my mouth from his.

"My bike!"

"*Your* bike?" he teases, following my gaze. "I thought you gave it back to me."

I step out of his grasp so I can move closer and run my hand along the handlebars. Then, it hits me. I spin back around to him. "Isn't this the same spot where you left it that day?"

He nods and glances away, down the hall. "I couldn't move it."

Oh.

Regret socks me in the stomach yet again.

"I'm sorry," I say on a soft whisper.

He glances back to me, and I'm surprised to see the residual hurt left in his gaze. Before, he would have tried to hide it, but not now, not if we're going to try to move on. He extends his hand to me.

"C'mon, let's go order lunch."

Not much has changed around his house since before I left. There's no new furniture or décor, and he's still using paper plates and Solo cups. I can't let it go on for another second, so while we wait on our Chinese food to arrive, I force him to unpack the dishes he's kept stowed away in his cabinets for too long.

I am surprised to find Harry the goldfish swimming around on his kitchen island. James has upgraded his original tank, and now he's basically swimming in a fishy paradise.

I beam and turn toward James. "You kept him."

He shrugs. "Of course. What else was I going to do? He's my fish."

"Wait—you didn't pull the classic kids movie gag, did you? Where the fish died months ago and you just replaced him with one that looks the exact same?"

"Are you saying you don't recognize Harry?" he jokes.

"Can I feed him?" I ask, bending down so my face is level with the tank. Harry spins in a little circle and a few bubbles float up to the surface. It's all very cute.

When our lunch arrives, we take it into the living room and sit in the center of the floor, envisioning what he could do with the space. I don't insert myself into the design plans, not yet anyway. This is his house, and maybe one day I'll share it with him, but it feels presumptuous to assume that will be the case now, after we've only just started to get back on track. Still, he wants my opinion.

"Do you think we should put up curtains?" he asks, pointing to the row of floor-to-ceiling windows that display a gorgeous view of the backyard. It would soften the space a bit, but I don't think they're necessary, so I tell him so.

"You don't want to obstruct that view if you don't have to."

He agrees and admits he's been dragging his feet on hiring a designer.

"My life has been in limbo for too long," he admits, surveying the room. "I think it's finally time I start to get settled here."

I look down and chew on my bottom lip before asking a question that's been in the back of my mind. "James, when I left...you didn't—I mean, you weren't waiting for me to come back, were you?"

I asked him not to, not if it meant he continued to live like this. I feel guilty knowing he might have hit pause on his life in the hopes that I might return.

"It wasn't my intention. Up until I saw you at the gala, I was under the impression that you'd moved on, so I tried to do the same. A few months after you left, I started to go through the motions of dating. I needed plus-ones for a few events, and it was a good way to test things out without jumping into anything too serious."

Jealousy digs its sharp claws into me.

"Did you like any of the women?" I ask, focusing down on the noodles twirling around my fork.

"Yes," he admits with a sigh, and my stomach twists

into a tight knot. His answer shouldn't bother me, but it does. "They all fit the bill of what I was looking for."

Oh, I'm sure they did—smart, beautiful, perky, closer to his age, and probably begging to settle down and start flexing their ovaries.

I barely stifle a sneer.

"None of them lasted though," he reassures me, reaching over to still my hand. I've twisted and twisted my fork around so many times, nearly every single one of my noodles is wrapped around it in a heaping mess. "Apparently, according to most of them, I wasn't *emotionally available.*"

"That's too bad." I try to sound genuine, but he sees through my thinly veiled disguise.

"Oh, yeah?" he asks, pushing our plates aside and pressing up onto his knees. "Do you wish I'd tried harder to move on?"

I finally gather enough courage to look up and meet his eyes. "Not exactly...though I do feel bad for hurting you, for leaving like I did."

He smiles as he stands and extends his hand down to me. I let him pull me to my feet and then we're pressed together, hip to hip. His hands wrap around my waist and he squeezes gently. "I'm sure you'll find a way to make it up to me."

"I plan on it, but first, I have one question."

"What's that?"

"Do you have any emotions available now?"

 **EPILOGUE**

FOUR MONTHS LATER

It's the middle of the afternoon and sunlight streams in through the living room windows. A group of older women ranging from their late 50s to late 70s sit in a small semicircle conversing with each other in broken French. Mrs. Walters sits closest to me and I listen intently as she practices simple sentences.

"*Le chat brun.*"

"Good."

"*La pomme verte.*"

I shake my head. "Try it again, and this time emphasize the long m sound rather than the e. Like this: *pomme*, not pommay."

The next time she tries it, it sounds much better. She's learning fast, just like the rest of the women in our small French club. It all started a few months ago, after I first moved in with James. His neighbor Mrs. Walters came over to see if we needed help—though at 70, I'm not sure how exactly she would have assisted us with the moving efforts. Anyway, we got to talking. She asked what I did for a living, I told her, and when she heard I was out of work, she hired me on the spot. She'd always wanted to learn a foreign language, and she knew a few other women in the neighborhood who would jump at the chance to keep their minds active.

Our small French club started up pretty organically. We've met three times a week for the last two months, and I'm shocked at how quickly everyone's been catching on. I'd always assumed children were my preferred students, but these women have been really fun so far. They're all retired and dedicated to learning, so we've been tearing through workbooks and vocabulary, not to mention we've all agreed that if everyone can master a basic understanding of the French language by next summer, we'll all take a trip to France so they can put their newfound knowledge to practice.

It's the perfect arrangement for me. I have flexible hours, I still get to teach, and these women pay better than any of my previous gigs.

I stand and interrupt their conversations to let them know "class" has officially ended, though that usually doesn't mean much. It'll be another hour before everyone is out of the house, and I swear they do it on purpose in the hopes of catching James when he arrives home from work.

"Is that a car I hear in the driveway?" Mrs. Walters says, perking up in her chair.

"Oh! I bet James is home! It would be rude to leave now!" Mrs. Buchanan says with a wide smile.

I can't help but laugh. "It should be Ellie coming over to help me make dinner."

They all visibly sag in their chairs.

"But I'll let James know you all missed him. Maybe he can make it home a little earlier on Friday."

That gets me off the hook for the time being, and everyone stands and gathers their textbooks before heading to the front door. Ellie is already standing out front, holding the door open for them.

"Afternoon Ellie." Mrs. Walters stops and pats her arm. "Are you sure I can't set you up with my grandson?"

Ellie laughs. "He's only 17, Mrs. Walters."

"*Only*? Why, I was married at 17!"

They do this every time they see each other. Mrs. Walters thinks Ellie is the prettiest thing she's ever seen, and she won't rest until Ellie is dating her grandson—who, by the way, is currently in 11th grade.

"Tell him to send me a graduation announcement," Ellie calls behind her before following me inside. "Maybe the life of a cougar will suit me."

In the last few months, James and I have been slowly but surely settling into his house. *His* house—every time I say that, he insists I call it our house. I smile and shake my head at the thought that we've lived here together for three months. It's still pretty empty because he insisted on hiring an interior designer. He wanted everything to be perfect for us, not just a hodgepodge of his old furniture mixed with some of my things, though my yellow bookshelf did make the cut. It's sitting in one of the spare bedrooms, the room we've both agreed will make a good nursery one day.

"What'd you do today?" Ellie asks, whipping open the refrigerator and peeking inside for a snack.

"I went to SoulCycle this morning before I had to prep my lesson for French club. Oh, and Diego and Nicolás called."

"How are they doing?" she asks, bending low to grab some string cheese.

"Good." I sigh. "But Luciana still won't talk to me."

She frowns. "I can't believe it. I really thought she'd forgive you by now."

"Yeah, I thought so too." I still think about her all the time. How could I not? For that year and a half I was in

Spain, we spent most of our waking (and non-waking) hours together. I desperately want her to forgive me, but I can't push it. "Anyway, part of why they called was because they're still trying to find a good tutor. The girls haven't been practicing their English as much, and they're worried they'll start to lose it."

"Did you suggest they contact the agency?"

"No." I nibble on my bottom lip. "Actually, I recommended you."

She rears back in shock. "*Me*?"

I nod enthusiastically.

"But I don't even speak Spanish."

"You don't have to! That's the best part. The girls just need someone they can practice their English with. Seriously, Ellie, it's the best job ever."

It's a brilliant idea if I've ever heard one. Ellie has been working at the country club for far too long, living with Dad and wasting time on guys who don't deserve her. There's nothing keeping her in Austin. She should take the opportunity to leave and try something new—not to mention, working for Diego and Nicolás is a dream.

"What'd they say when you suggested that?" she asks tentatively.

I beam. "They said if you want the position, it's yours."

Her brows shoot up in shock. "Seriously?"

"Yes!"

I can tell she's not completely sold on the idea, and I'm nervous if I push too hard now, she'll say no before she even gives it a real chance. "Just think about it for the next few days and get back to me."

She nods slowly, seemingly already mulling it over.

I take out one last gun from my arsenal. "Oh, but be

warned, if you do take the job, they're definitely going to force Alejandro on you."

She frowns. "Alejandro?"

Realization dawns on me: I never told her about him. At the time, it was a strategic move. If she knew there were so many eligible, cute men in Spain I was turning down, she would have jumped on the first flight out of Austin.

"Hold on a second," I say, running to grab my cell phone. "I'll show you!"

The last time I spoke to Luciana before telling her I wouldn't be coming back to Spain was over text message. I show the conversation to Ellie.

Luciana: GUESS WHAT?! MY BF IS HERE.

Ellie reads her text and laughs. "Isn't she like 12?"
I laugh. "Not even."
"Who's her boyfriend?"
I smirk and tell her to keep scrolling.

Brooke: BF?! I leave for two weeks and you get yourself a boyfriend? Who?

A few minutes later she sent back a photo and to this day, I can't help but laugh. It's slightly blurry, but there's Alejandro standing at the kitchen counter chatting with Diego. He's wearing his leather jacket, and his jet-black hair is all wavy and sexy. He looks completely unattainable, but what makes me laugh is the fact that Luciana posed the photo as a selfie so both she and Alejandro could be in the photo together without him knowing. Her smiling mug is in the foreground of the photo, taking up 75% of the shot.

"Who is that?!" Ellie demands, pointing at Alejandro.

"*That's* Alejandro," I say with a gloating smile.

"*Holy…*" She grabs my phone and zooms in until everyone but Alejandro has been pushed off screen. Then, she leans back and releases a heavy sigh right before she lobs me in the shoulder.

"You left *THAT* behind in Spain?"

"OW." I snatch my phone back in anger and then lock the screen. No more Alejandro for her.

"No, seriously, Brooke—is he single?"

"I'm not sure. You'll have to ask Diego when you accept the job."

Her smile fades and her eyes narrow as she finally catches on to my little trick. "*If* I take the job, it's not going to be because of him."

I laugh. "Of course not. Think of Alejandro as a potential signing bonus."

Just then a car pulls up into our driveway and a little bolt of excitement spirals through me. I love that sound because it means in a few seconds, James is going to walk through the back door of the house and find Ellie and me in the kitchen. He'll smile in relief, hang his keys by the door, and loosen his tie as he approaches me to plant a kiss on my lips. He told me the other day that he still gets excited to walk in every night and find me here. I've assured him I'm not going anywhere. I'll be here every night from here on after, but it doesn't matter. To him, it's still a novelty to get to come home to someone he loves every night. He told me it's the best moment of his day, and I agreed.

In the last few months, James has kept a busy work schedule. The BioShield is weeks away from releasing to the public, and that means there's never been more work for him or his company. Still, he makes a point to be home every night at 6:00 PM and not a minute later. I glance at the clock and smile when I see that it's 5:59.

The back door opens and James walks in. His keys get hung. His tie is loosened, and with no regard for Ellie's presence in the kitchen, he heads straight for me.

"Welcome home," I tease as he grips ahold of my waist and tugs me toward him. My hips meet his as I wrap my hands around his neck and he bends low, planting a passionate kiss on my lips.

"Yeah! Hi! *Yoohoo.* Could you please stop grabbing my sister's ass cheeks while I'm standing right here?"

I laugh as James breaks away and finally turns to Ellie. "Oh, hey, didn't see you there."

She rolls her eyes and turns back to the refrigerator. "Like hell you didn't. For that, I'm opening the good wine."

"Oh yes!" I agree. "You have to. We're celebrating!"

James glances back and forth between us. "Are we? Why?"

I grin as I announce, "Ellie is going to take my old job and move to Spain!"

"We don't know that yet," she points out, opening the cabinet to pull out three wine glasses. From the sound of her voice, I can tell she's actually going to consider it.

"I think it's a great idea, Ellie," James says, maneuvering around the island to uncork the wine. I use the distance as an opportunity to take in the black suit he put on this morning, the suit that does funny things to my insides, even with his tie loosened and his hair a little messy.

"We have something to celebrate as well," James says. "Did you share our good news, B?"

I glance up to meet his gaze, not even slightly embarrassed at being caught checking him out. "What good news?"

He delivers a devilish grin before turning toward Ellie. "Your sister asked me to marry her last night."

She squeals, whips around, and nearly drops one of the wine glasses.

My mouth drops open and my face burns scarlet red. "JAMES!"

"Brooke! Did you really? Wait, why are you so red?"

"Because I did not really ask him!"

The incident he's referring to happened late last night. We were in bed together, tangled in the sheets. We'd already had sex and were supposed to be getting up to shower and get ready for bed, but neither one of us was in a hurry to move. I'd just had the orgasm to end all orgasms—like, I saw my life flash before my eyes—and James had finished moments after, collapsing down half on top of me, half on the bed. My hand was strung through his hair and I was breathing hard against his neck, my eyes still closed. I was surrounded by his scent, his breath, his weight, so overcome by how much I loved him.

"Marry me," I say on a whim.

He stills and then props his hand beside my head so he can lift himself up enough to look down at me. "What did you just say?"

I don't bother opening my eyes, but I let a lazy grin spread across my lips. "I think I asked you to marry me."

"Brooke, open your eyes."

"No, I can't. I'm dead. You—that just killed me."

He strokes his finger along my cheek, and then higher, around the corners of my eyes, trying to convince me to look at him. "Please."

I sigh and blink my eyes open, reluctant to reenter the world after what just happened between us. His face is only a few inches from mine and I'm shocked to see how wide and vulnerable his eyes are as he stares down at me. "Did you mean that?"

"Marriage?" I ask gently.

He nods, never taking his eyes off me.

Did I mean it?

"A little," I respond sheepishly. "Does that scare you?"

He shakes his head. "Of course not."

I rub circles around his shoulder blades, concentrating there for a moment so I have the courage to continue. "I don't want you to think we have to get engaged right away or anything. I guess I just want you to know I'm ready when you are."

"We haven't been together long," he points out, trying to see where I actually stand on the subject.

I smile. "Martha told me once, 'When you know, you know.'"

A handsome grin overtakes his features before he dips down and plants a kiss on my lips. When he pulls away, he whispers, "I know."

I kiss him again. "Me too."

With that, he finally pushes off of me and pads toward the bathroom in the buff. I ogle his derriere without a care in the world. He might look killer in a suit, but this is definitely how I prefer him. Just before he steps past the doorway, he turns back to look at me over his shoulder with an amused smile.

"Harry will be happy when I tell him."

Harry the goldfish, our first wedding RSVP.

I frown, trying for my best solemn expression. "I bet the last few years have been really hard for him. Me away in Spain, you moping here."

He nods in a mock agreement. "You can't imagine what it's like being a single dad these days."

I have to stifle a laugh to stay in character. "I'm sure you've done the best you can."

He grins and tips his head toward the shower. "You coming?"

"In a second."

He turns and walks away. A moment later, the sound of the shower running filters into the bedroom. I pause, stare at the doorway long enough to make sure he isn't going to come back, and then crawl toward his side of the bed and pull the top drawer of the bedside table open.

There, in the corner, is the small black velvet box I found the other day while I was cleaning. Inside, nestled tight, I find the antique engagement ring that leaves me breathless. It seems even more flawless than before, twinkling in the low light. I brush my finger across the round diamond, careful not to dislodge the ring from its cushion. My finger itches to try it on; I know it will fit, but it feels wrong to do it without James watching.

"B?" James calls from inside the shower. "Water's hot!"

I jump, close the black velvet box, and shove it back into its terrible hiding place before scurrying off the bed to join him.

"Coming!" I call back.

Soon, I remind myself, I'll get to put that ring on and never take it off. I smile at the thought.

 # ACKNOWLEDGEMENTS

During one summer in college, I worked as a cabana girl at a country club in Austin. My uniform consisted of khaki shorts and a bright orange polo. Paired with my red hair, it was quite a bold look. (*Yikes.*) Obviously, at the time, I didn't know I would use that job as inspiration for this book. If I had, I probably would have taken more notes. ;)

Though it might seem surprising, it was a really fun job. The members at the country club where I worked were much more down-to-earth than the members Brooke deals with in this book, though rest assured, I definitely dealt with my fair share of snooty jerks.

Also, yes, the moms at the kiddie pool were always SO GLAMOROUS; there were a few kids I was legitimately scared of, just like the tweens Brooke deals with in this story; and Andie Roddick *was* a member, but I never saw him.

• • •

Big thanks to Lance for helping beta read and co-write the second draft of this book! Also, thank you for taking the night shift with baby Hallie so I'd have enough brain power to write in the mornings. I would never have been able to get this book done without your help.

To my mom, THANK YOU, thank you, thank you for babysitting Hallie so Lance and I could hammer out the final details of this story. I am forever in your debt, truly.

Thank you to my editor, Editing by C. Marie, for continuing to work with me even though I threw this manuscript at you so last minute. Trying to schedule a book release after the birth of my first child was a little crazy to say the least. I honestly can't believe I made it to this point. I fully anticipated having to email you and postpone. *pops champagne*

Thank you to my readers for continuing to come back to my stories time and time again. There are so many good books for you to choose from, and I really appreciate your love and loyalty over the years!

Big thanks to the book bloggers and bookstagrammers who have read and shared my books. Without your support, my stories would have never found an audience.

All my love,
R.S. Grey

Find other R.S. Grey Books on Amazon!

The Foxe & the Hound
Anything You Can Do
A Place in the Sun
The Summer Games: Out of Bounds
The Summer Games: Settling the Score
The Allure of Dean Harper
The Allure of Julian Lefray
The Design
The Duet
Scoring Wilder
Chasing Spring
With This Heart
Behind His Lens

Printed in Great Britain
by Amazon